She cried to God for justice even as she vowed her own revenge . . .

It was old Doctor Cornish who first told Optimus Shute about the strange and tragic events that had taken place a generation earlier. He spoke of vengeance – not the hot-blooded variety, the kind that anyone might be tempted to, but the cold-blooded kind that slept in the brain like a cancer, biding its time before breaking out. And he spoke of a woman called Grace Pensilva.

Before long, Shute was compulsively re-creating the story on paper, the project absorbing all his waking hours. The obsession with Grace Pensilva had begun.

GRACE PENSILVA is Michael Weston's first novel.

His second novel, THE CAGE, is the winner of the Georgette Heyer Historical Novel Prize and will be published by Corgi Books.

GRACE PENSILVA
or The Vindication

Michael Weston

CORGI BOOKS

GRACE PENSILVA

A CORGI BOOK   0 552 12676 4

Originally published in Great Britain by The Bodley Head
Ltd.

PRINTING HISTORY

The Bodley Head edition published 1985
Corgi edition published 1986

This book is set in 10/11 pt Cheltenham

Corgi Books are published by Transworld Publishers Ltd.,
61–63 Uxbridge Road, Ealing, London W5 5SA, in
Australia by Transworld Publishers (Aust.) Pty. Ltd., 26
Harley Crescent, Condell Park, NSW 2200, and in New
Zealand by Transworld Publishers (N.Z.) Ltd., Cnr. Moselle
and Waipareira Avenues, Henderson, Auckland.

Made and printed in Great Britain by
Hunt Barnard Printing Ltd., Aylesbury, Bucks.

To Joan who made this possible

Acknowledgements

With thanks to Jack and Harry and Eric and Maud and Margaret and all the other old folk who told me how it was.

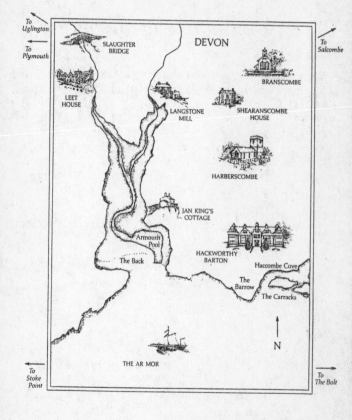

Part One

La vengeance est une plat qui se mange froid

French proverb

1

But for the lines of strain about her eyes and mouth, the young woman might have appeared beautiful. Some particular intensity in her expression, in her restrained manner of moving, picked her out from the other mourners and held his attention as the slow, hesitant procession formed up on the Plain and wound its way uphill towards him, past the Trafalgar tavern from which shouts of mirth came unabated, past the pound where a stray donkey was tethered in the trampled grass, past the fishermen's store whose doorway was flanked by piles of lobster pots, and came to a halt at the base of the steps that led up into the churchyard. The bearers, six stalwart, blue-jerseyed fishermen, shifted their burden on their shoulders before tackling the steep ascent from the dusty lane to the tombstone-studded grass. Even before she came close enough for him to see that face, whose grey-eyed gaze seemed capable of piercing the tangled screen of yew behind which he stood, he was obsessed by her, wondering who she was, why she was there so close behind the swaying bier.

The Vicar of Bigmore, gaunt and drooping in his dark vestments, fluttered around the church tower and began to read from his book. The words were inaudible, whisked away by the chill breeze, but that was of no importance, they were the same words as always and it was the identical ritual. The watcher behind the yew had followed it all too often before. It was a harsh world they lived in; death was a commonplace, no man was ever safe from that chill embrace. And yet he puzzled at the strange compulsion that had drawn him to

Harberscombe on this inauspicious day, risking recognition, to observe a ceremony so hackneyed and uninspired in its execution as to make grief a mockery and loss banal. The link that bound the watcher to the inanimate clay in the crudely carpentered coffin had nothing of affection in it. Was his attendance at the funeral an unspoken gesture of expiation for a secret guilt? He did not think so; he had killed many men, most of them in hot-blooded encounters, but not all, some had been struck down coldly in ambush, that was the nature of war. He had done his duty, fulfilled his debts of honour. And in this case, had he failed to strike, it could have been his body, not this other, that was carried to a cold grave. His long, wide-eyed face showed no sign of inner torment; his tall frame, wrapped in a handsome greatcoat, appeared relaxed yet watchful, like a duellist ready to shift on fast, purposeful feet.

The funeral cortege was advancing in undisciplined file along the shady side of the old grey church. In a village of cob-walled, thatched-roofed cottages, built with the materials prescribed by poverty, the church was the only building of style and antiquity, though the new farms, constructed of dressed stone and sporting small Georgian porches, spoke of a new era of rural wealth in the hands of the great landowners and their tenant farmers. Otherwise, this village was exceptional in having no old manor house or prepossessing mansion where the rich performed their tasks of music-making, embroidery, fox-hunting, card-playing, and dynastic matchmaking. Somehow, the secular branch of feudal society seemed to have left out Harberscombe, dismissing it perhaps as a barren waste, isolated from more smiling and prosperous farmland by an intricate network of wooded coombes and deep river valleys. Even the church had been loath to commit itself fully to this marginal parish, treating it as an offshoot of inland Uglington, providing only an illiterate curate and obliging the Harberscombe folk to carry their dead five miles, over steep, rocky roads to the mother church for burial. Only after centuries of petitioning the Bishop of Exeter was consent obtained for the establishment of the churchyard where now the clusters of plain slate slabs testified to brief lives and inevitable passing of the generations of Harberscombe families: the Triggs, the Coytes, the Wroths, the Luggers, the Crockers, the Terrys, the Kingdoms and the Kings.

There were no elaborate vaults in Harberscombe churchyard, no gilded tombs within the church. Its musty aisles, with peeling whitewash and the green stains of damp, had never sheltered the finery of lords and ladies, only country folk, smallholders, rabbit-trappers, fishermen. Their voices rang boldly under the twin barrel-vaults, shaking out dust from the crumbling, wheatear-carved ribs about the plain arcade. It was a weekly chorus of hope and harmony essential to a community always struggling on the brink of want and misery.

Now, another sound came from within its walls. Although he should have expected it, its abrupt clamour surprised the watcher into a sudden, unconsidered movement which might well have betrayed his presence. High in the tower whose strongly-buttressed shape spoke more of the fortress against marauding man than of aspiration to divine goodness, a bell began to toll. Insistent, deliberate, shaping the mourners' steps into a regular cadence, the monotonous bell was like a slow, expiring pulse, fluttering a little as it struggled to maintain itself until the coffin had reached the grave. When it did so, and the bearers laid it down on the twin poles that crossed the newly excavated trench, the tolling ceased. It had not lasted much more than a minute, but the mood it generated lingered on: resigned, hopeless, brazen, helpless.

The mourners were closer now, so close that, had there been a furtive tear coursing down one of their windburned cheeks, the watcher would have seen it. But till now, there was nothing but dignified, almost casual respect, not even grief, as though they were there more out of duty than from sentiment.

The Vicar of Bigmore was proceeding, perhaps a little hurriedly, with the service for the burial of the dead. There was no excuse for this speed, there was no haste in

Harberscombe, but his parishioners were aware that he was eager to have done with it and collect his fee.

'In the midst of life, we are in death,' he enunciated through yellowing teeth and the watcher saw a thin thread of saliva strung across the gap between his lips at the corner of his mouth as he spoke.

Without warning, there was a commotion. The young woman whom the watching man had picked out from among the advancing mourners stepped forward boldly and knelt in the fresh earth beside the coffin. Oblivious to the brown stain on the cloth of her freshly dyed black dress, she wrenched at the boards that formed the lid of the cheap deal box.

'Frank! Frank!' she shouted.

Around her, the villagers shuffled their feet in embarrassed silence.

'He's in there, poor dead Frank, you've nailed him down and you've forgotten him. But you shan't be allowed to forget; you shall have a last look, so you'll remember him,' she shouted at the mourners, throwing back her head so that her black hair made a wild mane about her face, and confronting each in turn with a hard stare. And all the while she was tugging at the lid of the coffin. Had it been better made, it might have resisted her. The Vicar stood aghast, his words trapped in his throat, silenced by the sacrilege of her act.

To the watcher it appeared that her gaze penetrated into the furthest recesses of their heads, divining their inmost thoughts. If he had not been so sure of the efficacy of his own concealment, he might have been excused for believing that she was weighing his. Her look lingered inexplicably on the matted yew-fronds that hid him. He saw the cold, piercing glare of her grey eyes; he saw the angular, unbalanced pose she had adopted, with her arms straddling the coffin and, for an instant he was afraid, afraid in a way that smacked of the irrational, and which he made himself shake off immediately. *She could not see him*, that much was certain. Her smooth oval face, with its serene white brow, pale cheeks stained with a red flush, tight lips, and delicate chin, was not turned on him, but on the obscure funereal symbol, the sombre yew.

14

And yet, although his conscious mind assured him this must be so, a deep primeval stirring in his bowels betrayed him and a prickling along his spine told him he was observed.

As if to confirm his foreboding, the woman moved. She reached into the open coffin with unerring grasp, wrenching the corpse's stiffened arms skywards in a defiant gesture, shaking them violently, as though her baffled fury could reinstil them with life. But those arms she held would hold no more. Each hand she brandished, clutched below the wrist, was hideously truncated, a fingerless stump.

'Look!' she commanded. 'Frank Pensilva's hands. Remember them, his fingers gone. With half a hand, he lost his grip on life. Remember them! Someone in Harberscombe, someone in your family, someone betrayed him. These hands were perfect, look at them now. And who's to blame? Someone amongst you. God willing, if there be a God, I shall see justice. If God saw this, he'd strike the guilty down this minute. Come God, let us see justice wrought.'

There was more embarrassed shuffling of feet; an old man cleared his throat; a woman clutched at her bodice and appeared ready to faint; the Vicar stepped forward, trying to re-establish order and authority on this barbaric scene. As he did so, another man emerged from the circle of mourners, took the woman by the shoulders and dragged her by main force to her feet. She resisted his help, clinging to the body till it half emerged and the swollen thick-lipped face was visible, but the man tore her hands away and raised her willy-nilly. Seething, she stood facing him, a quiescent volcano, containing her fury.

'Us couldn't do nothin' for un,' the man muttered. The woman was not listening. She coiled herself back inwards like a viper, then lunged forward and spat in his face.

The man wiped the spittle from his cheek with the back of his hand. It was a gesture that betokened more of sorrow than of anger. Turning from her, he knelt at the graveside in his turn and disposed the corpse once more in its coffin, hammering the lid home with his clenched fist. A nod to the bearers brought them out of the crowd, briskly performing their tasks of removing the poles that held the coffin and lowering it away with bights of crab-line.

The watcher examined the man who had aroused such animosity in the young woman. He had a sharp, keen face that some would have called foxy, fringed by auburn side-burns, and his dark tanned skin was typical of the local fisher-men, exposed to all weathers, and with a ruddy cheek. There was something familiar about the man, characteristics to which he could not put a name.

Meanwhile the Vicar was hurrying through the concluding words of the service. There was no sermon or eulogy: no money to pay for that. The Vicar of Bigmore considered him-self a man too poor for generosity.

Shovels bit into the dirt and the first crumbs of earth pattered on the coffin. The young woman seemed to have retreated into herself, standing bleak-faced as if unaware of her surroundings. Summoning up a compassion he did not feel, the Vicar made a summary attempt at offering her the accustomed words of consolation. She shrugged him off. Rebuffed, he hurried away. The mourners began to trail after him; they were not many and, now that the man was buried, they had their daily lives to attend to. Not only that, they were anxious to plunge into any kind of absorbing activity that would rid their minds of the disturbing image of the young woman holding up those dead and fingerless stumps that once were hands.

Soon, only two figures remained at the graveside. The man in whose face the woman had spat was the last to leave her there. His cheeks worked with emotion as he attempted to bring out the words to speak to her.

'I . . . shall . . . never . . . forgive . . . meself,' he enunci-ated slowly with painful pauses between the words.

'Nor I neither, Jan King!' was all her reply.

'No, I suppose I shouldn't expect it,' muttered the man as he walked away.

While they were speaking, another man had been advancing towards them. He had emerged from the church porch and the watcher guessed he was the bellringer. He

16

came forward by fits and starts, like a bird afraid of a cat, head cocked to one side, his mouth twisted sideways by a sporadic tic.

The watcher, who had been on the point of leaving, was held spellbound by the woman's subsequent behaviour. She stood, grasping the bellringer's shoulders, her brow pressed against his and whispering to him urgently. The watching man strained his ears to catch what she was saying. He knew only that she was questioning him, making him shake his large curly head in puzzled confusion until, finally, she stamped her foot and turned away. For the first time, the watcher thought he saw a tear in the corner of her eye, but from the set of her expression, he knew it to be a tear of anger and frustration.

'If that's all you can remember, Ivor Triggs, you're no use to me. What's wrong with you? There's been a betrayal and Frank's been lost by it. What's wrong with you? Can't you remember more? Away with you and toll the bell! Haven't I paid you? Why have you stopped ringing? They shall know, these Harberscombe folk, that my poor Frank is dead, but he's not forgotten.'

Ivor Triggs the bellringer stumbled away, but the woman ignored him. She was still speaking, but not to him, speaking in another direction, facing the grave, with her back to the watcher. She held herself firm, though quivering slightly, head down, arms crossed on her breast, fingertips showing over her shoulders, speaking low and rapidly as if confiding in the corpse. All her words were lost to the man in the yew, snatched away by gusts of the rising wind which carried torn scraps of cloud past the defiant bulk of the old tower whose pinnacles combed the wisps of vapour till they wept.

The first heavy drops thudded into the foliage of the yew. The man concealed there shivered slightly, turning up the collar of his greatcoat and putting on his flat three-cornered hat which he pulled low down over his face. He felt a compelling urge to be away from there. Before he went, he took a long last look at the graveside scene. The woman had stopped speaking and was turning slowly in his direction. Although he knew he must be invisible, the weight of her stare was heavy upon him as was the weight of his new knowledge that there was a bond between them. Just as there was a broken bond, but yet an enduring one between this woman and the dead man. A new bond that he had been unaware of bound her to him and filled him with concern. Who was this woman? the dead man's wife, his mistress? his first love? The wide grey eyes said nothing and everything; the face confronting him was a mask. If there was grief, she did not show it. Her savage beauty cut him like a sword. Had she been closer, had he dared to show himself, had he not been cast into his present covert role, he would have rushed forward to comfort her, trying to pull down that mask of indifference and let her weep as a woman should. But her face was hard, and the gulf between them infinite. He knew he was the wrong man, in the wrong place, at the wrong time. The air was full of her hostility. He had been a damned fool to come in the first place; now he must leave before someone discovered him.

Optimus Shute replaced his pen on the glass inkstand and sighed. He was tired; it was late at night; the candle beside him had burnt low and was guttering fitfully, sending the shadows dancing grotesquely around the walls of his study. Outside the window that November night all was dark. There was not a glimmer from the house opposite, the old man must have gone to bed early. Optimus felt alone, marooned on a small island of human fellowship in a great hostile sea of indifferent countryside. Branscombe was a small, unknown hamlet close to Harberscombe, but for all that, in the middle of nowhere. The Board of Education, in their infinite wisdom, had chosen him to settle this island and civilize it, with literacy and numeracy. It had been a hard pill to swallow.

He cast a glance at the last few lines of his copperplate handwriting. Was this really how it had been? How could he be sure he wasn't inventing things, feigning false emotions, overlooking vital facts? His mind was confused, his fatigue was not so much the result of the physical effort of standing at the high carved desk at which he wrote, but from the effort of imagination, reconstituting the past from scraps of evidence, sometimes self-contradictory, often puzzling. He was afraid that, in the recounting of it, he was lapsing into the melodramatic, and yet he did not wish to restrict himself to the dry bones of the story and a recital of scraps of hearsay without any attempt to see into the heads of his protagonists. At first, he had done nothing but glean information, with no idea of setting it down on paper, but a time had come when that had seemed natural. Now he was bogged down in a new set of problems. The project was absorbing all his waking thoughts, interfering with his school work. The inspector, when he came, was bound to notice. How had he become entrammelled in all this? That question at least was easy to answer. The fault lay with Dr Cornish.

As he prepared for bed, Optimus Shute recalled their first encounter. He remembered that morning in early September when the old man had summoned him over, sending Mrs Kemp to fetch him on some trumped-up pretext or other. He had been reluctant to go; the roofers were still at work, putting finishing touches to the new building; his trunk and carpet bag had yet to be unpacked, they lay in the doorway where the Kingsbridge carrier had left them; not only that, he had classes to prepare, his pupils would be putting in their first appearance next morning. But he had gone over, though with an ill grace, partly because the Doctor's summons was so pressing, and partly from curiosity to know what kind of a man he was to have for a neighbour during his stay at Branscombe.

Mrs Kemp, a portly woman who, he guessed, must be the Doctor's housekeeper, had half pushed, half ushered him into the farmhouse kitchen where her employer sat waiting. Immediately to his right as he entered the room was a large brick-built open fireplace in which some logs were smouldering under a blackened kettle. The fireplace was flanked by two doors leading to alcoves from which the oven and smoke room at the back of the fire could be reached. Dr Cornish himself sat at the nearer end of a long massive table, wedged tightly between it and the wall, along which a bench was fastened. It looked as though the table had been constructed in that kitchen; Optimus Shute could see no way it could have been wangled through the constricted doorway or, for that matter, how it could ever be got out again. At the far end of the table was a wainscot partition and, through the open doorway, he saw the Doctor's consulting room, though he was unaware of its function at that time, noticing only a kind of hatch or inner window set high in the wall on the far side of it.

'Sit you down, young feller,' the Doctor had instructed him peremptorily, as if Shute were just another patient, 'there's not much time, or rather *I* haven't much time.'

Nor I either, thought Shute, but held his tongue, half intimidated, half diplomatic. He settled awkwardly on the hard bench with something of the feeling of a schoolboy facing his master for the first time, an impression heightened by the untidy heap of books and papers on the table between them. To see his interlocutor he was obliged to shade his eyes with his palm against the morning light; the sun had just cleared the rim of hills that enclosed Branscombe and was flooding through the casement, dazzling him. What he saw of Dr Cornish, in silhouette, was a heavy grizzled head, balding on top and aureoled by the sunlight. In the penumbra, his features were puffy and lined, glowing with a faint redness that owed little to the embers of the fire and much to cheap brandy, or so Optimus surmised. His body, clad in an old-fashioned coat and splayed waistcoat, had the exaggerated corpulence of those who had become completely sedentary in middle age. He gave an impression of lumpishness, lethargy, world-weariness. Only his eyes were bright and quick, like a robin's, examining Shute minutely. Well, if he had anything important to say, he was taking an unconscionable time about it.

'A most perplexing case,' the Doctor continued inconsequentially, 'most perplexing. And a most remarkable woman, most remarkable. You're bound to agree with that, I'm certain.'

'Look here, Dr Cornish,' exclaimed Optimus Shute,

20

convinced that the old Doctor was in his dotage and that his mind was already wandering, 'look here. I'm a busy man; I've a thousand things to see to: primers to prepare, lessons to plan. I've been given the charge of young minds, Dr Cornish, I mustn't neglect them. Now come to the point, I've no time for social calls.' After his outburst, Optimus Shute sat nervously pinching at his thin straw-coloured moustache. Dr Cornish was slow to reply, even then.

'It's a long time since I've seen an educated man in Branscombe, Mr Shute, a man of culture, a man of intelligence. I mean to take advantage of it.'

He paused again and Optimus was distracted by a burst of hammering and the sight of the roofers coming up to the ridge of the schoolhouse across the road.

'You're young,' said the Doctor, 'but you're clever. You've been to college. You think you know all there is to know about human nature. Well, *I* haven't made head or tail of it yet and I've lived the best part of a lifetime. There are things that still puzzle me, Mr Schoolmaster, and one in particular, the one I've asked you over to talk about. It's been my privilege to see many strange things during my long stay here, odd events, confused, some might say pointless stories, but intense, some might say tragic. But the one that I've found most perplexing is this one here.' At this point the Doctor made a broad gesture with his arm over the papers that littered the table. As he did so, he became aware that the schoolmaster was wrapped up in a brown study.

'What did I last say, Mr Shute? You've not been listening, now have you?'

'Perplexing – perplexing is this one here!' repeated Optimus Shute as if recalling something learnt by rote, or noted during a lecture, without attempt at understanding.

'It's not enough to remember and repeat what you hear, you've got to try and understand, young feller, look into the heart of things. Wake up now, I'm addressing you.'

It might have been the vehemence of his remarks or the underlying emotion. Whatever it was, Dr Cornish stopped speaking suddenly and Optimus was concerned to see him fighting for breath and observe an increased flush on the old man's cheeks. What was that he had said about not having much time?

'Shall I call Mrs Kemp?'

The Doctor shook his head. It was evident that he was mastering the crisis by an effort of the will. The stifled wheezing died down and his hands steadied.

'Comes of being old,' he announced at last. 'I was like you once, though you'll not believe it, fresh down from college, full of crusading zeal, never a spare minute. You'll find it hard to keep that up for thirty years in Branscombe: this is the place God made and then forgot.' Optimus squirmed in his seat.

'Do you have to be blasphemous?' He began to rise, determined at last to take his leave. A hand shot out and grasped him between elbow and shoulder, hurting him. There was more strength left in the old man that he had imagined.

'Do you believe in vengeance, Mr Schoolmaster?' Optimus Shute looked blank. There was nothing in the preceding conversation to prepare him for the question. After a pause, the Doctor continued, 'I don't mean, do you believe in its existence, that's something we can take for granted, isn't it? No, what I want to know is, and you're the man to tell me, you've just been to a Church of England college where they debate such things, what's the modern doctrine? Do they accept such behaviour? Is it the New Testament or the Old that's in the ascendant?'

'It wasn't a question we –'

'No, I suppose not, there's not much reason to exercise the intellect in that direction in some college backwater. But here, here in the country, where there are real people, there are real dilemmas. As you'll find out . . . But to return to my question: to take a scholastic approach and define two aspects of it, there's the hot-blooded variety, the kind we all are tempted to, and thus excusable, and there's the cold-blooded sort, the kind that sleeps in the brain like a cancer and, when it does break forth, we have forgotten the affront that caused it. What are we to make of that, Mr Schoolmaster? And when there's a woman involved, wouldn't you think it somehow unnatural, shouldn't she be forgiving and kind, wouldn't you expect her to forgo satisfaction of some distant wrong, isn't that what you would expect? But I don't intend to burden you with abstractions, it's all in here, all in these papers, and a bit beside, in the memories of those who knew her, thought they knew her, those who are still alive. If you want the truth, you'd better hurry. You'll make more of it than an old house-bound doctor. But you won't find it wearisome, she was a most remarkable woman.'

Despite himself, Optimus Shute was beginning to feel stirrings of interest. 'You're talking about a real person, aren't you? What was she called?'

'Her name was Grace Pensilva.'

'I've never heard of her. Where was she from?'

'She came from Harberscombe.'

'You knew her then.'

'I scarcely met her – not while she lived, that is. But I heard much about her and, one night, a man they thought of as one of her victims lay here bleeding his life out on this very table.'

The kitchen seemed to have grown darker and the hammering outside seemed to come from further away. Optimus Shute stared at the table-top. It was made of massive pine boards that ran the full length of it. The wood was marked here and there with knife scratches and stains from a thousand suppers. Of blood, there was no distinct trace, though how the Doctor could still eat from that self-same surface, however scrubbed, Optimus could not imagine. In his mind, he saw the unconscious body being lugged in, with a scraping of hob-nailed boots on the flag-stones. When there came a hammering on the door, he was ready to believe it was the wounded man's pursuers.

'Come in!' shouted Dr Cornish without hesitating and the door swung back instantly. Looking over this shoulder Optimus saw a small man standing there. It was one of the roofers.

''Tis the Vicar. 'E've come to see 'ee, Mr Shute. And 'ee says 'ee be tired o' waitin'. 'Ee said to say 'ee'd come to greet 'ee, and if you weren't back soon, 'ee'd be leavin'.'

'Better go, young feller, no good will come of slighting the Vicar,' said Dr Cornish. 'Never mind these papers, I'll send Mrs Kemp over with them later.'

After the gloom of the Doctor's kitchen, the clear autumn light was blinding. Optimus was still rubbing his eyes when he came upon the Vicar of Bigmore, standing on the school-house step. In one hand he held the reins and his nag's mane, in the other was a willow switch with which he was tapping his boot impatiently.

'Still much to be done, Mr Shute; you *are* Optimus Shute, aren't you?' he greeted the schoolmaster without further introduction. 'I'll not detain you further, we both have God's work to do, no time to waste in idle talk with drunken old reprobates. I'll expect to see you at church in Harberscombe on Sunday.'

'Good morning, Mr Lackland. I do apologize. He called me over. He said it was important.' Well before he finished speaking, Optimus realized his mistake in taking the defensive. The Vicar's eyes glittered, like a hawk about to swoop; his nostrils quivered.

'But it wasn't, was it, Mr Shute? It never is. The man's a disgrace to his calling, a soak, a quack, an atheist. And what, pray, was so important that he had to discuss it on your first morning?'

'He wanted to talk about Grace Pensilva.' Before he met him and saw how young he was, Optimus had thought that the Vicar of Bigmore might be able to enlighten him about the woman in question, but this clergyman, who was studiously looking down his nose at him, was too young, a mere whipper-snapper not a year older than himself. There seemed no chance he could have known her.

'Grace Pensilva?' said the Vicar, with a sudden narrowing of the eyes. 'You mean the murderess. Well, let me tell you this: she's best forgotten. Raking over the ashes of old crimes is not what you're paid for, Mr Shute; you're here to teach respect and clean living to the younger generation. I'll thank you to see that none of them, none of them, d'ye hear, ever speaks a word to that evil old man that it's your misfortune to have for a neighbour.'

With that, he swung his leg over the saddle and spurred away down the lane that led to Harberscombe and Bigmore, spattering Optimus Shute with mud from his horse's hooves as he did so. The schoolmaster felt suddenly isolated and friendless. If that was the reception he was to get from other God-fearing folk hereabouts, it did not augur well for the future. But, he recalled with relief, there was work to do: four and twenty pupils to teach on the morrow.

When Mrs Kemp came over with a bundle of papers later that day, he flung them into a corner of the attic, fearful that they would distract him from his purpose. At eight o'clock next morning he would pull the bell and the children would file in. It was his duty to make them count and spell and become good Christians. By the look of things, it would be a harder task than he had expected.

2

The watcher turned, blundering through the yew branches
that whipped his face and stumbling over the roots that
trapped his spurs. He was making a devil of a noise, but what
matter? What mattered was that he was escaping from that
damnable place. He limped across the lane towards the spot
where he had left his hunter tethered in a gateway and
breathed a sigh of relief coupled with pain as he swung his stiff
leg over its crupper. As he straightened, a man's voice from
nearby, quiet but firm, greeted him unexpectedly, by name.

"'Tis an ill wind that blows you to 'Arberscombe, Mr
Genteel.'

Genteel looked down, involuntarily fumbling with the handle of his riding quirt. He had not expected to be seen by anyone who knew him. He had been abroad for so long and so little
at home at Leet beforehand that he knew almost nothing of the
villagers and he supposed them to know even less of him. Evidently, he was mistaken. If he had had any sense, if he had
listened to his reason, he would not have come. Turning in
the saddle, he saw that the man who was addressing him was
short, thick-set and strong, wearing a seaman's jersey and an
oilskin slung across his shoulders. His face was sharp and intel-
ligent, eyes close-set, pert nose. Genteel had seen it before,
only a few minutes back. It was the man in whose face the
woman had spat. That, in itself, was enough to make him
memorable, but there was a still earlier memory, a blurred recollection of features and voice, like part of a nightmare in
which the man's face snarled at him malevolently.

'I wasn't aware I had the honour of your acquaintance,' he

replied rather haughtily, jerking the left-hand rein to turn his horse and set it in motion.

'Us've met, Frederick Genteel, though you'll not remember me. Gennulmen don't 'ave much time for us poor fisherfolk.'

Genteel looked down from his full height on his high horse at the squat, burly figure who was closing off the lane to him. He had been so sure no one in Harberscombe would know him. After all, he had been back in Devon a bare three weeks. Before that, boarding school and his years in the Service had kept him away. As for Harberscombe, although it was on the fringe of the estate and a bare five miles from Leet House, he had never before set foot in it. Even now, he was hard put to it to explain the inner urge that had brought him here, through the maze of lanes that protected the village from the outside world. Now, he felt as if the network of lanes was nothing more than a trap, an ambush into which he had been lured, a journey from which he might never return. The drama of recent events in the churchyard had set his teeth on edge. He must, he decided, pull himself together. This was all ridiculous. He set his chin and challenged the fisherman. 'What did you mean, "an ill wind", just now?'

The fisherman was looking up with a leer, something insinuating, implying an unfounded complicity. 'Gentry never brought no good to 'Arberscombe, gentry means tithes and rents and taxes. Some might feel flattered to be visited by gentry, but not us 'Arberscombe folk, us don't take kindly to bein' watched by strangers. A man may be the Squire and still a stranger. Us be independent beggars, us can very well live our lives without un.' Genteel attempted a laugh at this, but even to himself the laugh seemed forced.

'There's not much love lost on the Squire, is there? And never has been. But who pays for the barns to be built, who drains the water-meadows, who buys the new bloodstock? The Squire has a job to do in this world and, if he's worth his salt, he does it, even when it involves riding out to a God-forsaken place like Harberscombe. There's precious little that's joyful to see over here.'

'Aye, us don't 'ave no great 'ouses, nor books nor music,

but us do 'ave good funerals, or so I fancy.' Once again, Genteel looked at the man narrowly. How much did he know? Had he, the hidden watcher in the yew, been watched, and for how long? What would this man imagine to be the reason why he, a gentleman and a stranger, would hide in a hedge to watch a funeral? But he was not completely convinced that this man had seen him there; perhaps he had only seen him emerge from it; perhaps not even that. Any kind of reference Genteel might make to the event would be compromising and a tacit admission of an involvement he refused to admit, even to himself.

'You're a sharp-tongued rogue if ever I saw one, and you're lucky I'm not the kind of squire that horsewhips tenants, or it might be *your* funeral.'

'I'm no tenant o' yourn,' said the man stoutly, 'I'm a freeholder, like my father before me.'

'What did you say your name was, if you're not afraid to repeat it?'

'Me name's Jan King, at your service.'

'Well, you'll serve me if you'll set me on the road out of Harberscombe. These lanes of yours are too like one another.'

''Twill be a pleasure. Which way was you wantin'?'

'Leet, of course, where else would I be going?'

'That be for you to know, Squire, bain't it?' As he spoke, he reached up and grasped the hunter's bridle, leading it firmly towards the crossroads at the angle of the churchyard. Genteel felt impotent and ill at ease. He didn't trust the man. Why should he? This man King must know he was unarmed: Genteel's coat fitted him so tight that, had he carried a pistol in his belt, its butt would have been apparent. Now, he was allowing himself to be led down a dim, overgrown lane, by a man he distrusted, a man who claimed to know him, a man who, in the past hour, had had a bereaved woman spit in his face at the graveside. If there were a question he ought to be asking this man Jan King, it was this: what had he done to merit such burning hate? But the question was never uttered. The fisherman halted at the crossroads, pointing down a lane which, to Genteel, was identical with the others and saying,

'I'd wish you a safe return, but there wouldn't be no sense to that, would there?'

Genteel sat his mount a moment in silence. Deep in his mind a strange conviction of a shared destiny, some pattern of future fate whose ultimate workings had been sketched out in the past and given fresh impetus, however cryptically, in this chance encounter, was taking definite shape.

'Hal King of Armouth, Hal King the pilot, isn't he your father?' he demanded abruptly, with a flash of recollection.

'Hal King was drowned four winters back.' Genteel had a distinct vision of a weatherbeaten old man perched on the gunwale of a sailing lugger, with his son beside him at the tiller, and he himself much younger then, trailing his idle hand in the water, and his own father Lord Mayberry, before drink and frolic spoiled him, speaking in his booming voice from the bow, 'Come on then, Hal, give the boy a chance, how about letting young Freddie take over?' And then, changing places with the other boy and feeling for the first time the tremor in the live tiller as the water streamed past the rudder.

Briefly he searched Jan King's features for the boyish traits he remembered from that far off day, but encountered only his bold, insolent eyes.

'I'm sorry, I hadn't heard. Been away, Mediterranean station. How did it happen?'

'Crossin' the bar. Ship 'ee was pilotin' went on the Back and fell to matchwood.'

'Tell your mother I'm sorry, I really am. I remember her now. I remember both of 'em.'

Jan King's lips curled into a smile that had no humour and much irony in it. 'Mother's gone too. But don't think you 'ave to burden me with more of your "sorrys", I can live without 'em.'

'Yes, I suppose you can.'

'Farewll then.' As he spoke, Jan King gave the horse a slap on the rump and, with the curtest of curt nods with the brim of his three-cornered hat, Genteel was away, digging his spurs into the hunter's powerful flanks. As he did so, the bell in the tower resumed its tolling. He did not look back. It was a relief to be off, even if he was as like as not to lose himself in the lanes. Harberscombe was behind him; he had no wish to return. He cantered along, trying to fix his mind on forth-coming candles and a sea-coal fire. Leet might have its prob-lems, and one in particular, but it was not heavy with death, it was not all anger.

As he rode clear of the close web of lanes he came into bleak, open countryside. This was not the way he had come, but he pressed on fiercely. The wind snatched at his coat and the rain flew at him horizontally, pummelling his face. It ran down from his forehead over his eyes as if he were weeping, but he felt no sorrow. The sensation he felt, and was reluctant to admit even to himself, was fear. It was fear that kept him digging his spurs into his unfortunate nag, despite the numb stiffness in his right leg, until they ran with blood. But his fear had nothing to do with substantial perils, it was inspired by and nourished from that afternoon's most telling image: the stern and ravaged beauty that shone from the face of the young woman at the graveside. It haunted him. The eyes that had bored into his concealment among the yews, as though with a supernatural awareness, pursued him yet. Steady, cold, implacable, in terrible contrast to the delicately cut lineaments of the surrounding face, they shone close behind him as he rode. He knew that he had only to turn his head slightly to see them, but feared to do so. Never before had he come face to face with such a woman's grief: it harrowed him. Fast as he rode, it dogged him still.

Optimus threw down his pen in disgust. There was no real evidence that the two men had ever met in this manner; what he had just written was pure speculation. Oh, it *was* possible, there was a genuine possibility that Genteel had ridden over to Harberscombe and stumbled on the funeral or, more likely, that he had been driven by some obscure prurient curiosity. No one would ever know: they were both gone. Jan King had been an illiterate, retiring, almost friendless man, and Frederick Genteel, if he did have such an encounter, had never mentioned it, nor did he allude to it in his later journal.

30

Other events that day were real enough, well attested to. Several villages could bear witness to the graveside scene: the sight of the young woman brandishing the stumps of the dead man's hands had burned its way into their memories, nor had they forgotten the moment when she spat in Jan King's face.

'Why don't you go over to Harberscombe and talk to Emma – Emma Troup can tell you all about her. You ought to be able to talk to Emma, she was a teacher too, in her time, if it *was* only a dame school. Yes, she'll tell you all about Grace Pensilva.' Dr Cornish had reined in his trap one cold autumn Sunday morning when he chanced upon Optimus who, free of his charges, was strolling pensively along, admiring the patterns of hoar-frost on the leaves. 'You haven't been neglecting Grace, now have you? You've got a tongue in your head, why can't you answer? Convinced you I'm a leper, have they? Take your time, young feller, but not too much of it, if you're too slow off the mark, you may be too late.' With a quick flick of his long whip Dr Cornish stung his nag into a shambling trot, shattering the ice that covered the puddles under his trap's grinding wheels.

It had been a full two months after his arrival in Branscombe before Optimus finally slackened in his resolve not to waste time on Dr Cornish's papers. He had been tempted more than once, just as he had been tempted by the glow from the Doctor's window. Branscombe was such a quiet place after the children had gone home. The Church Commissioners had engaged him like a South Sea missionary and his little school was an outpost planted on an island in a sea of ungodliness. In the eyes of the Church, Dr Cornish was the equivalent of a drunken trader. But Optimus Shute had a mind that craved provender. He soon found that his other neighbour, Farmer Stitson, of Butterwell Farm, had a conversation that never went beyond fat-stock prices and foot-rot.

More than once, as he walked home in the twilight, he saw the brightness of Dr Cornish's mineral-oil lamp streaming out of the uncurtained window and paused to peer into the kitchen where the old fellow sat rocking gently in his chair beside a roaring fire, his pipe and brandy glass beside him on the table. But for the steady swing of the rocking chair, the shawl-wrapped Doctor might have been dozing, his eyes were closed and Optimus supposed he was drifting in a sea of reminiscence. What was the old fellow really thinking?

But Optimus refused to allow himself to mount the steps and tap on the Doctor's door. However curious he might be, and the old man intrigued him more than he cared to admit to himself, he was determined to use his will-power to stay away from him. There was a strong foundation of truth in what the Vicar had said about him: Dr Cornish *did* drink immoderately; he *was* gross in his language. Several times Optimus had heard the schoolchildren imitating his outrageous expressions which they heard through the surgery window; if he was not an atheist or an agnostic, he was certainly not a practising Christian. At church times, the Doctor's stable door remained resolutely bolted. If he harnessed his trap it was to trundle off to a tavern. Dr Cornish could only be considered bad company for a novice schoolmaster and Optimus was well aware that consorting with him would soon reach the ears of Mr Lackland and the Parish Council. Optimus was on a year's probation and couldn't risk the luxury of contact with people of doubtful character.

One evening, after the first frosts, when there was an iron bite in the air that spoke of coming winter, Optimus sat at his own chill fireside, watching the flames glimmer. The minutes dragged by slowly, marked by the ticking of the American clock on his mantelpiece. It ticked loud and long in the empty, sparsely furnished room. His lessons were already prepared for the morrow, the children's slates had been looked over and ranged in their place in the schoolroom window. He had read the three books which he had brought in his trunk when he left college. Had he known he would have bought more, but how could he have known how barren would be the resources of Harberscombe village, still more those of Branscombe hamlet. There was talk of establishing a circulating library, but as yet no action. If only he had something to read.

And then he remembered: was there not a whole pile of

assorted papers up in his attic? What was it Dr Cornish had said about the person they concerned? 'A most remarkable woman'? And how had Vicar Lackland described her? 'You mean the murderess?'

Optimus half rose from his seat. Wasn't there something worth reading in all that? The story might not be edifying, but it was better than boredom. He stood up, took the candlestick from the table and made his way to the attic. Up there, under the bare slates and rafters, the draught made his candle flicker. A cluster of hibernating bats had already taken up residence in the gable; they hung like shrivelled figs among the roof-ties. Shielding his candle in a cupped hand, Optimus knelt among the papers. There were too many for him to take down all at once, and he would have to make an arbitrary decision, as there was no order that he could discern among them. He settled for a journal whose cover was inscribed with the year 18 –, and a sheaf of yellowing manuscript sheets bound with a faded blue ribbon.

He had been back at his fireside a full hour before he stumbled on anything in the journal that seemed significant. It was written in a small, practically illegible hand that he took to be the Doctor's, a surmise confirmed by a number of medical references, but its pages were often taken up by minutely described items of natural history, observations on a nuthatch, speculation concerning the meaning of barn owls' cries, an account of an unusual hailstorm when the falling hailstones had been mingled with red dust. Even when he read Dr Cornish's terse description of the night when they brought him wounded, half-dead Jack Lugger, he did not immediately link the event with Grace Pensilva. It was interesting in itself and opened his eyes to an era of lawlessness which appeared to have vanished entirely from the quiet country round Branscombe. The letters were a different matter and he found a certain compunction in reading them, a feeling increased by the passion they expressed.

That was the first of the long succession of nights that Optimus was to pass in search of Grace Pensilva. That was why he was standing now, at his writing desk, baffled and exhausted. Her enigmatic shadow seemed to beckon to him as he turned the dog-eared pages that Dr Cornish had entrusted to him, trying to make order out of chaos, separate dream from reality. And when he met Dr Cornish in the lane, he did not even see fit to admit to his cantankerous old neighbour that he had already sought out Mrs Troup and questioned her.

3

'I don't know as I ought to be answerin' a stranger's questions 'bout Grace Pensilva,' Mrs Troup had countered when the formalities were over and he had asked his first leading question.

'But what harm can there be?' protested Optimus. 'And I wouldn't be bothering you if I could avoid it. But there's no one else who knew her as you did. Didn't she help you teach at the dame school here? She was a bright girl, wasn't she? Out of the ordinary in a place like Harberscombe.'

'If you know so much, what're you doin' comin' round pesterin' a poor old body like me? Can't you tell it pains me?' Mrs Troup was a formidable old woman who dipped her head forward to study Optimus over her steel-rimmed glasses. She still had a residue of the impatient, dogmatic pedagogue about her. He also sensed a certain defensiveness which stemmed, no doubt, from an age before formal qualifications became the rule.

'It wasn't my idea in the first place, Dr Cornish said –'

'Dr Cornish is a meddling old busybody,' she interrupted, clenching her hands on her chair arms until the gnarled knuckles showed white, 'no one who gives a fig for morality has anything to do with that old quack. I suppose you already know what passes for diagnosis and treatment in *his* surgery. Dr Cornish knows nothin' 'bout Grace Pensilva, *nothin'*. If he's the one that's started you off on her, you'd best begin by forgettin' all he's told you.'

'Grace was a murderess then, that's what someone else is saying.'

Emma Troup sat up brusquely, gripping her chair so tight her arms were trembling. 'If you want to believe that, you're talkin' to the wrong person, Mr Shute, Grace Pensilva may have been many things, and not all of them honest, not in the general sense, but she were no murderer. If all you want is to confirm that opinion, you'd best keep your questions for Nancy Genteel, if she'll see you, or Mrs Coyte, if you can find her.'

'I didn't say I believed that, I merely said I'd heard it.'

'What you college-made teachers don't seem to know is you can't believe all that's fed to you as fact, specially not in places like Harberscombe. There's all sorts of prejudice, all sorts of resentment.'

'Precisely, and that's what brings me to you, Mrs Troup, I was sure you'd be above that kind of pettiness,' Optimus was pleased to see he had struck the right note, for the old lady relaxed visibly.

'Grace wasn't Harberscombe born, was she? I've heard say that Emma Troup was one of the few that ever showed her real kindness, truly accepted her,' said Optimus gently, propitiatingly.

'Small places make small minds, Mr Shute. I did no more than any Christian body ought to. It weren't as if the Pensilvas comed from far, they were only from across the Tamar, but Cornish is Cornish, for all that. Poor as church mice they were, but hardworkin' and old man Pensilva persuaded Charles Barker, the Steward over to Leet, that he was worth a try as a tenant. He was making a go of it too, and paying for Frank's schooling in Ashburton into the bargain when the cholera – 'twas the cholera that took them off you know, father and mother both. The boy Frank was too young to take over the farm, and anyway he was too unruly, too full of himself to stay and be a farm-hand, so he ups and signs on as a sailor, didn' come home to Harberscombe for many a long year and, if you asks me, 'twould have been best for Grace and for all concerned if he'd never done so. Harberscombe had no need of his foreign notions. Grace didn't see it that way o' course.'

'And Grace herself, what happened to her?'

'Old Miss Delabole took her on as a kind of lady's companion. That was on my recommendation, though Grace never showed no gratefulness for it, that weren't her way. But that was where she learned what social graces she had, that's where she learnt to talk like gentry, that's where she picked up French and I don't know what besides. Oh, Miss Delabole turned Grace into a proper lady all right! But she didn't leave her the money to go with it, though there was many as thought she would've done, Grace not least among 'em, or so I fancy. Grace were a misfit here. If she went wrong, it weren't her own fault. Grace weren't wicked, not at first anyhow, and the way she turned out were marked out by justice.'

'Justice?'

'Grace Pensilva had an idea of justice that didn' have nothin' to do with the law. Accordin' to her lights there was no justice to be had that way. No, 'twere all in her own head. In that she were like her brother Frank, that's where she learned some of they ideas, that's for certain, but she didn' go all the way with him, it weren't her idea to turn the whole world topsy-turvy with politics and what he called philosophy. A whole lot o' books he had, I see'd 'em, folk like Cobbett, Paine and that American called Franklin. Grace didn' fall for all that, though she loved the way Frank went on about it. But justice, that were a different thing, she said she knowed she'd never get it in the King's courts and she was sure Harberscombe folk would want to deny it to her. Never mind that, she *would* have it, she were obstinate were young Grace, might as well plead with a stone as try to deflect her. I tried it more'n once but to no purpose. Thought I knowed her, but I were wrong. Once she had made her vow, there was no shakin' her.'

'Her vow? What was that? What did she tell you?'

'She never did say exactly, though I found out more or less from what Ivor Triggs did tell me. I could guess the rest and she never denied it. It didn't take a clairvoyant to tell what it meant when she spat in Jan King's face in the churchyard, now did it? Dr Cornish has told you about that if he's told you anything, I'll warrant.'

'I'm still trying to puzzle out what it meant.'

'Oh that, that were simple enough: three men in a gig, one of 'em poor half-witted Ivor, the second were Frank, and the third, Jan King. Only two on 'em ever comed home, Jan and Ivor. 'Tweren't Ivor what gived 'em away to the preventives, too mazed for that. Who do that leave? 'Twas plain as a pikestaff to Grace.'

'But it might have been an accident.'

'An accident? To be run down by the preventives' boat on a dark foggy night, an accident?'

Optimus shook his head. 'No, but it might be.'

'Everyone knowed that boat were betrayed, but Grace were the only one to demand justice, her justice, justice on Jan for givin' the gig away and justice on the captain o' the revenue cutter what cut Frank's hands and sealed his death warrant.'

'So what you're trying to tell me is she was after revenge. You saw her soon afterwards I expect, what did she say to you?'

'Saw her afterwards? Course I did, many times, but I see what you mean, did I see her that night, after the burial? Well I did, I called round at the cottage she'd shared with Frank ever since she left Miss Delabole's and he'd come home. Almost ran into Farmer Wroth who was comin' out, he were their landlord and no need to guess at his business.'

'What did you talk about?'

'It weren't her vow, not then, Ivor hadn't told me about that yet. No, I just wanted to talk to her 'bout Jan King, tell her to live and let live. But she wouldn't listen, said I was just like the others in Harberscombe, protectin' our own and leagued against her.'

'So she vowed something. What was that? vengeance? And she knew who one man was, did she know the other?'

'She thought she did at the time, he had to come from Salcombe. The story, told from the preventives' side, were all over the neighbourhood.'

Optimus was beginning to feel he was getting somewhere. Mrs Troup wasn't telling him all she knew, not by a long

38

chalk, but she was opening up. 'So Jan *was* guilty, but the village protected him. What sort of a chap was he? You must have known him.'

'Jan King was what he was, a fisherman. I've no more to say about him.' Now she was getting cagey again. Well, he could afford to wait, come over and see her after Sunday service. She was a good woman, a strong believer who stood in the choir and bellowed the hymns with the best of them.

'Grace was lucky she had a friend like you to turn to,' he murmured diplomatically as he rose and began to don his coat.

'Grace didn' want no friends,' said Mrs Troup firmly, 'she didn't trust no one.'

'Not even you?' asked Optimus thinking, yes, and you don't trust me either.'

'Not even me. She wouldn't take no help neither, not even when Eric Wroth turned her out of the cottage. I told her she could come and stay with me awhile and help in the school till she found her feet, decided where she was goin' to, but she wouldn'. She knowed I'd try to put her off her purpose. That were why she went to work for Mrs Coyte over to Langstone Mill, she didn' have to. But she knowed Mrs Coyte'd never let her forget her Frank. So go there she did, and bowed her head and drank small beer while the time passed and it seemed she were resigned to everything.' Now that Optimus was leaving, the old woman seemed ready to talk again. Long days alone at the fireside with only memories for company, when she got going it would be like Robinson Crusoe telling his life story.

'She was very close to Frank, wasn't she?' His hand was on the latch. 'I wondered if you knew anything about that. I've been reading some letters. –'

'Whose letters? Frank's letters. I shan't ask how you've come by 'em, but don't expect Emma Troup to say nothin' about Grace and Frank, that's all gossip,' the old woman broke in with some intensity. 'If that's what you want to discuss, Mrs Coyte's the one you want, though you'll need a barrel of salt to go with her tittle-tattle. Now leave me. Can't you see I'm tired? I've had just about as much talking about

39

them old things as I can stand, it do bring back bad memories.'

'Just one last question,' said Optimus raising the latch, 'how would you describe Grace Pensilva? Would you say she was a good woman?'

'That's not an easy one for a Christian to answer,' said Mrs Troup, rubbing her interlaced fingers together to revive the circulation. 'On balance, she might have been, but then she might not. There's too much I never knowed about her. But I've tried to forgive her.'

The woman who had so disturbed Frederick Genteel was hovering wraith-like in the churchyard where her companion, poor Ivor Triggs, who had given over tolling, was shovelling the last of the earth on to the grave, his face working with an uncontrollable tic. Her own face was streaked with dirt where her passionate fingers had dug into it. Now the rain was dissolving the streaks and forming a series of blotchy runs down her cheeks, like tears of grief. And yet she did not weep.

'Not now,' she spoke to herself, in a voice not much above a whisper, 'not while they think they have reason to fear, but in the fullness of time.' She made a small, self-censored gesture towards Ivor, but withdrew her hand before it touched his sleeve. Was he listening to her? She did not think so. She imagined he was still at sea in his imagination, trapped under the upturned boat, listening to the water lap on the planking while his poor brain went over the disaster that had left him there, trying to make head or tail of a few shouts in the fog, the shattering of woodwork, the glint of weapons, sounds of threshing in the water as a man tried to swim away. 'We know, don't we, Ivor, we know what happened, we know what befell poor Frank, we know the name of his betrayer.'

'Ivor knows what 'ee knows,' said her companion leaning on his shovel.

'You'll see, friend Ivor, there will be a bitter harvest for more than one.'

'Bitter for sure, 'tis always a salt one for us fishermen. Us do reap, but us don't sow, bain't that the way of it?'

She left him there, patting the soil with his shovel, and half
ran, half walked, down into the village, past the Trafalgar
tavern, haunted by the reek of tobacco and brandy, stung by a
burst of ribald laughter, though whether at her she knew not,
past the wheelwright's shop where the lane expanded into a
bedraggled failure at a village green. Through an elder patch,
the massive stone barns round Home Farm imposed their
stark outline on the darkening fields. Further again, a row of
beetle-browed thatched cottages fringed the road to her left.
As soon as she cleared the last of them and turned the corner,
the wet west wind tore back her hood and slapped her face.

The cottage at which she halted had no lock on the door.
Like all its fellows in Harberscombe, it contained nothing of
value to a wandering thief, and among the village folk the
code of honesty was so strong that if one of them were to leave
a rip-hook or a bag of potatoes by the roadside unattended, it
would still be there when remembered next week. She lifted
the latch and stepped indoors on to the lime-ash floor. Under
the low joists made of timber from some ancient wreck, the
dim light filtering through the casement soon lost itself. The
edges of her plates, carefully ranged on the dresser, gleamed
faintly in the dusk. The scrubbed pine table surrounded by
four rush-seated chairs, stood bleak and bare in the centre of
the room. The fire which had always burnt bright and cheerful in the open hearth was cold and dead.

When the door had clicked to behind her, the young
woman unbuttoned her cloak, moving with the deliberation
of a sleepwalker. She hung it on one of the pegs at the back of
the door and, as her hand came away, it brushed the heavy
fabric of a seaman's jacket on the other hook. Impulsively,
she snatched it down and buried her face in the rough cloth.
She could smell the salt in it, the lingering sweat, reminders
of all the long tramps down to Armouth to catch the tide, the
buffeting spray rattling over the weather bow, the hard
hauling of kegs, the night runs inland with the loaded donkeys. While she waited, waited. For fear of the preventives he
would not let her ride with him.

41

Still she did not cry, although her shoulders shook. She was seeing his open face with its shy smile below the blond moustache and his eyes, those teasing, whimsical blue windows that opened his soul to her. She heard his tread on the floor as he slumped, dog-tired, into his favourite chair. The kettle sang on the hob and she brewed his tea. He took the mug in his berry-brown hands and carried it to his lips, drinking deep with a sigh and wiped his mouth with the back of his hand. The edge of his moustache was pearled with drops. His lips parted as if to say something to her, but there came no sound. Only the beating of a heart, pounding, insistent, her own heart, filled the room.

So loud was her heart, so compelling, that at first she did not hear the knocking on the door. When, finally, its loudness broke into her consciousness, she tried to ignore it, blot it out, but it would not cease. In despair, she flung the jacket into a chair, his chair, composed herself and pulled back the door.

'Well?' she demanded boldly, challenging the man who stood in the doorway. He ignored her attitude.

'I'll step inside, if I may; 'tes rainin' like the devil out 'ere. I don't want to get pnuemonia,' said the man as he brushed past her into the room, bringing cowshed smells and a stink of stale tobacco.

'If it's your condolences you've come to parade, you can take them home again. I want none of your sympathy. When things went well, this house never knew your tread.'

'You know me better than that.'

'I do. You're here on another matter. Out with it then, Farmer Wroth; you speak, I'll listen.'

'There's a place for you as dairy maid at Langstone Mill. You can live in, all found, and earn some pocket money.'

'Who said I wanted a job? When I need one, I've got a tongue in my head.'

Farmer Wroth shifted from one foot to another, twisting his wet hat in his hands. 'You won't be able to stay on 'ere, that's certain. Without Frank's money comin' in and with only the few pence you gets from 'elpin' Mrs Troup at the dame school, you'll never afford it. This place be too big for one woman anyhow.'

So that was it. Grace paused a while before answering. She had not thought of this. What had happened to Frank had been so unexpected, so sudden, she had had no time to consider its implications. Now Eric Wroth was down upon her, quick as a flash. He was a good landlord, good at being a landlord, protecting his interests, protecting his property. Without proper rent coming in, how could he be expected to maintain it? Who could blame him? That was how you made good in Harberscombe: you bought a scrap of land and tilled it in your spare time from labouring. With the profit, you bought more; when you had fields enough, you bought cottages and used the rent to buy more land, more horses. It was the only way off the treadmill of poverty which was the eternal lot of farmhands and fishermen. Farmer Wroth had taken that road; he was greying now, but in a lifetime of effort he had dragged himself up out of the mud and installed himself in a stone-built house, the one which had belonged to the Honourable Miss Delabole until she died recently. Eric Wroth had bought it from her executors, another bargain. Who could blame him? His father had been felled by a stroke following another man's plough.

'We've paid till Michaelmas.'

The farmer nodded assent. 'That leaves you three weeks till I gain possession.'

'At least you're no hypocrite, Eric Wroth, you're weeping no crocodile tears at my predicament. I suppose I should thank you for that. Well, you shall have your vacant possession, and much profit may you have of it. But now, for the present, this house is mine and I'll trouble you to vacate it.'

'Mr Coyte down to Langstone's a good man, accordin' to 'is lights. 'Ee were a friend to your father; 'ee'll be good to 'ee,' said Farmer Wroth as he set his hat on his head. The young woman nodded. She felt almost grateful. Although Eric Wroth always took care of himself first, there was some good feeling in the man.

'I'll see him tomorrow.'

'Say I sent you, Grace, 'ee's beholden to me, one way and another.' He stepped out quickly into the dusk, leaving her

43

confused. Where was she going? What road was open to her? It was illusory to think she was mistress of her fate. Only the routine of life offered some kind of security, some semblance of consolation. She took the flint and steel from the mantel-piece to light a candle. As it flared up, she saw a pale face staring in through the window. She bit her knuckle with fright before she recognized Emma Troup making signs at her. Reluctantly, she went to the door. Why couldn't they leave her alone with her grief? She could guess what good-natured, meddlesome Mrs Troup wanted; she would be full of kind suggestions and Christian resignation. Grace resolved to be uncommunicative, the woman would leave the sooner. But she knew that the cottage was no longer a sanctuary. To be alone with herself she would have to leave it.

A shadow among shadows, the man who had remained behind to fill the grave ranged his shovel in the church porch almost reverently, taking care to avoid making the slightest clink. Alone in the graveyard, generations of superstition crowded in on him and made the skin prickle on the nape of his neck. He would have been disturbed here after dark in any event, but now, after the things he had seen and the words he had heard, Ivor Triggs was unsettled and fright-ened. The rain pattered on the slate roof above him and the wind sighed in the yew. The tombstones were like black playing cards poised erect on a grey table, the wind whim-pered in the eaves and buffeted the tower. The ragged low clouds scurried over, their fringes fluttering like a woman's cloak.

He kept remembering her insistent questions: How dark had it been? If strangers had known the marks, could they have found the place? Had anyone in the gig made a careless noise, some sign that might have betrayed them?

All night she had questioned him, till his head spun and his speech was more jumbled than ever. Still she did not relent. Even to his poor puzzled mind there was some inkling of what she was driving at. How could the gig have been discov-ered, far out on a blank sea, on a black night, in a thick fog,

44

without some signal? If sense made sense, there had been a betrayer.

But he could not remember. Indeed he would rather forget, yet how could he? How could he forget the crunch of wood on wood, the flash from a dark-lantern, the hopeless struggle to pitch the last keg over the gunwale, water closing over him while he dug his nails into a thwart, finding his head trapped in the small space between it and the keel of the upturned boat, a terrible fear, Ivor Triggs couldn't swim, how long would the gig stay floating, and then a muffled shout from the nearby lugger, a voice, Frank's voice saying, 'Good Christ Captain! Have pity! 'Tis me, Frank Pensilva! Have pity!', a thud, then silence, the sound of oars approaching, and still more silence when he emerged from the hull and lay across it, the loneliness, the long night's loneliness till the dawn found him, drifting under the Barrow?

Her answer was not there, though he told her all that and repeated it. Detail by detail, she had prised it from him, but still there was something. Only much later had he remembered it, when the coffin was leaving the house and she had fallen in behind the bearers.

'Jan King did light 'is pipe,' he whispered and saw her stiffen. She looked straight ahead, ignoring Ivor; she had found what she wanted and had no more use of him.

Even so, when she spat in Jan King's face, he was unprepared for it, his slow mind had trouble linking the two facts together. Obscurely he felt he had been wrong ever to have told her.

The rain slackened and he left the porch, circling the church till he came to the steps that led down past the weathered Celtic cross to the deep-set lane and the lights of the alehouse. As he turned the corner, he let out a thin cry of fear: a hooded figure was hastening towards him. He shrank into the shadow of a buttress as she swept past him. She came within two yards without observing him, close enough for him to see her set face as she strode up the path to the graveside. And notwithstanding the instant recognition of her features, this was another person, not the Grace he knew,

45

Ivor Triggs did not know of what she was capable, but he feared her, following her compulsively as far as the place where the tower offered fresh concealment, as a whipped dog might follow his master.

But Grace Pensilva was not looking for Ivor. Her surroundings meant little to her. By the light of her candle in the cottage kitchen she had washed herself using ewer and basin, brushed out her hair, brushed it until it shone bright in the wall mirror that reflected her expressionless face. One thought was coursing through her head with the insistence of a Buddhist chant; it would not leave her, nor did she wish it to. It was to be the power that shaped her life. It was the expression of her will and she gloried in it. From being no one, existing dumbly on the edge of nowhere, she had transmuted herself overnight into a person with a purpose, a resolve she would never relinquish. After a prolonged stare into her own grey, unfathomable eyes, she had snuffed out the candle and stepped out into the falling night.

'No, Frank, I shall never forget you,' Ivor Triggs heard her say, as she stood at the graveside.

'All others may forget you here in the cold ground, but Grace will never, never forget, never forgive.'

Ivor Triggs cowered against the wall, expecting her to pass close to him on her return, but though her voice grew inaudible to him and then ceased, she did not come. When he found courage to look at the place where she had been, she was gone. Was she lurking round the angle of the tower? He held his breath: there was nothing but the wind worrying at the eaves. It was some time before he dared moved off, but soon he was running, running for the light and safety of his mother's kitchen.

Grace Pensilva had taken another way, leaving by the stile at the top of the graveyard and following the lane that led to the sea. There was more than one lane that left Harberscombe in that direction. One dipped into the ancient woodlands that hugged the estuary near Langstone Mill where the shallow River Arun ended its rush from Dartmoor to the sea. Another road ran past Okewell Court to the pool inside the Back at Armouth where the luggers and punts bobbed at moorings or dried out on the hard sand. This was the road the fishermen took on the quiet days when it was safe to cross the bar and tend their pots or set trammels and long lines. Its muddy floor was pitted with the hoof-marks of patient donkeys. Frank's boots had marked it once, but his prints were already overlaid by other traces. The Okewell lane was the lifeline by which half the Harberscombe families lived. It added a mile's trudge homeward to their daily stint, but they had known no other life, no lesser struggle. Harberscombe lay far back from the sea, as though hiding from Spanish or Salee rovers, sheltered in a shallow bowl that kept it safe from hostile eyes and let the rough winds fly over. Only by watching the tops of the elms could you tell how hard it was blowing.

She took the third road, a long straight lane that led out along a ridge towards the headland. The storm which had come in with the afternoon tide was at its height. The rain was over now, but the gale was pounding in from the south. Atlantic swells were rattling on the Bolt, sending up great plumes of unseen spray, too far off for Grace to see or hear them. Nearer at hand, Armouth Bar was an impassable mass of seething white as the rollers spent themselves upon the sand. At the head of the bay, Grace Pensilva saw the faint glow of a light in Jan King's isolated cottage. He was the only person to live down by the boats and his house was a sea-mark, having been built in that place to aid Jan's father, the Arun River pilot, to bring the Plymouth barges up into the estuary without touching the offshore reefs. What was Jan King thinking now, down there alone in that house? There were no distractions; he had nothing to do but repent. No doubt he feared her now, but that would pass.

The lane petered out in a field where the wet grass soaked her boots and weighed down the hem of her skirt, but she strode on. Not far ahead, the arching brow of the Barrow reared itself up, highest headland on this coast, where the wreckers of an earlier century were said to have lit their beacons to lure tall ships ashore.

She slowed as she felt the rough cliff-top gorse scratching her legs. Just a few yards in front of her, the unseen cliff fell away precipitously. At its foot, the waves were beating the jagged rocks in a continuous hissing roar. For a moment she felt as if she could willingly fling herself over, or allow a gust to take her and send her spiralling down. But she braced herself and waited.

Far out where the Eddystone lay in wait for wayward ships running blind before the storm, a patch of livid moonlight began to play on the backs of the heaving waves. As it sped shorewards, it broadened, spilling out to either side till it touched Bolt Tail on one side, and the rise of land at Stoke Point on the other.

Grace Pensilva had never been to a city; she had never known a theatre's brightness, but here, without knowing it, she was getting her first glimpse of the vivid drama that was to be her life, a life of incredible luminosity, high tension, and dark shadow. She had made her decision, the one fatal, inexorable, terrible decision in her brief existence and she was about to mould her life to it, becoming an actress, dissembling her emotions in a play of her own making. Even now, with her resolve taken, she had no idea of its implications. But if she had, she would not have wavered.

There, in the centre of the pool of moonlight, was the place where she knew her Frank had foundered, lost his life, had it snatched away from him. Her vow was fresh in her mind, she did not regret it. Never, she promised herself, never in all her days would she waver. Whatever the cost, she would pay it, pay it gladly. Little did she know how heavy the cost, how dreadful the reckoning.

But now, plaything of a wild wind, deafened by the surf and stung by the salt spray, she had no misgivings. The great natural crescendo of the storm enveloped her, bearing her up in a flight of passion that freed her constraint and let loose her sorrow.

She wept. She wept and her tears mingled with the salt sea spray on her face. She wept, and her tangled hair whipped back and forth across her brow. She wept, and her mouth, still the mouth of a child, quivered uncontrollably. She wept, and her hands, those hands she had just dedicated to their secret destiny, clenched and unclenched convulsively.

Then, like a curtain coming down over a tragedy, the clouds rolled in, the pool of moonlight fled and plunged her back into obscurity. She wept on. One such a night was not enough to quench her sorrow, the sorrow she clung to like a a lifebuoy. She would burn and burn, but to the world she would put up that same mask of indifference on the morrow that she had worn today. She would grieve him still. There would be time enough: the two she stalked had lives to lead, and she had time to kill.

4

Optimus did not fail to try and track down Ivor Triggs. Such a
witness, however unreliable, was not to be neglected. The
only trouble, as he soon discovered, was that Ivor had long
since moved away. Whatever the reason, his mother who,
willy-nilly, had been obliged to care for him, had given up her
cottage and gone off somewhere, taking the poor creature
with her. Poor Ivor was 'proper mazed', as the locals
expressed it. The few who remembered him affirmed that his
wits, already weak before the incident with the gig, had been
definitely deranged thereafter.

Thus unfairly deprived of his principal witness, Optimus
began diligent inquiries through the local carrier and postman, but all to no avail: Ivor Triggs and his mother, who must
be an old woman now, had vanished as if they had never
existed. Optimus was forced to fall back on more hearsay
testimony from unreliable sources and to rely more heavily
than he wished on Mrs Troup's reminiscences. Everywhere,
he encountered a climate of distrust and even Emma was
slow to outgrow it.

'Why do you keep on askin' the same old questions, Mr
Shute? Haven't you nothin' better to do than keep rakin' over
the ashes o' the past?'

'The truth, Mrs Troup, the truth and nothing but the truth,
that's all I'm after.'

'The truth! The truth! That's all some young folk go on
about. They think 'tis easy to get hold of, just like the
'rithmatic they learn you in college. The truth, I tell you, was
buried long since along o' Grace Pensilva and them as loved

her. And even if you had the truth, what would be the use on it?'

'I might manage to justify her.'

'Justify Grace Pensilva!' The old woman laughed with unwonted bitterness, as if at some unchanging incongruity, some irony in life that you met unexpectedly at every other turn in the road. 'Justify Grace Pensilva,' she continued, 'don't you know there's two kinds o' justice. There's your soft, Christian kind, that's all forgiveness, and there's the other that's all retribution, eye for eye and tooth for tooth. Go back to your Bible, Mr Shute, and you'll see if there's any mitigation possible, any justification.'

Where had Optimus heard this argument before? It had a familiar ring. Then he remembered: Dr Cornish. The old scoundrel knew his patients' minds better than they gave him credit for. Emma had paused and was polishing her glasses on her shawl. When she had finished, she stared at him intently.

'So she's not forgiven,' he said.

'Go and ask one-eyed old Scully if she's forgiven. He could tell you a thing or two about what happened in Salcombe if he had a mind to, but I'll warrant he won't, 'tweren't much to his credit.'

'What *did* happen in Salcombe? You must know something.'

'Only bits and bobs. I know Grace went there. She were determined to get a look at the captain o' the revenue cutter. Only when she got there, he'd gone and another man'd replaced him.'

'Scully?'

'If you know all that, what's the use my tellin' you? I s'pose Dr Cornish has already told you 'bout the man in the mask, the one what put paid to Frank Pensilva.' Optimus shook his head. 'Well, 'tis only hearsay, but that's what I heard, though why the revenue captain should've wanted to disguise hisself is beyond my understandin'. What I do know is: Grace Pensilva went off to discover his identity, but she comed back as ignorant as when she started. She never did get his scent, not while she lived in Harberscombe.'

'So you knew all along what she was set on. Others must've

had more than an inkling too. What about Jan King, surely he must have suspected her? He'd have been pretty dim if he didn't.'

'Oh, Jan King,' murmured Emma, her eyes suddenly vague and misty, 'poor Jan. Believed what he wanted to believe o' Grace, did Jan. But Jan weren't soft in the head, nothin' like that, but soft on Grace, that he were for certain. Grace knowed it, played cat and mouse with un, took her time she did, till he'd all but forgotten.'

'But you knew more than he did, you knew about her vow, surely *you* weren't taken in.'

'Taken in? Course I were. Grace never did speak again o' the matter. The days went past, the weeks, the months, until it seemed she had forgotten, and so did we, never thought she might be play-actin'.' Mrs Troup paused and sighed. 'I used to think I knowed young Grace, when she were with Miss Delabole we used to laugh a lot together, times she comed here to chatter. But the real Grace were *'ard*, Mr Shute, *'ard* as a flint. Once she were wronged, or thought so, there were no deflectin' her.'

'And you never told Jan about the vow, about what Ivor told you?'

'Not in so many words. You couldn't take what Ivor said for gospel. But I did warn him. Might as well preach to the deaf. Jan were struck on Grace, always had been, Jan wanted to think the best of her.'

'But to be so besotted.'

'Moonstruck – ah, Mr Shute, 'tis easy to tell you're a young un, you haven't yet learned the half of what a man in love'll believe of a woman. Oh, I can see you're a doubtin' Thomas, but I've somethin' here as'll serve to convince you.' She opened her sewing box and removed the shelves until she reached the bottom layer. After a period of ferreting about, during which she pricked her finger, she pulled out a small scrap of folded yellowing paper. After pulling it open and glancing at the interior, she passed it across to Optimus. When he held it up to the light, he saw there were nine words written across it, but he could not read them.

'What is it? Latin?'

'Latin! No, Mr Knowall, I thought an eddicated man would know better than that. Don't you know French when you see it? And the handwritin', surely you know the handwritin'?' Optimus nodded. He had seen it before many times among the papers Dr Cornish had given him, it had become almost as familiar as his own mother's in the monthly letters she unfailingly sent him.

'I know the writing all right, but I still can't read it. You know what it means, don't you?'

'I've had it explained, but you mustn't trust yourself to that. You must find a proper translator. Try Mrs Lackland, she were taught by French nuns up to Lunnon. She's lookin' for someone to help her with her good works about the parish. Give her a hand. One good turn deserves another, she'll explain it for you.'

'We'll see about that,' said Optimus, pocketing the paper and rising. A vague resentment was welling up inside him; he wasn't going to let Mrs Troup push him into anything. But he found it hard to contain the curiosity that was already gnawing at him to know the nine words' meaning.

'If you're too shy to approach Mrs Lackland, there's always Nancy Genteel to ask, she'll know the meaning,' murmured Mrs Troup teasingly, 'she's older now and must've lost some of her appetite for young men and horses. Have you been to Leet? Have you tried to see her?'

'They say she's not at home.'

'Aye, she's not at home, but by day you'll see a face at the window, and by night a lamp allus burnin'. That Nancy don't sleep much, and for good reason. What she wanted, she took, now she's got it, she's past sharin'. By rights Leet House ought to be haunted, haunted by her poor brother Frederick, but God knows where his sad spirit do wander.' She closed her eyes and set herself to rocking slowly.

It was time to leave. Although Mrs Troup was softening towards him more than a little, he was wise enough not to over-stay his welcome. Next time, he told himself, he would bring her some special tea from the grocer's. Bribery might work better than mere persuasion.

After walking some distance from her cottage, Optimus stopped and surveyed the landscape. Down there, deep in the woods, lay Langstone Mill; further off, in misty parkland, the crenellations of Leet House frowned over the trees; nearer at hand, Harberscombe nestled in a shallow declivity backed by the church and the sloping graveyard. At that distance, you could not expect to clearly discern figures standing among the tombstones, even if they had been there in reality. But now its occupants were present in his head and he knew he must hurry back to the schoolhouse and commit the next of their encounters to paper.

Two days later she was kneeling by the bed. All around her lay Frank's possessions which she had removed from his sea-chest. Her own few belongings were already packed into a leather bag, one of the few things Miss Delabole had given her. What had he owned? Little enough in all conscience. She picked up a walrus tusk, engraved with scrimshaw work showing the engagement between the *Chesapeake* and HMS *Shannon*. She would have to sell it for what it would fetch, though who would want it in Harberscombe she could not imagine. She was not in immediate want, a chamois leather purse contained a few gold coins: a couple of napoleons, a dollar and a South American piece with an image of Bolivar. But it was not these things that constituted Frank's treasure in Grace's eyes. On a shelf to one side of the chest were ranged a short row of leather-bound books: Cobbett's *Political Register*, a compendium of radical news-sheets, Benjamin Franklin's *Rules for Reducing a Great Empire to a Small One*, and best of all, Tom Paine's *The Rights of Man*.

Grace took up this last book and opened it, holding it up close so that she could read its small print in the inadequate light. She was so absorbed in reading it that she failed to hear the door behind her open softly.

'You'll strain your eyes, Grace. When *will* you give over reading?'

Grace whirled round in astonishment, slamming the book shut and clasping it to her breast. 'Oh, it's you, Emma! You

54

frightened me. Why didn't you knock?'

'Us don't need to knock on the door of a friend's 'ouse, not 'ere in 'Arberscombe.' For all the dignity of her position as mistress of the dame school, Mrs Troup had precious little book-learning beyond the ability to construe her Bible and prayer book. She could write a passable hand and do simple arithmetic. Her manner of speaking owed nothing to drawing-rooms or colleges. For all that, she had a kind heart, belied by her abrupt exterior.

'I suppose not,' replied Grace. 'I must be edgy.'

'What's that you're readin'?' inquired Mrs Troup solicitously. 'I 'opes 'tis religious, there be naught like religion to comfort a body in trouble.'

'Words, Emma, words, that's all it is,' said Grace, dropping the book into Frank's chest and closing the lid behind it.

'Oh, 'tis one o' they books your Frank was always on about. Well, you'd best 'ave done with 'em. No good'll come of readin' that rebellious nonsense. Frank would've 'ad more friends in 'Arberscombe if 'ee 'adn't tried to ram that stuff down people's gullets. This is England, not France, not America, us don't want that revolutionary stuff, us wants peace, us wants beef and ale and if us 'as to say "God save the Squire" to 'ave 'em, why so be it. Frederick Genteel's not a bad man, neither.'

'Frank's good sense was wasted here, we both knew it. This was the last place he should have tried to alter men's opinions, there hasn't been a fresh thought in Harberscombe since the Reformation.'

'I wouldn't go so far as to say that, but us be slow and careful, not like you young people what gets ideas from books. 'Arberscombe's no place for the likes of you. No doubt you'll be leavin'.' Grace shook her head. 'What's there for a bright young maid like you in this village? You'll make your way in the world, you will. Mark my words, you'll end up somebody, a proper lady. But 'ere in 'Arberscombe, there's nothin', not unless you marries the squire.'

'Don't be a fool, Emma, will you stop your romancing? Don't talk to me about marriage, and don't talk about leaving either. I've things to do here and I'll leave when I have a mind to.'

'No need to snap at me, I was only tryin' to be friendly.'

'I'm sorry, Emma, I'm still a bit overwrought.'

'As well you might be, poor dear,' said Mrs Troup, coming over and placing a comforting arm round Grace's shoulders, ''tis 'ard to face a loss at the best o' times and you and Frank were terrible close, wasn't you? Best thing you can do be let go and cry a little.' Grace shrugged away Mrs Troup's arm and stared stonily out of the window. 'What'll you do, Grace, if you stay?'

'Work.'

'Where? There's no work for the likes of you in 'Arberscombe.'

'Langstone Mill.'

'Langstone Mill? That old skinflint Coyte won't give 'ee 'arf enough to' keep body and soul together. 'Tis no place for you, Grace. There bain't nothin' 'ere, I tell 'ee. You must go away, leave 'Arberscombe, forget it. And forget your Frank, clear off and forget un.'

Grace swung round on Mrs Troup, her grey eyes suddenly cold and narrowing with anger. 'I won't! I won't! I won't!' she shouted. 'And I won't listen to you either. Why should I forget Frank? Why does everyone want me to? He was too good for this place, that's the reason, and you're all too happy to get rid of him.'

'Not so,' affirmed Mrs Troup, not to be browbeaten, and trying to keep her temper, 'us did know un for what 'ee were, a drifter, a wastrel, a big-mouth. Frank weren't the fine feller you took un for.'

'I forbid you to say that. I won't listen,' said Grace, covering her ears.

'I knows why you're staying in 'Arberscombe, Grace Pensilva,' said Mrs Troup with a sudden coldness. ''Tis vengefulness. Well, don't think I'll stand by and let it 'appen. Ivor Triggs 'ave told me somethin'; I won't repeat it, but I knows what you're up to. You'll not take the law into your own 'ands and get away with it. Forgive and forget, live and let live. If you won't give over, if you won't give me your word you've changed your mind, 'twill be my duty to warn 'em, and the magistrates too, if needful.'

'You shall never have it.'

'I'll give 'ee three days to change your mind. That's more than I ought to give 'ee. 'Eaven knows what you might do in the meantime.'

'Get out of my house,' said Grace in a toneless voice. 'I've told you, I won't listen to you.'

'There's none so blind as them as won't see,' muttered Mrs Troup, flouncing towards the door. 'Stay in 'Arberscombe if you must, much joy may it bring 'ee. But don't think you can stay friends with Emma Troup if you can't speak to 'er decent, if you won't show forgiveness.'

With that, she went out and slammed the door, leaving Grace alone with her thoughts. So that, as she had suspected, was how it would be: she could expect no real sympathy, no understanding from the people of Harberscombe. Blood was thicker than water, they were all cousins, Jan King was related to Emma Troup on his father's side. In the end, it boiled down to one thing: they would stand up for their own. They knew as well as she did that one of the men in the gig had sold out to the preventives. It could not have been Ivor Triggs, even before the incident unhinged his reason, he was too simple for that. Even if he had been tricked into it, Grace was sure she would have wormed it out of him by now; Ivor Triggs had never been able to keep a secret. Grace was convinced she knew the identity of Frank's betrayer; it was easy to arrive at by a process of elimination. And, if evidence were needed to confirm her deduction, there was Ivor's recollection of Jan King's having lit his pipe just before the arrival of the lugger. It was Jan all right and she knew his motive: jealousy. Jan King was jealous of Frank for having become the leader of their venture, jealous of his education and his intelligence, above all, jealous of his closeness with her, Grace. She knew from the way he had looked at her. Jan King could never be brought to understand that there was no place for him in her universe; Frank had been too bright a sun for that.

Knowing that Emma Troup was forewarned of her intentions was a blow. If Emma suspected her, others must also. She must be doubly careful. In the weeks and months to come, she must lull their suspicions. She did not yet know what she would do in response to Emma's ultimatum, but already she was formulating her reply, a reply that would put her off her guard. She knelt again and packed Frank's weather-stained clothes and his other possessions back into the chest. Tomorrow morning, she would walk down to Langstone Mill, with the chest on her shoulder. She knew it would be a hard road, but she was determined to take it.

Shortly after his talk with Mrs Troup Optimus had strolled down towards Langstone Mill, hoping to obtain further insight into Grace Pensilva's story by seeing the house where she had lived after leaving the cottage in the village which she had shared with Frank. The way led over the brow of a hill to a tract of ancient woodland, principally lichen-draped oak trees, but including a stand of enormous beeches and a few bracken-carpeted clearings. As he entered the last of these and faced the thicket of gloomy rhododendrons that fringed the woods, he became aware of a strange groaning. The air in the clearing was still, none of the rusty bracken shoots was stirring. The pervading sensation was one of decay, many of the bracken stems were broken and their heads were drooping into the faded grass. Tattered spider webs spanned the path, showing that no one had passed that way of late.

As he stood there, he seemed to feel a presence: it was as if Grace Pensilva were watching him. Optimus glanced over his shoulder, but of course there was no one. The solitude only added to an irrational sadness which was already weighing him down. But he knew that the sadness was merely the fruit of a romantic imagination. It was part of the pathetic fallacy that nature should seem to share in human grief. With a shake of his shoulders that was almost a shiver, he pressed on across the clearing, breaking the clinging filaments of web as he went. They clung to him like small restraining hands. For an instant he thought he heard laughter, a peal of untrammelled mirth, but it was only a jay, clattering off among the branches.

Langstone Mill was probably much as it had been when Grace had lived there. He halted at the edge of the wood, half expecting to see her come out of the door and cross the farm-yard.The grey buildings stood absolutely alone, cupped in a deep landlocked valley. Blue-grey slates on top of dove-grey walls, it was still half farm, half mill. A faint lowing came from the cow-house on one side of the yard. On the far side, facing him, the barn's doors hung open and the shafts of a waggon stuck out of its dim interior. On the right, the mill itself, which was part and parcel of the miller's lodgings, was set deep into the hill slope so that the leat ran straight to the chute at the crown of the wheel which kissed the eaves as it spun slowly. It was the groaning from the shuddering, ill-lubricated wheel and inner machinery that Optimus had heard in the clearing. There was a rational, down to earth explanation for everything.

Even so, there was no escaping the melancholy groaning which pervaded the valley from the sea-fed pond on his left to the stunted, knobbly apple trees that sprawled up the hill to his right. Even in the autumn sunshine, there was a sad, abandoned desolation about the place. What must it be like when the sea winds brought stinging rain up the winding estuary? Optimus felt it like a coldness around his heart.

And then a door opened at the head of a short flight of steps where the farmhouse overlooked the yard. A half-starved collie slunk out and Optimus waited to see who would follow. That must have been the door from which Grace emerged daily to cross the yard for firewood from the shed opposite. This time, it was not Grace, how could it be, but a bent, ageing, shock-headed farmer or rather miller, for he wore a soiled white apron. From the jerky way he moved, Optimus guessed him to be of a choleric disposition and, unwilling to risk a confrontation, he was ready to step back into the bushes when the dog smelt him and set to barking hysteri-cally and running towards him in a series of oblique zigzags, cringing and aggressive in turns. The miller's head swung round and he fixed the intruder with an unsmiling stare. Optimus was determined not to let himself be discountenanced. He strolled boldly down the intervening meadow to the farmyard gate, with the collie snapping half-heartedly at his gaitered legs. The miller awaited him, standing firm with his large dusty hands widespread and locked on to the top bar of the gate.

'Don't you know you're trespassin'?' he demanded when Optimus came close.

'This is Langstone Mill, isn't it? There's a right of way that comes down here. Mrs Troup told me so, she said it went right through the farmyard where you're standing and up the lane to Uglington.'

'She said that, did she? Well, you weren't on it, the path do run down by the pond. If you don't know that, you 'ad no good reason to come traipsin' round 'ere. Us don't 'ave no time for strangers.'

Optimus looked the miller in the eye coolly, astonished at his own temerity. Behind the man's screen of aggressiveness, he detected a sly evasiveness, a pair of eyes that shifted nervously. Like farmer, like dog, thought Optimus, his hand descending on to the latch. As he did so, he realized that one of the miller's eyes, the right, had a patch of white in the centre, as if splashed with flour; its iris had been destroyed and he was partly blind. 'Your name is Scully, isn't it? And you've a son called Andrew that goes to school in Branscombe. I'm Mr Shute, his schoolmaster.'

'Why didn't you say so in the first place? Come on through, Maister, come through and be welcome.' Optimus smiled a thin smile at the miller's change of tone; a man wasn't often valued for what he was, but for the title men hung on him.

'What's become of the Coytes who used to live here?' he inquired innocently as he picked his way across the muck-strewn farmyard.

'Gone, long since, and good riddance to 'em,' grunted Scully. 'Always behind with the rent, they were. Old Barker, the Steward over to Leet, threw 'em out.'

60

'That's how you got here, is it? Well in with Barker were you?'

'Charles Barker owed me a favour.'

'No doubt you knew a thing or two about people round here that was worth money or at least preferment. Your old job saw to that.'

Scully halted and looked at Optimus searchingly with his good eye. 'What d'you mean, my old job?'

'You were with the preventives, weren't you?'

'Who told you that? That old gossip Mrs Troup, weren't it?' Optimus shook his head; the miller scowled. 'Who was it then?'

'I'm not at liberty to tell you.' There was no point in revealing to this man that Dr Cornish was aware of Scully's background and had passed on his information. 'Anyway,' Optimus continued, 'there's nothing to be ashamed of in that, is there?'

'Harberscombe folk never took kindly to the customs men.'

'I suppose not. Well, you needn't worry: I shan't go round blabbing about it, not if you're helpful.'

'Helpful? How can I be helpful?'

'You can tell me what you know of Grace Pensilva.' The change in the miller's face was alarming. For a moment, Optimus thought the man might strike him and he caught Scully sneaking a glance with his good eye at the cleaver which was stuck in the chopping-block beside the wood pile. But the man controlled himself and answered Optimus's question with another.

'Grace Pensilva? Who might be Grace Pensilva?'

'She lived here once – in Mrs Coyte's time, that is. I thought you might have heard something.'

'In this house? There's nothing of hers here, nor've I never heard tell of her neither.'

Optimus shrugged his shoulders in mock resignation. He knew Scully was lying, but there was nothing to be gained by disclosing that knowledge. He changed the subject. 'Where's your boy, Mr Scully? I don't see him about here anywhere, his mother either for that matter.'

Scully scowled darker than ever. 'We don't see eye to eye, the wife and I.'

'She's left you then.'

'In a manner of speakin'.' Scully was evasive, not sure what to say. 'Threw 'er out's more like it. Couldn't put up with 'er 'olier than thou expressions. Never in this world, Mr Shute, will you find a woman that's worse than the kind that's got religion.'

'And that's where your boy is, he's gone to see her,' Optimus surmised our loud.

'Aye, but he'll be back directly. The boy's mine, I've brought him up, I've taught him proper respect for his father.' Yes, you have, thought Optimus, remembering the weals he had seen on the young man's legs and back. Spare the rod and spoil the child was an honoured precept in more than one Harberscombe family. A man like Scully could swing a vicious belt and be no less a jealous father. Scully was sly, Scully was secretive, but his boy was the chink in his armour. When the time came, Optimus thought he knew how to get at him.

'You must find it very quiet here alone, Mr Scully.'

'I've a good conscience,' muttered Scully. 'I've work aplenty, Mr Shute. If you'll excuse me, I must get back to me milling.'

'I thank you for your welcome,' said Optimus with feigned courtesy. 'A pity though about your memory. If you should ever recall something about Grace Pensilva, you know where to find me.'

There was another gate at the far end of the farmyard where the steep, rutted lane began to climb to the road. Optimus opened it and passed through, uneasily conscious of the miller's single eye glaring on his back. As he slipped the hasp into the staple, he looked up. Despite his talk of work, Scully had not moved.

'Let sleeping dogs lie, Mr Schoolmaster,' came his voice in little over a hoarse whisper, 'that's a good saying to remember.'

'The wheels of God grind slow, Mr Miller, but they grind

exceedingly small. How's that for another?' After that, Optimus never looked back. The hissing splash of the water hurrying down the rotten chute to the turning wheel faded slowly, overwhelmed by the wavering bass groan that emerged from the machinery. Though Scully had volunteered nothing, he now knew more of Grace Pensilva, knew it only intuitively perhaps, but none the less, knew with some certainty that he had passed a place still haunted by her uneasy spirit.

5

Dr Cornish heard the doorbell ring, but did not move to answer it. He looked up and watched it quivering at the end of the spiral spring the blacksmith had set it on so that it would jingle long after its chain had been released. Dr Cornish's foot was paining him again abominably, it was the same gout that had been plaguing him for twenty years, but close acquaintanceship hadn't made it any more acceptable. It pained him while he sat almost motionless in his rocking chair, but he knew it would pain him even more were he to stand up. Mrs Kemp would answer the door eventually. She had taken her knitting to the parlour and would be nodding over it by the fireside. If the bell were rung hard enough, she would hear it, she usually did.

After a second, more timorous, pull at the bell, there was silence, and then Dr Cornish heard footfalls on the cobbles; his caller was going away. It was dark outside and, even when whoever it was reached the lane, he wouldn't be able to identify him. The Doctor didn't think it was one of his patients; they usually had the good sense not to disturb him after supper. He was full of curiosity and sat up in his chair with his fingers twitching.

'Ho there!' he shouted, 'stay where you are. Wait a bit, where's your patience, can't you spare a minute till we get the door open?' He opened his mouth to shout to Mrs Kemp, took a deep breath, then changed his mind about it. Mrs Kemp hadn't heard the bell, she wouldn't hear his bellowing either. Instead, he snatched an old hickory stick from the chimney corner and flung it at the inner door that closed off the

64

passageway to the front of the house. It was a good throw, the Doctor's arm still had some strength in it, he congratulated himself, and the stick struck the panels with a squib-like crack before clattering on to the flagstones. Dr Cornish cocked his ear and waited.

There was silence: the footsteps outdoors had stopped, but there was no sound of Mrs Kemp's slippers approaching. Damn the woman and her deafness, she was probably asleep into the bargain. When she dozed off, it would take a cannon to awaken her. There was a renewed shuffling outside the door. 'Don't move!' he shouted again, 'I'll get it open for you.'

When he climbed out of his chair and started to cross the room, he beat the air with his right hand ineffectually. The stick he should have leant on was lying in the far corner. When his bad leg touched the ground the pain was exquisite. It was only a few steps, but when he reached the door, he was already panting. He had to balance on one leg while he unshipped the iron bar that was slotted across the door frame each night to supplement the lock in the centre and the bolts at top and bottom. With a hop to one side, he wrenched it open and looked out into the night. At first he saw no one, the pool of light from the kitchen fell on vacant cobblestones. Only after a while did he see the faint blur of a white face in the obscurity at the head of the steps. With an impatient gesture, he waved the stranger forward.

'Oh, it's you!' he muttered ill-temperedly as the man's face became clearer. 'Why didn't you say so? So you've decided to come over at last, have you? The mountain has decided to come to Mahomet, has it? Well, you've been a confounded long time making up your mind to it.'

'I only wanted to ask Mrs Kemp for some sugar. I forgot to order a bag last time I saw the grocer and now I've run out.'

Dr Cornish sniffed. 'Not much of an excuse to call out a neighbour at this hour, now is it? Still, there's hospitality at stake and you must have some. Come in boy, don't just stand there, you're letting all the heat out of my kitchen.'

Optimus Shute approached tentatively, with something of the shyness you would expect of a young colt being lured into a tight corner by a horsebreaker. He was wary of the warmth and comfort which enveloped him as he neared the fireplace. 'I mustn't stop,' he muttered defensively.

'No, don't do that,' grunted Dr Cornish, 'you mustn't waste your valuable time here jawing. Well, it's taken you long enough to decide to come over, you must stay long enough to let us get a proper look at you. Take that candle, young feller, and go through to the parlour. Tell Mrs Kemp to come out here quick, she can find you some sugar; better than that, she can make us a grog to drink away melancholy.'

Meekly enough, Optimus took the light and set off into the dark passageways. It was a sprawling house, starting from an ancient medieval core, which was now the kitchen and extending drunkenly in two directions, up steps, round corners, enlarged whenever its owners had come into some money. He passed the surgery and couldn't resist a sidelong glance at the small wainscoted chamber containing nothing but a couple of chairs. Facing the chairs was the internal window through which Dr Cornish was said to look down from a small chamber on a higher level, questioning his patients concerning their symptoms and examining them visually, without ever actually touching them, before prescribing the old-fashion remedies he usually made up himself for them. Whatever the truth about the Doctor's methods might be, the two rooms were certainly there, just as his informants had described them. Further on, he found Mrs Kemp snoring over her knitting and had to shake her shoulder to wake her. She showed no astonishment that he should be there, merely gathering up her bits and pieces in her big, work-worn hands before following him back to the Doctor who was already ensconced in his rocker.

'Two bumpers of grog,' the latter instructed her, 'and don't be mean with the rum, or the lime juice either, and don't forget the demerara; this young feller's run out of sugar, he needs sweetening up a little.'

Optimus considered turning down the grog, but what was the use, old Dr Cornish wouldn't listen. It wasn't an invitation, it was a prescription. He promised himself he would sip it slowly. He wasn't really a teetotaller, though he had allowed the selection committee that chose him for Branscombe School to think so without contradiction. He was sure the Vicar took the occasional glass or two, why shouldn't a schoolmaster? It was only hellfire Methodists who pretended all alcohol was poison. He settled into a round-backed chair facing the Doctor and waited.

'Well, what d'you make of her?' demanded Dr Cornish as soon as Mrs Kemp had shuffled away to the dairy in search of ingredients.

'A pity the old lady's so deaf,' replied Optimus.

'I wasn't talking about Mrs Kemp, you fool,' snorted the Doctor. 'You're not that obtuse, are you? You can't be. What I mean is, are you getting close to her, have you made any progress?'

Optimus Shute wasn't really ready to admit that he was involved in Grace Pensilva's story. He wasn't eager to admit it to himself, but he supposed someone had been talking about his inquiries, perhaps the Troup woman, and the news had filtered back to Dr Cornish.

'I've glanced at some of the papers you gave me,' he admitted, 'but I'm not getting anywhere. I haven't even summed up how the whole thing started.'

'Real life stories don't have neat beginnings, or neat ends either. That's something you'll learn, boy, if you make a study as I have. I suppose you're mulling around what happened in the churchyard or perhaps, if you've obtained a grasp on that, you're puzzling over what exactly did happen in the gig. What if I were to tell you that didn't matter? The event in itself was banal, it would have led to nothing if it weren't for the nature of the people. It was Frank and it was Grace Pensilva; otherwise it would have fizzled out like most other stories. You've understood that, at least, you must have. What did Emma Troup have to say about the two of them?'

'There are certain things Mrs Troup doesn't like to discuss; she said I should ask Mrs Coyte –'

'Knowing full well that Mrs Coyte left Harberscombe years ago,' broke in Dr Cornish. 'What a squeamish, namby-pamby,

Pharisaical woman she is! Everyone in Harberscombe knew they were close, closer than normal; only a few were ready to discuss it in public, though there were always whispers. Mrs Coyte, in particular, was always insinuating things; she was a sharp-tongued old devil, but was always first and loudest with her amens in the Wesleyan chapel.'

'What exactly did she say?'

'Consanguinity.'

Optimus was shocked; he hoped the Doctor was exaggerating, and he suspected his own face was flushing as it often did when he was confronted by an embarrassing subject. He was relieved when Mrs Kemp interrupted them with two steaming glasses of grog on a tray.

'Go on, it's not poisoned,' insisted Dr Cornish, taking one for himself. Optimus sipped at his glass tentatively. 'Don't look as though you eat much either,' grumbled the Doctor. 'Look at him, Mrs Kemp,' he continued, raising his voice to a shout, 'thin as a rake. You'll have to feed him up a little.'

'I can look after myself, I'm not incapable.'

'Never mind that, it's all very fine to be independent, but Mrs Kemp can as easily cook for three as for two, she'll come over with supper. Pay her if you want to. You're tired after a long day in the classroom, you don't want to go cooking when you could put your feet up and think, think about Grace Pensilva. Eaten tonight, have you?' Optimus nodded vigorously, but unconvincingly. 'Bring us some ham and a loaf from the pantry, Mrs Kemp,' thundered the Doctor. 'And you, Mr Shute, throw another log on the fire; can't you see I'm too old and inform to do that kind of thing. Go on, stir it up a bit, we need some warmth so we can talk a little, there's quite a few questions at the back of my mind that I want to put to you. About Jack Lugger for example, and Uncle Bill Terry; you should have seen Uncle Bill by now. Uncle Bill's one of my successes, a doctor has to have some, you know. Ought to have died years back, ages ago, from a heart attack pulling pots, but I brought him round and he's lingered on, beyond a man's alloted span of threescore and ten. Uncle Bill can tell you a thing or two about Jan King, so can Jack Lugger, if you can find him in Cornwall, but take *his* information with a pinch of salt; the man's a liar, he'll tell you he got that scar across his face when he was in the navy, but I know better.'

'Was it from smuggling?' asked Optimus, his eyes lighting up with new interest.

'You're all the same, you new people, when you hear the word smuggling you're all ears, it's so romantic. Well, let me tell you something, it wasn't like that in real life; it was hard, dangerous, chancy work, and a man didn't do it for pleasure. It was sheer necessity that drove men to it, even Jack Lugger, whatever he says nowadays. No one ever made more than a decent living at it, never a fortune, and it's a good thing the whole bloody business is over.' He paused and looked deep into his glass. 'I'm not saying smuggled liquor didn't taste better; it did, it does, but there's precious little of it left nowadays. The laws have changed and the people with them; it's tamer now in Harberscombe. There's a tale or two I could tell you about the old days, if I had a mind to.'

Despite his good resolutions to take an ounce of sugar in a twist of paper and run back across the lane to the schoolhouse where he had left a light burning in his room to give the impression he was there, studying, Optimus lingered on late into the night, wrapped up in Dr Cornish's wandering conversation, or rather monologue in which the names he had read in the stack of papers kept coming up in a different context, filling in blanks in his understanding and opening up new, unsuspected vistas.

When he had started at college, he had believed he would learn a great deal, some large fraction of the sum of human knowledge. Now that he had left college and its dogmatic certitudes, his ignorance was being revealed to him piecemeal: he soon discovered that the slovenly old fellow, Stitson, who kept Butterwell Farm, was possessed of a vast lore concerning animal husbandry, weather, tillage, fat-stock prices, nuts and berries from the hedgerows, phases of the moon, etc. etc., whose existence Optimus had never suspected, having believed that country folk were limited, slow-moving blockheads, and that farming was an occupation of childish simplicity. Likewise Dr Cornish: his style and practices might be old-fashioned, but the man knew, he knew so much that Optimus was browbeaten. It was a surprise to find something which was beyond his understanding.

On the point of leaving, and swaying slightly on the balls of his feet, Optimus remembered something and groped in his pocket for a paper which he handed over to his host without explanation.

'Can't make head or tail of it,' grunted Dr Cornish, turning it this way and that. 'Now, if it were Latin, Greek even, I might have a fair crack at it. But it's not, it's French I suspect, and I never learnt the language, unpatriotic to pick up the froggy lingo, not just that, all their ideas were wrong, all that equality nonsense, not our English way. Know who can read this for you? Mrs Lackland. She's a fast filly by all accounts, though a bit long in the tooth, she'll lead you a merry dance, I'll warrant. Educated by French nuns, she was, no wonder they're so high church, with all that incense, she and her husband.' Dr Cornish paused for a long minute, gazing at the scrap of paper. 'Well, even if I can't tell you what it says, I can tell you who wrote it, if you don't know already.'

'Who was it then?'

'Grace Pensilva, you should know that, you've seen her handwriting. Tell me what this says when you've had it deciphered. Who gave it to you?'

'Emma Troup.'

'Sly old fox, she told me she had nothing of Grace's, but she gave it to you, didn't she, I said she'd trust another pedagogue, now didn't I?'

Outside the house the air was chill, but Optimus scarcely felt it, he was warmed by an inner fire, part grog, part human sympathy. He looked up into the starry dome that sat like a roof over deep-set Branscombe, and smiled to himself. Orion was striding high over the lip of the hills. Grace Pensilva had known those selfsame stars. Perhaps now, from some distant fastness, she was watching him, her eyes shining among those innumerable points of light.

That night he wrote nothing, he was too befuddled, too

uncertain, but the next night he did, and the three thereafter. And he put the scrap of paper Mrs Troup had given him to one side, in an envelope, waiting for an opportunity to have it translated by Mrs Lackland. Mrs Troup had told him to see the Vicar's wife and involve himself in her good works around the parish. Now he had a second reason for doing so. But when he looked across at her narrow, unsmiling face the following Sunday as she stood clasping her small brown hymnal and heard her shrill earnest voice, he was filled with misgivings and put off the encounter. Mrs Lackland would not be content to translate his paper, she would want explanations; Optimus was not prepared to give them. Grace Pensilva, or at least a certain shadowy, imaginary Grace Pensilva was his and his alone, he did not want to share her with a person he assumed to be unsympathetic. Grace Pensilva remained locked up under the hinged desk-top in his study, he was not yet ready to bring her out and subject her to the gaze of common people, her existence was a secret he had not yet admitted, not even to Dr Cornish, though the latter suspected it.

There was a clatter of hooves on the cobblestones outside the Fortescue tavern and the landlord, sensing business, scurried across to open the door, rubbing his hands on his coarse grey linen apron as he went. The man who was dismounting outside was past middle age, plump, affable-looking, not at all the picture you would associate with his calling. But the landlord knew him of old and sprang forward nimbly to take the reins and hitch them to a ring in the wall intended for that purpose.

'Welcome to Salcombe, Mr 'Awkins, welcome to the Fortescue. 'Tis donkey's years since us've seen 'ee. What brings 'ee all the way from Plymouth on such a squally mornin'?'

'Wouldn't you like to know?' replied the horseman, pulling off his gloves as he bustled past him. 'Where's your guest? Tell him I've come to see 'im.'

The landlord's face registered alarm. 'I don't like to, your

71

'onner,' he explained, with a quick, uneasy glance at the door on the far side of the room. 'Never knowed such an unsociable bugger – oh, sorry, your 'onner, friend of yours 'ee may be, but us can't abide un. 'Ee do take 'isself for God Almighty, never a word for poor mortals like we. Don't 'ardly drink neither, a poor fish of a man, if you asks me, and 'tiddn as if you could tell from 'is face if 'ee be frownin' or smilin'.'

The small knot of cronies who spent the whole day by the tavern fireside nodded their heads in assent and pulled at their tankards. To be abstemious was evidently considered no virtue in Salcombe.

'Never mind that, where is he?'

''Ee be in the snug, your 'onner. But 'ee've gived orders that no one shall disturb un.'

'We'll see about that,' said Mr Hawkins quietly. He crossed to the snug door and tapped on it twice with the antler-headed riding quirt he carried. There was no response while he waited patiently for a minute, perhaps longer. Finally, he pushed it open and stepped inside without further ceremony.

'Knock, damn you!' bellowed the man who was sprawled in a seat facing the small grate on the opposite side of the room. 'Won't you ever learn good manners?'

'I *did* knock,' murmured his visitor. The man in the chair made a visible effort to pull himself together: he straightened, snapped shut a notebook in which he had evidently been writing some time before, and swivelled slowly until he faced Hawkins.

'I'm sorry,' he muttered, 'didn't mean to bark at you, Hawkins. I'm not myself these days. Close the door, won't you?' Without turning round, his visitor clicked it shut with the flat of his hand. His whole attention was captivated by the bizarre impression the man at the fireside was producing on him. When the man spoke, there was no lip movement to accompany the words, no expression to lend additional meaning. Only the eyes glowed and the lips and teeth were dimly discernible through three small holes in the soft leather mask which covered his face from brow to chin. Even though he knew the person who was thus disguised, the effect was disconcerting.

'A dirty business,' continued the man in the chair, 'a damned dirty business. I'm sick to the teeth with it.'

'Don't say that,' answered Hawkins, crossing to the fireside, spreading the skirts of his coat and fitting himself into a chair facing the masked man. 'You've no reason to be discouraged, in fact you've started splendidly. Their lordships are delighted, really delighted, they have charged me with telling you so.'

'I don't give a tinker's cuss for their lordships' opinion. I know what I think myself, I know what I think *of* myself. I've had enough of this business, I'm getting out of it.'

'You can't do that, Mr –'

'Brown!' interrupted the man in the mask savagely. 'Don't forget, the name's Brown. You were about to let out another one, weren't you? If you open that door over there, you'll find Landlord Barlow crouched by the keyhole.'

'You can't do that, Mr Brown, not now, just when you're getting results. Of course, it would have been better if you'd laid hands on one or two of them, so they could've been judged and transported to Van Diemen's Land, or picked up a good load of contraband so we could share the percentage. Still, I mustn't diminish what you've achieved, Mr – Brown, you've struck a mortal blow at the smugglers, destroyed their confidence, they're all looking askance at each other, wondering who'll be the next to peach on 'em. You've put paid to Harberscombe as a nest of smugglers, it won't revive for many a long year. Now, you must strike again while the iron is hot, put the fear of God into every smuggler along this coast.'

The masked man kicked a dull red log across the grate, sending a shower of sparks up the chimney; he shivered slightly. 'It makes a man feel cold, the isolation, the distrust, the hatred. Some people would laugh it off, some people would be ready for more, waiting hopefully for that tap on the window, that tug at the arm in the street, ready to turn round and talk to the informer. I've done it once, in this selfsame room, heard the scratching on the pane and let the man in. He sat just where you are sitting and I asked him how much

73

he wanted for his information. It was surprisingly little, much less than I was prepared to offer. I almost had the impression that he would have given his friends away for nothing, for some other reason, but I didn't put it to the test by beating him down, I was too excited at the prospect of making a capture. It doesn't happen every day, now does it? That was what I was here for too, wasn't it? That was why I never showed my face, never gave a name other than Brown; it was the secrecy, the anonymity that helped him come forward. Well, now I don't want another tip-off, I don't want to get sucked into another equivocal situation and play God with men's lives. I can't help feeling I'm doing something dishonourable, playing fast and loose with the code of conduct I was brought up in. Putting down smugglers isn't like fighting the Frenchies with Lord Nelson.'

'It's a patriotic duty, for all that. We can't sit back and do nothing while they run off with the king's revenue.'

'*You* can't, Hawkins, it's your job, you're the Collector of Revenue. But *I can*. I can say enough is enough, and I'm saying it. Here –' he reached into his pocket and pulled out a paper which he extended to Hawkins. 'No need to read it, it's my letter of resignation.'

'But, Brown –'

'There aren't any buts that will move me. When I agreed to do this I did so for one reason, it wasn't for love of their lordships, it wasn't to protect the revenue. You know very well why I accepted: I needed the money, needed it desperately.'

'Aren't we paying you enough? I'm sure their lordships –'

'I'm not interested,' cut in the masked man, rising and taking down a cutlass from the mantelpiece. He unsheathed it and held it in the light of the fire, studying it closely.

'What's the matter?' asked Hawkins.

'There's a stain on this somewhere and I can't get rid of it. All the time I was with Captain Troubridge and Fell, there was never a stain. But here, in my own country, I've stained it. I've made a mistake, a mistake I tell you, Hawkins, and I'm regretting it. You don't know, do you, you don't know, when it's

74

one of your own that dies, how they look at you afterwards. The eyes, Hawkins, the eyes, goddammit, they look right through you. I can't forget them, I'm not made for this work. When they look at you like that, it brings you up with a jerk. You see, Hawkins, *you* don't stand at the cutting edge, you keep back a little. Oh, I don't blame you, I wouldn't be any different. You'll find a new captain, easy enough. It was quite providential you rode over, I was going to send that letter on the evening mail. Now it won't be needful. No hard thoughts, Hawkins. Will you shake hands on it? We'll part good friends, won't we?'

'I'm still trying to understand.'

'Don't bother.'

'Where will you go? Home?'

'I don't know yet. I don't feel clean enough. You know your Bible, don't you Hawkins?'

Hawkins nodded. 'I've had a Christian education, for my sins.'

'Well, tell me, we're told what happened to Judas, how he felt, how he hanged himself on a tree, but what about the man who gave him the money, who was he, how did he feel afterwards, what end did providence reserve for him, did he live out his days in honour and prosperity?'

'Cease thinking those black thoughts,' commanded Hawkins. 'It's the solitude, the isolation. When I sounded you out for this job, I did so because everyone else who had ever held it had lacked moral fibre, they'd been unprincipled ruffians, every man Jack of them. Well, you've proved my point Mr – Brown, only a man of quality, someone immune from corruption, could make a dent in the smuggling trade. And now you want to throw in your hand, just when you're on a winning streak and could solve all your money problems at a single throw. You're too squeamish, too squeamish by half, Mr Brown. Tell me you'll reconsider.'

The masked man shook his head. He sheathed the cutlass, belted it around his waist, picked up his notebook and pocketed it. 'When I look back over what I've written down in the past few weeks, I'm ashamed of myself.'

'You did your duty, sir, no more no less.'

75

'Those eyes, those terrible eyes, Hawkins, if you'd seen them, you wouldn't say that.' He paused and put a hand to the mask that covered his face. For a moment Hawkins had the impression that he intended to tear it off, but he merely patted it. 'Those eyes look right through you, Hawkins, and you know they'll find you, wherever you are, there can be no hiding place.'

Jack Lugger took the bitter end of the crab-line from Uncle Bill Terry and paced out the regular eleven fathoms to the ash tree by the wheelwright's where he made it fast with a clove hitch. Uncle Bill took his clasp knife from his pocket and severed the rope where it emerged from the bale. The knife was keen, but the rope was hard and stiff, forcing him to saw the blade back and forth vigorously. Lugger ambled back and the two of them grasped the line, leaned back like competitors in a tug-of-war, and heaved against the dead weight of the tree. After a few violent jerks, they released the tension and spun the line in their fingers. This was a precaution taken by all wise fishermen before putting in the corks and fastening their lines in the crab-pots. If the twists were not removed by stretching the line like this, it wrapped itself into long awkward kinks as soon as it went into the water. The kinks were hard to get out in a boat and they could make tangles, tangles that could trap a man's leg and whip him over the side after a sinking crab-pot.

Uncle Bill Terry was bending to take the rope's end from the bale and start another crab-line when Jack Lugger nudged him. He looked up quickly and saw Grace Pensilva sail past them. She ignored the two fishermen and made her way up the curving lane past the alehouse and the church until she vanished where it turned towards Armouth and Langstone.

'She were always a proud one,' said Jack Lugger, spitting into the dust. 'But she'll 'ave to come down a peg or two now, that's certain, for all 'er learnin'.'

'Poor li'l maid, none the less,' said Uncle Bill, taking advantage of the interruption to tap the ash out of his old clay pipe and recharge it with plug tobacco. 'She've lost 'er Frank and that be hard enough, but to go out to service, that will be 'arder.'

'Took 'erself for a proper lady when she were companion to that Miss Delabole over to Shearanscombe, picked up a world of book-learnin', gentrified 'erself, she did. No doubt she thought the old woman'd leave 'er money. Well the old skin-flint didn't; blood's thicker than water, left everythin' to a cousin in Cornwall, she did. All she left Grace were a few books and ideas above 'er station. 'Tiddn' no good to play the clever miss with no name and less money.'

'Grace be a good girl accordin' to 'er lights,' said Uncle Bill. 'She bain't afraid to work in 'er fashion. She did care for that old bedridden Miss Delabole for more'n a twelvemonth and never asked for nothin' special. She could've 'ad a place in the will if she'd asked for it.'

'Too proud, too proud by 'arf; that be 'er trouble,' said Jack Lugger sourly.

'Grace Pensilva be like this cord,' said Uncle Bill, flexing a piece of new crab-line between his hands. 'She be new, and she be 'ard, and 'twill take time to knock the stiffness out of 'er. But she's strong stuff, she'll bend, but she won't break.'

'Too proud to show grief like other folk,' insisted Jack Lugger, 'and too proud to bury 'er Frank with proper resignation. She bain't our sort, she bain't a proper 'Arberscombe person.'

Grace herself had realized long since that she was not a proper Harberscombe person, she was not from one of the established families, the Triggs who were married to the Terrys, who were married to Troups, who were married to Kings, who were married to Stitsons, who were married to Luggers, who were married to Coytes. Not only was their blood inextricably mingled, but the very thoughts of Harberscombe people seemed to take a predictable, inward-looking slant. The Pensilvas were interlopers, new arrivals with no roots in the village, and worse still, not Devon folk, but Cornish. How long, how many generations would it take before the Pensilvas became true natives? Grace shrugged her shoulders and walked on. What did she care, she asked

77

herself, for the good opinion of Uncle Bill Terry, or Jack Lugger, or the half-cut topers who stared out at her from the Trafalgar Inn?

She paused at the top of the hill after taking the right-hand lane and looked down at Harberscombe through a gateway. There were long chaplets of thatched-roofed cottages, squat and bedraggled under the elms, a few stone-built, slate-roofed farms, the alehouse, the church and the churchyard where her Frank ... She shivered momentarily, feeling the coldness of cold soil pressing against her skin, then hurried on. The high banks of the lane closed in on her until she had the sensation of being some hunted, burrowing creature. These earthen banks, more than ten feet tall and topped with hawthorn, hazel, and ash that grew inwards over the cramped track, formed a kind of green tunnel. There was almost no sky and no horizon.The villagers took these strange claustrophobic thoroughfares for granted, but to Grace they symbolized narrow minds and crooked ways.

After a sharp double bend that might have been contrived as an ambush by some iron-age artificer, the lane broadened inexplicably into a short stretch of highroad on which three carts could pass with ease. It afforded an unusual prospect over the undulating landscape and Grace made out the grey Tudor towers of Leet House among the autumnal trees of its wide park. Between her and the great house the road lost itself in the hoary oak-woods that crowded in on the Arun estuary's tendrils. Though she could not see them from this point, she knew that the herons were standing, timid and tattered as clowns, along the banks of the secret creeks. Confirming her thought, a flight of duck rose with a clatter of wings as if disturbed by a poacher, wheeled in the sky and flew seaward, away from Langstone Mill.

The lane dipped steeply and the oaks closed over her. Grace hugged her shawl around her shoulders. It was cold here, a primeval coldness where the sun never shone and the trees were heavy with lichen and moss. Deep ruts scored the roadbed rock, cut downwards by thousands of carts that had passed this way down the centuries, grinding towards the tidal ford by which they could cut off a full five miles, five steep laborious miles of the journey from Harberscombe to Leet on the far side of the Arun. But before she reached the place where the carts emerged on to the slipway, Grace reached a crossroads. A ride branched off to the left and flanked the estruary towards the sea at Armouth; facing it was the lane used by waggons carrying corn to Langstone Mill. A few grains which had fallen from leaky sacks had germinated in the mud and straggled upwards, frail and etiolated.

Grace took this way and soon found herself passing through a tropical-seeming forest of evergreen rhododendrons whose knotted stems sprawled round her like the limbs of gigantic insects. It was a relief to her when she broke clear and entered a bracken-strewn clearing.

She halted. Despite the autumnal chill, there was a memory of warmth here, a recollection of another time when she had known this place. Those same bracken stalks which now hung shattered had been brightest green, freshly uncurled, basking quietly in the summer sun. The heat had shimmered all over the clearing and there had been a murmur of bees; a woodpecker's tapping sounded deep in the wood, from the waterside had come a heron's croak.

She was lying on the grass under a tent of bracken stems that arched over her like cathedral vaults. Inside that traceried space, a congregation of tiny insects were going about their important business. She watched a red and black beetle cautiously probing the air in front of it with flickering feelers. Was it aware of the hugeness of the other world, the world she knew, or was it as unconscious of the concerns of human life as men and women are of the lives and loves of beetles? Did these minute creatures have loves and hates? Were they capable of passions? She bit off a blade of grass and manipulated it between her lips to form a probe with which to make contact with the beetle. But when the sharp point touched it, the insect flung itself off the leaf where it had been lingering and disappeared among the plant stems. Grace lay back on the grass and let the sun play on her face while she chewed at the grass with her eyes closed.

79

Was it the tugging on the grass, or was it the shadow that fell on her face? She opened her eyelids and there, closer than a full moon, gazing down at her and nibbling at the other end of the grass, was a face. The smiling eyes seemed to mock at her gently, the shaven cheeks shone pink and youthful, the hair glistened like the halo of a young god.

The lips munched voluptuously at the grass and the ivory teeth were maculated with green fragments. She watched mesmerized as the lips descended and approached her own. The lips vanished, too close to be seen and she sensed them brushing hers. The eyes were no longer smiling, they were veiled and vague. Looking at their glistening surface, she knew that she could not see into them any more than she could see into the beetle's red and black carapace. Yet she thought she knew how he felt, and she knew how she felt, knew that a strange current was passing through them, knowing that because he was there, because it was him, she was in another state, more intense than common experience.

The taste of the grass in her mouth, a green taste, a slightly sweet, rasping-edged taste, she remembered it now and she remembered his tongue, probing her lips like the beetle's flickering feelers, and she remembered his breath on her cheek, long hot lingering sighs, and she remembered his hands on her flesh, hands that sought out the nipples of her breasts, and she remembered the weight of him, bearing down on her like a hot sun, making her sight swirl and her knees buckle.

And when she came back to herself, when she was free again and could look at him, sprawled in the grass beside her, she saw the beetle climb out of the scrub and on to his forearm. What had it made of all that? Was it aware of their passion? She turned her flushed face to ask him, but when she opened her mouth, he covered it with his cupped hand and his worried eyes invited her to hear the silence. And she understood: the woodpecker had ceased his work, even the bees seemed to have paused, the quietness hung over the glade like a stifling blanket, an ominous expectancy.

Somewhere, not far off, there was an abrupt cracking from

a dry stick. A startled jay flung itself out of an oak and flew off screeching. His eyes were dark with concern as he pushed up on one elbow and peered through the bracken. They both heard, or thought they heard, retreating footsteps.

The spell was broken. This place that they had thought so unknown and secret had been violated. As if touched by a chill, Grace shrugged on and buttoned her blouse. She waited while he searched the surrounding woods for signs of the intruder. She felt anxious, marked by the hidden observer, stained by a touch of lascivious disapproval.

Grace watched herself rise from the bracken and steal away into the woods. Even now, she had the sensation of being observed by someone hidden in the rhododendrons. Though she knew it was preposterous, she felt naked, vulnerable, as if reproving eyes were fixed upon her.

Shortly after the clearing, she emerged from the under-growth and came to a fork in the ride. This was unfamiliar territory, he had never brought her this far. Farmyard sounds came to her from beyond another clump of trees. She took the left-hand, downward path and, almost immediately, felt she was mistaken. A few steps more and she was certain of it: the path debouched from the rhododendrons on to a stone-built dyke, separating the estuary from an impounded pond on the far side of which stood the cluster of buildings which must be Langstone Mill. Grace realized that she must retrace her steps to circumvent the pond, but before she did so she was brought to a halt by a figure she saw standing on the dyke.

Barely twenty yards ahead, motionless as a heron and similarly long-legged and squat-bodied, stood a man with a gun. He was hunched, long-necked, narrow-shouldered, pot-bellied, dressed in breeches and gaiters, waistcoat and a full-sleeved shirt. His hair stood up on his head like a ragged crest. Around the bulge of his cheek Grace could see the bushy tip of an auburn moustache. For the moment he was unaware of her presence, but she suspected that any sudden movement on her part would attract his attention. The man was leaning over the edge of the dyke at a point where a culvert allowed the sea water to run in and out of the estuary. The first, fan-like wave of rising tide had penetrated the culvert and was reaching out across the dull lead-hued mudflats inside the pond. The man seemed to be observing something in the water, something invisible to Grace, but which now absorbed both their attentions. Though she still had an urge to slip away, curiosity got the better of her.

Slowly, with infinite precaution, the man brought the stock of his shotgun up to his cheek. The barrels, inclined downwards at the water, wavered slightly from side to side as he tracked his target. Grace saw tiny ripples wavering across the skin of the calm water.

The explosion, following the dry click of the flintlock mechanisms, sent a volley of echoes reverberating round the folds of the Arun estuary. Two resentful herons flapped anxiously away from the far side of the dyke where they had been feeding. A cloud of shouting rooks blossomed from a spinney on the far hillside. A flight of oyster-catchers flashed red legs as they took off and skimmed seaward, squeaking in alarm.

The man had dropped his gun on the grass and was wrestling with a long pole that had a kind of net on the end of it. Drawn by her inquisitiveness, Grace took a few steps forward, peering at the place where the shot had sent up a column of fine spray, like steam.

The man noticed her and lost his preoccupation with whatever it was he had shot at in the water. He made as if to drop the pole and pick up his gun. The second barrel had not yet been fired and he could still use it. She stood irresolute, staring back into his ruddy face with its bushy moustache and unsteady eyes. There was something wild, insecure and impetuous about the man that made her uneasy. But she was not prepared to turn back now that she had recognized him. He was the man she had come to find.

As she resumed her advance across the dyke, the man's eyes dropped and he resumed his task, ignoring her now that she had brooked his first challenging stare. The spray had subsided and the water was beaded with innumerable bubbles among which twitched a succession of glistening shapes.

They floated belly-up, stunned by the detonation, their swim-bladders distended so that they could no longer stay in their element, and their ventral fins flicking in useless fanning gestures.

'Seven at one blow!' exulted the man in a peculiar, strangled voice. 'Never seen nothin' like it, 'ave 'ee? Shootin' fish, I mean.' Grace shook her head. The man did not appear as menacing as he had at first. 'A man's got to 'ave a bit of sport. Gentry do 'unt foxes, farmers do shoot pheasants, labourers dig badgers, fishermen trap rabbits, Jack Coyte d'shoot mullet.' He laughed a throttled laugh.

The first of the fish were already landed and were gasping their lives out on the grass, their mouths pouting and drawing back ineffectually. Grace flinched at their fishy smell which was mingled with the whiff of burnt powder.

'Why don't you put them out of their misery?' she demanded.

'What for? They'll die soon enough in the air, same as us would under water, 'tis natural. Fish don't feel nothin'.'

How do you know? Grace felt like exclaiming, but bit her lip, repressing the impulse. This man was doing no more than express the ordinary countryman's indifference to cruelty and suffering. The animal world to which they were accustomed knew no squeamishness. Why should man show a tender regard for suffering among animals when he would cheefully slaughter his own kind? Did the hawk show pity? Did the stoat feel remorse? Humanity had no place in a system that was equally ignorant of the concepts of justice and revenge. 'I've come to see you, Farmer Coyte.'

The man licked his teeth and landed another mullet. Then he looked at her and raised his eyebrows.

'Mr Wroth sent me. He said you had a vacancy.' Farmer Coyte licked his teeth again and ran a hand through his thinning shock of hair.

''Ee said that did 'ee? Well I might and I might not. What be your name, young woman?'

'Grace – Grace Pensilva.'

Farmer Coyte sucked his yellowing teeth loudly. ''Twas

your Frank then that . . . Well, 'ee'd've done better to've kept clear o' that trade. No good never comed of it. I don't 'old with strong liquor, nor do Mrs Coyte. You don't take after un, do 'ee?'

'Do I look like a smuggler?'

He seemed surprised by the bold directness of her question. He studied her closely. 'I didn't mean that, I meant be you a drinker?'

'I'm not that either.'

'And a Jacobin? Be 'ee one o' they trouble-makers?'

'That's none of your business. Do you think I'd say so if I were?'

'Don't look much like a dairy maid neither.'

Grace shrugged and made a wry face, he had a point there. 'You can but try me. I can start at quarter day, that's but three weeks off.'

'Three weeks' time, eh? Mistress Pensilva will start in three weeks' time, will she? Well, I've news for 'er! 'Tis tomorrow she'll start or never.'

'But I must go to Salcombe first, I've urgent business there.'

'Suit yourself. If you're down by the mill by six in the mornin' us'll give 'ee a try. One minute later, the work goes to another.'

Grace knew her face was burning with resentment. She was sure he was only making this condition to spite her, to assert his power over a mere dairy maid. If she had said nothing about her own concerns, he would have been in no hurry to set her to work. Already he had returned to his preoccupations with the fish, dismissing her. Grace realized the futility of arguing with the man. The bristly moustache told her something about him: short-tempered, dangerous to cross, canny, censorious according to his narrow lights, Farmer Coyte and his wife were pillars of the newly built Methodist chapel on the fridge of Harberscombe Plain.

She glanced across at it as she hurried home; its expensive granite façade was built in the Classical manner to differentiate it from Church of England buildings. There was something in the strict hardness of its lines that repelled her, yet

84

she knew there were good people, simple Harberscombe folk who went there. It must have something to offer besides self-righteous privations.

Uncle Bill Terry and Jack Lugger had finished making up the new crab-lines, which were hanging from a spar outside their shed ready to be loaded on a donkey. The two men were sprawled in the shade of the ash, an earthenware flagon of cider, a hunk of bread and a wedge of cheese between them. The wheelwright's dog was asleep on the dusty road outside his shop. There was no traffic to disturb it.

'Pride goes before a fall,' muttered Jack Lugger, 'that Grace Pensilva don't look none too 'appy.'

'Grace 'aven't 'ad much reason to feel 'appy in 'Arberscombe,' replied Uncle Bill. 'She never knowed 'er mother properly and 'er father followed the poor woman to 'er grave before Grace 'ad 'er tenth birthday. If Miss Delabole 'adn't took an interest in the poor maid and if Frank 'adn't come 'ome to care for 'er, God knows what'd've become of 'er.'

'Well, that Frank could've stayed away, 'ee've brought no good to 'Arberscombe, never knowed 'ow to turn an honest penny,' grumbled Jack Lugger. 'And as for puttin' on airs, 'ee were worse than 'is sister, if that was possible. All that talk of 'is about equality, what good could they furrin notions do us 'ere in 'Arberscombe? Any fool can see there's no equality possible in this world. There be poor folk like us, and there be *the* quality. There bain't no common ground between us and no way for a poor feller to rise either. Shake your fist in the Squire's face and 'ee'll grind your face in the dirt. That Frank always wanted to persuade someone else to do the fist-shakin' and the shoutin'. 'Ee weren't so quick to stand forth 'isself. More concerned to play Robin 'Ood and feather 'is nest were Frank Pensilva. Good riddance for us, that's what I say. As for that Grace, 'twill be as well for 'er to quit 'Arberscombe. Us 'aven't no need of 'er sort 'ere. Let 'er go back to Cornwall, that's where 'er folk did come from, that's where she ought to be welcome.'

'Grace were born 'ere,' chided Uncle Bill gently, 'she've a

right to live, just like the rest of us. But there be precious little for a clever young maid 'ere in this village, nor never will be, I fancy. That Grace'll leave 'ere 'fore long and no need of your promptin'. No, Grace won't stay 'ere, but us will, won't us, Jack. 'Arberscombe'll always want for poor fishermen.'

'Sooner she goes the better, and take 'er fine airs with 'er.'

'The way you go on about Grace anyone'd think she'd gived you the cold shoulder. If you aks me, you're more than a bit struck on that maid yourself, Jack Lugger. If she gived you a smile, you'd soon change your tune and put your pride in your pocket. I've seen 'ow you looks at 'er.'

Grace let herself into her cottage and sat down at the table without removing her shawl. She too would have to put her pride in her pocket. What else could she do? If she wanted to remain in Harberscombe and keep faith with Frank, there was no alternative. She must work for a living and if she wanted the job at Langstone Mill she must take it. Vacancies, even for dairy maids, did not long go begging. Six months or a year might pass before there was another, and there was no question of sharing the poor income that Mrs Troup derived from the dame school. No, if she wanted to fulfil her vow, she would have to eat humble pie and conceal what airs and graces she had developed. She wondered if she would have the strength and steadfastness.

6

'No, I can't say I ever knowed 'er, not special. I thought I did,
'o course, the way you think you know a maid what 'ave
growed up beside 'ee in a small place like 'Arberscombe.'
Uncle Bill Terry spoke slowly in a deep bass voice that was
particularly incongruous, coming as it did from his bent
wasted frame. Optimus had sought him out one afternoon
when winter was teetering on the verge of spring, following
him down the Okewell lane to Armouth beach where he
found the old fisherman sitting splay-legged on a low stool,
with a half-finished crab-pot between his knees. While he
spoke, he worked steadily at his pot-making, taking willow
rods from a pile on the floor beside him and fitting them into
the framework, almost without looking, so accustomed was
he to his task, though Optimus wondered how anyone could
make such an elaborate shape. 'You'll 'ave to ask someone
what knew 'er better. Janet Coyte was forever on about 'er, 'tis
a pity she'm gone away, she'd've answered better'n I could.
And Eileen Wroth, she 'ad a soft spot for Grace, she'd tell 'ee
another side to the story. Outlived 'er 'usband 'ave Eileen
Wroth, and sold up and gone to live in Plymouth somewhere.
You'll 'ave an 'ard job to find 'er, but you're set on it, bain't
'ee? No one cared much about Grace Pensilva 'ere while she
lived, and no one tried to find out much thereafter, not till you
came to teach school at Branscombe, that is. More'n a few
people be askin' what could be the reason for it. They think
you might be after a treasure.'

'A treasure?'

'Aye, they say Grace and Jan made a mint o' money by

moonlight and that they must've buried it somewhere. There's been a deal o' diggin' over there near Jan's cottage,' here Uncle Bill jerked a horny thumb at the derelict house that stood on a knoll on the far side of the stream-bed, 'but I know better. There was money all right, but that Grace took it with 'er.'

While he talked, Optimus was observing the old fisher-man's face. It was the consistency of old tanned leather, leather that had once been crimson, but had had the colour washed out by wind and weather, creased and rubbed bare in a dozen places. Though his head was bald in the centre, it was fringed by curly grey locks and his mutton-chop whiskers still showed a hint of their former rich chestnut. The lines that scored his cheeks so deeply followed the creases of frequent smiles and his expression suggested a man who made the best of things and tried to think well of his neighbours. But the arresting thing about his face was the fact that while one side was lively and mobile, the other had long since fallen into a kind of dull paralysis.

Having fitted the last of the willow rods from the pile into the crab-pot, Uncle Bill struggled to his feet and limped to the back of the shed in search of a fresh bundle. There was a pile of them, heaped up nearly to roof level. He grasped one of them and began to tug it, with his breath wheezing loudly as he did so.

'Here, let me help,' exclaimed Optimus, clambering past him and pulling at a bundle near the top of the pile.

'I bain't that far gone yet, young maister,' said the old man, but he allowed Optimus to get the willows for him. ''Tis me 'eart,' he explained, leaning back against the wall and filling his clay pipe, ''tis the old ticker what do let me down. I put paid to un when I pulled that store-pot. A man never knows when 'ee's beat. I were young and proud in they days. Dr Cornish said I were lucky to live through it. But 'ere I be, more'n twenty-five years on.'

Optimus was only half listening, his attention had been caught by a shape he saw in the shadowy roof: a long slim hull, clinker-built, light and racy, unlike all the other

Armouth boats, hung suspended from the roof-ties. Was it, could it be? He dumped the bundle of willow rods beside Uncle Bill's stool and questioned him. 'That boat up there, it's a pilot gig, isn't it? Who does it belong to? It's not for sale, is it?'

'There bain't no one to sell un to 'ee,' grunted the old fisherman, pressing the hot ash into his pipe with his horny thumb. 'No use thinkin' on un.'

'Isn't it the one that Jan –'

'I said 'twern't no use thinkin' on un,' broke in Uncle Bill, with a tinge of anger to his voice. 'Us should've burnt un long since. Last time I did see Jan King alive, 'twas in that gig. 'Ee should never 'ave done un up, Jan King were a fool to go back to the trade, but a man be mazed every time when there be a woman at the back of it.'

'What did Jan King feel about Grace Pensilva? You ought to know, you were partners, weren't you?'

'Aye, partners. Jan King were a good partner while it lasted. What did 'ee feel about Grace?' Uncle Bill puffed at his pipe. 'Why, 'ee wanted to trust 'er. Proper moonstruck over that maid were Jan King, no use tellin' un not to play with fire. Jan believed what 'ee wanted to believe and when she comed 'ere with un, 'ee were in the seventh 'eaven, or so 'ee thought. More fool 'ee to put faith in 'er.'

'You didn't care for Grace Pensilva, did you? What was wrong with her?'

'In they days I couldn't be sure, never got close to 'er, but now I think she spent all 'er time weavin', weavin' a trap like this 'ere crab-pot, a trap for Jan King to swim into. She 'ad to be cold to do that, cold and 'ard, she sailed under false colours, did Grace Pensilva.'

'But what about Jan, was he blameless? Someone gave the gig away that night. Are you sure Jan King had nothing to reproach himself with?'

'All I can say is, it weren't 'is nature.'

'Perhaps his nature didn't show any more than Grace Pensilva's did.'

'Look 'ere, Mr Schoolmaster, 'tis a long time past, 'tis all dead and forgotten, what be the use in rakin' over cold ashes?

89

Let sleepin' dogs lie, bain't that a good motto?'

'I just need to know, that's all. Someone got me started on this thing and I can't get it out of my head.'

'Even if I wanted to 'elp 'ee, and I bain't sure I do, an old man's memory bain't better'n a sieve. I've told 'ee all I've a mind to for the present, I'm goin' 'ome along, and if you've any sense you'll do likewise, 'twill come on to rain shortly.'

Optimus looked out of the wide double doors of the boat-house. Between the two headlands, a band of pewter-grey cloud fringed with a skirt of flying rain, was marching across the sea. The old fisherman was already tucking his head and shoulders into a sack whose corner he had punched in to make a hood. In another minute the door was clapped shut and Uncle Bill was perched on his sad-eyed donkey, jogging as fast as he could up the lane towards Harberscombe. It was none too soon, the rain had already obliterated one of the headlands and was approaching the other. Optimus turned up his coat collar and made for the dilapidated cottage. He was in no mood to go home so soon and would take his chance of a soaking if the rain did not soon blow over.

The back door of the cottage was ajar, its latch was broken and one hinge had given way making it sag on to the floor. It scraped loudly as Optimus pushed it open and stepped inside. No one had lived in the house for years; there had been one family who had tried it, but they had moved out after less than a year, unwilling to say why, so Emma Troup had told him. Standing in the empty house, with the rising wind rattling the sash windows at the front of the house and sighing in the chimneys, Optimus himself felt uneasy. It was impossible to imagine brightness and jollity in this shadowy place, yet he had perforce to admit that it had existed. In this kitchen, whose curtains hung in sooty threads, whose floor was littered with the fragments of a broken chair, Jan King had passed a few months of what, to him, had seemed like happiness.

Climbing the creaking stairs, Optimus halted on the landing. Open doors led to each of the two bedrooms. The rain was already tapping on their windows and in one case, finding

90

a broken pane, was staining the floorboards. According to Emma Troup, the Leet estate had obtained the house when Jan King failed to return and pay the peppercorn rent he owed them. Thenceforth, they had maintained it, but only as much as was needed to keep it from falling into absolute ruin. Its two chimneys and broad bulk still served to guide the vessels as they steered between the reefs and across Armouth bar. Now, while Optimus looked, the rising surf was tossing on the seaward side of the Back, the curious whalebacked hump of sand and shingle that ran out from the western shore, closing off more than half the estuary opening and making it a safe harbour. Behind it, in the Pool, the few remaining Armouth luggers swung at moorings. First they yawed one way and then they lurched back. That, Optimus thought, was how it was going with his investigations. Every so often, he would go off on a new tack, make some fresh discovery, feel he was getting somewhere as a new perspective was opened to him and then, abruptly, some other piece of unexpected information, some object like the gig he had just found, would appear, the chain of truth would snub up tight and jerk him round into a new direction. His mind was already cluttered with scraps of fact which, at best, was really unreliable memory and, at worst, prejudiced hearsay, and brought nothing but confusion to the simple pattern he had formed in his head and which was now the basis of his imaginary narrative. In a curious way, it seemed that his fabrication was 'true', perhaps because it had come to him effortlessly, like a revelation, as though Grace Pensilva were dictating it to him. It was repeatedly disconcerting to find that there were other viewpoints, other 'facts' that could not be reconciled with his first mental picture, though it was curious how many events seemed to have come to him intuitively. But reluctantly he now accepted that parts of his narrative would have to be rewritten if he wished to lay claim to a historian's mantle. Perhaps the right way was to wait until all possible research was complete. That was the ideal solution, but he knew that, if he adopted it, the project would soon founder completely. With all its faults, Grace Pensilva's story

91

must continue as it had begun, disorganized, self-contradictory, halting, imaginative. For all his frustration, for all
his doubt, a picture of Grace Pensilva was coming through to
him.

Over the mantelpiece in the left-hand bedroom was a
cracked mirror. Optimus approached it with some trepida-
tion. It was as though he expected Jan King or Grace Pensilva
to stare back out at him. Long ago, he was certain, that mirror
had watched one or both of them. Now it was charged with
dust and flecked with grey patches where the silvering had
capitulated to the corrosive sea air.

Behind this fog, all he now saw, dimly reflected, was his
own thin, studious face, clean-shaven though hardly in need
of a razor. His wispy moustache was a gesture, an assertion of
his manhood. It needed trimming, but he lacked the incen-
tive; smartness counted for little in Harberscombe. Looking
into his own eyes, he tried to fathom their brown pools; there
was passion there somewhere, passion like Grace Pensilva's
but he was yet to discover the woman to awaken it. He ran his
fingers through the waves of his abundant hair and felt the
electricity.

Or was it something else, some presence, that made the
nape of his neck prickle? Grace Pensilva was there behind
him, but he dared not face her. In abrupt, blind terror he ran
downstairs, out of the house and into the rainstorm. Fear kept
his eyes averted from the upstairs window through which he
felt her watching him. The cleaning rain drummed on his
face, making him sense his skull, but could not wash away
the thought within.

The Sunday after Mrs Troup gave Optimus the paper, Mrs
Lackland, the Vicar's wife, waylaid him as he left the porch
and stepped into the churchyard. Despite the fact that he had
been told she would be able to translate the French for him,
he had been loath to approach her. Something about the way
she stood in her pew, with her head thrown back, her bosom
projecting in a manner that was definitely unbecoming, and
her bright eyes darting unashamedly about, restrained him,

as it had on earlier occasions. When he knew she was glancing at him his own eyes had fallen demurely to his hymnal while he made a show of searching for the next number. He suspected she had caught him blushing. This time there was no escaping her.

'Ah, Mr Shute,' she exclaimed loudly, 'I'm so glad to see you. Mrs Troup tells me you're keen to help with the good works I'm involved with around the parish.'

Optimus licked his lips, trying to decide how to answer. 'She did suggest it.'

'And you agreed, I'm sure you did. How splendid! You must come round to the Vicarage immediately, have coffee and discuss it. There's no time like the present. I know you'll be a wonderful asset. Here, give me your arm and escort me. Mr Lackland is never away from church on time, he *will* stay talking.'

A few moments later, Optimus was seated in Mrs Lackland's curricle, bowling along the Bigmore road and uncomfortably aware that the narrow bench seat was keeping the whole length of his haunch and thigh against her silken dress. The warmth of youthful flesh came through to him, promoting involuntary stirrings. He sat bolt upright and stared straight ahead, hoping she would fail to notice. At every turn of the wheels, Optimus became more embarrassed. He ought to be making conversation, but the longer his silence was prolonged, the more difficult it became to break it. Furthermore, although he knew it could not be true, he had the distinct impression that Mrs Lackland's silk-encased knee was pressing against his own in a rhythm that accentuated the jogging of the vehicle.

'Your husband,' he blurted out and paused, seeing her turn suddenly and stare at him, 'your husband is so conscientious, so good, so devoted to saving the souls of the sinners in Harberscombe parish.'

'Mr Lackland is exclusively devoted to the hereafter, Mr Shute. He eschews all fleshly delights. Lent is his favourite season. Hell and damnation are forever in his thoughts. Mr Lackland does not approve of dancing. He will have no incense in his churches –'

'But Dr Cornish said he had Romish inclinations,' exclaimed Optimus, instantly regretting it.

'What does Dr Cornish know about it? He hasn't been seen in church in all the time I've been here. He knows nothing of my husband. But I do! Mr Lackland does not laugh on Sundays, his weekday smiles are sparing. The things of this world concern him not.'

Optimus was flabbergasted. A sidelong glance showed him that Mrs Lackland's cheeks were flushed under their powder and rouge; her eyes flashed with anger. 'He must be grateful that God has sent him such a devoted helpmate whose good works take care of his parishioners' material wants while he devotes himself to the cure of souls. Mr Lackland does not concern himself with me. He is like Milton, he believes woman to be the Devil's creation, an inferior being to be suffered, despite her imperfections, for want of a better alternative.'

'Isn't that Bigmore Vicarage showing through the trees?' asked Optimus, trying to change the subject. 'How fine it looks! What a lovely prospect!'

'I hate the place!' she exclaimed, stamping her foot and sending a delicious tremor along his thigh. 'He told me nothing of this district, its isolation, its lack of good society, the poverty of the living. He *implored* me to marry him. I could have found a thousand better husbands, kind considerate men who would have been happy to settle close to my dear parents at Tunbridge Wells. I could have played whist at parties, met people who did not damn Paris fashions and rail at painted faces.'

The crunching of gravel under the wheels was good to hear, offering some relief from his embarrassment. It signalled that they had turned off the lane into the vicarage driveway. The Vicarage was a tall Gothic mansion, reminiscent of a Scottish castle, all angles, towers and turrets. Optimus sprang down and held the horse's head while they waited for her servant to take it.

'We can only afford Treebie, and you can see how old and slow he is,' complained Mrs Lackland as a somewhat dithery

94

old man emerged from the house. 'Tell Margaret to bring us coffee!' she shouted, with her lips close to Treebie's ear, before she flounced up the steps into the parlour. Either the old servant was too deaf to hear her complaints or he concealed his chagrin under a bland exterior.

'Coffee's a bit of a luxury, but one must indulge oneself now and again, mustn't one?' the Vicar's wife murmured as she poured from the pot that buxom Mrs Treebie soon set on the table. Optimus, whose meagre salary made tea itself seem sybaritic, held his cup and saucer as steady as possible, but they still rattled when his hand trembled. He sat perched on the edge of a chair, facing her, and kept his eyes away from her tightly buttoned bodice.

Mrs Lackland was not, he discovered, terribly interested in discussing her planned good works for the parish but questioned him closely on his past, his life at college, his interests outside the classroom. 'I'm a dull dog really, never had any adventures, no great enthusiasms,' he admitted ruefully.

'But you *have*. You're crazy about Grace Pensilva.'

'Who told you that?' What did she mean, crazy about her? Optimus knew he was intrigued, but he certainly wasn't crazy about her.

'Mrs Troup.'

'Mrs Troup's a dreadful gossip. And she exaggerates terribly.'

'You *are* a silly boy. Everybody knows you've been asking questions. You can't keep your passions secret in a place like Harberscombe. You are bewitched by her. Admit it!' Optimus was tongue-tied. Something deep inside him refused to allow his vision of Grace Pensilva to be sullied by this flippant female. 'She said you had a paper you were going to ask me to translate for you. Do you have it with you?'

Optimus shook his head. 'It's at home,' he mumbled.

'Oh, Mr Shute, you *are* a fibber. I can tell you're lying, you can't look me in the eye and repeat that, can you? No, of course not. But I know what it is, you're a shy boy, aren't you? Don't try to deny it; I've seen you staring at me in church,. You really must act more discreetly. Come now, where's the paper? Hand it over!'

She held out her hand imperiously and, although he hesitated, he realized that she was only making him do something that he himself had been too timid to undertake earlier. He dipped into his pocket and took out the paper.

'What's this?' she asked as she unfolded the grubby scrap, holding it between fastidious fingertips. 'Did Mrs Troup give you this? I thought she'd nothing left.'

'Dr Cornish gave it to me,' said Optimus, lying gratuitously and biting his lip in secret vexation. This woman was leading him like a pig by the nose and he hated it.

'How intriguing!' Mrs Lackland crossed the room and went to a mahogany cabinet which she unlocked with a key from her purse. Reaching into the back she took out an old, scuffed, leather-bound volume, a small book, scarcely larger than a prayer book, and turned to the flyleaf, holding Optimus's paper alongside for comparison.

'Well?' asked Optimus after a long silence. 'What is it?'

'Come and look.'

He crossed the room and stood looking over her shoulder, trying not to be influenced by her musky scent. 'Well,' she demanded, 'do you see what I see?' Optimus stared at the open page. There in bold handwriting was written a single phrase:

Revenge is a kind of wild justice

He trembled slightly as he read it, but hoped Mrs Lackland would fail to notice his emotion. 'Well?' she repeated.

'It's in English, I can understand it.'

'I don't mean that. Haven't you noticed the similarity? It's identical.'

'How did you come by that book?'

'I bought it from Mrs Troup. She said it had been Grace Pensilva's. She sold me all the books she had. I was once as excited as you are, when I first came here and heard the story. I like her, she's such a romantic figure.' While she spoke, Optimus was turning the books in his hands, rifling through its stiff, old-fashioned pages and reading the faded gold letters on its spine. Yes, there was no doubt about it, the handwriting

96

was identical. And he could have told Mrs Lackland that it corresponded with the writing on other documents in his possession, but he held his peace about that.

'*The Rights of Man*?' read Optimus questioningly. 'What kind of a book is that? Who wrote it?'

'A man called Paine, Tom Paine. Do you know what my husband says? "The Devil's second name, it was Paine!" That's what he says. Paine was a revolutionary. If Lackland knew I had this book, he'd thrash me. It's lucky he never pries in my bookcase. He thinks all I read is Maria Edgeworth, for edification, that and the Bible, of course.'

'But what does it say on the paper?'

'What the devil are you skulking in here for, woman?'

Optimus looked up in astonishment. Mrs Lackland was glaring at Mrs Treebie who was standing in the doorway. 'How long have you been there? You know I won't have you spying on private conversations!'

'I only comed back with more coffee,' replied Mrs Treebie, refusing to be browbeaten.

'Well, next time you come into a room, announce yourself. Put the pot on the table and leave us immediately. Lackland sets her to spy on me, I'm sure of it,' she concluded once they were alone again. 'Now where was I?'

'You were about to translate the paper.'

'Ah yes.' She held it up to the light. '*La vengeance est un plat qui se mange froid*,' she enunciated carefully. 'It means: revenge is a plate – no better – a dish which – which is eaten cold. That's it, more or less. You've got the sense of it. "Revenge is a cold dish" will do, but it doesn't convey the French meaning completely. How intriguing! It explains a great deal about Grace Pensilva, for she was the one who wrote it, she had to be. You say Dr Cornish gave it to you; how did he come by it?'

This was just the kind of questioning that Optimus had been dreading. The last thing he wanted to do was share Grace Pensilva with this woman. But regarding its provenance, he could afford to be truthful. 'I don't know. He never told me.'

'You are a deep one, Mr Shute, why do you make it so difficult to approach you? What's your Christian name anyway? We've no need to stay formal. Mine's Diana.'

'Well, Mrs La – I mean Diana – it's Optimus. I'm being as open as I can; I can't help my own nature.'

'No, I shouldn't expect it. You're still a boy really. But that's better than being a whited sepulchre like Lackland. Here he comes now. Not a word to him about what we've been discussing. It's like a red rag to a bull. Sit down and drink your coffee. We'll have time enough to pursue this later.' Optimus pocketed his slip of paper while Diana Lackland hurriedly replaced the book in the cabinet and locked it. Wheels could be heard approaching. 'Now, about those good works,' she began, with a broad wink, 'isn't it time we were planning them?'

When Grace reached the farmyard next morning it was still half dark. The air was cold and the clamminess of the night dew clung to her cloak. As she approached, the air had been shaken by a cock's thin crowing but now it had fallen silent. A fawning collie sidled out of its kennel in the shadows and began to lick her hand. For a moment she thought she had arrived before anyone was about, but she was soon undeceived. The house door, at the head of short flight of steps, swung back and revealed a sharp-faced woman beckoning to her with a candle-lantern. Grace climbed the steps and followed her into the dairy.

The chill, low-ceilinged room seemed vast to her after the cramped space in her cottage. All around the whitewashed walls were slate-topped workbenches and its centre was monopolized by a long, scrubbed deal table. Polished cans of milk and cream stood on the benches and other empty receptacles, together with quart, pint and gill measures, hung from nails in the walls and the beams overhead. The woman placed her lantern on the table and faced Grace.

'Let's see your 'ands, young lady!' she commanded, pointing into the pool of light by the candle. 'Put 'em 'ere, let's look at 'em.' Grace dropped her belongings and did as she was bidden. 'Bain't she a proper little lady?' said the woman in a sarcastic tone. 'They 'ands 'aven't never knowed 'ard labour. Well, if you stick it 'ere, which I doubt, you soon won't know 'em.'

'You're Mrs Coyte,' said Grace, trying to maintain a mild exterior.

'None other,' said the woman. 'You'll find us different 'ere. I bain't none of your Honourable Miss Delaboles. Us don't sew samplers 'ere, us don't embroider, us don't speak French. Us be true-blooded Devon folk, us knows all 'bout 'ard work. Either *you'll* learn too or –'

'I'll learn,' interrupted Grace. 'I'll learn, never you mind about that. Just show me how.'

''Appen I will,' said Mrs Coyte. 'But I've not said I'll 'ave 'ee yet, 'ave I? There be somethin' you aven't reckoned with, I fancy: us be a God-fearin' 'ousehold, us be chapel folk, us don't 'old with your sort o' carryin' on.'

'What do you mean, carrying on?'

'What I mean is, I've got a young boy 'ere, not far off bein'a man and –'

'And?'

'Stay away from un. Stay away from un, that's all.'

Grace looked at Mrs Coyte in amazement, she appeared unable to believe her ears, but the farmer's wife was deadly serious, there was no doubt about that, her face had the pursed up look of the Pharisee. 'What makes you say that?'

'Ah,' cooed Mrs Coyte knowingly. 'I 'as me reasons.'

'Come on, woman, be frank, out with it!' exclaimed Grace, losing her temper at last. Mrs Coyte smiled a thin smile, triumphant at touching a raw nerve.

'What I means be this, when a woman 'ave done it once, second time don't cost nothin'. Now, my Ronald, 'ee've got expectations, 'ee'll be a miller one day and a farmer too. I don't want you gettin' no ideas, I don't want to see no cradle snatchin'.'

'And you won't. You can be sure of that. I'll not waste myself on your precious son, Mrs Coyte, whatever his "expectations".'

99

'No need to get on your 'igh 'oss with me,' snapped Mrs Coyte, 'I knows I be right to 'ave me suspicions. Janet Coyte bain't the sort to invent it. I've seed 'ee, Grace Pensilva, seed 'ee with me own eyes, seed 'ee with a certain person. 'Twas a mortal sin, Grace Pensilva, and you knowed it. 'Tis in the prayer book!'

'I don't know what you're talking about,' Grace answered. But she did. She could tell the woman wasn't bluffing. There was an electric tension between them, a clash between freedom and rectitude. 'I've nothing to reproach myself with.'

'That may be your opinion, 'tisn't the opinion o' Christian folk.'

'I'd best be going then.'

'No, don't go. Stay 'ere if you like. Us'll give 'ee a chance. Us'll do the Christian thing, us'll give 'ee a chance to repent, Grace Pensilva, repent and mend your wilful ways.'

'And if I don't choose to?'

'Then good riddance. But you'll stay, there bain't no other work for a young maid in 'Arberscombe. You'll stay and you'll watch your conduct. If you can't bother, I'll watch un for 'ee. And remember, if you let your lewd thoughts stray to my Ronald, Janet Coyte will talk. There be plenty o' folk in 'Arberscombe will sit up and listen.' She paused and snuffed out the candle between finger and thumb, leaving the room in the cold bluish dawn light. 'Us can't be wasteful, can us? 'Tisn't as though Mr Coyte were the landowner, there be rent to pay at quarter day,' she remarked, leaning forward with her stiff arms propped on the table to either side of her. 'Well, be it go or stay?'

The bitter smell of the snuffed candle stung Grace's nostrils. It was like incense at a sacrifice. This was a sacrifice, her sacrifice, for Frank. She looked Mrs Coyte in the eye, knowing there would be no love lost between them and that the farmer's wife would haze her as hard as she could. 'Stay,' she answered and for the second time Mrs Coyte smiled her thin-lipped smile.

Before the week's end, Grace's hands were red and raw. They were forever in icy water, scouring out the pans, or she would be crouched on a three-legged stool, pulling at a cow's teats. That was the only time she ever felt warm, in the dim shed where the cows were crowded together, filling the place with their hot breath and the smell of their steaming dung, with her brow pressed to the cow's twitching flank, sending hot jets of milk into the pail that rang musically when empty and later dulled to a rhythmic hiss.

The mill house was cold, even the kitchen. Mrs Coyte kept the stove burning low, only stirring the embers in the Lidstone grate when it was time to do the cooking or scald the cream. Grace went cold to bed and shivered under a thin blanket in a damp, mouldy room alongside the great mill-wheel that covered one side of the building. All night long, the water spouted from chinks in the closed-off chute and splashed down over the spokes of the wheel.

It was a relief to get up in the morning, cross the yard where sheets of brittle ice covered the puddles, bend over the chopping block and wield the cleaver in her ravaged hands, until the splintering twigs drew blood. Fiercely, she swung the cleaver down from above her head, making it sever the kindling and thud into the chopping-block. In her head, the sound was the sound of a cutlass biting into the lugger's bulwarks, and she heard Frank's pathetic, 'Pity! Pity!' With her eyes closed, she saw the tall, cloaked figure, the inflexible captain, darker than the darkness of night. She hated him, the unknown stranger.

She did not feel her hands, they were numb at first, but the fervour of her work sent the blood coursing through her veins and set her mind racing. Day after day she followed him, the man with the pitiless cutlass who had maimed her Frank and sent him to perdition. To look at her face, as young Ronald Coyte often did, standing with head cocked to one side like some great awkward bird, you would never have suspected her of having any other than seraphic thoughts. A light smile played around her lips as she shadowed the faceless one who was, in the fullness of time, to feel the weight of her vengeance.

At all times, she remained conscious that the success of her enterprise would be jeopardized by the slightest revelation of her real purpose. The face she must show the world was a visage of dissimulation, an illusion of slow forgetfulness and resignation. How else could she avoid the results of her resolve from becoming common knowledge? At best, people would try to dissuade her, Emma Troup was proof of that and only time and apparent indifference on Grace's part would allay her suspicions; at worst, insuperable obstacles would be set in her path by those who felt it right to protect the two men who had taken her Frank from her.

She knew she could have no confidant to share her secret and bolster her intent if ever it wavered. As the days passed, she knew that it would be put to the test. Only the inner fire that burnt in her imagination, fuelled by unquenchable memories of the precious person who was irrevocably lost, could sustain her.

The captain of the revenue cutter was alive somewhere, going about his daily business. In her mind's eye Grace spied on him, tracked him, sidled up close to watch the way he laughed, pretending to share his humour, pretending to admire the cut of his coat, the whiteness of his stock, but all the while probing the depths of his remorseless eyes in search of the soul that hid there. She would find it, some day she would have it. If the execution were slow, so much the better. She desired nothing more than to have obtained the man's completest trust against the day when she would charge him with his fault and –

'Penny for your thoughts.'

She looked up, it was young Ronald, one shoe curled around the other, nervous hands clasped, watching her. 'I was thinking of my sweetheart,' she lied, knowing that the very word would embarrass him. Ronald was but a callow boy. Mrs Coyte was wrong to worry about him, he was still wrapped up in tree-climbing, birds'-nesting, leaping brooks, snaring rabbits.

'I just see'd a grebe,' he told her. 'Leastways, I think 'twas one, down by the pond 'ee were. Will you come to see un?' Ronald was a shy boy, unsure of himself; Grace had discovered that already. Dominated by his mercurial father and shut out by his lifeless, loveless mother, he had begun to hang around Grace, waiting for a chance to talk. He had already told her about the place by the bridge where he hid himself to watch the mallard and teal among the reeds; he had brought her a buzzard's feather and showed her his collection of sea shells. Oddly enough, Grace did feel a kind of love for him, nothing like her feelings for Frank, but concerned, intrigued, protective, possibly maternal. She derived a wry pleasure from fulfilling the need his mother was not even aware of. The drawback was that, occasionally, something he said or did reminded her of Frank, and once her mind came back to him it set to ruminating by itself, like a seething pot in which memories rose unbidden to the surface and taunted her with their fearful joy and their unrepeatable uniqueness. Yet it was these recollections which furnished the gall that kept her from acceptance and forgetfulness. The thought of what had been was one thing, the thought of what might never be was another. That bitter gall sustained her like a stimulant at which she sipped whenever lassitude seemed likely to overwhelm her.

'I can't come now, with your mother watching,' she told him, 'she'll say I'm slacking and send me away. You don't want that, do you? Leave me alone for now, can't you see I'm working?'

Ronald sauntered off and she thought of Frank all morning, thought of Frank and his executioner, the revenue officer. Suddenly, she was seized with a fear that the officer might be getting away from her. She realized that unless she went to Salcombe soon, he might move on to another posting. That same afternoon she asked Mrs Coyte for the day off but her mistress made no secret of the perverse pleasure she took in refusing her permission to go to Salcombe.

''Ardly a week 'ere and Miss Pensilva do want an 'oliday! Proper little lady of leisure! Who's to feed the ducks? Who's to do the milkin'? Who's to clean the dairy?'

'But if it's a Sunday?'

'Work for mortal man never ceased because 'twas the Sabbath. Now, if 'twere permission to come to chapel, or even to go to church and 'ear that idolatrous Vicar, that might be different, that I might agree to. No, you shall stay 'ere and mind the farm while us do go to Chapel. Us'll pray for 'ee to see the light, Grace Pensilva, pray for 'ee to find the way to repentance. Us be all sinners, but there be one sinner, the worst of all, for whom the gates shall remain for ever shut, the sinner what won't repent. Give me a good Christian reason why I should let you go to Salcombe and I'll think about it, till then, get you back to your chores, young lady!'

And so, on Sunday, Grace watched her master and mistress, wearing the boots she had blacked for them and carrying their big black prayer books, climb into their little black trap behind a black Dartmoor pony and jingle off, followed by their long-legged son Ronald, perched on a raw-boned hack which Farmer Coyte had just paid good money for so that the boy could go hunting. Grace watched them depart without regret; she felt no need of their sort of forgiveness. Once they were safely away up the hill she went to her room, took out one of Frank's books from the chest Mr Wroth had brought down in his cart for her, and wrote a phrase on the flyleaf. After that, she sat a long while, turning the pages as if reading. If Mrs Coyte thought Grace would work while she herself was away in a warm chapel, surrounded by the consolations of religion, she had another think coming.

7

'So you've taken my advice and decided to 'elp Mrs Lackland in 'er good works. She do visit the sick, and see that the poor do get their dole money, like the Squire's wife should, if we 'ad one. 'Tis bad luck for a village to lose its Squire, and more so when 'ee be a young one and kind-'earted like Frederick Genteel were. 'Twere a sad day for 'Arberscombe when 'ee went off·to Malta and the estate fell into the 'ands of that Nancy.'

Optimus was back in Mrs Troup's parlour, using the excuse of bringing her a packet of fudge from Salcombe, in order to pump her for more information. Somehow he had thought that, by going to Salcombe and asking around, he would learn much more about Grace and the captain of the revenue cutter. But he had been disappointed: the Custom House held no record of the event he was interested in, nor did he discover the name of the captain who had commanded the lugger at the time in question. The clerk was helpful enough, but there was a month's gap in the archives, as though someone had deliberately expunged any reference to the person Optimus was seeking. Where the records stopped, a Captain Trahearne was posted to Bridport; where they took up again, the new captain's name was Scully. When Optimus asked the shopkeepers and innkeepers in the town what they could tell him of Grace Pensilva, they had all heard her name and had an idea of her exploits, but none of them could tell him anything of the anonymous captain. He felt thwarted, almost angry that he was unable to trace Grace's movements in the weeks after she began life at Langstone Mill, still less discover what she too had undoubtedly been seeking: the preventive captain's identity.

'Nancy?'

'Squire's sister, though Frederick weren't never the real Squire, that were Lord Mayberry, their father, what never comed down 'ere, but stayed up Lunnon, gamblin' away all 'is substance in Boodles and they other clubs. That was 'ow young Frederick and the 'Onnerable Miss Nancy was always kept on a tight rein for the lack of it.' Mrs Troup paused and popped a fresh lump of fudge into her mouth, mumbling it between toothless gums. 'You do know 'ow to get round an old lady, don't 'ee, Mr Shute. 'Tis bald-faced bribery and corruption, but don't give over for I do like it. That Frederick Genteel were proper smitten by Grace Pensilva, forgot all about rank and station 'ee did, and she weren't no different, though she were quick to deny it. Ever since she seed 'im ride over with the hunt, she was taken with that Frederick, but that be another story and 'twill 'ave to wait for another day and a new bag o' fudge.'

'But what about Salcombe, you'll tell me more about that now, won't you? You must know, did she go there? What did she discover?'

'Oh aye, I'll tell 'ee that, can't 'ave our new schoolmaster losin' 'is beauty sleep worryin' over Grace Pensilva, can us? I'll tell 'ee, but you won't be much more forward for all that. Grace invented an old aunt, sick and like to die in Salcombe, to convince Janet Coyte to let 'er go there, but when she did, the bird 'ad flown. Not just that, but a masked man don't leave much trace, do 'ee?'

'What do you mean, a masked man?'

'The revenue captain, the one what put paid to 'er Frank, no one ever knowed who 'ee were, never gived a name and always wore a mask o' chamois leather. Folk said 'ee were sent down from Lunnon special 'cause all the other preventives sold out to the smugglers, they said 'ee were gentry, too well-off to close one eye in exchange for a cut. Any'ow, 'ee were the only one ever to catch the moonlighters red-'anded.'

'So Grace never knew who the second man was.'

'Not then, she didn't, but she may 'ave found out there-after. She weren't one to let go, she were like a li'l terrier when she did get 'er teeth in. She would follow un round the world if she 'ad to. Course, I didn't know that at the time, 'ow could I, if I'd knowed 'ow 'ard she were, 'ow vindictive, I'd'a tried 'arder to keep poor Jan King away from 'er. Not that 'ee would've listened, 'ee were smitten with 'er too, just like Frederick Genteel, only more so. That were the way of it, there were somethin' about Grace that made men look twice, and then made fools of 'em. And you're the same, if I'm not mistaken. If Grace were 'ere today, you'd be eatin' out of 'er 'and, just like the rest of 'em.' 'Emma Troup took another lump of fudge and licked her lips after it. 'Grace Pensilva weren't sweet like this, bitter-sweet she were. That were what made men run after 'er, she 'ad precious little time for 'em, she weren't like the other village maids, she were different.'

'What made her different?'

'Some of it were in 'er looks, but it was more in 'er nature. She were fastidious, like a cat; she walked by 'erself. You 'aven't never see'd 'er likeness 'ave ee? Well, as you're a nice young man, better than I thought when you first comed 'ere, I shall show 'ee summat what I've never showed to another, not to a living soul since I came by it.' The old woman stood up stiffly and waddled across to a chest of drawers topped by some Staffordshire dogs and other china ornaments. She pushed her glasses back up her nose and ferreted through the drawers, eventually pulling out a black satin bag, orna-mented with jet that was too stylish ever to have been one of her own accoutrements. Puffing a little, she flopped back into her chair and fiddled with the bag's drawstring. Optimus watched without real interest; it was obvious that the bag was too small to contain a real portrait.

But when Emma Troup dipped her pudgy hand into the bag and came up with a small gold locket, surrounded by delicate filigree work, and started turning it round and round in her fingers, vainly searching for the catch that would open it, Optimus could not long restrain his impatience. He knelt beside her, took the locket gently but firmly and held it suspended from its chain while it spun slowly. The filigree which surrounded it completely was of a fineness that he had never seen, it challenged his young eyes to discern its details. On one face of the locket was engraved a ship-portrait, exact in every detail that Optimus was aware of, a brig perhaps, though he was not knowledgeable enough to tell for certain. On the opposite face was a heart and two interlaced pairs of initials in such florid script that he could not immediately decipher them. Of a catch with which to open the locket, there was no sign.

'I only did manage to open un the once,' said Mrs Troup commiseratingly, 'and even then I didn't know 'ow it 'appened, just comed apart in me' and, and when I shut un, I could never get un to open again for the life o' me. But you'll manage, I 'spect, with all your clever tricks.'

Optimus was not sure; the locket swung inches away from his eyes, tantalizingly. When he took it in his hand and palped it exploringly, the catch still eluded him, nothing in the filigree or the plain ring that held the chain responded to his gentle pressure, the joins between the two engraved faces and the body of the locket were almost imperceptible and had none of the incisions which commonly allowed one to open a pocketwatch with a penknife.

'I'm getting nowhere,' he admitted finally. 'Look here, I'm going to ask you a special favour, will you let me take it home with me? I'll take great care of it and bring it back next week without fail. You can trust me.'

'I don't know,' said Mrs Troup. 'Oh, you're honest enough, but 'tiddn' that, I just don't like to leave un go out o' my sight. 'Tiddin' for what 'tis worth neither, if I was after what 'tis worth in gold, I'd've sold un long since to one o' they young men what comes by to buy trinkets. I've never showed un to no one, once you does that, the thieves come runnin'.'

'But how did you come by it?'

'Grace Pensilva comed back 'ere once, not everyone do know that, and fewer did see 'er, only two or three. That be when I got un.'

'She gave it to you then.'

'I didn't say that, not zackly, but she did want me to 'ave un, leastways, I think so. 'Tis somethin' I'm very attached to, 'tis all I 'ave to remember 'er, and Grace and me was close, though she never said nothin' nor me neither, she knowed I cared for 'er and likewise, in 'er own way, which she kept to 'erself; she 'ad a special thought of Emma Troup. Weren't I the only one 'ere who tried to understand 'er, didn' I try to change 'er mind, keep 'er from doin' what she 'ad in mind. For 'er, for 'erself I did it, I stood up to 'er. I told 'er 'twasn't justice, I told 'er if she must pile one wrong upon another, she wouldn' 'ave no rest. Grace took no notice, but that didn' mean she didn' 'ear what I said, nor know the spirit in which I said it.'

Optimus lowered the locket gently on to the table beside the satin handbag. Sometime, he would ask Mrs Troup about that too. He had learnt already that the answer to each question came at its appointed hour. He relinquished the chain and it tinkled on the locket as it fell.

'Go on boy, take un!' He was astonished at the offer and hesitated to pick it up again. 'Go on, take un. Nobody much didn' care 'bout my Grace in 'er lifetime, and I'm not long for this world to remember 'er. You take un, don't bother 'bout bringin' un back neither. But you won't sell un, will 'ee? Promise me that. Promise you'll not forget 'er neither.'

To Optimus's surprise, slow tears were collecting in the old lady's eyes and coursing slowly down the deep furrows on either side of her nose. He had not thought her capable of much emotion, the professional, composed exterior assumed by the teacher had concealed it from him. 'I thought you didn't approve of her, I thought –'

'You thought a lot of things, Mr Shute, but you didn't know nothin'. Course I didn' approve of what she did; didn't I know what 'twould do to 'er? D'you think I didn' tell 'er? She didn' listen course she didn', that were 'ow she were, I didn' 'spect it. But when she'd gone, didn' I miss 'er. 'Arberscombe were a grey place without 'er.'

Optimus gathered up the locket gently and prepared to take his leave. He would have time aplenty to discover the secret of its catch. At the last moment, a thought occurred to

109

him. 'Remember that paper you gave me, the one with the French on it? You said she gave it to you; when was that exactly?'

"'Twas in that locket, I found un when I did open the front and see'd 'er picture. You 'aven't told me yet what was writ on it.'

'Revenge is a cold dish.'

'Ah, that's what she thought, right enough, though it were bitter fruit when 'er comed to taste un.'

Frederick Genteel aimed a kick of his riding boot at the pile of logs that smouldered on the hearth. A shower of sparks flew up the broad chimney followed by tongues of flame that illuminated his face in the dimness. Evening was closing in on the saloon, casting a merciful veil over the frayed tapestries that upholstered the furniture. Everything in this room was familiar to him, from the staid portraits on the walls to the chinoiserie cabinets and the gaming table. When his eyes lighted on that, Genteel took a deep breath and blew the air out of his pinched nostrils with a sniff of disapproval.

Perhaps divining his thoughts, his sister Nancy turned from her place at the tall window where she had been staring out into the dusk and spoke. 'Father has written that he intends to come down here soon.'

'Heaven forbid! All that'll happen if he does is that he'll bleed the place white to pay his debtors. Lord Mayberry lives in Town, in the style to which he is accustomed, selling the seed-corn of next year's harvest.'

'Well said! Just like an eldest son. So that's why you've come home: to protect your investment. Long live primogeniture and the entail!' The bitterness in her voice was there, just as he remembered it. Nancy had never forgiven God for not sending her into the world as a boy. Even her clothes betrayed it. Unless obliged to, she never wore anything but her riding habit. 'That's why you've slunk home,' she concluded, 'admit it.'

'I came home,' said her brother, striving to remain patient, 'because Napoleon's beat and the wars are over, because the

110

navy no longer needs all its captains, because Father didn't lift a finger to influence the Admiralty.'

Nancy smiled her thin-lipped smile at this. 'Come now, Freddie, it's not like you to be bitter, you're supposed to be above that sort of pettiness.'

'You mean I should leave it to you.' There they were, Genteel reflected, at it again like cat and dog. However long he stayed away, the pattern was always repeated. If anyone was bitter it was his sister. The very way she stood betrayed it, head advanced, shoulders slightly hunched, predatory, bird-like. And yet, she *was* his sister Nancy and, but for the whims of fate, he would be in her predicament. Heaven knows, he tried to be sympathetic, get close to her, but that only raised her bulwarks the higher. 'I'm sorry, I didn't mean that.'

'Yes you did. Can't you keep your apologies to yourself? You're a man, aren't you? This place was miserable enough before you came back, but it was bearable while I didn't have you to remind me of my station.'

'Your station?'

'Breeding stock, a mare to serve under some stupid, over-endowed young stallion that Father picks out for me, to mend our fortunes.'

'But Nancy, if you'd only get about a bit, travel up to Town, meet some nice feller on your own initiative, you might –'

'Don't you know me yet, don't you know your own sister? Do you think to convert me to marriage, exchange one tyrant for another. At least, if I stay as I am, I'll outlive the present one. May he gamble, may he drink, may he whore to his heart's content, he'll snuff his own candle the sooner.'

'Nancy! He's your father!'

'I suppose so. Anyway, I wish he wasn't. And if *you* weren't so damned hypocritical, so damned forbearing, Freddie, you'd wish him gone too. Admit it!'

Genteel's long face stayed impassive. If it had been lighter in the room, she would have seen the hurt in his eyes. In the firelight, she could see his strong jaw, lined cheeks, and the circles of shadow around those eyes, each picked out by a tiny point of reflected light. 'It's getting dark,' he murmured. 'I

111

must light a candle. What a place Leet has become, with hardly a servant.'

'Always the diplomat,' Nancy complained, 'always changing the subject.'

'What's for supper?'

'How should I know? I don't care either.'

'Not much of a homecoming, not much of a welcome, is it?' he asked rhetorically as he carried a glowing twig from the fire to the candelabra on the oval table. 'If only you knew how much I wish I was back in the Med. The light is clear out there, blue sea, blue sky, red rock, white rock, dark green trees; none of this damned eternal greyness. But I'm going to stay here, a while at least.' The candles flared up and there was no mistaking his determination. 'If I can't be a gentleman warmonger, I can be a gentleman farmer. Father can have no objection to that. If I succeed, it'll raise his revenue, he'll have more cash to gamble. We'll all be better off in the long run.'

'In that case, I'll take some of my share in advance. You won't begrudge me the wherewithal to buy a new hunter. The only possible pleasure here is hunting. You owe it to me, it'll be partial compensation for having to put up with you and your moralizing.'

'I'll talk to Charles about it.'

'Oh, you and your Charles Barker. Who is he anyway? God Almighty? All that he ever does is put a damper on everything.'

'Charles Barker is a good steward. If Father didn't cream off the profit, worse than that, mortgage the capital, Charles could buy you anything you wanted: gowns, jewels, anything.'

'Forget the jewels, damn the gowns, just let me have my hunter. I'm sick and fed up of being ridden on a short rein.'

'Then do your share in the house!' snapped Genteel, suddenly overwrought, as he limped across to ring the bell for supper.

'What's wrong with your leg?' she asked. 'It seems to be hurting.'

He doubted if her solicitude was genuine. 'An old wound,' he grunted.

'I didn't notice it the first time you came home three weeks ago.'

'It comes and goes. Riding makes it painful.'

'Where have you been all day then?'

'Around.'

'Can't you give a straight answer?'

'Riding to Harberscombe last week brought it on again,' he replied and instantly regretted it; once she had a bone to gnaw, she never let go of it.

'Harberscombe? I didn't know we had any land there.'

'We haven't. I just lost my way, that's all.'

Nancy shook with malicious laughter. 'Frederick, the great navigator, lost five miles from home, among the hayseeds, I don't believe it. There must be some woman you're after, that's what makes you limp, you sly dog you!'

Frederick Genteel shook his head; it was not a warm homecoming.

Someone was knocking on the door. How long the knocking had been going on, she did not know. She put her book into the chest and closed the lid swiftly. Who could it be? Whoever it was had not contented himself with hammering on the rough oak panels, she heard the door swing back and the scrape of boots on the flagstoned kitchen.

'Anyone at 'ome?' A man's voice, calling gruffly 'Anybody 'ere?' The sound of opening doors as he explored the dairy and looked into the parlour. In a moment, he would be climbing the stairs.

Grace tiptoed on to the landing, avoiding the boards that creaked. Down below there was silence. Whoever was down there must have heard her and stopped in his tracks. There was nothing for it but to go down. She descended the stairs as resolutely as she could, not wishing to betray her alarm. After the first half-dozen steps she saw his tall leather boots and knew him for a seaman, an impression confirmed by his serge trousers, tanned hands and blue jersey. When she had come down the stairwell far enough to see his face, she almost laughed. Was this the man who had momentarily scared her?

113

'They're not at home,' she told him. 'Nobody's home. Mr and Mrs Coyte are gone to chapel.' As she spoke, she fixed him with an unwavering stare, locking on to his eyes which returned her look for a moment only and then escaped her, wandering off sideways to a corner of the room. It seemed a long time before he replied.

'It bain't the Coytes I'm come to see,' he muttered lamely.

'Then who is it you're wanting, Jan King?' she challenged. A new silence fell and it amused her to observe the extent to which this strong man was humbled and inarticulate in her presence.

'You,' he answered finally, with a fleeting glance at her face to judge her reaction.

'Me? What business can you have with me, Jan King?' Jan King shuffled his feet and turned his hat in his hands. 'Come on, out with it! The Coytes will be back any minute. I don't want them seeing a man in the house. I know what they'll think.'

'It's about – about Frank . . .' his voice trailed away.

'Well?'

'I come to tell you –'

'You don't have to tell me anything,' she broke in. 'Ivor Triggs told me everything I need to know, Jan King. You sold out to the preventives. I despise you.'

'I came to say –'

'You came to say what? Do you think you can pay me back with excuses? Do you imagine you can compensate for my Frank with explanations? You can't bring him back to me, can you? He was supposed to be your friend too, wasn't he? Wasn't he your partner?'

'I came to say I'm sorry.'

'Sorry? What's sorry got to do with it, man? You're guilty! If it weren't for you, Frank Pensilva would be living and breathing still.'

'Forgive me, Grace, I've been thinkin', wonderin' what I might've done more, if I'd swum back, could I 'ave saved un? – I 'eard un shout – "Pity!" 'ee did shout and I turned back, but 'twas 'opeless, what good could a man in the water

114

do against a boatload o' preventives? Before I could think twice 'ee did shout again, "Pity!" – after that, nothin', 'ee were pulled under – and then I 'eard the stroke of oars, the cutter were after me and, if it 'adn't been for the fog – '

'If it hadn't been for the fog, all the world might have seen your treachery. You thought there would be no witnesses. Ivor Triggs couldn't swim, you knew that, and you never imagined he was alive there, under the capsized gig. No, Jan King, don't expect me to believe it was pure luck that you were able to get clear and swim ashore. That was no accident. It was no accident that you showed a light in the gig either. You're a Judas, Jan King. What've you done with the money, what've you done with the reward the revenue captain gave you? Much good will it ever do you!'

'There bain't no money, never was, never shall be.'

'Then how did he find you, answer me that, on a black night, in the middle of nowhere?'

'I don't know – I don't know –'

'And I suppose you'll say you don't know the name of the revenue captain.'

'I don't know that neither, why should I, I never met un. I tell 'ee, Grace, I can't understand it.'

'Well *I* can, and when you say you're innocent I don't believe you. You're a Judas and you betrayed him. My Frank was a fine man, too good to be wasted on folk like you and a place like Harberscombe. Frank Pensilva didn't bow the knee, Frank Pensilva was ready to stand up and fight, Frank Pensilva wasn't afraid to deprive the king of his iniquitous excise duty. Frank Pensilva believed in the rights of man. But you ignorant, cowardly people, you prefer to touch your forelocks to the lord of the manor, the constable, the taxman, and suffer, suffer as the landless men of Harberscombe have always suffered, generation on generation. I despise you. Without Frank you were nothing, without Frank you'd never have bought the gig and got started, you didn't have it in you. Frank told me what you were like, but I didn't believe him, not then. But he was right about that too. He was right about so many things, Frank was –'

Jan King straightened up suddenly, a rush of anger seemed to stiffen him. 'Frank Pensilva weren't the angel you thought 'ee were – not by a long chalk – nowhere near perfect. Full o' newfangled foreign talk 'ee were, what with 'is, "in America we did this" and "in France they do the other", 'ee did make us sick to the teeth with 'is talk o' revolution. 'Ow could us start a revolution 'ere? But 'ee weren't so quick to step forth and say such things to the Squire's face. 'Ee knowed full well 'twould bring a man no other reward than transportation. That brother o' yourn were a sham, Grace Pensilva, us never trusted un.'

'Be quiet!' hissed Grace, gripping the edge of the table till her knuckles showed white. 'I won't hear you say so.'

'"Tis God's truth, Grace, I can't tell no other.'

'The truth! What do you know of the truth?'

'I 'as to say it, Grace, your brother were a waster.'

'I won't hear it! I won't!' Grace was stiff with fury. It seemed to Jan King that she was capable of almost anything; that, had there been a knife on the table, she would have lunged at him. And then, abruptly, she mastered herself, the cataleptic rigidity left her body and her face regained an expression that might have been mistaken for a smile. 'You said you'd come to say you were sorry,' she said levelly, 'well, I've heard you say so. You can leave now.'

Jan King hesitated, disconcerted by this abrupt change of tone. 'And am I forgiven?'

'Forgiveness, what's forgiveness to do with it? If you're blameless, as you say you are, what's there to forgive?'

'I didn't think much to your brother, but I keeps thinkin' I might 'ave done more to save un. Perhaps 'twould've been better if I'd drowned with un.'

'That's for you to decide. You can't expect Grace Pensilva to absolve you, it's too soon, I've had no time to get over it, can't you understand that? Now go, I've grief enough without you coming here to revive it.'

She turned her back on him and began to climb the stairs. He took one step after her but stopped. What had she just said? Too soon? She was right, of course. He lingered another agonizing minute, then left.

8

By the time Grace reached the top of the hill above Salcombe, the morning was already far spent, for the road from Harberscombe was long and hilly. She had left just before dawn, with a small basket on her arm, a basket containing bread and cheese for her lunch and a small pat of butter that Mrs Coyte had insisted on giving her to take to her old sick aunt who was the pretext for the journey.

'Don't let old man Coyte see it,' she had whispered, covering it with a napkin, ''ee don't believe in givin' nothin' away. But to give to the poor be to store up treasure in 'eaven, or so they tell me. The old lady'll remember me in 'er prayers, won't she?'

Grace smiled to herself as she thought of it, she had told the tale of her aged aunt so well that she herself had almost believed it. The old woman was the excuse she needed to come to Salcombe and now here she was, about to arrive there. Although she lived a bare ten miles away, she had never visited the town, never seen anything larger than Harberscombe village, for that matter. This small town had always seemed as remote as the distant face of the moon; she was totally unprepared for the sight that was gradually revealed to her as she began her descent.

Ships: tall-masted ships of more kinds than a skilled seaman could easily put a name to, dozens of them, moored in the stream, grounded in creeks with their bowsprits poking into the trees. She stopped with a gasp at their loveliness, the wonder of it. Until then, all she had known of men's works were the old grey church and the low-lying farms scattered

117

about the quiet Harberscombe landscape. Great ships had crossed her horizon, but only as small white clouds, progressing serenely from headland to headland, diminishing to nothingness. Nothing had prepared her for this, this amazing demonstration of man's creative genius. Looking at the intricate network of rigging, she wondered how anyone, least of all a poor woman like herself, could understand and assemble constructions of such complication. Somewhere among that motley fleet was the revenue cutter and, not far off, must be her captain.

The Custom House was shut. As it was Sunday, she was not surprised. In any case, she had not intended making herself known there; her plan was to make her inquiries indirectly. The problem was where to begin. The quays and hards were dotted with seamen from the ships lying off in the harbour among which a number of skiffs were constantly plying. Many of the seamen were three sheets in the wind, despite the hour and the disapproving glances of the faithful who held themselves aloof, clutching their prayer books to their bosoms like talismans, as they returned from church and chapel. Grace made inquiries of several people, including a young servant girl drawing water at a conduit, but no one seemed inclined to talk of the revenue cutter or her captain. She was beginning to think she had embarked on a thankless task when a man in pea-jacket and sailor's trousers emerged from the Fortescue tavern and accosted her.

'Whither bound, me beauty?' he hailed her, ranging alongside. Grace walked on, nose in air, ignoring him. 'Come now, darlin', I've seen 'ee tackin' back and forth in the street 'ere and makin' no 'eadway. Luff up a minute, won't 'ee, and speak with a fellow voyager who might be of help to 'ee.'

'I thank you, but I've no need of your assistance.'

'No need of my assistance,' he laughed, 'that's a good one! Why, I never did see a vessel in more of a tangle; you're all in irons, your sails is aback and you're makin' nothin' over the ground.'

'Look here,' Grace exclaimed, halting suddenly and setting her hands on her hips. 'I have my own business to attend to

118

here. I've no time to waste listening to your frivolous talk, still less to attend to a man who can't use plain language.'

'But that *is* plain language. The language of the sea's precision itself. 'Ow can I 'elp it if you don't know it? What I've been sayin' is you've lost your bearings, and if you've any sense you'll let your friend Ben Barlow lend you 'is services for a pilot.'

Grace pondered a moment: she had heard all about sailors, they were notoriously ingratiating, frivolous, fickle creatures, but this Ben Barlow had a broad, kind face, with twinkling eyes surrounded by wrinkles, whether from smiling or screwing them up against the glare of sun on water she wasn't yet certain. 'Well, Ben Barlow, what do you know of the revenue cutter?'

'The revenue cutter?' Ben Barlow seemed taken aback in his turn. 'What can a nice young lady like you be wanting with the Revenue? I'll tell 'ee straight: the preventive men are a poor kettle of fish, and no friends o' mine neither.'

'Well, if you won't be helpful, what's the use of talking?'

'Avast! Didn't say *that*, did I? Come, sit on this wall 'ere and tell us why you're in search of the revenue cutter.'

'Why I'm in search of the revenue cutter is none of your business,' said Grace, but she sat on the wall all the same. There was something likeable about Ben Barlow. He perched on the wall beside her, reaching a long pointing arm across her shoulder and letting her sight along it. 'There 'tis, that one's the revenue cutter, the big lugger under the stern o' the schooner.'

'Which one's the schooner?'

'Don't know a schooner when she sees one! Why, the girl's green as grass.' He noticed a cloud of annoyance settle on her brow and continued hastily, 'No 'arm meant, I'm sure. But everyone 'ere in Salcombe knows a schooner afore 'ee can tell a cow from a donkey, us do know 'em by their rig. The schooner's the one with the foremast shorter than the main. Now do 'ee see 'er?'

Grace recognized the vessel he meant, picking her out from the confusing forest of masts. The lugger, close astern, was nondescript, poorly kept and appeared to be deserted. Grace's disappointment showed in her face, though she tried to keep it out of her voice. 'I should've known her crew wouldn't be aboard her.'

'Aye, they're mostly ashore Sundays, but you won't find 'em prayin' in church.'

'One of them would be well advised to do so.' There was a hard inflection in her voice that caught his attention and made him stare at her, trying to weigh up who she might be and what she might want with the preventive men. She didn't look the type, but you never could tell. Her face looked honest and straightforward enough, her eyes were steady and grey, but she gave nothing away. Only the tone of her voice hinted at controlled emotion. He guessed that what had brought her here was a lovers' quarrel, perhaps one of the preventives had jilted her after a brief romance in an out of the way village. Her clothes seemed to bear this out, she was a country wench, close to poverty, clean and neat, but threadbare. It was her manner of speaking which didn't fit; although she had a trace of West Country burr, she spoke like a lady.

'Well, there she lies and that's all an honest innkeeper can tell 'ee.'

'You're an innkeeper?'

'What's wrong with that?' Ben Barlow put on an offended air.

'I took you for a sailor.'

'The one don't rule out the other.'

'Then you must have met the lugger's crew, you must know her captain.'

Ben Barlow shook his head. 'I don't know nothin'.' To his surprise, she fumbled in her basket and produced a pat of butter. 'If I gave you this, would it help you remember something?' Ben Barlow laughed, he threw back his head and let fly a resounding peal and Grace had the impression that everyone in Salcombe must be looking at them. She prepared to leave, but Ben Barlow put out his hand and grabbed her arm.

'You don't 'ave much idea what might serve to bribe a

120

seafarin' man, do 'ee darlin? Now, if it was a pint of ale or a nip o' grog you was offerin' . . . Anyhow, tell us straight, what is it you want with the preventive men exactly?'

'I want news of the captain of that lugger, his name and where he lodges. It's a personal matter.'

'There'll be no 'arm done if I tell 'ee?'

She considered a moment before answering. 'I don't think so.'

Ben Barlow jumped off the wall and dusted his trousers. 'Stay 'ere while I look in the Fortescue and the other taverns to see what I can find out for you, Miss – what did you say your name was?' touching his sennet hat jauntily.

'Grace, Grace Pensilva,' she smiled at him, a slow, warm smile that lit her face and made him remember her long after their first encounter. It stayed with him as he hurried across to the Fortescue.

Grace gathered her skirts closely about her knees and twisted her body to face the panorama of the estuary where punts, skiffs and bumboats were criss-crossing among the larger vessels. She was trying, by deliberate absorption in the life of the harbour, to distance herself from the disquieting collection of passers-by who now crowded the street. There was a succession of rolling, drunken men and slatternly women proceeding from one tavern to the next, jostling each other and exchanging obscenities. Grace concentrated on a frigate, examining the rigging where the topmen were manning the yards, shaking loose the sails, then furling them again according to an elaborate drill. She closed her ears to the noise around her and lost herself in the repetitious, formalized movements, watching the white sailcoth rise and fall in the still air.

'What ho, me lovely!' A sudden stench of brandy and bad breath claimed her attention. Trying not to give a start, she looked out of the corner of her eye and discovered what she had feared: a tall, gangling drunk with a Vandyke beard, tousled hair, and tarnished gold braid on his coat, was ogling her. His bloodshot eyes were challenging her to look around and face him. When she failed to do so immediately, he swayed on his heels a moment as if ready to leave, but changed his mind. With great gravity he placed a large tattooed hand on her knee. She tensed and shied away from him.

'Lookin' for the captain o' the revenue cutter, aren't 'ee, me darlin', leastways that's what a little bird just told me.' Grace looked with disgust at the froth of saliva trickling down his chin. 'Come now, darlin', take a swig o' this. Drink up and we'll go up to your place.' He gestured with the brandy bottle which he held in his free hand, towards the tiered jumble of gables and slate roofs that struggled up the hillside. So this was the captain; he would be an easy man to hate.

Optimus was so excited he could not contain himself. Regardless of prudence and his good resolutions, he ran across the lane, scattering the chickens and making Farmer Stitson of Butterwell Farm look up in astonishment, nearly losing his tall felt hat in the process. With a quick pull at the bell, he sprang into the kitchen and stopped in the midst of the floor, astonished to find the room deserted. The bell at his shoulder was still jangling long after he stopped, but the rest of the house was silent as the grave, there was not even the usual clicking from Mrs Kemp's knitting needles. Optimus stood irresolute, with the dangling locket swinging from the gold chain that was looped around his fingers.

'Dr Cornish!' His voice rendered no echo in the low-ceilinged room, it was as if it were stifled. Something kept him from setting off to explore the rest of the rambling old house; although Dr Cornish was friendly, he was not familiar and never took Optimus beyond the kitchen and the parlour. He was about to slip out of the door and try to swallow his disappointment, when he heard a faint sound, like a groan, coming from a small curtained-off area to the left of the fireplace. Optimus had never seen the curtains drawn back and had never really wondered what might be concealed there. A similar alcove on the opposite side of the fire contained the scullery and Optimus had always assumed that the curtains concealed the entrance to a smoke-room. Even now, he was unsure whether he had really heard a groan, it might have been the pot-hook swinging in the chimney.

There it was again. This time it was unmistakable. Optimus was frightened. He knew it was irrational, but the feeling gripped him nevertheless. In all probability, old Dr Cornish was behind the curtain, taken suddenly ill while Mrs Kemp was out of the house. But he was not sure of that, he was not sure what lay in the tiny room which it concealed. Even if it were only the Doctor whose groaning he could still hear from time to time, Optimus did not know what to do, he had the layman's visceral fear of illness. Would he have to touch the old man? He shuddered.

Another long drawn out groan decided him; he stuffed the locket into his pocket and pushed the curtain aside. What he saw shocked and disgusted him. Dr Cornish was lying, limp as a rag doll, between the wall and a row of kegs of brandy. Optimus knew it was brandy because of the smell, a pungent reek that came from a leaking spigot and a pool on the floor beneath it.

The old fellow was drunk, disgustingly drunk. His eyes were turned upward leaving a strip of white showing under his partly opened lids, his breath came in long shallow hesitant gasps. His face was purple-red, it was bright at the best of times, but now it had an unhealthy tinge. This was the side to Dr Cornish that Vicar Lackland and Mrs Troup found so disgraceful and unacceptable. He was on the point of tiptoeing away when the old man's eyes fluttered open. His lips moved and it was clear that he was trying to say something, but though he was enunciating with painful slowness, all that came out was an inaudible whisper. Even then, Optimus might have left him there, wallowing in the stench of his depravity, were it not for a certain look in the Doctor's eyes, an intelligence too bright to square with drunkenness. Reluctantly, he knelt beside him and put his ear close to the Doctor's lips. 'Medicine bottle –'

'Where? Which one?' Optimus could all too easily imagine the number of seemingly identical bottles that must litter the surgery, among which he would have to choose at random.

123

'– table drawer –' the answer came at the end of an agonizingly long wait. Optimus sprang up and hurried to fetch the bottle. Even then, his pains were not at an end, he soon discovered that he would have to find a spoon in the scullery and administer the medicine slowly between the Doctor's scarcely-parted teeth, willing his patient to succeed in swallowing it. An hour later, he was still there, but the Doctor's condition had altered surprisingly.

'Others he saved, himself he cannot – You know the quotation,' said the old man, with a self-deprecatory grimace. 'Oh, I can counter the symptoms all right, but as far as the malady itself is concerned, I can only accept my fundamental incompetence. When I started, I was just like you, I thought all sorts of things were possible, I thought I could do practically anything, but now, God knows, I realize my limitations, I understand the limitations of human knowledge.'

'So, in the end, in your heart of hearts, you're a believer.' Optimus thought that the Doctor's recent brush with death had given him a renewed sense of reverence.

'An amusing observation,' countered Dr Cornish, with an unexpected twinkle in his eye. 'When I mention God, I might as well be addressing Zeus or Woden as that narrow-minded, vengeful, Jewish Jehovah of yours. And I don't confuse the unknown with the unknowable. As regards the latter, it may not even exist. In due time, with a proper scientific approach, mankind may well penetrate all the secrets of the universe.'

'Discover the elixir of life?'

'There are no simple solutions; there is no philosopher's stone. Indeed, any true philosopher would tell you that the concept is an illusion, an alchemist's avaricious dream; were all things transformed to gold, where would be the value of that rare metal? But what am I doing, maundering on philosophy when I should be thanking you for saving my life. Another half-hour and I should have been done for. When Mrs Kemp came back from the butcher, she would have discovered she had overbought her provisions, and she'd have lost her employer into the bargain.' He glanced up at the clock on the mantelpiece. 'She should be home any moment.

You'll stay to supper won't you? It's rabbit stew, ready cooked, out in the larder, won't take her long to warm it. And you can tell me what you've been up to. A little bird told me you'd been hanging around the Vicarage, cultivating that Mrs Lackland, a fast hussy if ever I saw one. What she sees in that Vicar of hers, I can't imagine. Watch your step, young feller, she'll have wound you round her little finger before you know it.'

'It was Mrs Troup's idea that I should help with Mrs Lackland's good works,' said Optimus stiffly. 'There's nothing at all between us, absolutely nothing, she's a married woman.'

Dr Cornish laughed at this, but soon regretted it, a small spasm brought his hand up to his chest. 'Don't make me laugh,' he chortled, 'it might be fatal.'

'You were better when you were at death's door, at least that stopped you teasing me.'

'I beg your pardon, Mr Shute, I should treat you with more respect. Now tell me, to what did I owe the honour of your visit?'

With an involuntary gesture, Optimus clapped his hand to his pocket. The locket was still there. How could he have forgotten it? With exaggerated slowness he dragged it out by its chain and, with his elbow on the table, held it swinging just above the stained woodwork. After giving him a long questioning look, the Doctor reached out his own hand and took it.

'Ever seen that before? Mean anything to you?' asked Optimus.

Dr Cornish turned the locket over and over in his palm, studying it closely through his spectacles and feeling for the catch which would open it. He shook his head. 'Can't say I have, but the initials, they suggest something. Still, it might be a coincidence.'

'What about the initials, out with it!' exclaimed Optimus with rising excitement.

'Not till you've shown me how to open it. I want to see what's inside. Quid pro quo.'

When he had taken the locket back, Optimus had a moment of self-doubt. Would he be able to do it? Over in the schoolhouse he had spent hours examining it, twisting and turning it, pressing it with his fingertips. When it sprang open he hardly knew what he had just done to achieve that result and was not sure he could repeat it. He had taken a magnifying glass and studied the tiny mechanism in an attempt to understand it before allowing the case to close again. That was after his eyes had drunk their fill of the image which the open case then disclosed. Now, holding the locket in one hand, he pinched the little ring where the chain was attached between finger and thumb, imparting a peculiar pushing and reverse twist, then pull and twist again to it until the cover flipped open.

'Well?' he asked Dr Cornish when the latter had spent a great deal of time gazing at the interior.

'Ah,' said the Doctor in an abstracted manner, as if daydreaming. 'I was younger then. But I've grown old. That never happened to her, did it? She'll always look like this, in my memory, in your imagination.'

'It is her then?'

'Of course it is, I was more than half convinced already, when I saw the initials.'

'You promised you'd tell me.'

'You must have studied them yourself, what are they?'

'FG, that makes some kind of sense, I've guessed who that must be, but the other ones, GD, they aren't right, are they? How do you explain it? And what about the portrait?'

'A most excellent likeness, no one in Harberscombe could have painted it. Those are the same penetrating eyes, the same expressive mouth. Had you noticed the artist's signature?' Optimus shook his head. 'No, I thought perhaps you wouldn't have, it's written too small, only a person obliged to wear spectacles with a magnification like these would pick it out. It's a strange name, "Scicluna" – "R Scicluna".'

'It sounds foreign, not a bit English.'

Dr Cornish drew a whistling breath between narrowed lips. 'You've given me an idea. You know about the episode in Malta, someone must have told you, wasn't it mentioned in my papers?'

'I've not read everything yet.'

'I suppose not,' Dr Cornish sounded disappointed, 'why should you, you're in no hurry, you've got all the time in the world.'

'Tell me about it.'

'Another time, I'm too tired just now, all washed out, it's suddenly hit me.'

'I'm sorry, I was forgetting what you'd just been through. I'll leave you in peace if you like.'

'No, don't go. Stay to supper. Just a little human companionship to remind me I'm still alive, that there's something to live for . . . She's beautiful, isn't she?' He held the open locket in the palm of his hand so they could both see it. 'No wonder they loved her. I suspect you're in love with her yourself, that would explain why you're immune to the charms of Mrs Lackland. Well, you're safe enough, she can't harm you, not now. Not that you would have anything to fear, she had nothing to reproach you with, had she? Oh yes, she was beautiful all right, but she wasn't forgiving. And when she loved a man, she knew no reason, she wasn't satisfied with half measures, she absorbed him utterly, or tried to. She loved not wisely but too well. And a man might feel that her kiss was the kiss of death, certainly that was the case as far as Jan King was concerned, and Frederick Genteel too, for that matter, though that was different. No, Optimus, I may call you that, mayn't I? Grace Pensilva wasn't a good person to love or be loved by. Before you become more closely involved with her, I'd like you to consider the proposition that what is fascinating in her character is wilful, compulsive, dangerous, and that she was driven by something pathological, obsessive, something which men of an earlier, darker age, would have called a demon.'

Optimus slept little that night. He had opened an exciting new door and he was anxious to know how Grace was faring in Salcombe.

*　　*　　*

'You mistake me,' said Grace, taking the man's hand firmly and lifting it off her knee, but he clung to her skirt and petticoat so that the movement bared her leg to the thigh.

'As 'andsome a pair as ever I did see,' he continued, bending forward to peer under her petticoat. 'My predecessor 'ad exquisite taste; 'twill be a pleasure to replace him.'

Grace saw red. This lout was not going to have his way with her. She clenched her fist and hit him behind the ear. The weeks of farm work had made her strong and she was astonished at how stunned the man became. He loosed his hold on her skirt and staggered back, putting his hand up to his ear. It came away marked with blood. 'You'll pay for that, darlin',' he muttered menacingly as soon as he could pull himself together. 'No one injures Cap'n Scully that way and gets away with it. I'll show you somethin', I'll give you a lesson you won't forget!'

He stowed his bottle in his pocket and lunged forward, dragging Grace off the wall and trying to pinion her arms. The pressure of his embrace, the stink of spirits and stale sweat, made her head reel, but she braced herself and bit savagely into his other ear. The man gave a yelp of pain and moved one hand to shake her off. Taking advantage of his diminished grip, Grace sprang away a couple of paces, then turned to face him. Already they were hemmed in by a ring of spectators, baying for more blood. 'Go on, dearie,' screeched a toothless old hag in a bonnet, 'go on, hit un again!'

But Scully had turned nasty. He was a big powerful chap, with shoulders like an ape. The pain had sobered him a little and his eyes had narrowed viciously. With a sudden terrible sinking feeling in her stomach, Grace watched him pull the bottle from his pocket and smash the punt off its base with a quick flick against the wall. Holding it by the neck, with the jagged remnants of its sides pointing at her, crouching on wide-spread feet, the man sidled towards her. 'Cap'n Scully'll put 'is mark on you, me beauty!' he announced between whistling breaths.

Grace broke and ran. She forced her way through the ranks of the surrounding crowd and rushed down the cobbled street, fearful that she might trip over her skirt and that he would be upon her. She had no need to look back to know that he was following; the pounding of his feet was close, apparently getting closer. She cursed the long heavy skirts that were hampering her movements. Where was Ben Barlow? If he were the true friend he had pretended to be, he would help her, and now was the time she needed him. There was only a slight chance he was still within earshot, but she was so desperate that she shouted all the same. 'Ben! Ben! Where are you? Help me! Help me!' But he did not appear.

Ahead of her the street seemed to come to a dead end where a tavern displaying an antiquated coat of arms for a sign, closed off an alley. Grace did not want to be trapped in a tight corner so she turned uphill towards the church. Within a few strides, she was gasping for air. The road was so steep and her clothing so heavy that she was sure the man would catch her in a moment.

Seeing a stone lying by the roadside, she snatched it up, whirled round, and flung it at him. She had no time to take aim; it was a desperate act, but luck was with her. It struck the man full in the face. He halted. Blood poured from his forehead. He was only a few steps away, swaying like a pole-axed steer. And then, half-blinded, but impelled by a dark animal will, he came on at her, slower than before, but aching for revenge. Grace turned and ran again. It was like a nightmare. The hill seemed steeper and her strength was ebbing. Her skirts clung to her knees like detaining hands.

And behind her, sooner than she had anticipated, she heard the wheeze of Scully's breath, the thudding of his feet. Her own breath was rasping in her throat. A violent stitch was catching her under the ribs. Another few steps and she would be forced to stop. She looked wildly around for another stone to fling, but there was none. A terrible lassitude was invading her limbs; was this what Frank had felt drowning? She wondered how it would feel when the jagged glass entered her flesh.

She stumbled to a halt, one hand pressed against a wall while the other fumbled to open the neck of her dress. Her breath came in long sobbing gasps, her heart pounded. The realization that the footsteps had stopped came upon her gradually. When she dared look around, she saw her pursuer lying prostrate on the ground, the last fragments of his bottle scattered around him. Another man was bending over him. She recognized Ben Barlow. He looked up and saw her. 'Run!' he cried urgently. 'Keep runnin'!'

'I can't,' she gasped.

'Can't you 'ear 'em comin'?' he asked and she became aware of footfalls lower down the hill approaching round the bend in the road. 'We can't stay 'ere talkin'. I just struck a King's officer, that's an 'angin' matter.'

Suddenly Grace realized why the man called Scully was lying in the dust; Barlow had hit him from the side as he rushed past an alleyway below the church. If Scully's followers caught Ben Barlow, he would be up before the assizes.

'I'm winded, I can run no further.'

'Quick,' said Barlow, 'catch on to my shoulder.' Half dragging, half carrying, he hurried her into the church. It was quiet and dim inside and completely deserted. A smell of burnt candles hung in the air from the recent service. He pulled her into a chapel and made her kneel, head in hands as if praying. They both heard the shouting mob pause where Scully lay, hesitate a while and then set off with renewed cries up the hill.

'Thank you,' Grace murmured.

'You came to see the captain of the revenue cutter, well, you 'ave, I 'ope you're satisfied,' he whispered.

'Did he see you hit him?'

'Keep your voice down! There's someone comin'.' Had anyone seen them slip inside? She heard footsteps approaching over the gravel and someone stopped in the doorway. A long shadow lay across the paving stones. Once again, Grace felt her heart beating. Whoever it was must hear it too. She bowed herself in silent prayer: praying for the man to go away. After an agonizingly long time, the shadow moved and feet crunched on the gravel again.

'Thank Christ for that!' Ben Barlow sighed with relief.

'Well, at least I know who killed Frank Pensilva,' said Grace in a flat tone.

So that was why her name had seemed vaguely familiar, thought Ben Barlow. He studied her out of the corner of his eye, between praying fingers. Who was she? His wife probably. If she had come here to know her husband's slayer, she was in for a disappointment. ''Tweren't Scully,' he announced quietly.

'Not Scully?' A cloud of anger and frustration fogged her mind. Scully had seemed just right. It was easy to imagine him wielding the fatal cutlass. 'He's the revenue captain, isn't he?'

'Scully 'asn't been skipper o' the cutter more'n a fortnight.'

'Who was it then?' Grace could not keep the anger out of her voice.

'Don't know.'

'What d'you mean, don't know? You must know. If you keep a tavern in Salcombe, you must know the name of the revenue captain.'

Ben Barlow dropped his hands from his cheeks and turned to face her. 'No one knowed 'is real name. Called 'isself Brown, 'ee did.'

Grace stared back at him; there could be no doubting his sincerity. 'But you must know what he looked like.'

'Never see'd 'is face, wore a mask, mornin', noon and night. All I can say is, 'ee seemed like a gennulman, not like that Scully.'

Grace pondered. If this were true, she was no further advanced than when she left Harberscombe. What she had just heard was incredible, outrageous, but she would have to believe it. She groped for a solution. 'Find him, find him for me, find out where he's gone. I'll make it worth your while to do so.'

'You can keep your money,' said Barlow. 'I shouldn't do it for that. But I can't 'old out no 'opes o' success, there ain't nothin' to go on. I'll try though, if you'll tell me why you wants to find 'im.'

'I can't tell you now, but you will try, won't you?'

'Aye, I'll try.'

'Thank you, thank you. Here, take this, it's good butter, I made it myself, it's all I have to offer you.' Amazingly, throughout all the chase which had just occurred, the butter basket had remained hooked over her elbow.

Ben Barlow took the cloth-wrapped butter pat and stood up. 'I'll be leavin' now,' he told her, 'you stay put till the 'ue and cry's died down, then go by the back lanes at sunset. Good luck to 'ee.'

When he had gone, Grace felt lonely and despondent. For the first time she realized the enormity of the task she had set herself. The captain of the revenue cutter had moved on already, tracking him down was almost an impossibility. Even if she did trace him, how would she find the money to set off in pursuit? She would be lucky to get back safe to Harberscombe, there were long miles to walk and a scolding Mrs Coyte at the end of them.

Grace sat silent. She had made her vow. Though it might take a lifetime to fulfil it, she must not relent.

9

As the primroses came out in the banks, brave yellow harbingers of spring, followed by catkins and bluebells which his pupils brought to school and set in old jars in the windows, Optimus became filled with perplexity. His mind was forever drifting from the classroom, following Grace Pensilva in one direction or another. He too was living out her long drawn out penance at Langstone Mill. When he left her in Salcombe, accosted by the rough captain, he could hardly wait to return to his desk, pick up his pen and discover how things had turned out for her. Even when Mrs Lackland drove over unannounced to visit the school, he was too distracted to rise to the occasion. As she left and he accompanied her to her curricle, she whispered to him, 'What's come over you, Optimus? You're so withdrawn. Are things getting on top of you? And you haven't been round to the Vicarage lately,' she added reproachfully. 'My good works are languishing for lack of assistance.'

Optimus stared into space. He was well aware of Diana Lackland's attractiveness and he had a shrewd suspicion that she was setting her cap at him. But her availability was disquieting. Had she been younger, simpler, he might have coped with her, but her scent, her rouge and powder, her mobile lips, made him restive.

'I'm sorry, I've been preoccupied. There's so much to think of. These children are a proper handful. It's all I can do to keep ahead of them.'

'There's no need to lie to me, Optimus Shute. Lackland keeps me informed; you've been hanging around that dreadful old Dr Cornish.'

Optimus couldn't resist a glance at the Doctor's window, in case he was watching them and listening. The lane was very narrow and he would be sitting only a few feet away. Mrs Lackland had been raising her voice as she spoke and didn't appear to care if the Doctor heard her. 'Everyone knows,' she continued, 'if Lackland knows, and he's not the most perspicacious of persons – I should have said *parsons*,' she corrected herself with a brittle laugh. 'But do as you please, I can manage without you. Evidently civilized converse over tea or coffee are not enough to satisfy your appetite: you must have strong drink and scandal. Well, don't count on my influence with Lackland when the time comes to judge your performance on probation.'

'You've got it all wrong,' muttered Optimus. 'I feared I might be trespassing on your hospitality by coming round too often. And it might not be proper to visit the vicarage in your husband's absence.'

'Silly boy,' said Mrs Lackland, poking Optimus with her whip-handle, 'how strait-laced you are, how old-fashioned! No one bothers about that sort of thing nowadays. And Lackland has absolute confidence in me, he trusts me implicity. As he should, shouldn't he? Or is it yourself you don't trust? – Why, I do believe the boy's blushing! – So I can expect to see you after church next Sunday, can't I?' Optimus nodded dumbly. 'Well, don't you dare forget,' she added as she gathered up the reins. 'I don't enjoy playing second fiddle. Be warned,' and here she tapped him on the shoulder with the folded whip, 'a woman scorned is a woman armed. My revenge will be terrible.'

With a crack of that whip she was off up the lane, scattering mud and chickens. She was jealous, that was clear enough. For her to be jealous of Dr Cornish was bad enough. Thank God she didn't seriously suspect her rival was Grace Pensilva. Wearily, Optimus returned to the classroom. If he could keep his thoughts off the clock, the day would soon be over.

That evening, when Optimus looked over his account of Grace's Salcombe adventure, he was shocked by the explicit savagery of it. What would happen if it fell into Mr Lackland's hands? Would he not say that it was the product of an isolated schoolmaster's fevered imagination? That would not make it any more excusable; the existence of such indiscreet writings would cast a shadow on his suitability for the formation of young minds. Quite apart from that, there was the perpetual question that nagged at Optimus every time he set down his pen: am I exaggerating, was it really like this? Biting his lip in frustration, he locked the manuscript in his desk and hurried out of the house.

The dark lane along which he strode was full of the delicate scents diffused by the spring flowers. How different from Diana Lackland's artificial perfume! An owl hooted from a barn on Butterwell Farm and a bat flitted close to his head. Likewise, Optimus let his mind flit from place to place, recalling scraps of conversation – things that Emma Troup had said; Dr Cornish's reference to an episode in Malta; the initials on the locket: FG was certainly Frederick Genteel, but GD made no sense at all, although the portrait was undoubtedly Grace Pensilva's; then there was Mrs Treebie, something told him she knew a facet of Grace Pensilva's personality. Above all, there was the memory of his latest conversation with Uncle Bill Terry. Optimus had gone to see him at his cottage with the intention of renewing his offer to buy the gig that hung in the boathouse. Despite its age, it was a trim craft and he burned to own it and explore the estuary. But Uncle Bill had not been more accommodating than on earlier occasions.

''Tis not for me to sell. By rights it do belong to Jan King. ''Twere 'is property and 'ee bain't 'ere to say yea or nay.'

'But he's dead, isn't he?'

'Who's to say? Never was no body to prove it. Without a body, without a will, 'tiddin' right to dispose of a man's possessions.'

'But he wouldn't have gone away like that with never a word, never a letter, never once coming home. It wouldn't be like him, would it?'

'Who's to say what would or would not be like un? Jan King were a young man what kept 'isself to 'isself. 'Ee went off with

135

Grace Pensilva in that gig and 'ee never comed back, nor she neither, not then, and the boat were found floatin'. Course, I knows what I thinks, so do us all in 'Arberscombe. No one expects un to come 'ome all of a sudden. Missin' presumed drowned, that be our verdict. 'Ee were a good man, Jan King, I didn't take to un at first, but when I come to know un better, 'ee were a good partner to me.'

'Yes, I know you were partners.'

'After what 'appened to Frank, Jan were sick o' the trade and us went fishin' together. Oh aye, I could tell you a thing or two about Jan, if I'd a mind to, young feller.'

The tide was coming in slowly over the sands, drowning the Back and spreading in a steely sheet towards the slipway on the far shore. The two men stood patiently, leaning against the high side of the lugger while the shallow river water trickled around their feet. 'Another quarter hour,' said Jan King, 'we'll soon be afloat.'

''Arf an hour, more likely,' replied Uncle Bill, 'you young uns be all impatient nowadays.' He tapped out his old clay pipe on the gunwale, and pulled out his pouch to refill it. With an automatic gesture, he offered it to his companion, only to see the other shake his head. 'What, Jan, still not smokin'?' he inquired, tamping down the tobacco in his pipe with a horny thumb.

'Can't seem to find no taste for it,' said Jan.

'No, I s'pose not,' replied Uncle Bill as he fiddled with his tinder-box to produce a light. The men stood silent for a while longer, the elbows of their jerseyed arms hooked over the boat's gunwale behind them. It was one of those slow neap tides with not much of a rise and high water would be around midday. ''Ow long since us've been partners, Jan?'

'Nigh on a twelvemonth.'

'You've been better'n that Jack Lugger,' said Uncle Bill, puffing reflectively on his pipe, ''ee were all talk and no pull, a man 'ad to pull twice to make up for un.' He thought back to the time he and Jack Lugger had parted company. Without turning his head, he could see the old tarred boathouses, the

136

boilers where they barked their nets and sails, and the pilot's twin-chimneyed cottage, where Jan King's father had lived before him. It was all in his mind's eye, clear and sharp as a painting, he would carry that image to his grave with him, it was where he had worked ever since he could remember. And he remembered Jan King coming out of the cottage and coming down to the beach to talk to him while he and Jack Lugger were offloading crab-lines from a donkey. 'Mind if I ride along of you tomorrow?' he had asked when he closed with them. He spoke with studied casualness and directed his question at Uncle Bill only.

'Thinkin' of earnin' an honest livin'?' broke in Jack Lugger with pointed insolence.

'There's not much in pilotin' these days,' Jan King had replied quietly, trying to ignore the provocation.

'No, there bain't, but I've always heard Jan King never lacked for a couple of guineas to rub together. That gig o' yourn've bin a proper money spinner. It've paid you better'n it 'ave Ivor Triggs. It've paid you better'n it 'ave Frank Pensilva.'

'What's that you're sayin'?' demanded Jan King, his fist clenched involuntarily.

'I've 'eard men've been paid good money for smokin' lately,' continued Jack Lugger slyly.

'Leave the poor begger be,' Uncle Bill had said gruffly. 'there's bain't no use makin' a chap suffer, and you're apt to get a bloody nose into the bargain.'

'Didn't think Jan King were the long sufferin' kind,' said Jack Lugger, 'I never saw no sign 'ee carried a conscience.'

'I've nothin' to reproach meself with,' exclaimed Jan King.

'That bain't Grace Pensilva's opinion,' countered Jack Lugger, 'and I'm more'n 'arf inclined to agree with 'er.'

'Grace Pensilva can think what she likes! I don't care twopence!'

'Oh, you don't, me beauty! Well that bain't what some of us thinks. All 'Arberscombe do know you'm soft on Grace Pensilva, proper mazed about 'er. But I thinks there be more to it than that, you were jealous, Jan King, jealous of 'er brother. That be the reason why –' Suddenly, Jan King had him by the scruff of the neck, shaking him like a fox shaking a chicken. Uncle Bill wondered whether Jan King was sufficiently roused to kill his tormentor. The memory of having Grace Pensilva spit in his face must still rankle. But Jan controlled himself, shoving Jack Lugger away violently so that he stumbled into the shallow stream where he knelt, rubbing his neck, all the truculence gone out of him. Jan King began to walk back to his cottage, but Uncle Bill detained him.

'Don't take on so, Jan,' he remembered calling, 'don't pay no mind to that Jack Lugger. Come along o' us in the mornin' and welcome.'

'I won't ship with no squealer,' spat out Jack Lugger.

'No need to come if you don't want to,' said Uncle Bill, 'us can manage without 'ee.'

'But we'm partners, Uncle Bill, you can't leave a man without a livin'. What've I done to deserve such treatment?'

'Slandered a good man,' Uncle Bill heard himself saying. 'I shall choose who do sail along o' me. I don't want you no longer. You can try rabbit trappin', or if you can't turn your 'and to that, you can go to the hirin' fair and try for work as a labourer, that'll teach 'ee a lesson in 'ard graft. You'll wish you'd tried 'arder when you was sailorin'.' He paused and looked straight at Jan King. 'Us'll soon see if this chap be better.'

'Thank you,' murmured Jan King before resuming his walk towards the cottage, 'you'll not regret it.'

''Twon't be long afore 'ee'll be lookin' out for the Frenchman,' called Jack Lugger as he set off in the other direction. 'You'll soon see if I bain't mistaken.'

That was months back, and Uncle Bill had had no reason to regret his decision. Jan King worked hard in the lugger, pulling pots with the strength of two, where Jack Lugger had been content to stand and watch. If Jan King felt the stirrings of desire to go back to the smuggling trade, he never showed it, but he never discussed the old days either, still less did he ever speak of the night when the gig had foundered. Since

138

that time, never once had he smoked a pipe, never once had he been seen to take strong liquor. When they came in from sea, he would go up to his house and spend his time alone there, while Uncle Bill returned to the village. That was his way, always had been, he was a quiet one.

The lugger stirred under their elbows. The tide had risen sufficiently to lift it out of the mould it had made for itself in the sandy river-bed. They felt the tremor and the slight lurch as it rose and took life again. It was time to climb aboard: five minutes more and there would be water enough to row seaward.

As they did so, Uncle Bill paused and pointed up the estuary. 'Bain't that a beautiful sight?' he said quietly. Less than a quarter of a mile away was a strange vision: a pack of hounds had left the slipway on the far shore and was crossing the estuary obliquely. The dogs were running and gambolling around a solitary horseman. What made the scene peculiar, unreal even, was that they all appeared to be walking on the mirror-smooth water.

'That's the first time this year I've seen the Master out cubbin',' said Jan, ''ee do bring the young dogs 'ere to train 'em to cross water.'

'They bain't all young,' replied Uncle Bill, 'I can see Destiny out front, and there be 'Armony, I've heered 'er barkin'. Tell you what, Jan King, us'll leave off fishin' tomorrow and go to the meet at 'Arberscombe. 'Tis no good to work all year and never see no sport. Will you come and watch it?'

Jan King did not reply immediately. He was watching the leading hounds pause when they came to the swirl of deeper water where the river-bed cut into the sandbanks. The red-coated huntsman came splashing up behind them, sitting straight-backed on his big-boned roan. The horse surged through the pack and beyond them till it was fetlock-deep in the running water. He took the small silver horn that hung from a cord around his neck and blew repeatedly, a peculiar gliding note. Still the hounds hesitated. Without looking round, he blew again louder and suddenly the first of them launched off and began to swim after him, crabbing across the

139

current. Soon all the others were following closely.

'That old Destiny would follow 'Arry Baskerville any-where,' said Uncle Bill, 'Old 'ee may be, but 'ee won't give up. Us'll have some proper sport tomorrow, I'll warrant you.'

'Meanwhile,' said Jan, ''tis time we went fishing.'

Their lugger was floating. There was no wind; they would have to pull until the breeze came in. Jan shipped the long sweeps while Uncle Bill got the anchor. Then, side by side, they pulled steadily, with the sweep-leathers thudding in the tholes and the stem sighing happily as they drove it through the water. Facing landward as they were, they were not the first to see the Frenchman .

It was Grace Pensilva, pausing to wipe her brow in the middle of the long row of turnips she was hoeing, who was the first to see him. She had been watching Uncle Bill's lugger creep seaward, and she too had seen the huntsman crossing the estuary. Ahead of her, Mrs Coyte was hoeing steadily along a parallel row of seedlings. In a moment or so she would turn round and scold Grace for slacking.

The field that they were hoeing was just under the shoulder of one of the hills that hemmed in the Arun. From where Grace stood, she could see a narrow wedge of estuary water between the two points that rose on either side of the Arun bar. She was high enough to see over them to a narrow strip of bright horizon, but it was not here that she saw the Frenchman.

The first sign was an increasing triangle of russet sail push-ing out from behind the western headland. Then came a black mast followed by a white topsail and a dun mainsail. Already, Grace was almost certain of its identity. The vessel was astonishingly close inshore, as if to taunt the authorities. It emerged with painful slowness from behind the rocks and she guessed that it had been caught in the bay by the long calm that had fallen after nightfall. Now, with every stitch of sail set, it was hauling itself inch by inch across the water, taking advantage of the flowing tide to make some easting. Far off to the west, Grace observed the sails of ano-ther ship, a small brig, that had come round from Plymouth;

in all likelihood it was in pursuit, but was too far off to offer immediate danger.

Now, the nearer vessel was almost completely clear of the headland. Grace made out a small dog house, the only upper works to break the smooth line of the gunwale. Behind it, a tiny figure stood at the wheel, and behind him was another man, probably the captain. Next came the stumpy mizzen with its red sail. Underneath was the steeply raked counter. There was not a shadow of doubt, it was the Frenchman.

'Do I 'ave to be the only one who ever works in this neighbourhood?' Mrs Coyte had turned round angrily and was shouting. 'There's more than half the field to finish before sundown. Come on, girl, were you born lazy? Stop moonin' around and begin to earn your wages.'

Grace took her hoe in both hands and began cutting. She said nothing of the ship which was creeping across the river-mouth; Mrs Coyte was too short-sighted to see it for herself and, if she knew of its existence, there would be more vituperation. She followed the farmer's wife across the field slowly, unwilling to quicken her pace. She would do what she must, no more, no less. The blade of her hoe bit sharply into the soil with a noise that made her think of steel severing flesh at the butcher's. That was the last sound her Frank had heard before he . . .

The mechanical repetitive work went on. She liked it, it numbed her. But she stole a glance at the sea from time to time to look at the Frenchman. The distinctively rigged vessel seemed to linger a long while in the centre of the bay, as though showing itself, waiting for some sign, some signal. The captain would be looking out for Frank's successor, someone with whom to set up a new trading relationship. There had been no brandy landed at Armouth since . . .

'What's the matter girl? Stop your dreamin'!' Mrs Coyte had taken her by the arm and was shaking her. 'Bestir yourself or I'll 'ave to speak to Mr Coyte about hirin' a more willin' worker. I should've knowed you'd got a lot of false notions when you was companion to Miss Delabole. You're at Langstone Mill nowadays, Grace Pensilva, 'tis not bezique

141

and whist, 'tiddin' patience nor sampler-work, 'tis real-life work, 'ard grind, us folk must toil while your gentry dance and sing. And 'tis no use dreamin' you can go back to moon-lightin' –' Here Grace looked at her narrowly, wondering if she had somehow managed to discern the Frenchman. 'There bain't no one in 'Arberscombe ready to go along of 'ee, not with a woman. No, there bain't no easy money to be 'ad, young lady, so you'd best step briskly till you do catch up with me.'

In the sultry heat of that morning, Grace found it hard to hold her temper in check. She wanted to shake off Mrs Coyte's hand, slap her pinched white cheeks, but this was not the time, not yet. She shrugged her shoulders and turned to her work without a word.

'A ne'er-do-well, just like that Frank, you be,' Mrs Coyte shouted after her. 'Made for each other, out o' the same mould you was. But I prays for you, every Sunday in chapel I do pray for you, I prays for your sins to be forgiven, so you'll see the light and repent.' Grace's face was burning, she knew that, but she refused to be baited. She hoed her row fiercely under the hot sun, feeling the farmer's wife's eyes heavy upon her.

Before she reached the end of the row, she felt a cool breath on her cheek. It was the breeze, the sea breeze, it cooled and refreshed her, carrying away her anger. She cast a glance out to sea, at the place where the Frenchman had lain like a model ship upon a mirror. It was no longer there.

Aboard the lugger, Jan King sat at the helm with his face turned resolutely away from the Frenchman. Both he and Uncle Bill had seen it when they had stopped rowing and pulled their boulter. 'Friend of yourn out there,' said Uncle Bill, 'bit of a stranger.'

'And can remain so for all I care,' muttered Jan King as he began to haul in the rope back of the boulter. Every two fathoms a hempen leader went off for a couple of feet, with a hook at the end of it. Baited and shot the night before, the boulter was a night line with which to catch bait for the crab and lobster pots.

''Ee must be up to summat, comin' in so close,' said Uncle

Bill. 'No doubt 'ee've found someone down toward the Yealm to land 'is produce. 'Twill be fetchin' a good price now, there bain't much on the market since you and Frank stopped tradin'.'

'Give over, will 'ee, Uncle Bill. Don't talk about it. There's no use remindin' a man o' past mistakes. They're all over and done with. Come on, find us the gaff and 'elp me land this conger.'

''Tis comin',' announced Uncle Bill. 'Breeze be comin'. Let's get the sail up.' The older man's eyes had already made out the early cat's paws ruffling the water out beyond the point. There was still no wind where they sat, dead on the water, but Jan too saw the signs and knew it wouldn't be long coming. He stowed the bait-knife and helped Uncle Bill with the halyard.

The wind came, softly at first, like a lover's caress, so soft that the boat hardly felt it and Jan had to swing his head from side to side to judge its direction from the coolness on his cheek.

'If you want to speak to the Frenchman, now be your chance,' said Uncle Bill. 'If you've second thoughts about fishin' for a livin', this be the time to say so. 'Ee've caught the wind too, 'ee 'ave. 'Twill be the devil to come up with un.'

'Good riddance,' exclaimed Jan King. 'And, if you've a mind to remain good friends with me, you'll say no more about un. Give us an 'and to set the mizzen, 'tis time we was off to the Carracks and catched they lobsters.'

After they rounded the Barrow, the Carracks hove into sight, a group of low rocky islets with a narrow gutway running between them and the reefs that stuck out from the shore. There were some pots there which they must pull after shooting the ones they had brought out with them.

But it was not lobsters that Jan King was thinking of as he pulled the pots. What engaged his mind was a memory triggered off by a glimpse of a dark sea-cave in a projecting shoulder of cliff between two coves. The place where he and Uncle Bill were working was a wild spot, impossible to approach in rough weather. In calm spells they came and

143

fished here, for the ground was good, crawling with big black lobsters.

What Jan King now remembered was a lazy Sunday afternoon when he had rowed out here alone in the gig, exploring every cranny in the coast. It had been a hot summer day, calm as a looking-glass. Beneath the gig the shallow sea-floor was perfectly visible. Long corridors of sand led between weed-covered rocks towards small beaches. On the rocks, the oarweed waved its palmated fronds and the bladder-wrack shivered gently. Spider crabs strolled across the sand. They had little growths of vegetation springing from their jagged backs. A vivid green wrasse was nibbling at barnacles. He had been so engrossed in the wondrous garden under the boat that he had not immediately noticed that he was not alone.

It was the shrill laughing voices which finally caught his attention. Seemingly muffled by the hot hazy air, they came from behind a serrated range of tall stony teeth that projected offshore beside a cave. Jan paddled across to investigate until he could see through a narrow gut that separated two of the innermost rocks, like a keyhole opening on a room beyond a door.

What he saw was a cluster of heads bobbing above the surface. There was much splashing of arms and peals of laughter. One of the swimmers stood up and he saw the top half of her naked body. The others flung water at her until she subsided. It was the village girls who had come down to remote deserted Haccombe Cove to swim undisturbed.

Before they noticed him, he gave a quick pull at the oars and moved the gig into the shelter of the rocks. He paused a moment, wondering what to do next. Then he remembered the cave. He knew the cave as he knew every nook hereabouts. It narrowed quickly from its gaping mouth, then formed a dog-leg that communicated with the cove on the other side. If he traversed the cave, Jan would be within yards of the swimming maidens.

The gig's keel grated on pebbles as he hauled it up on the hot beach. He hurried away to the cave mouth, wading through lukewarm water in a shallow pool. In the obscurity ahead, the wet hummocks of smooth wet rock glistened like sleeping seals or the body of some strange monster. He advanced warily, climbing through a constricted passage and arriving in a wider chamber with a sloping sandy floor. The echoes of the girls' shouts were audible again and a shaft of sunlight illuminated the silvery shale where the cave wall ended. He moved on carefully, his bare feet silent on the soft sand.

Just short of the bar of sunlight, he halted, staying hidden in the protective obscurity of the cave. There, so close that he could see the colour of their eyes, the drops of water pearling their shoulders, the maidens were gambolling in the water. He had never seen so much nakedness before. He caught his breath as the splashing young women rose out of the depths and bounded towards the shallows. Their bodies shone fresh and golden in the sun. Two of them ran towards the cave and he cringed back, fearful that they would discover him, but they stopped just short and lay down on the sand which clung to their wet bodies in shiny flakes like gold-dust as they rolled over.

Time almost stood still. Jan leant against the chill rock of the cave wall and drank in the compulsive spectacle. He could feel his flesh stirring and there was a suffocating tension in his chest. One of the girls, lying on the sand close beside him, was reaching out to touch the other on the nipple of the young breast. He bit his lip.

'Peeping Tom!'

The scornful, accusing voice shocked him and made him swivel round in alarm. It was a girl's voice. To have been discovered was bad enough; to have been discovered by a woman was worse. He wondered what retribution a crowd of enraged maidens might exact from him. But even more unnerving was to see that the speaker, outlined in a faint glow from the far side of the cave, was naked also. The smooth contours of her body simultaneously excited and frightened him. As his eyes adjusted to the gloom, the chiaroscuro of her breasts and belly became visible and the details of her features, framed in long tresses of black hair, were also revealed. She was beautiful, terribly beautiful, more beautiful than any of the maidens in the open air; she was superb, wonderful. But she was angry.

'Away with you!' she ordered, her eyes glinting fire, motioning to him to come back past her to the cove from whence he came. As he complied, bending his head sheepishly he saw what should have been evident to him earlier; a line of footprints, smaller than his own, leading back into the recesses of the cave.

Where the young woman stood, the space was so narrow that he was forced to brush against her. He winced as though burned and stumbled blindly through the pools, stumbling blindly on the uneven rock. From behind him came a shout of mocking laughter.

He sped into the sunlight, racing over the painful pebbles to the gig and pushing it savagely into the water. Even as he rowed away, her laughter followed him. He heard it now as he pulled the last of the string and baited it. The laughing girl had been Grace Pensilva.

'Your mind bain't on the job, that be certain,' Uncle Bill was telling him. 'Look 'ow you've stowed that crab-line. Thinkin' o' some maid or other, I'll wager.' Jan looked up from his work. Was the grinning old man who was leaning on the looms of the oars up forward a mind-reader? 'Written all over your face, boy,' continued Uncle Bill. 'Just one word of advice though, if you'll listen to an old-timer,' Uncle Bill was suddenly low-toned and serious. 'If 'tis that Grace Pensilva you'm thinkin' of, forget 'er. She'll never bring no good to 'ee. Forget 'er and find another. There's maids aplenty that'll care for 'ee more'n she would.'

'Time us was goin' 'omealong,' was Jan King's muttered reply as he busied himself with raising the sails. Soon they were clear of the Carracks, out in open water and bowling along in a fresh breeze. They began to round the Barrow, a huge rounded headland like a sleeping lion. Two other Armouth luggers had also set course for the estuary. Uncle Bill was watching them closely.

'Us can beat they beggars if you'm more than 'arf an 'elmsman,' he declared. 'But first off, us must 'eave these pots over. This spot'll do as good as any.' Suiting his action to the word, he took a pot from the pile and launched it over the side. The lugger was already surging ahead, and the line went snaking after it. Jan stood in the stern, one hand on the tiller, the other feeding the fleeters and buoys over the gunwale. As the lugger was lightened by losing the pots one by one, she bounded ahead, sending sheets of spray over the weather bow and setting Uncle Bill to bouts of laughter.

'Us'll show 'em a clean pair of 'eels,' he chortled. 'Slacken that sheet a bit and bear off a little. Us'll see the river in not much more'n a moment. You steers like a proper Armouth man, Jan King, I couldn' do no better.' Jan King was warm with pride. He looked out ahead for the break in the cliffs where the estuary lay hidden. Another pot splashed over the side and the line began to buzz over the gunwale. He would make up his own mind about Grace Pensilva, he told himself. She might change in time, hadn't she herself said so? What could be wrong with admiring her? Now that her Frank was gone, sooner or later she'd need somebody. She was over there somewhere, in the folds of the hills around Langstone Mill, he could imagine her, though he could not see her.

'Foot!' Uncle Bill's cry did not immediately register with him. 'Look to your foot, boy,' the old man shouted again urgently. Even then, Jan was slow to respond. He looked down. Unbelievably, one of the long loops of crab-line that he had flaked down so carefully had been kicked sideways so that it formed a rapidly closing bight around his leg. Already, the rough cordage was burning his ankle. A sudden jerk unbalanced him and he felt himself being drawn helplessly towards the transom.

It happened in a second. One moment he was standing there, basking in the pride of his helmsmanship, the next he was being pulled over and close to drowning. Suddenly, the rope slackened. Uncle Bill was beside him, holding the razor-sharp bait-knife. The coil of rope was still round his leg, but it was no longer tugging. The end which had joined it to the pot was vanishing over the stern.

'You'll owe me for that,' said Uncle Bill, 'that were a good pot and you'll 'ave to replace un.'

'I owes you a deal more than that,' said Jan ruefully. 'More'n I can ever repay you.'

Grace Pensilva had seen the returning luggers, but she was unaware of the small drama that had almost snatched Jan King from her. It was much later before the hoeing was finished and she could set off home. Mrs Coyte, stiff-backed as usual and hoe on shoulder, marched ahead of her down the steep lane that led to the mill. The cool of evening was closing in and Grace flinched at the greater coldness she anticipated at Langstone Mill. There was no joy for her there in that clammy hollow. If she had been imprisoned there by an agency other than her own sweet will, she would have found means of escape ere then, but she had so convinced herself of the inevitability of her sojourn that flight was impossible.

A horse was thundering up the lane towards her. Its hooves were pounding on the bedrock. Mrs Coyte had already turned the corner far ahead and it must have passed her without stopping. When it burst into sight, she made out a gangling figure astride it. The horse snorted as it laboured up the slope. It was practically a runaway and its rider struggled to rein it in when he saw her.

In the early dusk, the iron horse shoes struck sparks from the stones, the horse filled most of the narrow lane and Grace flung herself into the bank to avoid it. Looking up, she saw the rider clutching at his hat with one hand, the reins in the other, silhouetted against the darkening sky. The horse had stopped beside her, flanks heaving and froth dripping from its bridle.

'Oh, there you are, Grace,' cried the young rider. 'I've been looking for you all over.'

'Your mother said I must go hoeing. Didn't your father tell you?'

'Father went to market this mornin'. He've just come

home.' He stopped speaking, still breathless, waiting for a reaction. 'Haven't you noticed nothin'? – What do you think o' Lightnin'? Aren't he a wonder? Father just bought un for me.'

'He's got spirit.'

'He can run too. Will you ride home with me? I can hold un.'

'No, thank you.'

'Frightened?'

Grace laughed a little as she set off walking. 'Wouldn't you be?'

'You don't trust me.' He sounded hurt. 'I'm more grown up than you imagine.' He rode a few yards in silence close behind her. 'Oh yes, I'd almost forgotten; there's other news I forgot to tell you. Concerns you special.'

Grace walked on quietly. 'There was a man come to the farm today, a seafarin' man, askin' for Grace Pensilva.'

'And?'

'I didn't care for the look of un,' said Ronald, trying to sound important. 'I suspected he had something to do with the Revenue.'

'What did he look like?' Grace felt her heart beat suddenly fast and louder. Who was it? It might have been Ben Barlow, with the news she wanted about the masked man's identity. And then again, it might be Scully; he might still be at the mill, awaiting her.

'Didn't pay much attention. Can't remember nothin' special.'

'What did you tell him?'

'I said you'd gone away. I said you'd gone back to Cornwall.'

'Why did you say that?' Grace stopped in her tracks and turned to face him.

'I thought he might want to harm you.'

There was still sufficient light coming through the canopy of trees for her to see his face. He seemed genuine. 'I'm grateful,' she murmured. 'Where is he now, is he still waiting?'

'He left three hours back. I was glad to see un go. Didn't take to un.'

'Did he say anything else? Did he leave a message?'

'Said he might come back, that's all.'

'And his name?'

'Never said. And I never thought to ask un.' They came out of the woods and Langstone Mill lay at the bottom of the meadow below them. 'Father's in a good mood. Tell you that too, did I? Well, he's sold a score o' bullocks for a great profit. That's why he's bought me Lightnin'. He was in such a good mood when he came home that I felt brave enough to ask him the question .'

'What question? Stop spinning it out, tell me!'

'Whether I could ride Lightnin' to hounds tomorrow. He said yes to that too. Then I asked if us could all go. He said yes to that too. Even you can have a holiday, if you come to watch me.'

He galloped off down the slope and Grace stood still a moment, leaning on her hoe, willing herself to calmness. A single window gleamed with candlelight. She did not wish Mrs Coyte to see she had been troubled.

10

Mrs Treebie twisted and turned her hands in her apron as she stood in front of her two questioners. On the tea-tray she had set on the low table, the teapot had grown cold already.

'But what exactly was her relationship with Frederick Genteel,' asked Mrs Lackland almost severely. 'You can speak out here, we're not children.'

'I don't rightly know,' said Mrs Treebie with another twist of her apron and a glance at the clock, 'I only knows that Jan King weren't pleased the way she 'ung about un.'

'And how did things turn out between Grace and Jan? Do you think she ever loved him?'

'I don't rightly know that neither, Mr Shute. I weren't more'n a young girl in they days. She did live in 'is 'ouse though.'

'The cottage at Armouth?' asked Optimus.

Mrs Treebie nodded. 'Us never knowed what went on there. The other girls didn't like to go near there, they was frightened, thought 'twere 'aunted, and it did 'ave a strange feel to it, even to this day it do. No one 'aven't lived there since, 'ave they? If it weren't for the story o' the treasure, no one much ever'd 'ave went there.'

'What did people say about treasure?' Optimus persisted.

'They said there 'ad to 'ave been one, they said Grace Pensilva were so successful a smuggler there 'ad to be a mint o' money tucked away somewhere. Nobody never found nothin'. Oh, she were a great smuggler all right, none better, there 'ad never been a woman like that in these parts, nor 'aven't been after. But she never left no gold at Armouth. If you asks me, she took it with 'er. She wouldn't leave nothin'

151

round 'Arberscombe, she weren't set on returnin'.'

'It's Frederick Genteel that interests me,' said Mrs Lackland, 'I'm intrigued to know how Grace, a poor dairymaid, came to know him.'

'I can tell you that,' said Mrs Treebie confidently, 'I were there when she first set eyes on un. 'Twere outside the Trafalgar. 'Twere the same day 'is sister ran into young Ronald Coyte, though no one thought nothin' o' that at the time. They remembered 'ow Grace spoke to the Squire though.'

'What sort of a man was Squire Genteel?' asked Optimus.

''Ee were a fair man, a good man accordin' to 'is lights, that be what Feyther said and all who paid their rent to un. When 'ee upped and left, they 'ad time to regret un. That Nancy screwed 'em for every penny she could get, and Ronald Coyte 'elped her. Never ploughed nothin' back into the estate. Took after 'er feyther, she did.'

'She's still living over in Leet House, isn't she?' asked Mrs Lackland.

'Aye, she be still over to Leet, but she don't see no one. Shut up in that great 'ouse alone she be, alone with 'er conscience. Only Ronald do ever see 'er. 'Ee've come over old of late, 'ave Ronald; it comed on 'im sudden. One week 'ee were ridin' 'er 'orses to the point to point and the next 'ee was all grey and bent-up like. Folk say she used un.' Mrs Treebie put her hand up to her mouth, shocked at what she had let slip.

'He wasn't just a stable-hand then?' questioned Mrs Lackland, hastening to follow up her advantage.

'Don't rightly know,' said Mrs Treebie, avoiding her eyes and bending over to feel the teapot. 'This 'ere be cold. I shall 'ave to make fresh for 'ee. That be what comes o' too much talkin',' and she bustled off to the kitchen.

'There, didn't I tell you she knew something interesting? Aren't you glad you came, Mr Hermit? And now I've got you here, I shall claim my part of the bargain, you shall talk to me. Oh, you can't imagine how I yearn for civilized conversation. Talk to me about Mr Trollope's novel: the one I left on your desk in the classroom.'

'That was you, was it? I thought so. Well, I haven't read it.

152

I've been too busy for fiction.'

'What a bear you are,' laughed the Vicar's wife. 'All you can think of is that tomboy, Grace Pensilva, and all you've time for is drinking and yarning with that old soak, Dr Cornish. What can it be that so enchants you in his society? Could a mere woman be privileged to share in it? Do you have enough influence to procure me an invitation to one of the Doctor's soirées?'

'I don't really think you'd find it as amusing as you suppose,' Optimus muttered. 'You'd soon tire of an old man's ramblings interspersed with sententious comments from a young schoolmaster.'

'That's what I like about you, Optimus,' laughed Mrs Lackland. 'You're not like stuffy, pretentious old Lackland; you're so modest, so self-deprecatory, so – young! And you're not even aware that half the village girls are swooning over you.'

'Stop teasing! You really must!' said Optimus, half rising from the sofa where he was perched uneasily.

'Silly boy,' said Mrs Lackland, catching him by the arm and replacing him in his seat. 'I didn't mean to annoy you. You ought to be pleased to be the object of such adoration. But you know what it is, don't you? You're so quiet, so polite, so retiring, so handsome, I really can't blame them. If I weren't a married woman –'

'Precisely, you've hit on it exactly. And if I weren't the schoolmaster, with a position to maintain in this inward-looking society, I'd be free to have all the affairs I liked with the young ladies you mentioned.'

'It's possible to rise above such petty Pharisaical attitudes: your Grace Pensilva did so.'

'And they haven't forgiven her yet, have they? Don't expect me to follow her example, I haven't half the courage. And, you mustn't take this the wrong way. I'm afraid I ought not to spend the Sunday afternoons alone with you here like this. Never mind that it's completely innocent, people will be talking.'

'But Mrs Treebie's here all the time.'

'Exactly,' Optimus lowered his voice, 'and you know her

gift for romancing. I really shouldn't come here.'

'I thought you liked me.' There was a catch in Mrs Lackland's voice. 'I thought our friendship was worth more than such petty considerations.' She had pulled a cambric handkerchief from her sleeve and was twisting it nervously. Optimus imagined he saw her dabbing furtively at her eye with it. He sat, stiff as a ramrod, hands on his serge-trousered knees, conscious of the tightness of his starched collar.

'It's not that at all. I *do* admire you. You're the only really clever person I've met since I came to Branscombe. But we mustn't give these village people a chance to destroy your reputation. Why don't we do some good works, as you first suggested, visit the old and the sick. We could spend the occasional hour together.'

'The occasional hour! Oh yes, that defines your devotion to me exactly. I know you, Optimus Shute; it's *your* reputation you're so set on protecting. Oh, Optimus, you can't know what it is for a woman of spirit to be cooped up in this dull Vicarage. If only I'd known when I met Lackland – but it's no use crying over spilt milk, is it? And we must, they say, be thankful for small mercies. All right, next week we'll take the curricle and pursue our good works in public. But it's so long to wait. Would you mind if I called at the school again? I could catechise your classes.'

'It wouldn't be prudent, Mrs Lackland.'

'How hard you are, *Mister* Shute, so *reasonable*! And do you have to persist in calling me Mrs Lackland? You could say Diana. There's no need to stay so formal.'

'I'm only trying to protect you, Mrs –'

'Diana!' Her voice had an edge of hysteria, still close to tears.

'All right – Diana,' he repeated lamely, 'and it's a nice name, it suits you. "Queen and huntress, chaste and fair," isn't that what Ben Jonson would have called you?'

'There, you *can* be kind if you choose.' She dabbed at her eyes that met his with a new shining. 'Mrs Kemp told me you were a nice person. You see, even old Mrs Kemp's smitten on you. She's the one who told me you spend hours on end writing.

154

It's true, isn't it? What is it, a novel?' Optimus shook his head. 'You're so mysterious,' she went on, 'but I think I've guessed it: you're writing about Grace Pensilva, aren't you?'

'No.' The baldness of his lie surprised him. He had no need to lie to her, there was nothing disreputable in what he was doing. But she was sapping an inner citadel, threatening his secret self, and his special relationship with Grace Pensilva. To allow Mrs Lackland to invade it would be to sully a pure emotion.

'What is it then?'

'I'm making notes, preparing a primer.'

'Oh – how splendid, how meritorious.' It was obvious she only half believed him.

Just then, Mrs Treebie came in with fresh tea. She coughed a discreet warning of her presence. In her white apron and starched cap, it was hard to imagine her listening at the key-hole.

'We've been waiting, Mrs Treebie.'

'I've been as quick as I could. Mr Lackland don't buy 'nuff coal to keep the stove 'ot all afternoon.'

'I won't have you saying that. My husband has to live according to his circumstances.'

'Well, it weren't all the fire's fault. The postman comed with this 'ere letter.' She took an envelope from her apron pocket and handed it over.

'And you needed all this time to read it.' Mrs Lackland examined the flap carefully for signs that it had been steamed open. Mrs Treebie drew herself up tall.

'I don't care for your hinsinuation! If you'm goin' on that fashion, you shall 'ave my notice, Treebie's too. Then us'll soon see 'ow easy you finds replacements.' She stumped out of the room, with a brow like thunder. Mrs Lackland took a knife and slit the envelope. Optimus had already noticed that it was addressed to her husband.

'I know what you're thinking,' she protested before he could speak. 'Lackland has no secrets from me. I *always* open his correspondence. He approves, he says it expresses his confidence.' Her eyes dropped to the written page and, for a

155

minute, she was lost in study. 'Splendid,' she murmured finally, with a smile haunting her waxy lips. 'Splendid news. The new curate's coming. He's a Cambridge man, it's his first appointment, he's full of crusading zeal. Thank God *he* won't be a dog in a manger.'

The tea Mrs Treebie had brought was cold, but her mistress did not notice. Optimus put down his cup after a single sip and stood up. He had heard the sound of wheels in the drive and did not want to be trapped into another stilted conversation with the Vicar. 'I really must be leaving.'

'Well, go – go! Don't waste your valuable time with a real woman. I don't need you, Optimus Shute, and you've been too blind to see which side your bread was buttered.' Now that he was being dismissed, Optimus felt a pang of remorse and impending loss. When she was stormy like this, Mrs Lackland was exciting, even desirable. Diana, moongoddess, hot on the heels of Actaeon.

'If you want me to accompany you next Sunday . . .'

'I'll know where to find you. Yes, Mr Shute, I'll know where to find you.'

The small triangular crossroads between the Trafalgar tavern and the church was already crowded when the Coyte family party approached it. Farmer Coyte, straddling an unkempt Dartmoor pony, led the way, followed by his son Ronald, perched high on his restive hack. Next came his mother on foot, unsmiling and pensive, as though totting up the time they were wasting by taking this unjustified holiday. Grace brought up the rear, keeping a discreet ten paces behind her employer, in part because it was her duty to do so, in part because it suited her to keep her distance from the Coytes. Her lips formed a wry smile when she looked at Ronald's old hunting-pink jacket that she had taken in for him. It still floated round his bony adolescent frame. But she had formed a sneaking liking for Ronald, the least obnoxious of the Coytes; he was so different from his skinflint parents. Given half a chance, he would soon squander his inheritance. He was a bit of a dreamer and she could pardon him his awkward pride and vaingloriousness.

156

All Harberscombe was either at the meet already or fast approaching. The Trafalgar was doing famous business, full of chatter and smoke and so packed that its customers spilled out into the roadway. Grace saw Uncle Bill Terry, tankard in hand under the low doorway, talking to Jan King who was facing away from her. The yeoman farmers were mostly mounted, sitting on big-boned hunters and hacks. They were at home on horseback, but looked ill at ease in their clean breeches and hacking-jackets. Farmer Wroth and his wife were comfortably seated in a shiny black trap, on the edge of the gathering. Farm labourers, dairymaids, hedgers, rabbit-catchers, the blacksmith, the carpenter, the wheelwright, all were there, jostling the blue-clad fishermen and ribbing them gently for not being out at sea on such a good day for lobstering.

'They'm comin'!' shouted a slip of a boy, pointing up the lane. Heads turned quickly and a momentary hush fell. In the silence, the distant yelping of dogs became audible. Almost at once, talk started up again, more excitedly than before.

It was a few minutes before the first of the hounds appeared in the lane, followed closely by his fellows. On their heels rode the Master, seated easily on his roan. He was flanked by his two whippers-in and followed by a bunch of gentry. Harry Baskerville ignored the latter. Although he was a commoner, his established position as Master allowed him to assume an air of unbrooked authority.

The horses and dogs milled around in the centre of the crowd while the landlord came out of the Trafalgar with a stirrup-cup. The gentry exchanged occasional comments in nasal voices, but remained aloof from the people around them. But when Ronald Coyte's horse shied abruptly, cannoning into a grey hunter on which a smart young woman was sitting sidesaddle, and making her spill her drink, she spoke to him severely.

'Damn fool!' she snapped, brushing the wine off her habit with a white-gloved hand. 'Can't you control your mount, you young blockhead? If you can't do better than that you ought not to be permitted to ride to hounds. What's your name anyway?' Ronald Coyte was silent, tongue-tied with embarrassment. The woman turned in her saddle and spoke to a man behind her. 'Who is it, Charles? Fellow ought to be horse-whipped for his dumb insolence.'

'Name's Ronald, ma'am, Ronald Coyte, miller's son from Langstone.'

'Why can't he say so? I want him punished. I think he did it deliberately.' The knuckles of her ungloved right hand showed white where she gripped her antler-handled quirt.

'Don't go on so, Nancy,' murmured the rider beside her. 'Can't you see the boy's overawed? He didn't mean it, he's new to hunting, that horse of his isn't used to crowds, it'd be a handful for anyone to hold in. But I wish his father had invested the money in rent instead of in horseflesh.' He too swung round in the saddle to address the man behind them. 'Remind me to look up old man Coyte next week, he shan't get away with non-payment for ever.'

'Fine brother you are!' grumbled the woman, not caring who heard. 'Why don't you stand up for your sister, Frederick Genteel?'

'Hush, Nancy. You know how to stand up for yourself well enough, I fancy.' The woman shrugged her shoulders angrily and turned to Grace Pensilva who was standing close behind her.

'Here, gel, take this glass and find me another.' Grace showed no sign of having heard her. 'What, is everybody deaf round here or something?' the woman spat out. 'Here, take this and step lively.' As she spoke, she made a menacing gesture with her quirt.

'I'm not your servant,' said Grace quietly, 'ask the landlord, he'll send a serving maid.'

'Why, you cheeky hussy!' The woman raised her arm as if to strike her.

'Forget it, Nancy, we've no time for more drinking, the morning's half gone already.' Frederick Genteel had reached across and was holding her elbow in an iron grip, anxious to hide his recognition of Grace.

'Let me go!' she hissed. 'Let me go! People are watching us.'

Nancy Genteel's pale cheeks showed patches of red brighter than the touches of rouge she had put there. For the moment, he ignored her.

'Shall we move off, Mr Baskerville? I think we're all ready and waiting. Which way are you thinking of taking us?'

'Hackworthy Barton,' said the Master. 'There's been more'n one fox sighted in the woods there.' He looked down at his hounds, set his silver horn to his lips and blew as he dug his heels into his horse's belly and trotted off. The hounds were all around him, the whippers-in urging them on up the steep slope behind the church. Frederick Genteel dropped his sister's arm suddenly and slapped her horse across the rump, sending it jogging after them. She tossed her glass into the hedge as she went and gripped her reins tightly. Behind her, the rest of the riders fell in, followed by the waggons and traps and the walking followers.

'Might as well ride as walk, Grace,' said Farmer Wroth as he came up with her. 'Jump up along of us. There'll be great sport today, I knows it, in my bones I knows it.' As she climbed into the trap behind him he murmured, 'And my congratulations for standin' up to Miss Nancy like that. There bain't many 'ere as would've dared it.'

'Aye, but our Grace 'ave found a friend at court,' said Mrs Wroth primly. 'Did you see 'ow Squire did look at 'er? You've made a good touch there, my lover.'

'I don't think so and I don't want to,' said Grace, 'and I'll get down if you don't drop the subject.'

'Don't take on so, Grace,' said Farmer Wroth, 'Eileen were only teasin'. Come on now, let's see a smile on your face, 'tis an 'oliday. And you can tell me what life be like with the Coytes, and 'ow much you enjoys it at Langstone Mill.' Grace laughed at that; she liked Eric Wroth for his sardonic sense of humour.

Behind them in the tavern doorway, Jan King drained the last of his tankard. Already the place was almost deserted and the huntsman's horn was growing fainter.

'Come on, Uncle Bill, we'll never catch up with 'em.'

'No, boy, you go on and enjoy it. I 'aven't the wind for that

159

sport, not no longer. I'll stay and keep the landlord company, I'll be 'ere when you do come back later. If you do catch a fox I'll buy an ale for 'ee.'

Jan King hesitated. They were alone now. Farmer Wroth's trap, with Grace Pensilva sitting in the back of it, was vanishing from sight round the corner at the top of the road. Jan put down his tankard and set off running.

Half a mile ahead, the hounds had caught their first scent. Two couple of them had pushed their way under a five-bar gate on the long straight lane that led to Hackworthy Barton and were snuffling among the young turnips. Harry Baskerville was sure they were on a false scent, they were too indecisive.

'Come back, Tearaway,' he called, 'come back, Destiny, come back, Trouncer, come back, 'Armony!' But Harmony would not listen, she had just caught the scent again and was off down the slope with the others giving tongue close behind her. Soon, all the pack were through the gate and in full cry down the valley towards the scrubland and woods at the bottom.

'We must make the best of a bad job,' said the Master to the whippers-in. 'You two go down and see if you can draw that covert. It'll be hard work, it's overgrown in that waste ground just like a jungle, but push right through if you can. I'll ride on round with the rest of the hunt through the Barton and be there to meet you. That way we'll be fresh when Reynard puts in an appearance.'

'Good thinking,' said Frederick Genteel, who had come up with him. 'Any fool can ride helter-skelter after a pack, but it takes a man with brains to catch foxes hereabouts.'

The Master's face creased into a repressed smile as he trotted off. It was a pleasure to know that someone else appreciated that the South Hams wasn't your Quorn or Pytchley country. Up there, there was next to nothing to hold back the huntsman, just a hedge or a ditch or two that a horse could jump over. Down here, it was all banks, ten-foot-high earthen banks, topped off as often as not with a hedge of hazel and blackthorn. There wasn't a horse born that could jump 'em;

the only way was to use the gateways, and only a huntsman with years of experience knew where those gateways lay. The Harberscome Hunt ranged over country that was easier to get in to than get out of. Harry Baskerville was the man who knew how. He cantered ahead cheerfully, followed by farmers and gentry.

Farmer Wroth reined in the trap beside the gate where the hounds had vanished. 'Us'll 'ave as good a view 'ere as any. Us can't go down in the coombe in this outfit. If us stays 'ere, us'll see some sport and then mebbe us can follow when us sees the line they're takin'.'

Soon, a knot of other people was grouped in the gateway. Some stood on top of the hedge, others pushed into the field. Because of the lie of the land, they had a grandstand view of the way the hunt was progressing, or rather was not progressing.

'They'm proper bogged down in that old platt,' exclaimed Farmer Wroth, standing up in the trap which wobbled dangerously. 'Charlie and George be losin' the pack in all they brimbles an' stuff. Can't think why 'Arry ever let 'em go there.'

Several bystanders nodded knowingly. They could hear the hounds' muffled yelping and occasional shouts from the whippers-in as they crashed through the undergrowth. But they were hidden in the dense woodland, the only visible sign of their presence was the cloud of rooks they had sent protesting upwards.

'Pity us bain't bird 'untin',' muttered one wiseacre. 'Master Baskerville 'ave found they aplenty. 'Ee do seem to 'ave lost 'is touch where voxes be concerned.'

'Don't be too sure o' that,' exclaimed Farmer Wroth. 'Look where 'ee be to! 'Arry 'ave took the 'unt round through 'Ackworthy Barton; they be 'eadin' for t'other side of cover.'

As he spoke, the first horseman rode clear of the cluster of farm buildings at the head of the coombe and rode swiftly along a level track that crossed the grassfields to a point above the patch of woodland. They galloped from one gate to the next, Master and gentry in the van, crowded by Ronald Coyte whose hack was of better mettle than might have been expected, and a troop of bouncing farmers. At their rear came a pack of village lads, running strongly on foot. Each time the riders pulled up to open a gate, the runners closed with them, but by the time the Master reined in above the covert, the hunt formed a long straggling line all the way back to Hackworthy Brown.

Suddenly the crowd burst out laughing. A tall gangling figure, all in black, seated on such a scrawny diminutive pony that his feet seemed to be brushing the grass on either side of him, emerged from the Barton and came flying across the hillside as though shot from a cannon, overtaking all and sundry.

"Ee be a proper flyer, that Vicar,' commented the same wiseacre, 'makin' up for lost time, 'ee be. 'Ee do keep 'is feet on the ground to save 'is 'oss the work of transportin' 'im.'

"Tis you what'll be transported, if 'ee gets to 'ear what you'm sayin' about un,' said Mrs Coyte primly. "Aven't you got no respect for religion? I bain't Church of England meself, but I gives respect where respect is due.'

All this time, the unfortunate Vicar was attempting to rein in his runaway steed. It was clear that horsemanship was not among his accomplishments and it was a gateway jammed with mounted farmers that provided the obstacle that finally brought the pony to a halt.

Now it was the Master who was claiming the watchers' attention. He had come to a halt at the top of a small field immediately above the covert and was summoning the hounds with strong blasts of his horn. From the diminished noise they were producing it appeared that they were making their way, slowly but surely towards him. When some of the riders came up with him and pressed on towards the wood, the Master called them back peremptorily.

'If there be a fox in there and 'ee do break cover, us'll 'ave a good run for our money. 'Twill be proper sport, won't it, Grace? There bain't nothin' like a good 'unt for amusement,' said Farm Wroth.

'Do you suppose the fox thinks so?' asked Grace innocently.

'Old Reynard be a wild thing, runnin' do come natural to un,' grunted Farmer Wroth. ''Tis all like that in nature, kill or be killed, animals don't give no quarter.' Grace was tempted to say more, but held her tongue. She wanted to say that men weren't animals, not necessarily, and that a pack of hounds, a troop of mounted men, and a whole village on foot did not add up to the kind of odds the fox would find in nature. But she knew her neighbours, they were not evil folk, they did not hate foxes, they even had a sneaking admiration for their wildness and independence, and if they chose this way to kill them, it was more ritual than revenge, a throwback to ancient days when hunting had been a necessity and their quarry a hedge against hunger.

Among the runners on the far hillside, Grace had descried a familiar figure: Jan King was steadily overtaking the others. He ran purposefully with a long loping stride that carried him economically over the ground. Jan was a hunter, probably unbothered by the moral problems involved in the process. And, as in nature, Jan King the hunter could, at the same time, be Jan King the hunted. There was no law to state that hunting should stop short of the summit of the animal kingdom. Was she not herself a hunter, bent on destruction, however justifiable her motive? Grace bit her lip momentarily, but Farmer Wroth, who saw her do it, thought it was out of impatience to see the fox appear.

And the fox did come. An old dog fox came sidling quietly up out of the woods into the field at the head of which Master Baskerville sat waiting. The fox came a full fifty yards up the slope, casually, unhurriedly, as though unperturbed by the barking of the dogs behind him.

'Oolaloolaloo!' shouted Farmer Wroth, jumping from one foot to another, waving his hat over his head, and making the trap rock in his excitement. 'Can't you see un, 'Arry? 'Ee be there, right in front of 'ee.' No matter that the words could never carry the half-mile that separated him from the Master.

Harry Baskerville had not moved. He still sat his horse, with one warning, restraining arm held out behind him to keep the other huntsmen from advancing. At this stage the fox might do one of three things: it might run back into the wood and go to earth or slink past the hounds that were pursuing it, it might decide to make off diagonally, round the top of the wood and then down to the stream that followed the valley to the sea at Haccombe Cove, or it might come on uphill towards him. If it went back into the wood, chances were that it would get away, unless the village lads decided to dig it out of its den. There would be precious little sport in that for the huntsmen. If it ran for the stream and the hunt followed it, they would soon be bogged down in the marshland and baulked by the heavy growth of blackthorn and elder. Not only that, the hounds might lose its scent in the water. But if the fox came sufficiently far uphill for its way back to be cut off by the emerging pack, it would be forced into a run across country, open country apart from the banks, with no covert to hide in until it reached the cliffs around the Barrow. This was the way which would offer the riders good sport. He held his breath and waited.

Grace Pensilva also held her breath, though for a different reason. She was willing the fox to turn back, turn away, go anywhere but upwards towards the huntsmen. The old fox had stopped, he was standing with one forepaw raised and head cocked slightly upward, at the edge of a patch of kale that filled the top left-hand corner of the field. It was as though he had heard a movement inside it, or perhaps he had been distracted by Farmer Wroth's yelling. He swung his head slowly from side to side as if undecided whether to continue. In the gateway at the head of the field Harry Baskerville sat motionless as a statue.

'Go on! Go on!' Farmer Wroth whispered loudly, 'Go on, Reynard, let's see 'ow an old fox can run.'

Grace's heart was in her mouth. Why couldn't the fox make up his mind? Why hadn't he noticed the Master in the gateway? Was he blind or something? Turn back, turn back, she tried to send her unspoken thought to him. But still he wavered.

It was the noise of the Vicar's pony blundering into the bunch behind the gate that finally attracted the fox's attention.

164

He turned his face deliberately towards the place where Harry Baskerville sat and for a moment seemed to stare him out. Then, unhurriedly, he turned tail and began to lope back towards the covert.

'God damn the bloody imbecile who did that,' exclaimed the Master, looking over his shoulder for the newcomer who had scared off the fox. 'Whoever he is, he's a disgrace.' His eyes sought out Ronald Coyte, but to his astonishment the young rider was sitting his horse quietly, with no sign of recent movement.

''Tweren't me,' protested Ronald.

'Whoever it was, the blockhead, he's made us lose our fox,' grumbled Baskerville, unappeased. 'He'll have me to answer to afterwards, I'll know who it was, sooner or later.' He looked back down the hill to where the fox had been, fully expecting him to have disappeared into the covert. Instead, the animal had stopped again, facing downhill; something held it spell-bound. The Master craned his neck to stare in the same direction. Someone was trying to break through the hedge in the bottom corner. A moment later a bedraggled figure emerged, leaping out from the top of the bank, a lithe young man in a seaman's jersey. He ran swiftly along the edge of the wood, cutting off the fox's line of retreat. Even then, the fox was swift enough to have out-distanced him and reached the stream-bed, but he hesitated.

'Well done, Jan King,' exlcaimed the Master, 'you deserve to follow the hounds on horseback, unlike one or two I have to put up with.'

From her vantage point on the other side of the valley, Grace had seen the fox turn back downhill and had felt a surge of relief. Had her prayer got through to him? Her disappointment when he stopped again was all the keener. She could not understand his vacillation; the bottom of the field, screened by the elms at the top of the wood, was hidden from her. She wanted to scream to the fox, tell him to move, put as much distance as possible between himself and the cold-hearted riders. Time was running out: the yelping in the wood was getting louder.

Jan King and the fox stood facing each other across twenty yards of open meadow. There was a sweet smell in the air from the wild flowers in the wood. Seen from so close, the fox looked a poor thing to have mobilized such an expedition against him: he was woefully thin and the hair on his brush was greying. He seemed not to be looking at Jan but past him into the obscurity of the tree-trunks. Almost immediately, Jan discovered the reason: first Tearaway, then Harmony, then Destiny, then Trouncer broke through the screen of hazel, on a broad front, baulking the fox. Harmony let out a long howl and the others joined in and yelped in unison: Jan King saw the saliva dripping from their open jaws.

'That were a fine peal,' said Farmer Wroth contentedly, ''ound've seen somethin'.' With lead in her heart, Grace watched the fox turn round yet again and slink into the kale patch. Once he had entered it, there was no sign of him, but he had to be there somewhere. She was not the only one to have seen him enter, Harry Baskerville was trotting down the field, calling the hounds forward with his horn while the huntsmen followed him.

When the hounds ran into the kale she could see it waving, like the ripples made by fish in shallow water, as the hounds quartered it. The fox had to be in there somewhere, but they were taking their time finding him. 'Where be your nose, Destiny?' called Farmer Wroth. ''Tis time you found un.'

More and more hounds ran up from the wood and plunged into the kale. Behind them walked a man; she did not recognize him at first, only an attitude he struck when he stood still told her it was Jan King. So he had been the cause of the fox's turnabout.

'Gone away!' screeched Farmer Wroth. 'Gone away! Can't nobody see un?'

He was pointing with quivering whip at the place where the fox had slunk from the kale and crossed two yards of open ground that separated it from the overgrown bank where, once more, it vanished. Grace too had seen the small movement and now she saw the first of the pack reach the spot, sniff the air and plunge into the undergrowth in pursuit of it. Again their yelping rose in intensity. Several of the huntsmen galloped to the spot and milled about aimlessly.

'Sit down, Eileen, sit down, Grace,' ordered Farmer Wroth. 'If we'm quick, us'll catch up with 'em before they gets movin'. Old Reynard 'ave took off for Cliff, there'll be a fine chase to see behind the Barrow.' He cracked his whip beside his pony's ear and they were off, bowling along down the lane to Hackworthy Barton.

Meanwhile, the Master had touched his spurs into the roan's flanks and was trotting swiftly back through the gate, forging his way between the hesitant riders. In his head he had already calculated the best course to take, bearing in mind the fox's probable destination. There was no straightforward way to follow him: the system of banks, oddly-placed gates and short stretches of lane formed a labyrinth which had grown over the centuries until it was incorporated into Hackworthy Barton. The shortest distance between two points was never a straight line, and the obvious course led, as often as not, into a blind alley. Harry Baskerville ignored his hounds; they would track the fox without his prompting; he bore off to the right where a gate led to an overgrown lane. Frederick Genteel and his sister Nancy also turned swiftly to follow him, Jan King ploughed through the kale, which was nearly thigh-deep, and sprang into the bank through which most of the pack had already vanished.

As Nancy Genteel rode out of the gateway and dug her heels into her hunter, it shied abruptly, baulked by the parson on his ridiculous pony. She reined in sharply to control her mount but it reared unexpectedly. Sitting side-saddle as she was she had only her balance to maintain her. At the last moment she made a grab for the horse's mane, but her gloved hand slipped and a jerk unseated her. She fell ingloriously sideways and backwards while her scared horse made off across the field. To have fallen was bad enough, but to have kept one foot caught in a twisted stirrup was worse and might possibly be fatal. Her hunter's hooves were pounding into the turf beside her as it careered off wildly. If it reached a gateway it would dash her brains out against a gatepost.

167

Frederick, who was slightly ahead, had not observed the incident. The other riders sat bewildered and inactive. Only Ronald Coyte reacted swiftly: he galloped after the runaway horse, in an attempt to restrain it. Encouraged by some sharp whacks from his quirt, Ronald's wayward stallion took off like the wind, racing after Nancy Genteel's thoroughbred. But it had crossed half the field already before he got close to it. He dug in his spurs, though his horse hardly needed the encouragement, overhauling the runaway steadily, from withers to shoulder. Ronald had guided Lightning to the opposite side from that on which Nancy Genteel was being dragged and bumped along mercilessly. Now, as he closed with the hunter, he reached out and made a grab for the flying reins. His first attempt was unsuccessful. Out of the corner of his eye he saw the gate approaching.

By now, Frederick Genteel had noticed his sister's plight. The shouting and commotion had made him turn round. He too spurred after her, but he knew that his own help would come too late. Her only chance lay in the hands of Ronald Coyte, the awkward young farmer.

Ronald Coyte had managed to snatch a rein, but the frightened horse was not responding to it. And the gateway was terribly close, the gate had been left open by the riders as they rode over from the Barton. There was no room for two horses and a sliding woman to pass through the narrow entrance. In an instant Ronald knew he must rein in himself and let the others chance it.

Instead, he stood up in the stirrups and flung himself forward and outward, clasping his arms around the hunter's small head, and twisting violently, putting all his weight into the movement. If he pulled hard enough, the horse would be unbalanced. During a painfully long moment he was aware of the stumbling animal's flailing hooves, their iron shoes that might kill the fallen woman instantly or maim her for life more likely.

The hunter yawed towards Ronald and half fell on top of him. He scrambled clear as best as he could, astonished that he had no bones broken. On the far side, Nancy Genteel's inert body lay across her hunter's twitching hocks. Her brother was reining in and sprang down to kneel beside her.

'Nancy, Nancy, are you all right? Can you hear me?' he asked urgently. After a moment her eyes opened and she quivered a little. Then she sat up, pushing Frederick aside, and disengaged her foot from the stirrup. She climbed to her feet stiffly, straightened her muddied clothes and began tugging at the hunter's reins, trying to make it get up. Her other hand still gripped her quirt, her face was pinched and determined. She ignored her brother, she ignored her rescuer, she ignored everyone. Once her hunter was on its feet she rubbed its nostrils and petted it until it ceased snorting and wheezing.

'Help me mount,' she instructed Frederick.

'Are you sure you want to? That horse of yours is still terribly nervous.'

'Do I have to ask a stranger to help me?' It was clear that Nancy would not be thwarted. With a resigned sigh, he gave her a shove upward and deposited her unceremoniously into her saddle., She steadied herself and adjusted the reins, making ready to set off after the hunt.

'Aren't you going to thank your rescuer?'

'Rescuer?' There was no recognition in her voice, she had not bothered to glance at her recent benefactor.

'If this young lad hadn't stopped Hector, you wouldn't be sitting up there now, without a scratch. Don't you think you owe him a word of thanks?'

'I suppose so.' For the first time, Nancy Genteel swung her glance round to the youth who was preparing to mount his own horse which Charles Barker had just brought back to him. When she recognized the same person who had annoyed her outside the Trafalgar tavern, her eyes darkened momentarily, but her glance lingered into a stare that took him in from top to toe, reappraising his gawky but muscular appearance, the down on his upper lip, his apprehensive yet occasionally bold expression. Still, she did not address him directly. 'Have him come over to Leet, Mr Steward,' she instructed Charles Barker. 'I want to take another look at him in a day or so. If it turns out he's good with horses, if he knows

169

how to master wild horseflesh, we'll find a place for him in the stables. But I'll talk to him first, I want to know if he's got a tongue in his head as well as a feel for the saddle. Now let's get moving. The Master will kill the fox without us if we sit here jawing.' With a slap of her quirt she was off, as stiff and wilful as ever.

'Tough as old boots,' muttered Charles Barker to young Ronald. 'God knows whether you ought to be glad or sorry she's taken an interest in you. Come on now, we'll talk later.'

The group which had lingered round Nancy Genteel now had to contend with the foot followers, the waggons loaded with labourers, the traps and dog-carts. They cursed as they squeezed past in the overgrown lane and whipped their horses into a gallop as soon as they emerged into open grassland.

''Tis an 'andsome sight,' said Farmer Wroth when they thundered past him. 'I 'aven't never seed nothin' to match it, there bain't nothin' like it to stir up the blood, not in 'Arberscombe.'

Far ahead, where the rounded head of the Barrow rose above the plateau which extended inshore of it, the Master, his whippers-in and a small knot of horsemen were hot on the heels of the pack whose barking was still faintly audible, punctuated by blasts on the huntsman's horn. Well out in front, seemingly unhurried, the fox, reduced to a speck at that distance, was trotting up the slope.

'Tally ho! Tally ho!' yelped Farmer Wroth. 'Keep goin' that way, Maister Vox and us'll 'ave 'ee.'

Frederick Genteel, riding his hunter at a smooth gallop, led the second bunch of riders past the foremost of the foot followers. Their leader, loping steadily with no sign of fatigue, was Jan King. 'Well done, young feller,' called the Squire encouragingly, 'you deserve to have a horse to carry you.'

'Don't need un,' shouted Jan, 'I'm well enough as I am.'

From where Grace sat on the bouncing trap, it seemed impossible that the slow-moving pack and the erratic horsemen could ever come up with the light-footed fox. But she was mistaken. Whether because he was getting tired, whether from age, whether from indecision, he stopped again and turned to look at his pursuers. Perhaps he sensed that by running out to the end of the Barrow, he was letting himself into a trap.

'If 'ee do take off for 'Accombe Cove, us'll lose un for certain,' exclaimed Farmer Wroth, sensing the fox's probable intention. He could see that if the fox doubled back, taking advantage of a dip in the land along the cliff, he would pick up such speed he could easily outflank the pack and the leading huntsmen. Harry Baskerville seemed to have formed the same opinion, he had reined in and was trying to call the pack to heel.

The fox did not wait to allow him to complete the manoeuvre, he streaked off down the slope and it seemed that nothing and no one could stop him reaching the rise on the far side of the dip and scurrying down to the marshes at Haccombe.

But there was a runner who had foreseen this gambit: Jan King had broken away from the others and was striding obliquely down into the dip, converging with the fox's line of escape. He ran faster than ever before, he ran with his arms held high and his feet barely kissing the ground, he ran so fast and so lightly he felt like a seagull gliding, he ran effortlessly, he ran like a wild creature. And the wild fox saw him coming and deviated from his route. To his right a narrow fringe of gorse and brambles separated the grassland from the cliff edge. Although he could not see it, Jan knew what was beyond that lip: a steep, tussocky no man's land for fifty yards or so and then sheets of smooth brittle shale falling almost sheer to the sea hundreds of feet beneath. The fox too knew this ground, it was wild country, riddled with dens and earths.

Runner and quarry came within yards of each other before the latter doubled back yet again and wormed its way into the bushes. Behind him, all across the hillside, the hunt in full cry converged on him. Harry Baskerville was the first to arrive and reined in when his horse came to the cliff edge. Over his shoulder he saw his baying pack arriving at full pelt. Destiny was foremost as usual, followed by Tearaway and Harmony. The Master took in the situation at a glance: there was no sign of the fox, it had slipped down over the short bank of red eroded earth and was crouching under the grassy lip that overhung it. He could not see it, but his sixth sense told him that it was there. What he could see was that, if the heavy hounds did not slow before they dived into the bracken, their momentum would carry them out over the lip and into emptiness beyond it. He shouted, he waved, he blew his horn at them. They paid no heed, their blood was up, the lust to kill devoured them.

The Master watched in horrified fascination as the leading hounds breasted the bracken. First Destiny broke through it and sailed into space with an eerie yelp like tearing silk that might have been a warning to check his followers. But if they heard it, Tearaway and Harmony were so close they could not obey it. They too flew off the edge and were carried a good twenty yards down the sloping bank before they touched ground. Their claws scrabbled at the sea-grass, they bit at the bracken stems as they flashed past, they howled a last lingering howl as they dropped downward over the glistening shale and were instantly flattened and silenced on the huge, sea-washed boulders beneath.

'God damn!' Harry Baskerville swore, not at the fox but at himself for having led the hounds into danger. The remainder of his pack, less impetuous, had slithered to a stop and were lining the cliff edge and baying at the fox who was still out of sight beneath them. What caught the Master's attention now was a small patch of bracken about thirty feet below them. He could see that what had allowed the bracken to take root on the grassy slope was the loose earth from an old excavation. At some time a fox or a badger had lived there. Old Reynard probably knew this, that was why he had chosen this place to slip over the cliff. If he reached the earth, he would be safe there.

Jan King had come to the same conclusion. From where he stood on a slight point that projected from the cliff, he could look back and see the fox, flattened like a wet rag against the earthen bank, red on red, you had to know he was there to see him. The baying dogs were only a couple of feet above him and, in a minute or less, one of them was sure to drop down and send the fox leaping for that ultimate shelter. Jan King had climbed these cliffs before, he knew them well, he knew the places it was possible to go, and he knew their treacherousness. He hesitated. A drop of moisture had touched his forehead. He looked up. It was rain, rain from a cloud sweeping in from the sea. It told him something: if he moved fast over the dry grass he could reach the earth reasonably safely. If he waited, the grass would be soaked, slippery as a skate's back and it would be suicide to try and cross it. He poised himself, dropped over the lip and took the few diagonal strides that carried him to the earth. Even then he almost lost his footing and dropped away, but the mound of soil in front of the earth was there to save him; looking down he saw that it was an old earth, the mud was packed smooth and weathered, a blade of fresh grass was poking through it. But the hole was still there, too big for a rabbit, too small for a badger. He balanced on the mound precariously, aware of the soughing sea behind and far below his feet. If he looked back, he would feel dizzy and be drawn downwards.

Above him, men, women and hounds lined the earthern bank. The riders had dismounted and come forward to the very lip. He studied their faces: they were mostly flushed with exertion or anger. Even the children had a sharp, predatory look. Nancy Genteel slapped her boot with her quirt.

'Go get 'im, Trouncer!' she ordered the old hound that stood slavering on the quavering lip. When he failed to jump she pushed him with her foot.

'That's my hound you're pushing, Miss Genteel,' cried Harry Baskerville, beside himself with sudden fury.'Don't you know I've lost two good dogs and a bitch already?' Nancy Genteel made no more answer than to give the heavy dog a final shove that toppled him over. His clawed feet slid over the grass a moment before they found purchase, but he obtained a grip on the narrow ledge. His nose wrinkled abruptly and his thick lips peeled back, revealing his fangs, set in a long snarl. It was clear that he had seen the fox.

The fox did not wait for the hound to seize him, he darted

down the slope towards the bracken patch, moving lightly and surely on his tiny feet. Perhaps he had failed to understand the meaning of Jan King's dash, perhaps the man had been hidden from him by the fronds of bracken, perhaps the hunter's absolute stillness deceived him. Now a mere six feet from safety, he found himself confronted with his old enemy, the foe he had managed to avoid, cheat and mystify down the years until his coat grew grey. The man was standing waiting, with his feet planted right in the mouth of the den. There was absolutely no hope of springing past him. The fox flattened himself on the grass and cast anxious eyes to either side. Behind him the pack was baying more fiercely than ever before and a crescendo of whoops came from his human pursuers. They were spread in a broad arc along the cliff top; even if he broke for one side or another, they would have him. A flurry of rain came sizzling into the grass beside him. If he had had a clear run across country the rain would have saved him, it would have washed out his scent.

Emboldened by Trouncer's success, three other hounds thudded over the parapet; it was only a matter of moments before one or another of them would spring, regardless of the consequences to itself, and land on the fox's back. The latter cast a glance over its shoulder and crept a few feet closer to where Jan King was standing. Looking down at it, he sensed its desperation. When the hounds pounced, he sensed it would run headlong over the cliff.

'Hoy, hoy, hoy!' lilted Nancy Genteel, in a high-pitched voice, an ancient, wordless, hunter's cry. 'Hoy, hoy, hoy! Kill 'im, Trouncer, kill 'im!'

As Trouncer began his dash and the fox twitched, looking back and tensing his muscles to dash away from him, Jan King reached down swiftly and coolly, snatching it up by the scruff of the neck. He held it at arm's length, scratching and yapping, full of blind fury. The fox squirmed so violently Jan feared he would drop it. He had to hold it high because the hounds were now in the bracken around him, snapping at the fox's brush.

'Give the hounds their due!' ordered Nancy Genteel. Jan

hesitated, he was not used to taking orders, and the fox was his, hadn't he just caught it? 'Drop the bastard! Give the hounds their due!' repeated the Squire's sister sharply.

'Jan King!' came another woman's voice from the crowd. 'Jan King, you'll do no such thing.' It was a quiet voice, but firm, and all heads turned to see who was the owner of it. She stood erect and unyielding, arms by her sides, fists tightly clenched. Jan King transferred his glance to her and they stared each other out.

'Mr Shute! Mr Shute!' There was someone at the door, someone calling him. It sounded like Mrs Kemp. Reluctantly, he put down his pen and made his way towards the kitchen which opened on to the road. Damn the woman, he was just at a critical point. There was the fox: he had become so engrosed in his own account of the hunt that its fate was a matter of concern to him. What would Jan King do? What would he have done was the real question. And what would happen to Jan King himself, poised there on that unstable perch, with the hounds jostling him and the rain beginning to fall more heavily? Optimus knew the spot, knew it exactly; he had scrambled down there one afternoon when walking over the Barrow. Even then, on a dry day, he had found the grass treacherous and slippery. For a moment panic had seized him, alone there with only a few gulls sailing over the blue void for company, and he had stood petrified, afraid of making the slightest movement.

When he opened the door, it was not Mrs Kemp as he had expected, but a woman in a blue poke-bonnet that he did not immediately recognize. When she spoke, however, he was able to place her.

'I just 'ad to come and see 'ee. There was things I wanted to say, but couldn't, not with 'er listenin'. Can I come in? I don't like to stand 'ere in the road, that Dr Cornish 'ave got terrible good 'earin' for 'is age, I don't want to share my thoughts with all and sundry.'

When Mrs Treebie was comfortably seated in the one ladderback armchair that graced his kitchen, Optimus stirred up

175

the fire to make tea. He had got over his initial annoyance at being disturbed and was full of curiosity to know what she would tell him.

'Jan King were my cousin,' Mrs Treebie began. 'Course 'ee were older than I and us weren't close, but I knows a thing or two, that be only natural. Now I d'know as 'ow you be terrible interested in that Grace Pensilva. Well, fair 'nuff, but I can't allow 'ee to get it all one-sided. Jan King wouldn't 'ave gone back to smugglin' if that Grace 'adn't talked 'im into it. She did worm 'er way into 'is confidence like: made un feel 'ee could trust 'er. She were like a cuckoo in 'is nest, she did move in and take all 'is substance. She were like the ivy round a great tree, she did stifle un.'

'Can you remember what happened on the day of the hunt; how did it end exactly?' Optimus prompted her, trying to get down to brass tacks.

'I were no more than a li'l maid then, weren't I? 'T'was all new and strange, but lookin' back on it now I understands it better. When Jan were in danger of 'is life, she did 'elp un, not for the reason 'ee thought, not because she cared a fig for un, she 'ad 'er own reason an' didn't say it. Played cat and mouse with Jan, she did, just like with that Scully from the Revenue, just like she tried to with Squire Genteel, though in that case 'ee weren't so easy and she got 'er comeuppance, leastways that be what Janet Coyte told me 'fore she went away, and I 'opes so, for Jan's sake, I 'opes she did meet with God's justice. 'Eart-'ole an' fancy-free she were, till she took up with Frederick Genteel an' she thought to lead un the same merry dance as the others, but us bain't made o' stone, not even the Grace Pensilvas of this world. Followed un to Malta, she did, when 'ee left Leet all of a sudden. Course, she were gone from 'Arberscombe even earlier, couldn't never come back, not with the questions 'bout Jan King we 'ad ready to ask 'er. I often wonders 'ow much she knowed 'bout the Squire before she left, 'tis sure she were sweet on un. I see'd 'er meself walkin' 'cross Leet park with un one night when by rights she were keepin' 'house wi' Jan King. You ask Charles Barker, 'ee'll bear me out, she were a double-dealer.'

176

'But what about the reason she might've had in the first place, what about Frank Pensilva?'

'Oh, Frank, Frank, Frank, that brother of 'ern, 'ee weren't no angel. If only she'd knowed, she didn' 'ave no reason to worship un, other maids in 'Arberscombe did know un better'n she did. No, they were like peas in a pod, took after each other, they did: two-faced. When that Grace did make out she' ad a soft 'eart for the old fox on the cliff, she were only play-actin', like with poor Jan, an' all too well she done it. Sent un to torment un better, she did. 'Ard as nails, she were.' Mrs Treebie picked up her bag and adjusted her bonnet; it was evident she was leaving. ''Twere Grace's fault that poor Jack Lugger did lie bleedin' 'is life out on that table opposite. Dr Cornish tell you that, did 'ee? No, I s'pose not, 'ee couldn't see that side of 'er, 'ee weren't alone in that, there were many a man what couldn't. Oh, there be a mint o' things I could tell 'ee 'bout Grace Pensilva, but I must be leavin' now. Parson Lackland will be waitin' for supper. That be what 'tis to be a servin' woman, never a life to call your own, but 'tis what God sends and us must bear it.' She paused with a foot on the threshold. 'Not a word of this to Mrs Lackland, mind. I don't want 'er sayin' I'm gossipin'. 'Twas to set the book to rights I comed 'ere. Not that I've nothin' 'gainst Mrs Lackland, she do pay me regular. But you d'know that already, I do believe you 'preciates 'er more'n 'er 'usband do. You should come round more often.'

With a broad wink, she left and Optimus was alone with the hissing tea-kettle that, until then, had sung forgotten. He lifted it off the hob and returned to his desk upstairs, but the thread of his story was gone; Mrs Treebie had broken it. Worse, she had opened up new avenues of inquiry, unsettling what certitudes he had. He had already licked his nib and dipped it in the ink, but now he put down his pen and stared at the sheet of paper. What he saw through it was Grace Pensilva; her grey eyes stared back at him as they had stared at Jan. Close beside her, with a small young face on a child's shoulders, yet recognizable, was the girl who had become Mrs Treebie. She was looking up at Grace with a frank, open stare that showed

177

something of her present resentment. All the other participants in the cliff top scene seemed frozen in their actions. Try as he might, Optimus could not will them into motion.

With a sigh he tidied the sheaf of papers on which he had just written. Tomorrow evening he would try again and, when that chapter of Grace's life had been consigned to paper, he would walk over to Leet House and see Charles Barker. Now that the evenings were longer, such a stroll was becoming possible, though he would have to come home in the dark. Tonight, as he sat thinking, the daylight was slipping away from him. He opened the flap of his desk and ranged his writings in the drawer. The gold locket glinted up at him. He took it out and carried it downstairs where he played with it in the firelight, seeming to feel it with the same slim fingers that had once accepted it. The side with her portrait in it fell open at once and he threw some twigs on the embers to make a flame the better to study it.

But then, as he turned it towards the light, he must have made some new move unwittingly, for the far side, which he had thought solid and unopenable, swung back with the faintest of clicks. Within it, another face, a man's face this time, stared out at him. And a wisp of hair, so small that he barely saw it in the flickering firelight, fell out on his knee. He picked it up carefully between finger and thumb. Though faded, it still had something of its original bright reddish brown, the same colour as the man in the portrait.

Optimus knew he was looking at the features of Frederick Genteel, he felt no need of corroboration. They were much as he imagined them: firm, direct, classical, no doubt the artist had used some licence here for that was the style of the period, but there was something amused and whimsical about the eyes that owed nothing to neo-Hellenism and all to Byronic romanticism. Optimus thought that here was a man he would have liked. Was it any wonder that Grace Pensilva had fallen for him? Fallen for him, was that the right phrase? There was so much that was doubtful, equivocal, in their relationship, and Optimus now realised that he was only just beginning to scratch the surface of it.

178

11

'You'll let him go,' Grace Pensilva continued levelly. 'Look at him. Hasn't he been ill-served enough? And hasn't he given you sport, a good run for your money? Give him a fair crack of the whip, he deserves it. You've run him to earth, now free him.'

Jan King still held the fox above the yapping dogs that jostled him. Why, he was asking himself, should he obey her? What had she done to make him beholden to her? Nothing. Not that he himself wanted to kill the fox. She was right, old Reynard had already given them a good run for their money. What was the sense in killing him? But Grace was asking him to deprive the whole hunt of their due. Would they ever forgive him?

Frederick Genteel, who found himself standing beside her, felt an involuntary surge of admiration for this girl. He had realized who she was from the outset. When his sister had threatened her with her quirt outside the Trafalgar tavern, he had known her immediately for the young woman who had stood at the graveside while he hid in the yew. Something deep in his bowels told him to fear her yet, at the same time, he was taken by her defiant spirit. Now she was challenging the whole of hunting convention. The fox had to die: everyone knew that. But she was oblivious of the resentment provoked by her action or, if she noticed it, she ignored it. She also ignored the abrupt beating of the heavy rain that began to stream down her set, unwavering face.

'Hold your tongue, gel!' snapped his sister, the Honourable Nancy, her knuckles white on her riding crop's antler handle. 'Give the hounds their due.'

Grace Pensilva did not respond. She appeared not even to hear the imperative, venomous voice. Her whole attention, her whole being, was concentrated into the locked stare she was exchanging with Jan King, willing him to do her bidding. The contest was going on too long; she feared that her initial power was slipping away from her, that Jan's own will was reviving to challenge her and comply with the general blood-lust of the hunt.

'Enough,' came a tired, drawly voice beside her, 'enough. The gel's right, we've had a good run for our money. Let him go, boy, there's no need to kill him.' Jan King's eyes flicked across to the speaker, Frederick Genteel, whose long rain-streaked visage had lost some of its usual bland condescension and showed earnest concern. Had the Squire's voice had a shade more authority in it, Jan King would have offered an involuntary resistance, the resistance of the freeborn, independent seaman, but there was something in Frederick Genteel that his father Hal King had known about which was now showing through. Despite, or perhaps partly because of the elevation of his station, the thousands of acres in his father Lord Mayberry's possession, the exaggerated respect with which he was surrounded, Frederick Genteel gave signs of an uncommon humanity and a shy sensitivity.

The fox wriggled fiercely in Jan's grasp and he was aware that the animal was attempting to take advantage of his inattention to break his grasp and escape. Yet, for all his defiance, the fox was merely a small, pathetic creature whose only sin was to be a poacher and whose peculiar quality was wildness; quite a few men in Harberscombe were not unlike him.

When he stepped back out of the mouth of the earth and dropped the fox into it, there was a groan of disapproval from the line of frustrated spectators, but they could do nothing. The fox had not paused to thank his benefactors, but had slipped unceremoniously into his burrow, leaving the hounds to snuffle round disconsolately. But Harry Baskerville was secretly pleased; he had lost three of his best hounds already and feared that the rain-wet grass would take a higher toll of them if they lingered. Setting his horn to his lips, he blew the recall and they turned their heads, beginning to lumber up the slope. It was none too soon: their clawed feet skidded frequently on the glistening mat of sea-grass.

Grace Pensilva faced the Honourable Frederick Genteel who was turning up the collar of his riding coat. 'Thank you,' she said in a voice not much above a whisper. The Squire nodded, a little curtly, then strode off towards his mount, starting a general movement away from the cliff top.

'Bleddy spoil-sport,' muttered Mrs Coyte, but not so loud that the Squire could hear her.

The hounds scrambled up the bank, aided by helping hands from Harry Baskerville and his whippers-in. Already the riders, hunched and bowing away from the rain and the rising wind, were beginning to trot away. The cliff edge was almost deserted; only Grace Pensilva remained in her place, as if entranced, with the gusts tugging at her skirt and the stinging drops streaming down her face and matting her hair. It was as if she were peering out into the squall in search of a phantom ship, the Frenchman perhaps, or was it her brother she sought?

There was no one left to observe her now, the whole hunt was hastening away up the hillside. The one man who might have seen and been intrigued by her expression, had other preoccupations. Jan King was on all fours, frantically trying to hoist himself up across the short stretch of slippery grass that separated him from safety. He had covered two thirds of the distance in one swift dash, but had lost his impetus and was sliding back, ineffectually attempting to find a grip with his stiffened fingers and the welts of his hobnailed boots.

When Grace came to herself and became aware of him, she did not know how long he had been engaged in the attempt. Her dreamy state might have lasted a few minutes or only a few seconds. She realized that, had he stayed where he was, at the mouth of the burrow, he would have retained a safe foothold, but he had been shivering in the cold rain that penetrated his threadbare jersey and there had been no sign that the squall would soon be over. He had been forced to leave the temporary security of that place and now there was nothing between him and a slide to destruction but the grassy slope and a few isolated stems of gorse and dead bracken.

She found herself regarding him with the same kind of dispassionate curiosity that a small child will feel for a spider trying to climb out of a bowl. She knew he would attain a certain level and then slide back. If there were an urge to reach down and aid the creature, there was an equal revulsion from touching it.

But Grace Pensilva was not watching an insect; she was watching a man. And not only was she watching a man, but a man whose life held a particular significance for her, a man whose fate was her special concern. Even so, she was not fully conscious of his real peril until he made a fresh dash for the top, coming within three feet of it, a mere arm's length from where the fox had sheltered, when an imprudent lunge lost him his grip and sent him in a long anguished slide down the slope to one side of the bracken patch, until it seemed that nothing could stop him.

A frail gorse stem checked him. He grasped it with one hurried hand and lay there, trembling uncontrollably, although the trembling of itself might break the stem and send him sliding the last few yards to the edge of the sheer cliff. Slowly, slowly, he raised his head and looked upwards in mute appeal, no daring to hope that someone might still be there or, if they were, that they would care to help him.

Grace's eyes showed him no special sympathy; she had shown more for the fox. She watched him for what seemed an interminable time without speaking, then turned away for a moment. What was she thinking? With grim, overwhelming clarity, he suddenly realized that the only person aware of his predicament was the one who thought she had reason to vow him an undying hate. What exquisite satisfaction it must be giving her to watch his futile efforts and his impotent quivering on the edge of annihilation. She would stay there immobile, with that strange look on her face, that might have been a secret smile, until the gorse gave way and he vanished into

182

oblivion. He opened his mouth to speak to her, to implore her assistance, but no word came forth. The gusts of wind snatched at him and, behind his back, far below among the rocks where the hounds had died, he heard the sob and weep of the sea.

Why didn't he speak? What was wrong with him? Was he lily-livered or something? Grace watched his lips working convulsively. The man was almost at the end of his tether. Was it still possible to save him? She glanced over her shoulder: the whole band of huntsmen was toiling up the flank of the Barrow towards Hackworthy Barton and the warmth of their homes in Harberscombe. With the wind buffeting their ears and the rain on their backs, they were not likely to pay much heed even if she did shout to them.

'Help!' The single word came to her through the mists of her conjecture. It was quiet and dry like an insect's creak and, like an insect's cry, it was insistent. It was the last word from a man on the verge of dying.

She turned and ran; she ran like a woman possessed, slithering on the wet ground, screaming till her voice grew hoarse, persisting till first one, then a cluster of heads looked round at her. Even then it was not over, she had to reach them, breathlessly to try and explain that they had to turn back, hurry, hurry, with a rope from a waggon, or form a human chain, risking their own lives to do so; bravely confronting their blank faces, faces of folk who found it hard to agree to help the man who had just brooked their disfavour.

And all the time she had the compelling vision of what she would find when she returned to the cliff top with the rescue party: an empty slope, a broken gorse stem, a tiny inert figure spreadeagled among the boulders.

'Come back, Mr Wroth,' she implored, 'come back, Ronald, come back and help Jan King, he's in terrible danger!'

By the time Optimus reached Slaughter Bridge over the River Arun, the evening was far spent and the shallow valley was suffused with that peculiar golden light that colours certain Devon sunsets. The small purling river ran over reddish stones towards a spinney on the left bank. The other side was a water meadow, trending gently uphill and dotted with handsome trees whose placing looked haphazard, but was really part of a scheme invented by a landscape gardener of the previous century, to the place where the ancient mansion showed itself a little at a time: here a tower, there a tall mullioned window, now a long battlemented roof. A winding drive led from the gatehouse on the far side of the bridge across this park and up to a monumental terrace on which the ancient pile now stood. Apart from some grazing sheep, the meadow seemed deserted and the great house was closed and lifeless, grey windows in grey walls, buttressed with black shadows that deepened in the failing light.

From Dr Cornish's description, this must be the place, no doubt of that. A hundred yards downstream would be the shallow pool where the last of the rising tide spent itself at the extreme head of the estuary. It would be just beyond the clump of trees, there where the river curved to the right. Optimus determined to spend a few minutes exploring the place more closely. It looked so tranquil that one could hardly imagine anything violent occurring in the vicinity. He dropped down beside the bridge's abutment and followed the grassy bank towards the spinney.

'Don't you know you're trespassing? You're on private property! Go back immediately!' Startled, Optimus swung towards the speaker. He felt uneasy. There was no doubt about it, in a sense he *was* trespassing. But his unease turned to real fear when he saw his challenger: a stocky, rather unkempt figure in outmoded clothes had stepped out from behind a tree and was pointing a gun at him. It was a light fowling piece whose barrel glistened in the twilight, covering half the face of the man who was sighting along it. Whoever he was, he looked as if he knew how to use it; Optimus took him for an aged gamekeeper.

There was no use giving in to his fear and taking to his heels; the man might pepper his behind with birdshot. He must brazen it out.

'I'm Optimus Shute, the schoolmaster from Branscombe

and I'm come to see the mistress of Leet,' he asserted, trying to make his voice sound steady across the water. Though not strictly true, his pretext was well chosen; if he had business with the lady of the manor, who was a mere underling of a gamekeeper to stop him?

'Come to see her ladyship, have you?' Something in the man's diction told him that this was no ordinary gamekeeper. 'Well, you'll be disappointed; she'll not receive you. Nancy Genteel hasn't seen anyone these last twenty years, or rather no one's been privileged to see *her*, one person only excepted.'

Optimus was pleased to see that the gun's muzzle was no longer aimed at him directly. The speaker was so consumed with repressed bitterness that he could not keep it steady. But he was still menacing and Optimus thought it would be prudent to beat a retreat as soon as possible. 'Well, if it's not possible to see her ladyship, I'd best be stepping homeward,' he announced with a slight move in that direction.

'Stay where you are!' The gun was suddenly trained on him again. 'Stay where you are! First tell me what was your business with her.'

'It's a personal matter.'

'Well, young man, let me tell you, I don't believe you. D'you know why? – I'll tell you! If you'd really intended to visit Nancy Genteel, you wouldn't be on that side of the river, now would you? No, you've some other purpose: out with it!'

Optimus could see the irrefutable logic in what the man was saying. If he had really intended going to the great house, he would have crossed the bridge, entered the gates beside the lodge, and walked up the drive across the park. But he had had no intention of trying to see Nancy Genteel that evening; if he had hoped to meet anyone it was Charles Barker, but he did not want to disclose this intention to a gamekeeper. From what he had heard, the old Steward no longer wielded much influence on the estate and was something of an outcast. 'To tell the truth, I'm a bit of an amateur historian; I was curious to see the place where a certain incident once happened.'

'A certain incident?'

'Yes, my friend Dr Cornish has been telling me about

something that happened here years ago when Jack Lugger –'

'You're a friend of Dr Cornish's?' broke in the man, lowering his gun and hooking it into the crook of his arm. 'Why couldn't you say so in the first place?'

'You didn't ask me,' replied Optimus, with a slight smile of relief. 'But who are you, then? You frightened me with that gun of yours; I'm not used to being shot at.'

'Charles Barker, at your service,' said the man, touching his cap in a rather waggish way. 'But tell me, what's your interest in Jack Lugger? To my mind he wasn't worth anyone's trouble to investigate. Jack Lugger was a windbag, nothing more.' As he spoke, Charles Barker advanced to the river bank, so that the two of them were conversing more normally across the narrow stretch of water. Optimus observed his frayed, slightly outmoded clothes, and his lawyer-like manner of talking.

'But he was shot here by the pool, wasn't he?'

'Who told you that? Not Dr Cornish, I hope. He's not usually given to inexactitude. No, young feller, Jack Lugger wasn't shot here; it was up the road towards Uglington. The preventives arrived late from Plymouth and caught up with the rear of the party. But walk down and see the pool, if you like. There's nothing there now to suggest blood and thunder.'

Proceeding on either bank of the River Arun, the two of them strolled down to the pool. Optimus stood in the shade of the trees that grew just above it, watching the smooth water, flecked occasionally by a fish rising to take a fly. At its downstream end the river snaked away across the meadows, bordered with flags and sedge, dotted with clumps of willow, vanishing round a swell of land to the left of the wooded estuary. From the way the current was flowing gently, it appeared that the tide was down. Dr Cornish had explained that it reached this point, the head of navigation, only briefly, for a few minutes twice a day. He imagined it flooding almost imperceptibly into the pool with a mantle of sea-froth until the current ceased flowing completely. He imagined the men waiting in the trees with their ponies tethered; he imagined he heard the soft thudding of oars between thole-pins, coming from somewhere down beyond the willows. He saw the dark bulk of the boat come into sight round the last bend, with a single figure erect in it, and come gliding across the pool until its bow grated on the shingle.

'This was the place they landed the goods though, wasn't it?' he inquired, seeking corroboration.

'Off and on,' agreed Charles Barker. 'It was a good place to meet the tinners from the moor when they came down to collect it.'

'And what was Jack Lugger's role in all that?'

'Oh, he was a sort of go-between, on his own he'd never have done anything. That woman was at the back of it; without her they'd never have got started.'

'That woman?'

'You must know who I mean, if you've heard of Jack Lugger you can't fail to have heard of Grace Pensilva.'

'Grace Pensilva? Grace Pensilva, the name rings a bell, but I can't place her.'

'Grace Pensilva, damn her innocent looks, was the source of all our misfortunes. You must be new here if you don't know Grace Pensilva. But this isn't the place to stand talking, it's getting chilly.' Charles Barker glanced over his shoulder at Leet House as if concerned at being observed. 'Come over to the lodge and take a glass of toddy by the fire. Any friend of Dr Cornish's is a friend of mine.'

Optimus followed him willingly enough, taking the longer way over the bridge. Charles Barker was hanging his gun along a beam by the fireplace when he arrived. 'Come in, come in, pay no attention to the clutter, you have to expect that with an old bachelor. We've known better times, all of us. I suppose I should be grateful that she hasn't turned me out altogether, but she still needs someone to keep the accounts, her precious Ronald was never up to that, though he was up to other things, I fancy.'

Optimus realized that Charles Barker must be talking about his mistress, Nancy Genteel, and the Ronald he mentioned must be the Coyte boy. He installed himself on the

187

settle next to the thin fire and studied his surroundings about which the Steward had shown himself so defensive. The room had a neglected, soiled appearance, with smoke-begrimed cobwebs in the corners.

'Oh, I know what you're thinking,' exclaimed Charles Barker. 'Why doesn't the old codger have a skivvy, surely he can afford one? Well, let me tell you, since the Squire went off so sudden and left the estate to that Nancy and her Ronald, my heart's not in it. At first I dreamed he'd come back and set things to rights, but now I know better.'

'Frederick Genteel, you mean; I've heard of him,' said Optimus, 'he left long ago, didn't he? But why?'

'He never said, not even to me, but it was so soon after Grace Pensilva made fools of Mr Hawkins and Captain Scully that I couldn't help putting two and two together. I know Hawkins suspected Frederick, someone had to have tipped her off. But the worst was to see how cock-a-hoop it made his sister Nancy when she was sure he was leaving.'

'So Squire Genteel knew Grace Pensilva?'

'Too well for his own.good, she had him spellbound. They used to walk round the park together; I came upon them more than once, sitting on a log and talking. Frederick told me it was about poetry, William Wordsworth or someone, he said it was a wonder that a girl with her simple background could have such sensibility.'

'Do you think they were –'

'Lovers?' Charles Barker completed for him. 'Not in the sense you mean, not while I knew them. But poor Frederick was entranced by her. No sooner had he met her at the hunt than he was off to Langstone Mill, on the pretext of squeezing rent from Farmer Coyte, but really in the hope of running into her. It was a strange link that held them together. "The meeting of true minds" was how he described it to me before he went angling one evening; that was the pretext he used to cover his assignations with her. I can't say I myself disliked her then or distrusted her. She was a wild one was our Grace, and there's something in most of us that's captivated by wildness. But wild things don't have much conscience, do they?'

'Grace Pensilva didn't have a conscience?'

'I don't think so, not as far as Frederick Genteel was concerned. As for Jan King, why she taunted him with her relationship with Frederick; she flaunted it, she drove him wild at it. She used Jan King and, when his usefulness was over, she did away with him, at least that's what everyone believes round here.'

'Do you believe it?'

'There was no positive proof, was there? No body, only circumstantial evidence, both of them vanished one night, their boat found floating, and never a sign of him after that. And there was more than one motive –'

'Money?'

'Oh there was that, plenty of it so they say, but there was another thing.' Optimus raised his eyebrows questioningly. 'Her brother, her brother Frank. You see, she thought Jan King had a hand in betraying him.'

'But didn't she go and live with him, weren't they partners?'

'You already know that, do you? Well, at the time that seemed reasonable enough. Jan King was fairly besotted with her, always had been, and she had had time to relent, to come round to the idea that she might be mistaken. You mustn't look for too much logic where Grace Pensilva was concerned, she was the kind of woman that – that even a cussed old lawyer might fall for.'

'You don't mean that you too –?'

'Oh no,' laughed Charles Barker, 'it didn't get that far with me, I was too much of a cold fish, I fancy. That's probably why I'm still single. And she never set her cap at me, not like the others. Women like men of action, I suppose, not dry as dust book-keepers. That would explain why Grace followed Frederick to Malta, if for no other reason.'

'You think she was attracted by him?'

'I'm certain of it, unless she was more of a play-actor than I took her for. No, she fell for him all right, perhaps not here, but later when they were both in Malta. He wrote to me from time to time and mentioned it.'

'From the way you say it, it was a one-sided affair; he wasn't really interested.'

'Not entirely. He was charmed by her, but I'm not sure there was passion. Later on, in Malta, she was an embarrassment, or that's how I read it.'

'Could I see the letters? Do you still have them?'

'Curiosity killed the cat; you're the most inquisitive young man. Even if I did have them, it would be too late in the day to go looking for them. And there's privacy involved, letters are somewhat confidential, aren't they? I'll have to think about the matter. For a person who merely wanted to see the place where Jack Lugger was shot, you've covered a lot of ground. Before I say more I'll have to know your interest.'

'I'll be frank, my interest is Grace Pensilva. It was your friend Dr Cornish who put me up to it; I didn't want to get involved. Now I'm up to my ears in it.'

'Well, enough's enough for one night. Here, drink this toddy and let's change the subject.'

'I was hoping you'd be able to tell me about Malta. Dr Cornish said –'

'Dr Cornish is a presuming old busybody. He ought to know I know nothing about the place, never been there, don't want to see it, everything about Malta has bad associations for me, it did no good to Frederick. No, you've come to the wrong door to find out about Malta.'

'But the letters, they must have told you something. And hearsay. And wasn't there any kind of report when Frederick –'

'Look, I don't like to be pumped, perhaps it's the lawyer in me. Whatever your reasons for investigating this business, and for all I know you're nothing but a treasure hunter, it's a private matter. Come on now, let's change the subject. Have you ever seen the ceremony of the glove at Uglington? It's how they open the summer fair there, most picturesque, part of our folklore, every newcomer should see it.'

'Just one last question,' Optimus pleaded.

'All right, but I won't promise to answer it.'

'How did it come about that Grace Pensilva left Langstone'

Mill and moved in with Jan King at Armouth?'

'Mmm, lots of people could tell you that. It all came to a head at Farmer Wroth's harvest home, and that damned Ronald Coyte had a part in it. I sometimes think she put him up to it.'

'She?'

'Nancy Genteel. But you've got me going again. I won't have it. Drink up that toddy, it's past your bedtime, young feller. Mine too, for that matter, but come again if you've a mind to.'

On the way home in the dark Optimus was sure he passed close to wounded Jack Lugger.

'Who was that gel who spoke up for the fox?' asked Frederick, trying to sound casual. 'Her face is familiar somehow, but I know nothing about her. But you know everything about these parts, Charles, nothing escapes your attention.'

Frederick Genteel was sitting on the table in the estate office with his legs dangling. His polished boots were spattered with mud, for he had just come in from riding.

'I thought you knew her, from the way you looked at her,' said Charles Barker and Genteel flicked a glance at him. Was it so obvious, was there any overt sign of a link between him and this singular woman? He hoped Charles was only teasing. 'Spirited filly,' he continued. 'Grace is her name. Her brother Frank, he was a bit of a misfit, was drowned not long since, in a brush with the Revenue. Whole county was abuzz with the story.'

'Oh?' With a show of absent-mindedness, Genteel poked with an inquiring finger at the piles of bills that littered the table, as if seeking something.

'It happened just before you came back to live here. Otherwise you'd've heard of it. Feller's name was Pensilva, worked by moonlight. Not only that, he had a lot of lunatic ideas he'd picked up abroad. Made no secret he was agin authority. Mr Hawkins wasn't the only one to say good riddance when Frank Pensilva caught it.'

'And his sister Grace?'

191

'Ah yes, his sister.' Charles Barker permitted himself a knowing smile as he spoke. 'Come down in the world has our Grace, used to be lady's companion to Miss Delabole.'

'You mean the old battleaxe, over at Shearanscombe, the one who inherited all that land up-country?'

'She wasn't such a battleaxe as you imagine. Bit of a recluse, that's all. That's why you didn't get to know her, Grace either while she was there.'

'But *you* did.'

'Oh, Charles Barker gets to know everyone, he has to, he's forever out dunning for rent, arbitrating over who trims what hedgerow, who owns the water-rights, et cetera, et cetera.'

'So you know where she's living now, don't you?'

'You *are* persistent,' laughed Charles Barker, 'I'll give you that Freddie, you *are* persistent.' With deliberate slowness, he cut open an envelope and scanned its contents. 'This'll interest you,' he murmured, placing it on the table.

'Answer my question, you devious jurist, you!' Frederick reached across to where Barker was sitting and grabbed him by his linen stock and shook him gently in mock anger.

'Hadn't I mentioned it? – Langstone Mill.'

'What? Is she related to that skinflint Coyte? He's behind with the rent again, isn't he?'

'Jack Coyte is *always* behind with the rent. But she's not related to him, as far as I know. She's an orphan. Not much of a life for her now, she merits better than to work as a skivvy for the Coyte family. Mean and self-righteous into the bargain, they are. Worst possible combination.'

'The estate seems full of tenants like that, Charles, riddled with hopeless payers. How can we be expected to repair their barns, build sea-dykes, drain their land, when their rents aren't forthcoming?' He picked up a handful of bills as he spoke. 'All I seem to do is pay, pay, pay. There's never an end to it.'

'They know when an estate's mismanaged,' said Barker, leaning back in his judicial manner. 'They know when it's being bled white like this one, with your father extracting every penny. Who can blame them? But I'll tell you something, Freddie: they know you're back here, they know you're taking an interest.'

'All very well to say that, but the old beggar's about to come down here and spoil it.'

'That's what this letter's about. Why don't you read it?'

Genteel took it up and scanned it. A broad smile creased his lips and brightened his habitually serious face.

' "My dear Charles," ' he read, ' "You will be desolated to hear that my gout has worsened and enforced a postponement of my projected visit." ' Genteel slapped his thigh. ' "I pray you to inform Frederick and Nancy who will, no doubt, share your disappointment. Though I regret that I shall not be able to inspect the estate which, I fear, may be suffering from my son's over-enthusiastic meddling, I trust I shall continue to enjoy its meagre fruits and I look forward to the usual remittances, to be sent to me early, if at all possible – Yours indigently, Mayberry." – Well, the old fellow certainly hasn't lost his sense of humour.'

'It'll mean more rent-collecting.'

'Never mind, I'll do my share of it. For a start, we'll squeeze old Coyte for what he owes us. What irks me about Farmer Coyte is that he doesn't have to depend on his crops like the rest of 'em. He's got the corn-mill to bring in income. Every sack that's ground in Harberscombe has to pass through Langstone Mill. And we should be getting a royalty on it. Of course, I wouldn't expect the old skinflint to declare every last sack he grinds, it wouldn't be human nature if he did. But to plead poverty the way you say he does, that's the last straw and he must pay for it.'

'What shall we do about it?' inquired the Steward, chewing his pen. 'Give him notice? Quarter day's coming up shortly.'

'No,' replied Genteel with a pull at his flowered waistcoat, 'I'll ride over and dun him personally – What're you grinning about, Charles, you simpering monkey?'

'There couldn't be another reason Freddie – a certain dairymaid – or could there?'

'You lawyers are all the same, can't credit a feller with a simple motive,' grumbled Frederick, but still grinning. 'All

I'm trying to do is bring in the money so we can maintain Father.'

'Most noble of you, Frederick, most altruistic!' Both men turned quickly to face the door where Nancy Genteel was standing. Now that they had noticed her, they smelt the stable on her. She was forever currying her horses after her wild gallops. When she did this work, she wore breeches and looked more mannish than usual.

'Someone has to see the books balance,' said Frederick quietly.

'Well, there's money coming in at last. I can smell it. You'll be thinking of your sister, won't you? I don't ask for much, not compared with Father. Just a few guineas for a proper thoroughbred. I've had enough of second-best, enough of playing second fiddle. And don't just sit there looking censorious and solemn, damn you. It's my due and I shall have it.'

'We'll see,' said Genteel propitiatingly. 'I hope we can manage something.'

'No, you won't see,' spat Nancy. 'You'll do it! Or I'll find it my duty to write to Father and inform him you're concealing his revenues.'

'But it's for the good of the estate.'

'Damn the estate! We must live today, not tomorrow. Think it over. But don't take too long over it: there's only one answer. Off you go and extract our due from Farmer Coyte. Tell 'im it's for your sister.' She turned to leave, then added over her shoulder, 'And by the way, if you see that young Ronald, find out why he hasn't appeared yet. I suppose you *did* give him my summons, didn't you, Barker?' Without waiting for an answer, she was away and the courtyard soon echoed to her hunter's flying hooves.

'Good riddance,' said Genteel with some resignation. 'God knows, I try to treat her like a sister, but it's a rough road to follow. About that Ronald, have you approached him?'

'I hoped she'd forgotten. We can't afford to pay him.'

'Well, you can see *she* hasn't. Perhaps it'll be best to humour her. No use meeting Nancy head-on.'

'Takes after her father,' said Charles Barker, rising. 'What's

194

bred in the bone will come out in the flesh.'

'I suppose so,' said Genteel, rising in his turn, 'though I can't see where that leaves me in all this. Perhaps I take after Mother.'

'Who's to say?' murmured Barker as he began to sort the papers on the table. 'If she'd lived, this might all've been a different story.'

Genteel sighed as he left. So much could turn on the influence of a woman. If he was honest with himself, it was a woman who was determining his actions now. As he rode towards Langstone Mill, he knew that what drew him, like a moth to a flame, was a woman, though he sensed the danger. That woman was Grace Pensilva.

One person who was not concerned with thoroughbreds, or with grooms, was Grace Pensilva. In the coldness of her room she slipped her warm body into her clammy nightgown and shivered in her turn. She slid into bed, snuffed out her candle, turned her face to the peeling whitewashed wall and tried to compose herself for sleep. Outside her window, the chute from the mill-leat gushed and gurgled, spitting its choked-off flow over the immobilized wheel. A dying man might sound like that; a man drowning, or a man at the end of his tether before letting go and plummeting over a precipice. Grace closed her eyes tight, but her ears still listened. They heard an erratic thudding, like a man's boots digging into the turf. But she knew the sound: it was Ronald's nag, penned up in the stable and drumming its hooves in its stall. In a kind of dream, she imagined herself setting him free, vaulting astride and riding him bareback over the cliffs while he ran headlong. In her imagination, she rose above the scene and saw herself galloping, her night-clothes fluttering, her face set in the pale mask of the avenger: pale horse, pale rider. She shrieked, or dreamt she shrieked: the horse was leaping to destruction.

She awoke shaking, sat up and shivered. The night was long, it would not soon be over. Later, she dozed fitfully until the first light entered her chamber. When it did so, she rose, opened Frank's chest, took out some letters that were hidden beneath an inner drawer, and read them slowly. It seemed only minutes before she heard Mrs Coyte clanging the pans in the dairy. It was time to rise. She pulled on her working clothes, went down and milked the cows and carried the pails into the dairy.

'Work aplenty to make up this mornin',' announced Mrs Coyte with relish. 'Us can't spend our days out 'untin' and not make up for it after, can us, me beauty? 'Twas all very well to play the lady and 'ob-nob with the gentry, but now we'm back at Langstone Mill, bain't us, Missy? Down 'ere, Grace Pensilva be 'er real self; she bain't naught but a skivvy.'

Grace bit her tongue and held back her answer. She went out and cut wood, she fed the chickens, collected the eggs, tethered the goat in a new position and began to muck out the stable. Young Ronald, with a straw in his mouth and his legs dangling, watched her from the hayloft. 'Farmer Wroth be 'avin' an 'arvest 'ome, over to Shearanscombe,' he announced.

'What's the point of telling me,' she answered with hardly a pause, 'you know I don't attend that kind of thing.'

'Why not?'

'If you must know, I'm still in mourning.'

'I thought you might like to see the place again; you 'aven't been there since Miss Delabole died, I reckon.' Grace made no reply, but continued shifting straw and dung with her fork. 'Well, if that bain't enough to lure 'ee, there'll be folk aplenty to meet there, I do believe the Squire's invited.'

'What should I want with Frederick Genteel?'

'Why, to thank 'im for takin' your side over the fox.'

'Look, Ronald, there's a very good reason why I shan't be going. I've had no invitation. If Eric Wroth had wanted me there he'd've asked me himself.'

'Exactly. But 'ee forgot, didn't'ee? When 'ee remembered 'ee told me to pass on the invitation.'

'Well, tell him I'm not going.'

Ronald looked crestfallen. 'I'd 'oped . . .' he began and stopped in mid sentence. Grace was about to make a sharp answer, but saw his long face and softened.

'You'd hoped what?'

'I'd 'oped you'd go along o'me; I needs a partner.' Grace smiled; he was but a boy really.

'Why don't you ask one of the village maidens?'

''Tis you I wants, you don't make mock of me like they do.'

'I'll think it over,' said Grace a little doubtfully.

'Oh, thank you!' In a trice he had jumped down, given her a peck on the cheek and run out of the doorway.

Otherwise, it was a day like any other, full of habitual chores that taxed her young body and dulled her spirit. But that very dulling was what she thought she needed. She threw herself into the repetitive monotony of it until her train of conscious thought came to a halt and her anxieties sank into a blur of sameness and exhaustion. If she was doomed to spend her life in servitude, it had better be dull servitude. If there were hope and that hope constantly disappointed, it might break her spirit. But if she knew her station and toiled accordingly, she would be like a thousand, ten thousand, a hundred thousand, a million others, tied to the treadmill of life. And indeed, what else could there be? There was no other possible order; all men could not be farmers, still less lords and ladies. Since Piers Plowman had followed his team down the long furrow there had been no alteration: the labourer had sown and the farmer had reaped. The poor man had lain down in a cold bed and been thankful for his supper.

That night, as the four of them sat round the deal table eating the clear broth and the stale bread that Mrs Coyte doled out to them, Farmer Coyte cleared his throat portentously. 'Ronald tells me 'ee do want to take Grace for a partner at the 'arvest 'ome.'

'What blamed nonsense,' snapped his wife. 'There be no need for 'er to go off gallivantin'. She must stay 'ome and sleep like any other body that 'as to work on the morrow.'

'I don't know,' said Farmer Coyte. 'I bain't sure 'bout that.'

'What do you mean, you bain't sure? Us don't pay 'er for nothin'.'

'Squire Genteel comed over this mornin'.'

'What 'ave that got to do with it?'

'Ee comed over 'bout the rent.'

'Money, money, money,' whined Mrs Coyte, 'why do they always come after our money?'

'If we don't pay, 'ee says us'll 'ear from the Steward and it'll be notice for Lady Day –' He paused to let the message sink in. 'But there were something' else: 'ee did ask after our Grace 'ere, would 'ave spoke to 'er if 'ee could, but I couldn't find 'er. Any'ow, 'ee wanted to know if we'd all be going to Eric Wroth's 'arvest 'ome, an' I catched 'is drift immediately. I told un, maybe.'

'What for?' his wife asked blankly.

''Aven't you got a brain in your 'ead? Can't you see 'ee be smitten on Grace? The more 'ee do see of 'er the less 'ee'll come after our money.'

'Ah! Would that were true; I do 'ope so. Well, Grace, you shall go, and welcome,' said Mrs Coyte, suddenly converted.

'What about the person concerned?' demanded Grace. 'Who said I wanted to? You never heard me say so.'

'Ungrateful hussy!' exclaimed Mrs Coyte. 'After all us've done for 'ee, taken 'ee in, given 'ee work and lodgin'! Go you shall and enjoy it. 'Tiddn' every maid do 'ave the Squire ask after 'er.'

Grace was beginning to shake her head and dig in her heels when she saw Ronald's doleful face across the table. It wasn't his fault that his father and mother were so despicable. She relented.

'Oh, very well, I'll go, but not for your sake, not to save you money – I'll go with Ronald because he asked me.' As she spoke, Grace thought of the irony of Mrs Coyte, who had started by warning her against being a cradle-snatcher, now pushing her off to the harvest home with her precious young Ronald. A faint smile haunted her lips as she finished the meal in silence.

When the great day came, Ronald went on ahead of Grace; he had volunteered to help Farmer Wroth to prepare his barn for the festivities. She was held back by Mrs Coyte until she had finished the milking and tidied the dairy. It was late in the day when she went up to her room and pulled her grey dress from the chest by her bedside. It had been fresh and new when she was with Miss Delabole who had insisted on buying it for her. 'A gel has to have something decent to wear, it brightens her spirit,' the old lady had said to the dressmaker who made it. 'And worsted will do, but silk is better.'

Now the dress was a little crumpled and touched with the dampness that reigned throughout Langstone Mill, but it was soft to the touch and made her eyes sparkle as she slipped on her silver-buckled shoes. Her only worry was how her fellow villagers would react after the incident with the fox. It was some weeks back, but they had long memories, particularly where strangers – and Grace for all her years in Harberscombe was still a stranger – were concerned.

'Off so soon, maid?' cried Mrs Coyte querulously as Grace passed the kitchen.

'Tonight my time's my own, or so your husband's told me.'

'I wonders where you do find the strength. Not tired after workin'? Well, good luck to 'ee. Mebbe you'll find another Frank up there. If you found Frank good, Squire ought to be hundreds better.' Grace ignored her; she would not rise to the bait. She pulled the door to sharply after her and stepped off into the dusk.

She hurried up the steep hill from the mill, passing the cider orchard and crossing the leat. The lane doubled back on itself like a wounded snake, becoming steeper still, so steep that it sometimes defeated the loaded carts returning from the mill. She picked her way as daintily as she could through the mud and ruts that were now obscured by the over-arching hazel hedges' heavy shadows. The first bats came jinking down the lane, splitting the night with their acid cries. Grace put her hand to her hair, victim of age-old superstition or some obscure instinct, but brought it down again with an effort of her will. As she came to the first fork in the road the banks lowered momentarily; she heard the first owl hoot from across the valley, echoed soon by another from lower down the estuary; she paused to catch her breath.

Seen in this light, without the associations of travail and

199

narrow horizons, the Arun estuary was breathtakingly beautiful: the ridges of the hills dipped in soft folds whose green was still barely perceptible under the amber vault where slaty clouds sailed in ragged majesty. Around the skirts of the hills the ancient oak-woods billowed and frothed gently like the waves of some vegetable sea. And between them, glistening like watered silk, patterned by the channels of innumerable streams and the obscure blotches of the reed beds, were the mudflats, reflecting the first stars' glow.

Grace felt uplifted by an ineffable communion with the loveliness of creation. Her solitude did not detract from it. At that time of her life she had no thought of sharing and, for a moment, the overriding sense of her purpose did not intrude on and stain her perceptions. The image etched itself on her memory with a depth and precision that would render it unforgettable and, in the fullness of time, when she came back to it, its peace, its agonizing beauty would stop her in her tracks, with a feeling that was more than grief: a dagger to the heart.

She strode on. In half a mile she saw the high roofs of Shearanscombe House and the new barn alongside. It was a place she knew and she approached it confidently, drawn on by the lighted windows and the sounds of revelry. The downstairs windows were uncurtained and Grace peered into the parlour. It was impossible to look into that room without expecting old Miss Delabole to stare back at her through steel-rimmed spectacles from her seat at the sampler. But the seat was empty, its tapestry upholstery had already been shredded by the claws of the cat which slept there. Miss Delabole would have been horrified at the dirt and disorder. Her long-nosed, elegant ancestors glowered down from their oval frames at the casual negligence of everyday existence. They certainly disapproved of Farmer Wroth who had snapped up the property when it was put on the market by the old lady's indifferent executors, and who now allowed his chickens to run all over the carpet. Yet, despite the squalor, something of the old lady's spirit still hovered over the room.

'I may not be Julius Caesar,' Grace remembered her

chiding gently, 'they say he could read a dispatch, write out orders and listen to a messenger all at the same time; I do not pretend to that level of mental agility. But I certainly can listen and sew simultaneously. I pray you child, continue your reading.' It was strange to hear that voice and see Miss Delabole's chair in front of the long-case clock that ticked the hours away ponderously while Grace read quietly, vacant and woebegone.

'I believed you were dozing,' she remembered replying.

'I *never* doze, child, don't you know that already? I don't believe in relaxing. But I'll accept your excuse; you might think when my eyes are closed that I'm dreaming. It is not so. Would that I *could* sleep. I want you to know, dear child, that I am most sensible of the degree to which you are solicitous. There are those in the village, sharp-tongued gossips, who will have it that your kindness is not disinterested and that you believe, as I have no close living relatives, I will leave you a legacy. But I think I know my Grace better than that, do I not? Is it hope of gain that inspires your kindness?' Grace remembered shaking her head fiercely. 'You shall have your reward,' the old lady had continued, reaching out to stroke her hair. 'I'll not forget you. I could not have wished for a gentler daughter.'

Grace could not hold back a tear, old Miss Delabole had sounded so concerned, so sincere. And yet she had left Grace nothing, there had been no will. Treasures in heaven, that was all that Grace had earned during her time here, that and the French she spoke and the silk dress she was wearing.

A burst of music from the barn brought Grace back to herself. The door swung wide, followed by a wedge of yellow light that came towards her, making her pull away from the window, fearful of being caught spying.

'Why, if it isn't our Grace!' exclaimed Eric Wroth, outlined in the doorway by the brilliant light from within, his voice pitched high to cover the noise of concertina and fiddle. 'The last person I expected to come 'ere tonight, but welcome, welcome. Come on in, maid, and take a glass of ale.'

Grace gathered in her voluminous skirt to cross the dirty

yard. She was prepared for a transformation of the vast dim barn, but not for the magic scene that presented itself when Farmer Wroth handed her across the threshold with a gallantry worthy of an earl. 'Welcome back to Shearanscombe, me 'andsome,' he greeted her. 'What a pretty maid she be, proper little leddy.'

Grace paused a moment beside him, drinking in the splendour of the brightly lit interior. The whole place was ablaze with flames: the small flames of a hundred candles in a huge borrowed chandelier, swung from a beam in the centre, flames from sputtering torches set in the new cob walls, flames from flickering rush-lights that spangled the long farmhouse tables brought into the barn to carry the eatables. And with all this profusion of light went a multiplicity of shadows. High above her head was the reverberated geometry of tie-beam and king post and rafter, all interlocking and overlaid with each others' insubstantial images. Lower down, the silhouettes of the prancing dancers were flung about like huge, grotesque caricatures in a shadow-play. And there was the smell of good food: pies and cakes and tart and russet apples.

Above all, blending together into an impression that was more enchanting than any of its separate components, was the continuously changing, yet repetitive web of music. It was a wonder that a mere three instruments – a fiddle, a concertina and an antique bass viol – could produce such volume and excitement. What the players lacked in artistry, they made up for in gusto, playing together with an understanding born of long habit. If their tunes were old, they were all the more popular. Even the smallest children joined in the dance: pairs of tiny girls in elaborate dresses and polished black shoes that their parents must have skimped and saved for, were placing their feet carefully and maintaining grown-up faces. Sleek-haired young boys were pulled into the dance by their elder female cousins, or even their aunts or mothers, and stumbled through the steps as though they would never learn. Their contemporaries sniggered at them from the sidelines.

But the centre of the dance was held by the young farm-hands, the farmers' sons, the unmarried maidens, and the newly-wed couples. Many of the young men had more gumption than grace, but their partners kept them in line, pulling them by the arm where needful. Half-way down the barn, stately and tall in an unaccustomed formal black coat, Uncle Bill Terry called the sets in a sonorous voice. Behind him, grouped round a firkin of ale, were all the men and boys who could not or would not dance. Facing him, on the far side of the room, was a smaller congregation of women and girls, all laughing and chattering and flaunting their finery.

Grace joined the women, intending to make her peace with Eileen Wroth, but she had not been there a second when Jack Lugger sprang across and dragged her into the dance. 'How have you fared since you left fishing?' Grace asked by way of conversation.

''Tis no life labourin', said Jack. 'I thought fishin' were bad enough, but this be worse. I've tried rabbitin' too, 'tis short commons.'

'How about moonlighting?' asked Grace in a whisper.

'That be a fine jest,' laughed Jack Lugger as the dance ended. 'Never thought you'd ask me that. Why should anyone want to work in that trade?'

'If they wanted to pull themselves up by their bootstraps, they might,' replied Grace as Ronald Coyte came over to claim her. While she had been dancing she had watched the young lads picking on him, teasing him until his face reddened with embarrassment. It was the usual story: they were putting a shy boy up to asking a girl to dance.

'Beggin' your pardon,' he began, speaking to Jack Lugger 'Grace be my guest 'ere and my partner.'

'Run away and play, young un!' grunted Lugger. 'Can't you see I be talkin' to this lady?'

'No,' said Grace, 'stay here Ronald, I'll dance with you.'

'What about me?' demanded Jack Lugger in an aggrieved tone.

'Run away and play!' Grace laughed at him.

'Bleddy vox lover!' Lugger called after her as she and

203

Ronald stepped into the dance. It was a surprise to find that Ronald was light and sure on his feet and she was astonished that, despite her high-heeled shoes, he was taller than she was.

'I didn't know you could dance.'

'Feyther sent me to the dancing-master over to Uglington. 'Ee do want me to become a gennulman.'

Grace repressed a desire to laugh. The idea of quaint, skinflint old Farmer Coyte's son becoming a gentleman, by whatever means he meant to compass it, was ludicrous. Yet it was unfair on the boy to make him feel this. She smiled at him encouragingly and he danced all the better. Although his feet were a trifle large, he put them in the right place, unlike the other men who would later crush her toes and tear the hem of her dress.

Grace danced with a long succession of farmer's sons that evening, but she danced with Ronald more often than any. He had little to say to her, but that was preferable to the others' crude comments and invitations to the hayloft. If he clasped her a little too closely during the following dances, she put it down to his inexperience.

The band fell silent for a while, gorging themselves on pies and good ale. Everyone fell to talking, but there was a hush when Frederick Genteel and his steward walked into the barn. 'Welcome, Squire,' called Farmer Wroth, hurrying to greet him. 'This 'ere be me wife, Eileen.' Eileen Wroth curtsied awkwardly, as did several other women.

'Honoured, I'm sure,' she murmured. 'Will you take a bite o' supper?' But Squire Genteel was only half listening to her, his eye was roving round the circle of faces, searching for someone. When he found her, he tried a smile, but she ignored him. She felt his look, but turned to talk to young Ronald.

'We'em all friends 'ere,' proclaimed Farmer Wroth, 'within this place there be neither rich nor poor, bond nor free, us be all good Devon folk. Come on Maister Genteel and you, Maister Barker, drink up, us've got a lead on 'ee in that connection.' He turned to the musicians. 'Come now, I bain't payin' 'ee just to eat and drink; let's 'ave a tune out of 'ee, somethin' the Squire will like, 'ow 'bout "Lillibullero"?'

'Us can't dance to that,' said his wife, 'play "Sir Roger de Coverley.".'

As the band struck up, Grace saw Frederick Genteel strolling, with studied negligence, towards her. What should she do? Ronald had left her for a moment and she had no wish to cultivate the Squire to please the former's father. She edged away through the thick of the crowd until she reached the doorway.

Outside in the darkness she heard sounds of grunting, subdued squeals and giggling coming from the nearby cartshed. She knew what was going on in there; more than one couple had vanished from the barn during the past half-hour. The blind, obsessive bestiality of their farmyard love-making disgusted her. There was something irresponsible in these fleeting moments of lust that she could not condone. The village was full of love children conceived in this casual manner. Their mothers bore more than their share of the consequent opprobrium and misery, but the children were branded with the indelible name of bastard. They were the innocent and they bore the sanctimonious shame.

She was trying to decide whether to return to the barn or set off homeward when a dark figure approached her. He had been lurking in the shadows behind the door, and now, with the light behind him, she could not see his face. He reached out and caught her arm above the elbow. 'Let me be,' she snapped, trying to keep the fear out of her voice.

''Tis only me.'

'Let go of me!' she insisted.

'I only comed over to thank 'ee Grace. I thought you'd be 'ere dancin'.'

'Then why were you waiting outside, Jan King?'

'I never was much for dancin', never learned that down to Armouth. And I wanted to see 'ee private.'

'Well, thank me then, if you must and release my arm. You're still holding it, if you haven't noticed, and you're hurting me.'

205

'I don't know 'ow to say it.'

'Then keep it to yourself. The last thing I need is your gratitude.'

'You'm so 'ard, Grace. Why did you 'ave to save me when you won't talk to me after? Why didn't you let me slide over? That were what you wanted, weren't it, to punish me for your dead brother?'

'You're a human being,' said Grace, 'and you spared the fox, didn't you?'

'Well, I'm grateful. If there be anythin' I can ever do –'

'Hush,' said Grace, 'you owe me nothing. But I promise you, if ever I need your help, I'll call on you. Now go home and forget it.' There was a sincerity in her voice that cheered him unreasonably. He ran off into the night and Grace turned back to the improvised ballroom.

Frederick Genteel was waiting for her close to the doorway. He put out a detaining hand that she could not ignore. 'I feared you had left,' he murmured. 'Will you dance with me?'

'Would you take no for an answer?'

Frederick Genteel shook his head. 'The Squire still enjoys some manorial rights, I imagine,' he smiled reassuringly. 'Don't worry, I'll not eat you.'

Grace obeyed reluctantly. He took her hand and led her into the dance. His thin, bony fingers were cool, the lace on his shirt cuff brushed her wrist. Despite his insistence, he remained distant. 'You were with Miss Delabole once,' he remarked. 'You see, I've been checking up on you.'

'Am I supposed to be pleased at that? You've been asking after me at Langstone Mill too, haven't you? Do you think that kind of inquiry's good for a woman's reputation?'

'I didn't see it that way. Excuse me. You're not happy there, are you? You can't be.'

'Happy, what's that got to do with it?'

'That was a brave thing you did at the hunt,' said Frederick Genteel, taking a new tack. 'I admired you for it. It's not easy to confront a whole village. You're made of finer stuff than most, whatever your brother might have been –'

'My brother was a good man,' Grace interjected. 'He didn't

206

believe in your kind of world, that's all. He had principles, he believed in the rights of man, that's why the King's men destroyed him!'

'Perhaps he was, I'm not in a good position to judge. But what I wanted to tell you is this: if ever you need another position, something better than being a slavey to Mrs Coyte, there's a place for you at Leet, if you want it.'

'What sort of place?' demanded Grace, suddenly belligerent and halting in mid step, so that the other dancers turned to look at her. 'Let me tell you, Frederick Genteel, that Grace Pensilva isn't to be bought for a chambermaid's wages.'

'You misconstrue me,' protested Genteel. 'You turn everything on its head. Come, be reasonable.'

'Had I been reasonable, I should never have come to this gathering. My heart's not in it.' She turned to Farmer Wroth who was hovering nearby nervously. 'Excuse me, you've been kind, but I must be leaving.'

She broke away and ran off into the darkness of the lane. For a while she thought that someone might be following her, but she was confused by the echo of her own feet and the beating of her heart. At the corner she stopped and listened. Silence. She set her lips and strode on towards Langstone. She was glad she had quit the barn. For a while, she had felt at ease there and had given herself up to pleasure, blind enjoyment, carried away by the music and the human feeling. Now, alone, she could find herself again.

The sound of a horse's hooves made her look back apprehensively. A horseman, outlined against the stars, was rapidly approaching. She shrank back into the hedge, hoping that he would ride by without seeing her. But he reined in, with a flash of sparks where the horseshoes skidded on stone, and looked above her like an apparition. She felt her nails digging into the palms of her hands and her mouth was too dry to speak.

'Climb up 'ere, Grace, and I'll give 'ee a ride 'omealong.' It was only Ronald Coyte. She breathed out in relief and was glad it was too dark for him to see her harassed expression. Normally she would have refused, but this time she was glad

207

to be hoisted up on the saddle in front of him. The lane was steep, but the nag was sure footed; it knew its way better than either of them.

It was not long before she realized her error. Young Ronald, who had put his arms around her waist to steady her, was allowing his hands to palp her flesh and already a breast was cupped in one of them.

Although she repulsed him on that occasion, the following days confirmed that there was an alteration in their relationship. Something had brought about a change in him. No longer was he the timid, awkward boy she was accustomed to, but a moony young man, who seemed to burn with desire for her, following her as she went about her work, seeking opportunities to touch her surreptitiously. Whereas she had been used to romping with him like a boisterous puppy, his every move was now imbued with another significance. She pursued her daily tasks in an atmosphere of increasing tension, conscious of the danger of offering him the slightest encouragement. Her only respite, and she thanked her lucky stars for it, was that Ronald was often away on his horse, riding to Leet House where, so Farmer Coyte proudly informed her, he was being tried out for a groom at the stables.

And then, as if to chime in with her mood of growing anxiety, the weather broke.

Part Two

[The smuggler is:] A person who, though no doubt highly blamable for violating the laws of his country, is frequently incapable of violating those of natural justice, and would have been in every respect an excellent citizen had not the laws of his country made that a crime that nature never meant to be so.

Adam Smith, 1723–90

1

'Chilly afternoon, isn't it?' said Dr Cornish by way of greeting when Optimus stepped into the kitchen. 'Chuck a log on the fire, will you?'

Optimus was astonished; it had been a warm day and he himself was in his shirt-sleeves. To his sense the kitchen was overly warm already, but he did as he was asked, with a sidelong look at the old Doctor who was curled in his usual chair, with a woollen shawl draped over his shoulders, rocking gently.

'Well, did you see the pool where Jack Lugger caught it?' he asked. 'I saw you setting off in that direction and you weren't back till the early hours, were you?'

'You were wrong about one thing,' said Optimus.

'Oh, what was that, pray?'

'He wasn't shot at the pool at all, he was hit on the way to Uglington.'

'Who told you that? – Oh, you don't have to tell me; you've been jawing with that old rogue Charles Barker; trust a lawyer to be so finnicky about detail. What the devil does it matter exactly where they shot him. The important thing was that they brought him here and he lay there upon that very table, cold as a dead conger, and I had to try and save him. Precious little thanks I got for that, barring a little brandy. His wife talked to me as if it were my fault. Mine and Grace Pensilva's.'

'And was it?'

'Well, it wasn't true, though if he lived it was more by luck than judgement. Draw up your chair to the fire, boy, you must be freezing.'

'I'm not cold,' said Optimus.

211

'Not cold? Ah well, young blood, I suppose.'

'I'm trying to fit it in, trying to discover how Grace came to leave Langstone Mill and turn to smuggling.'

'Your guess is as good as mine, boy. When you get down to it, history is based upon conjecture, a certain number of verifiable events, but between them – nothing. I can try to remember what I said. Someone tells you what he heard that someone else said and you take it as gospel, you're avid for crumbs. In between, what is there? Oh yes, it's obvious that by the time Jack Lugger was shot, Grace Pensilva was a leading light in the smuggling trade. How did she get there? Was it because she spoke French and could bargain with Caradec, the captain of the Frenchman? Was it just because she had a stronger personality than the others? Why she left Langstone Mill is a moot point. To an extent, if we assume that her purpose was already fixed, she only needed a pretext. As for what she did, where she went, she had more than one option: she could have taken up service at Leet, Charles told me that once and he's not a liar. No, for me the interesting thing is that everything fitted in. Grace couldn't have known how things would turn out when she went to Langstone Mill, but something, call it fate, call it providence, seems to have chimed with her designs. Don't you feel that already? However determined she was in the first instance, she would never have done what she did if other things had fallen out otherwise. Aren't we all, to a large extent, floating leaves on the stream of life?'

'You said Jack Lugger's sister blamed Grace for what happened.'

'She claimed that it was too much of a coincidence that the preventives didn't arrive when she and Jan were unloading the boat in the pool and only struck later when Jack and the tinners were riding away from it.'

'That's not far from accusing Grace of the same thing *she* reproached Jan King with.'

'Well, she *did* bear a charmed life; it looked as though someone were protecting her, a person aware of the preventives' plans who was tipping the wink to her.'

'I've an idea who that might have been.'

'Well, you might be wrong. Grace Pensilva was so clever, so they used to say, that she could tell what Hawkins and Scully would think before they ever got round to it, she was always a jump or two ahead of them. When they shot Jack Lugger, that was the nearest they ever got to her. And there was no earthly reason why she should want to peach on him; she was well off by then, rolling in money, though there was no way in which she could spend it.'

'Perhaps Jack Lugger was scheming against her and she wanted him out of the way.'

'Jack Lugger wasn't in the same class. He might've been jealous that she, a woman, was in charge of things, but he didn't have the grey matter. Now, tell me, did you learn anything from Charles about Malta? You must have asked him.'

'He said he knew next to nothing, he'd never been there.'

'Charles Barker's a sly old fox, he keeps his cards very close to his chest, always has done. He knows more than he's telling, that's for certain.'

'He said there were some letters.'

'Letters, hmm. Well, people sometimes tell part of the truth in their letters. But he didn't show them to you, did he? No – that wouldn't be like him.'

'Well, how shall I ever find out what happened on Malta? Something *did* happen there, didn't it? Something between Grace and Frederick Genteel. Frankly, I believe you yourself know more than you're telling me.'

'Not much. Most of it is merely conjecture.'

'But Grace came home, didn't she? You saw her? You told me once you'd seen her and it seemed as if you'd seen her dead, and that only. But, if you were here when Jack Lugger was shot, you must have known her earlier.'

'I won't be cross-examined,' grunted Dr Cornish, 'don't imagine you too can play "Lawyer Barker" with me.'

'I'm sorry.'

'Poke up the fire a bit, there's a good fellow. Oh, how I wish I could feel warm again. They say it's warm on Malta. When she came back from there she wasn't the same, she was like a clock without a mainspring.'

'And she told you nothing about what she did there?'

'No, she was only interested in one thing.'

'What was that?'

'The past. She wanted to see her brother's grave and there was something else.'

'Yes –'

'There was something she learnt; it drove her distracted.'

'What was it?'

'I don't know. I'm feeling cold. I'm cold, I'm tired, you're pestering me.'

'But how shall I find out about Malta?'

'Go there.'

'But how can I? I haven't the time: I haven't the money.'

'Then you must learn patience.'

The weather broke: Jan King and Uncle Bill laid up the lugger for the winter. Armouth Pool was deserted except for flocks of migrant birds winging south for the winter. Jan King collected great piles of driftwood after the equinoctial gales that lashed the coast. At night he sat by his fireside alone, hands clasped, while the yellow flames from the salt-soaked wood flared and danced. He sat pensive, while the wind moaned in the chimney and the rain drummed on the roof. He sat unmoving, wrapped in his drowsy day-dreams until the night when he was aroused by a strange scratching on the window behind him. He turned to see a pale face regarding him through the streaming glass . . .

Optimus stopped writing and bit his lip. He held the page close to the candle and read it over; it was more or less how he imagined it had been at Armouth when Jan King lived there in the cottage alone; he could visualize the mess and disorder in that kitchen which Jan coped with as best he could. What he found difficult was to get inside the head of this simple, unlettered fisherman. What went through a man's head when the long hours stretched out before him and he could not read as Optimus himself would have done in that situation? Was he running over the events of the past months, was

214

he dreaming of the future, what kind of future would a man like Jan hope for? Did Grace Pensilva still figure in it? Was Jan mulling over his memories of Frank, was he jealous of the latter's hold over her affections? Was it reasonable to expect that Jan's juvenile passion for Grace could have survived the disdain she had shown him? And how had he felt about the unnatural attraction that Grace and Frank had felt for each other? He could not have failed to be aware of it.

Optimus pillowed his chin on his left hand and stared into space. That was not all, he feared he was leaving something out, neglecting what happened to Grace in those last days at Langstone. Holding the paper by one corner, he touched its lower edge to the candle flame, watching it suddenly blaze and curl into a brittle blackened fragment that burnt his fingers. Passion was like that, it flamed a moment then decayed into ashes. Before long, nothing remained of the fire that had been in it. Ashes to ashes, dust to dust, all loves and hates relapsed into nothingness. At least that was how he thought it must be. Optimus knew little of love and nothing of all-consuming emotion. He could understand the kind of feelings that drove Ronald Coyte, but there had to be more, something on another level of experience. Across the lane a light still burnt in Dr Cornish's window. He had to struggle with himself to resist hurrying over. Instead, he took a fresh sheet of paper, dipped his pen in the ink and tried a new beginning.

The weather broke. Great streaming veils of rain swept over the ruffled reaches of the estuary. The cold wind flung itself in from the sea and clashed the oak-tree boughs together in the streaming woods. The leaves, torn from the trees, whirled and tumbled a moment before sheeting the slopes with red and yellow like the dying flesh of gangrenous wounds.

The fishermen gave up the struggle, rescuing what pots they could in the breaks between the storms. Much of their gear was lost: some pots were fouled down in the oarweed, some were jammed for ever in the gullies between the rocks, some were cast up on the shore. It was the annual ransom they paid; the sea is a hard mistress.

As soon as the smack came by for the last time, they brought in their store-pots and ran their luggers up the river, far from the raging seas that pounded the Back and seethed in Armouth Pool. The ungainly crabbers lay on the mudbanks like stranded whales. The fishermen closed up their huts by the beach, strung their black baskets and panniers across their donkeys' backs for the last time and trudged homeward up the long hill to Harberscombe, leaving Jan King to lord it alone over Armouth.

Grace Pensilva had little thought for the beauty around her. Her task was chopping up turnips for the cattle and her cleaver thwacked persistently into the worn block as it clove them. What filled her thoughts was that morning's episode in the cowshed.

What a fool, why hadn't she accepted Frederick Genteel's offer and taken up service at Leet? Life at Langstone Mill was becoming impossible. Last night, when she went up to her room, she had a strange impression, a sensation that everything was not as she had left it. And yet, there was nothing definite.

In the morning, seated on the three-legged stool with her forehead pressed into the cow's flank, she was milking steadily when she felt someone touching her. Turning her head she encountered Ronald's leering face. Reaching into her bodice, his groping hands found her breasts. 'What do you think you're doing?' she demanded coldly.

'Milkin',' he replied, bringing his face closer and attempting to kiss her. She twisted round savagely and slapped him hard across the face, leaving the red marks of her fingers where his cheek now paled with anger. 'You shouldn't't've don that,' he muttered.

'You shouldn't have touched me; I'm not your plaything.'

'Soon you'll know who be the master 'ere.'

'I've but one master here, and that's your father. My contract's with him; it says nothing of dishonour. If you persist, I shall speak to him.'

'No, you shan't, Grace; one word to Feyther and he shall know all about you, all about you and that Frank o' yourn.

216

Not too proud to unbutton for that un' were 'ee?'

Grace struck him again.

'Mother did warn me against 'ee, but I were ready to forgive and to love 'ee. I did think –'

'You thought what? Oh, don't tell me, I know what you thought, you thought that because I treated you gently, not like your mother, I'd be a walkover; you thought that because I was only a servant – you thought that because I'd loved one person, it would be easy with another. Well, it's not; it's the opposite. Now clear off! Leave me! You've spilt half the milk and I must finish the milking.' Ronald rubbed his cheek, his eyes were clouded with resentment.

'You'll pay for this. Feyther shall see they things that Frank did write to 'ee. I'll give 'ee just one day to think it over. She said you was proud; she said you be too proud to give in to me, but I'll not take no for an answer.'

'*She* said? Who is *she*? Did someone put you up to this?'

'Never you mind.' And he was gone, and Grace was left wondering what Mrs Coyte would say when she noticed that the milk was short that morning; it had spattered her shoes and lost itself in the straw bedding.

As soon as an opportunity offered, Grace ran up to her room, opened the sea-chest and knelt beside it. Throwing its contents on the floor, she sought the packet of letters. They were not there.

When she looked up, Ronald was standing in the doorway. The letters she sought were in one of his hands and he was tapping them significantly into the palm of the other. Grace sprang up and tried to wrest them away from him, but he was much the stronger. Slipping the packet inside his shirt, he pinioned her wrists and smiled a knowing smile at her. Grace gave up the struggle. He released her and she retreated to the bed where she sat with her head in her hands. She appeared to be weeping.

'Well, what's it to be?' he demanded.

'I didn't think you'd stoop to this,' she told him in a broken voice. 'I thought you liked me. I liked you too, do you know that? Do you have to spoil it?' For a moment Ronald seemed

217

to weaken and give in to a wave of compassion. Her red eyes, her downturned mouth affected him. Then he straightened again.

'If you like me, if you love me, 'twill be all the easier.' He closed the door and approached her. She stood up quickly and went to the window where the mill-wheel turned and turned.

'I will not love you. I *did* care for you. Now, what can I do but submit? No, not now, do not touch me now. Your father and mother are below, they will hear us.'

'When?'

'Tomorrow they will go to market. Give me the letters and you shall have your way.'

'Can I believe you? Do I have your promise?' She nodded and turned to him. He was astonished at the change in her, she seemed to have softened amazingly, his toughness had paid off. She put out a hand and touched his cheek.

'I hurt you, didn't I, I'm sorry. You will be gentle with me, won't you? Now let me take the letters.' Delicately, she unbuttoned his shirt and slipped her hand inside. He felt the coolness of it on his skin, exciting him. He caught her by the shoulders, trying to embrace her. She gave him a peck on the cheek. 'There, there, poor darling, you'll soon be better,' and she wriggled free. 'Tomorrow, when they are gone to market,' she whispered. 'Now go, don't let them get suspicious.'

When he had left, she barred the door and sat on the bed, counting the letters. They were all there. Why hadn't she burned them? What had made her imagine that her room here was her own and would remain inviolate? Her thoughts went round and round like the turns of the mill-wheel. Langstone Mill was determined to grind her small, exceedingly small.

As night fell, Grace let herself out of the house silently. She carried the heavy chest on her shoulder with one arm and a bulky bag in the other. Without hesitation, she took the track that led past the dyke and plunged deep into the woods along the estuary. The grassy ride was littered with branches torn from the creaking trees and she stumbled often. She had no lantern to guide her steps and the low, racing clouds blanketed out all but the dimmest of light. More than once she dropped her burdens, but she gathered them up and proceeded. There could be no turning back.

When, at last, she broke free of the woods, she found herself at the top of a series of sloping meadows beyond which was the indistinct outline of the eastern headland on the one side and the Back on the other. The grumbling surf could be heard, almost felt, but showed as only a broad strip of pallid confusion. Where the land met the sea, the rectangular bulk of a small, two-chimneyed cottage stood out black and firm upon the surrounding greyness. But what made the cottage even more prominent was the amber glow, the only light in the whole landscape, that came from a window low down in its left-hand corner.

Grace hastened towards it. The wet meadow-grass clung to her skirts and a herd of inquisitive bullocks crowded in on her till she stamped her foot and shouted at them, making them break and run. Though she fought down her weariness and fear, she could not help feeling uneasy. She had escaped Ronald, she had the pretext she had been waiting for to approach Jan King, but what new experience was she running to?

As she approached Armouth Pool, the memory of her brother Frank came flooding back to her. She heard him laugh. It was as though he were there beside her, laughing at the elements as he had laughed at life. She stopped and looked: he was not there, but the place was full of him. Close behind her now were the ramshackle sheds where the fishermen kept their gear. A rough canvas patch, made of an old sail, was breaking free of the roof and flapping madly. Although she knew there could be no justification for it, she could not help peering into the shadows between the sheds, fearing to see someone, with pale dead face, lurking there.

There was no curtain across the cottage window. The light from within revealed a pattern of streaked grime and salt. Dimly visible through it was a small bare room, sketchily furnished with cheap deal furniture. On the table lay a knife, a hunk of cheese and an earthenware mug. Clothes were scattered on one chair in some disorder. In the fireplace set in the left-hand wall, a small pile of driftwood flared and spat as it burned low. Alongside it, hunched in another comfortless wooden chair with his back to her, sat a figure. He was not reading, there was no light for that. He might have been dozing, but his head had not dropped forward as sleepers' heads do. The firelight showed him only in outline and his shadow wavered across the room. He seemed utterly wrapped up in his solitude. She waited for what seemed a long time for the slightest gesture. There was none: he might have been carved in stone. She marvelled at his patience; the hours must pass slowly here.

She shivered. Now that she had stopped walking, the rain felt colder and the chill breeze was sneaking under her cloak. Dropping her bundle, she raised her hand and scratched at the glass with her fingernails.

At first there was no movement; he seemed to be trying to rouse himself from some deep reverie, turning his head slowly to face her. Even then, there was no immediate recognition. But he showed no sign of anxiety, though he might well have been wary of a visitor at that hour in so remote a place. Although his face was turned directly towards her, she was not sure he had seen her. She scratched the glass again. This time he rose, lit a candle at the fire and came so close to his side of the window that their faces were almost touching.

The face that examined Grace through the glass was familiar to her; it had the same deep-set, penetrating eyes close set on either side of a sharp nose, the same whiskered cheeks, the same expressive mouth. Now, instead of being petrified with horror as she remembered them from the incident on the cliff top, his features showed astonishment and concern.

'Come on in quick, maid, you'm soakin'!' he exclaimed as he wrenched the rickety door open. 'Come on in, you'll catch your death out there! 'Ere, give us that chest. 'Ow've 'ee managed to carry that stuff so far? Come on in! What be keepin' 'ee? Come on in and close the door.' Grace lingered outside, shaking with cold. Though she wanted to enter, first a bargain had to be struck.

'I'll not jump out of the frying pan into the fire.'

'What do you mean?'

'Can I trust you? Will you respect me?'

'Course I will, Grace, you knows me. But why 'ave you runned from Langstone Mill?'

'I could not stay there.'

'Why?'

'Young Ronald – and I thought that maybe you – you said that if ever I –'

'Ronald! The young devil – I'll whip un for 'ee – I'll whip un to an inch of 'is life – I'll kill un if you wants me to. Abuse you, did 'ee?'

'He would have done, had I stayed.'

'Well, that bain't goin' to happen to 'ee 'ere. Come on in, Grace, and welcome.'

'It'll be a bargain then,' said Grace, setting down her chest inside the doorway. 'Can I have your hand on it, will you swear that it won't be worse than at Langstone?'

'Out of the frying pan –' Jan repeated her expression. 'Well, you needn't worry.'

'Oh, but I do,' said Grace, gauging the firm clasp of his hand. 'You're a man, aren't you? I must have a room to myself. There's to be no pretence of love between us. I wouldn't be running from Ronald to be throwing myself at you, now would I?'

From the moment she entered the house, Grace seemed to dominate it. No longer was it his father's or his mother's kitchen, or his own even. In minutes the table was tidy, the clothes were hung by the door and Jan had been set to work stoking the fire.

Once everything in the kitchen was ordered to her satisfaction, Grace sat down at the table with her chin in her hands and looked at him with a kind of elfin twist to her lips as she spoke. 'You know, Jan, I think I may have misjudged you. I've a proposition to put to you tomorrow, a business proposition.

221

Meanwhile, it's time to sleep, will you show me my chamber?'

'Can't you tell me now?'

'I'm tired, doesn't it show? Tomorrow will be time enough. There's no hurry – unless you're anxious to be rid of me.'

When he had shown her to her room, Jan sat by the fire again. He could not sleep. Nothing had prepared him for this, though he had dreamed of Grace often. Now, he wondered, what would she be proposing that they do together? Whatever it was, he knew he would do it, so long as she stayed there at Armouth. This hearth was already warm with her presence.

Next morning, when Grace Pensilva woke, the house was silent. She went to the window in her nightgown and saw an unsuspected world. Although she had lived close to the sea all her life, within a mile at most and had, in recent times at Langstone Mill, slept within two hundred yards of the highest tides that mounted the estuary, this awakening at Armouth, on the shore of the open sea, was a revelation.

All night long the surf had worried at the arched shingle bank called the Back, the broad hump that sheltered Armouth Pool from the Channel swell. The waves had stumbled over the bar, curling into the cove where the boatsheds stood and Jan King's boats lay hauled up on the grass. The scend of the wave running along the beach had swept it clean and patterned it with fan-like markings flecked with flowers of foam. Only the topmost lip where the sand met rock and grass was striped with weed and jetsam. Here and there giddy flocks of oyster-catchers and curlew wheeled and piped, or ran nimble-footed after the sandhoppers. The grass at the beach head had been blasted flat by the gale and was still glistening with wetness. Beyond the shallow pool the flats stretched in a gradually diminishing pattern of water interlocking with sand and, through the midst of it, swinging in bold arcs, ran the dark hurrying river, swollen with the last of the falling tide.

It was all new, like a fresh creation, made overnight by the sea out of its bounding elements. The sky was full of new shapes, tufted billowing clouds of buff and white, coursing over the dappled water. The sea itself, smoothed under the freshening offshore wind, varied in tone between sombre purple and the clearest aquamarine. Grace threw up the sash window and breathed in the fresh, exciting air.

Far off, beside the low tide mark, a lonely figure was strolling among the pools. Suddenly, for no apparent purpose, he ran, flailing his arms like windmills. A host of lazy gulls stirred up by his progress, hovered and soared into a vast column. The running man was Jan King and all the estuary was his kingdom.

When Jan returned from his excursion he found Grace down by the boats which were in their winter station, pulled up on the grass beyond the tideline. She was standing beside the abandoned stove-in gig and looked unexpectedly gay and bright. There was none of the reproach he expected her to associate with the craft that had been salvaged with Ivor Triggs lying across it. Her eyes shone; the breeze tugged at her hair; her cheeks were glistening. He was fascinated by the way her white collar turned up against her neck and a tendril of hair waved across her eyes. 'Shall we go to sea then?' she asked.

'Not in that,' he answered.

'We'll use one of the others.'

'Don't you know what season it is?' he countered patronizingly. She ignored that, persisting.

'If you can get out there soon and find him, we can get started.'

'Find who?'

'The Frenchman.'

'Now, Grace, you bain't serious, be 'ee?'

'We'll need to find him before we can set up in business.' Jan King looked down and kicked at the turf.

'Don't count on me for that, I've swore to stay away from that trade. Weren't it enough for 'ee to lose your Frank? 'Twas enough for me, I 'aven't forgot, even if you 'ave. You said you'd never forgive me and now you'm sayin' us should start again together.'

'How else can we hope to escape from Harberscombe? What other way is there to make money? Don't you want to

223

become someone? What's the use of life on a treadmill?'

'I be 'appy enough fishin'. There bain't nothin' wrong with earnin' an honest livin'.'

'An honest living,' she repeated with heavy irony. 'That's an existence at best, that's what they want us to earn lest we get rich like them and dine off fine linen. There's no way in this world, Jan King, to better yourself with honest labour.'

'You'm fine one to talk. You tries to 'ave it both ways. First you blames me for what 'appened to your brother. I tell you, Grace, that did sicken me as it did you. Now you wants to lead me to it. Well I won't, I tell you. I vowed I'd never take to the trade again. One death be enough for me.'

'Are you afraid then? They say your father was a bold man and would cross the bar in any weather.'

'They say that, do they? Well, Feyther be dead and I be livin'.'

'No need to get stirred up,' said Grace quietly. ''Tis no more than a proposition, no doubt you'll be happy to see the back of me.'

'I didn't say that.'

'Well, think about it. Now, how about going to sea. It's a fine morning and you can try me out for a partner.' Jan looked seaward, he was evidently tempted.

''Tis safe enough now with the risin' tide, but the swell will break on the bar when the ebb starts runnin'.'

'We'll think about that later, when the time comes. For the moment, let's have some breakfast. Come up to the house and I'll make it for you.'

He found it strange to sit in his own kitchen and be served. It reminded him of the time his mother had been living. The house was warm, Grace had built up the fire and she had cleared away the cobwebs. Now, as she sat opposite him serving their porridge, she smiled at him and he felt that his long penance was over. A miracle had happened, Grace had turned to him for friendship and assistance. Oddly enough, he had Ronald Coyte to thank for that. Such were the curious workings of providence. He had never felt happier.

*　　*　　*

Diana Lackland did not appear at church next week. Optimus sought her vainly in her pew beneath the pulpit. After the service he approached Mrs Treebie discreetly and inquired the reason. 'The mistress be indisposed,' she told him.

'Is it serious? I'll walk over and see her immediately.'

'She said she were not to be disturbed, not by no one.'

Optimus was flabbergasted. He could accept the idea of Diana Lackland's being unwell, but as for her not wanting to see him, that was unthinkable.

'She can't mean it.'

'Indeed she can. If you goes round there pesterin' her, you'll find the door locked and bolted. She told my man Treebie to do it as I left, I 'eard 'er.'

'But what's wrong? I'm most concerned, I *must* see her.'

'Take my advice, young man,' murmured Mrs Treebie, self-importantly, 'leave well alone when you bain't wanted. 'Tiddn' no good to go after 'er. 'Aven't you seen Parson Lackland? 'Aven't you noticed what a foul mood 'ee be in?'

'What's that got to do with me? All the more reason for his wife to want sympathy.'

'Not from you, Mr Shute. I can't make meself no clearer. Mrs Lackland don't 'ave no need o' *your* consolation.' Even then, it proved hard for Optimus to take in. He felt an emptiness, the emptiness of rejection. Was this how Jan had felt? Worse probably.

Once Mrs Treebie had left he stepped into the porch where Mr Lackland was pressing the hands of the last parishoners. Optimus hovered until they had left.

'I'm sorry to hear of your wife's indisposition. Will you give her my best wishes for a quick recovery?'

'Indisposition?' exclaimed Lackland vaguely. 'But she's fit as a fiddle. When I left her she was playing piano duets with that new fellow Carfax. Said he was too tired from his journey to don his vestments, wanted to ease him in gently. I don't argue with her, learnt my lesson long ago.'

So that was it. Optimus mumbled something and blundered away. He hadn't expected to be so affected. But he was jealous, jealous of Diana Lackland. He didn't admire her, he

225

didn't love her, not in the way he loved his dream woman, but he *was* jealous.

What did he feel for her? Was it more than lust? He tried to remember Diana's face, but it would not come, only a mocking smile. But her body, the musky odour of it, the softness. And she had offered it to him, had he but known how to take her. Were all women like this? Was Grace Pensilva? No, he could not believe Grace capable of cheap flirtations.

For the first time in his life Optimus realized that his emotions were out of control. He was angry, jealous of a stranger, infatuated with a woman who rejected him. He clenched his fists and set off, half running, half walking, down the lane to the estuary.

When he emerged from the woods, a flight of startled mallard rose from the reed beds, followed by two sharp detonations that brought a couple of them tumbling downwards. A water spaniel went splashing after them and a man appeared from a hide in which he had been lying in wait. He waved to Optimus and came towards him after collecting the dead birds from the spaniel. Optimus was none too pleased; he would have preferred to have remained alone with his chagrin.

'Thought I recognized you,' shouted the man, who turned out to be Charles Barker. 'Here,' he said as he approached, 'you can take one of these home and share it with Dr Cornish. How's he keeping these days anyway?'

'Not too bright,' replied Optimus. 'There must be something wrong with him.'

'Sorry to hear it, but you know what the Bible says: "others he saved, himself he cannot save", that's always been the physician's lot. But you're not looking too pecker yourself; to tell the truth, you look as if the sky had just fallen on you. What's the trouble, crossed in love, young feller?'

Optimus shook his head. 'Just one of those days.'

'Well, I'll not press you further, but I know the symptoms. Master Frederick was like that once, mooning around all over the place. Come on, accompany me up the river; I've something to show you; I've found those letters. Now I've thought it over, you might as well see them; what harm can it do, they're both beyond redemption.'

Optimus trailed along unenthusiastically. Ten days ago, he would have jumped at the opportunity; now Grace Pensilva seemed only a shadow. Half his mind had become absorbed by the need for Diana Lackland. He found it difficult to concentrate on what Charles Barker was saying.

'That Scully at Langstone Mill,' the Steward went on, partly talking to himself, 'I never wanted him to have the place; nasty piece of work is Scully; it was Miss Nancy who insisted on it, said she owed it to him. The man's nothing but a layabout. Still, she could have done worse, she could have told me to reinstall the Coytes in there after her brother threw them out. But Ronald was enough for her, she was happy enough to have them out of the way; that Janet Coyte had a sharp tongue and didn't approve of how Nancy made off with her little darling.' They had crossed the dyke below the mill from which a fine thread of smoke rose from one chimney. Barker paused and looked back. 'You know Scully, of course. His child's a pupil of yours. But I suppose he hasn't told you what his role was in the preventives. He hasn't told you about his voyage to Malta either, I'll warrant. Scully doesn't give away information for nothing. He knows more about Grace Pensilva than most, but he's not proud of it. Grace made a fool of him, and he in turn made Mr Hawkins, the revenue collector, look foolish. He had reason enough to hate her and he didn't spare his hatred.'

'She got off scot-free when they shot Jack Lugger at the bridge, didn't she?'

'She did more than that, she masterminded a grand coup that had the Revenue all at sixes and sevens. Hasn't anyone ever told you about it; didn't Dr Cornish describe it?' At any other time, Optimus would have been astonished and delighted by the way Charles Barker was opening up and telling him all he knew; today he listened with only half an ear.

'This whole place is full of Grace Pensilva,' Barker announced as they crossed a narrow footbridge over the river.

227

'Over there, in those meadows on the edge of the park, out of sight of the great house, Frederick Genteel used to sit on a log and wait for her. She would row up the river in the gig, on the tide. Perhaps that was how he first got to know her, when she was learning the lie of the land for the smugglers. Be that as it may, it became a habit. Frederick would take his fishing rod – he never caught anything – and stroll away from Leet to the river. I saw them there many a time; he would bring a book in his pocket and they would read a little and talk, it was always very proper. I was in the secret, of course; Frederick used to confide in me, I was really the only friend he had here. He told me she was a woman of extraordinary sensibility. I think he was more than a little smitten with her, but he was rather unworldly, he didn't know how to exploit the situation.' As he walked, Charles Barker kept casting quick, almost apprehensive glances at the tall front of the great house which they were now passing. Optimus also scanned it, but there was no sign of a face in its windows. Nancy Genteel, who had inherited the Leet estate on the death of her father Lord Mayberry, now lived there alone, a recluse attended only by the master of her stables.

'Here we are,' said Barker when they approached the gate-house. 'You'll come in, won't you? But you're a dull dog today, seem to have lost the art of conversation. Women! Women! They're always at the back of it. Nothing like a woman to drive a man into the dumps and distract him. Thank God I've escaped it, at least so far . . .'

Optimus could see no better alternative.

The sea was smooth, with long gentle undulations that sucked at the rocks alongside where Jan King was rowing towards the western headland, making long kissing noises. Grace lolled in the stern enjoying the unfolding seascape as they opened up the long vistas beyond the Barrrow. Apart from their small boat the bay was absolutely empty and, except for Jan's house on the shore, there was no sign of human activity.

'There, it's not so bad as you pretended it would be, is it?' she asked with a smile. Jan nodded. He had said little but he had spent most of his time watching her, only glancing over his shoulder now and again to check his course as he rowed with a long, easy stroke. 'Isn't it wonderful to have it all to ourselves; it's as though all the world were ours. Do you think we'll be able to get along together?'

'I 'opes so.'

'Will you have the gig mended if I give you the money?'

'I'll think about it.'

'I can leave if you don't want me; I can go to Leet House and go into service.'

'Don't rush me. 'Tis too much of a turn around for me to take in easy.'

Their boat had passed the place where the storepots were moored in summer, holding the lobsters and crabs till the smack sailed round to fetch them. Ahead was a rocky islet, split from the point by a narrow gully. As they pulled clear of its lee, the wind caught them, a chill northwesterly blast that rippled the water as it sped seaward. 'Time us turned back,' announced Jan.

'What's that out there?' asked Grace, pointing over his shoulder into the part of the bay that had been revealed when they passed the headland. A yawl or ketch, under reduced sail, was coming up from the westward. 'Couldn't that be the Frenchman? What's the captain's name, Frank told me, but I've forgotten it?'

'Caradec,' said Jan, 'but I doubt if that be 'im, not at this season.'

'Can't you row out and see? He'll be passing not far from here.'

'I don't know. We ought to be getting back if we don't want to catch the ebb on the bar.'

'Please.'

'All right, but not for long.' Almost immediately he regretted it; the wind strengthened rapidly as they cleared the coastline. And it was clear that the ship was sailing so fast they could never intercept it. Jan lay on his oars after a hard pull and watched it make off into the distance.

'Well, was it him?'

229

'Aye, that was Caradec, that was his boat the *Ar Mor* all right.'

'Why didn't you try harder to catch him?'

'You'll see why when we start goin' 'omealong.'

As soon as their boat turned up into the wind, which Jan achieved with difficulty, spray started flying over the weather bow and, although he pulled manfully at the oars, they advanced painfully slowly. Jan was strong, but at times the wind was stronger and the small chop which had formed offshore almost stopped their progress. Jan thought quickly about the possible alternatives. They could run off to the eastward and try to get ashore further up the bay, but there was only one river and its bar was probably even more dangerous than the one at Armouth. They could press on slowly, in their present direction, but they could not hope to reach Armouth bar and the shelter behind the Back before the ebb was running strongly. 'You've got us into a proper pickle,' he muttered angrily.

'Move over, I'll help you,' said Grace, coming to the centre thwart beside him. Even that brief change-over made them lose several yards, but the weight of two rowers made more difference than Jan had expected. Grace pulled with a will and they began gaining, shutting in the coastline beyond the Barrow gradually but steadily.

Even so, their troubles were not over. Without looking round when they slid into the sheltered water under the headland, Jan could hear the swell breaking on the bar. And nearby to the eastward, where a submerged reef was nearing the surface as the tide fell, he could see other long waves rearing and breaking. It was not going to be easy to return to Armouth. However, staying out at sea in the night air, scantily clad as they were, was not to be considered. 'I'll take 'er now,' he announced. ''Twill be safer. You stand by with the bucket.'

For the first time, Grace felt uneasy. She had not understood, as Jan had, the sleeping power in the quiet swell they had found on the outward journey. Now, undercut by the fast-running ebb, the waves were rearing steep and high before tumbling headlong in a welter of foam. They seemed to be breaking right across the bar, making it impassable. And then, over her shoulder, she heard the roar of an enormous comber boiling over the reef.

Jan King had been sitting watching. He had positioned their boat just beyond the surf on the bar, where the river crossed it. But he was observing the reef where the waves succeeded each other steadily. Jan was watching for a certain pattern; they were not identical, there were spells of huge swells and there were lulls between them.

Grace sat clutching the rim of the bucket, perched on the stern thwart. They were on their own. There was no one to be seen on the shores of the estuary who might give the alarm or try to rescue them. But in fact, there was no hope of rescue: all the other boats were high and dry and, in any case, the surf was so high they would fare no better. Jan's face was impassive, almost relaxed. Grace realized that he was in his element, he knew the danger, he was familiar with it and was calculating it. If it were not for one thing, she might have admired him.

The comber which had just broken on the reef subsided astern of them and they felt it pass under their boat in a strong undulation. A few yards behind Jan's back the swell reared suddenly where the sandy bar shallowed. With a crash, it tumbled forward while a wind-whipped fringe of spray flew off the top and curled backwards. Jan waited to see what the next wave would be as it crossed the reef. It was much smaller. Before it had time to cross the intervening stretch of deep water, he leant back on his oars, making them bend with his determined effort. The swell caught up with the boat slowly and they were in the first of the backwash from the big comber before it reached them.

Although it was smaller, this new wave still towered above them. Its steep forward face was flecked with white and a crest was forming along its summit. Jan struggled to set his boat exactly at right angles to it before the stern rose and it was carried shoreward. The wave picked them up abruptly, their stern was so high that Grace had to cling to the transom to

231

avoid losing her seat. The bow creamed into the backwash, threatening to dig in and pitchpole them. They raced forward like a sledge on a mountain slope, with Jan heaving at the oars in an attempt to keep the boat straight. For a while he was successful.

And then, despite his violent efforts, it began to yaw to larboard, approaching the massive bulk of the half-sunken Back. The boat was traversing the wave at a tremendous velocity and heeling steeply to starboard. Meanwhile, the breaking crest was looming over them.

'Jump to larboard or we've 'ad it!' cried Jan as the lee bow began to take in water. The boat righted itself under their combined weight, but the crest swept over them. Half-waterlogged, the boat, checked in mid flight, hesitated a mere ten yards from the Back and lurched over the top of the wave.

'Bail! Bail for your life!' cried Jan, seizing the oars and wrenching the swamped boat back into the right direction. Grace did as she was told, mechanically, incessantly, with one eye over her shoulder at the next wave which was fast approaching. There was no time to empty the bilge, they would have to take the wave as best they could.

It came, and the water rushed into the bow of their boat, slowing it almost immediately. Grace waited for the crest to smash down upon her, but it did not; the wave was partly spent before it reached them. Heeling helplessly to starboard, they were carried towards the Back, so close that its individual pebbles were clearly visible. There was nothing they could do – the boat did not respond to the oars. Was this the way it would end? Grace looked at Jan, her companion in this crazy escapade, was it thus that they were fated to die together?

And then, as suddenly as they had been taken up in the cataract of tumbling surf, they were through it. Behind the Back, the Pool was almost calm and all danger was past.

Grace and Jan stood facing each other, almost knee-deep in bilge water. The tension had marked both their faces, they were bedraggled, slow-moving. Jan raised one hand and wagged an admonishing finger at her. Grace tried a shy smile.

'We made it,' she asserted in justification.

'Us made it,' he repeated. 'But whose damn fool idea was it anyway?'

'Mine,' said Grace stoutly. 'I'm not ashamed of it. You were splendid, you were magnificent. You look like a man, Jan King.'

'And you do look like a wet rag, Grace Pensilva,' laughed Jan, with unexpected good humour. She took her bucket and flung its contents over him.

'So do you, Jan King.' He reached out, taking her by the shoulders, shaking her. When he stopped, he leant back and looked at her.

'You'm a brave girl. Grace Pensilva.'

'Brave as a man?'

'Braver.'

'Shall we be partners then? Will you give me your hand upon it?'

'Do you want to stay at Armouth, along of a poor fisherman?'

She clasped his hand warmly and he forgot the waterlogged boat, his wet clothes and his recent experience.

'Jan King won't be poor for long; I'll see to that. Now, row us back to the cottage, we must dry ourselves if we're to escape pneumonia. I'll bail till we get there.'

Jan King could hardly believe it: a day ago he had been solitary, now he had this exciting, unpredictable woman for a partner. And her wondrous body showed through her wet clothes as she toiled with the bucket. Luck was running his way at last.

2

A black bulk emerged from behind the reeds and came up the winding channel. The night was almost pitch dark and only a faint sheen showed where the flood tide was running. Gradually, the lump defined itself into a boat shape, with a rower standing amidships controlling it with occasional quiet dips of the paddles. Apart from the place where she stood, the hull was covered with a tarpaulin, disguising whatever it carried. Where the reeds ended, a new dyke had been built to enclose new water meadows and the channel narrowed suddenly.

'Good evening!' A clear voice came unexpectedly from the right bank among the oak trees.

'Good evening, Frederick,' Grace replied without hesitation.

''Tis a treacherous channel to follow by night; take care, Grace, take care!'

'I'll travel when I wish; there's no law against it.'

'I'd rather you turned back.'

'What's the matter, do you know something?'

'Not for certain.'

'Then keep your worries to yourself.' Grace dipped her oars and propelled the boat onward. After a few hundred yards the tarpaulin in the bows stirred slightly.

'I might 'ave shot 'im,' whispered Jan. ''Ee were askin' for it, callin' out sudden like that.'

'More fool you if you had,' remarked Grace drily. 'Now keep your head down and your mouth shut. We're getting near the place and we want no trouble.'

Grace rowed standing up and facing forward with the oars

crossed in a way she had learned from Frank that was unfamiliar in Devon, but which allowed her to see where she was going. There was little work to do; the last of the tide carried them gently forward. A short distance ahead, to the right, was a clump of trees. Beneath them, there was a patch of intense darkness. The boat emerged into a small pool, where the river widened and cattle came down to drink at low tide. Grace scrutinized the shadows carefully. There was almost imperceptible movement down by the water. She knelt and picked up a brace of pistols which were lying already primed on the thwart beside her. She heard a horse neigh and stamp behind the woodland. Someone on shore gave a low, almost inaudible whistle. She answered it, but her lips were dry and her own whistle was little more than a hiss. However often this procedure was repeated, there was always a period of nail-biting anxiety until she was sure it was not the preventives who awaited her. And Frederick Genteel had tried to dissuade her. She was on his land, within sight of Leet House, but could she count on his protection?

"Ow be the wind?' came a voice.

'Fair from France,' Grace replied with a sigh of relief, recognizing Jack Lugger. He stepped into the shallows in his long boots and took the bow as it grated on the rocky bottom. Behind him, a cluster of diminutive fellows pressed forward.

"Ave you got the stuff?'

'Aye, but have our customers got the money?'

'Give us the bags,' instructed Jack Lugger over his shoulder. 'And Grace, put down they pistols, will you, you'm makin' me nervous.'

'Don't worry, I've never shot a man, not yet.'

'Grace don't need to, she be too blessed clever,' muttered Jan King, sitting up in the bow and beginning to help with the unloading.

'Well done, Jack!' said Grace when the work was finished. 'Your men work with a will, who are they?'

'They be tinners from the mines on the moor, and they've got a terrible thirst on 'em.'

'They won't need telling to hurry home then, will they?

Good night. I'll tell you when it's time for the next cargo.'

They separated swiftly and quietly. Grace guided the boat down the winding stretch near Leet House while Jan sat in the sternsheets and counted the money in the faint starlight that was breaking through the clouds. When they passed the place where Frederick Genteel had hailed them on the way to the meeting place, he looked up: it was deserted.

'You do see too much of that Genteel chap, Grace,' he grumbled. 'I don't like it.'

'You don't have to like it, you're not my keeper. You're not my husband.'

'Look, Grace, you don't 'ave to rub salt in the wound. Just leave 'im alone for a bit, will 'ee? For my sake. 'Aven't I been fair with 'ee? Enough be enough, I won't be made a fool of.'

'And how do you propose to stop it? Would you like me to leave Armouth?'

'Always the same damn question. Course not, but 'aven't us made enough money to call it quits and go off together?'

'Nearly, Jan, but not quite.'

'And we'll go then? You promise?'

'We'll leave Harberscombe for ever.'

'I bain't sure I wants to. Wouldn't you stay with me, I'd be good to 'ee –' As he spoke, the noise of an abrupt fusillade came from up the river where they had been. Jan looked round in alarm, half expecting other shots to ring out around them, but there was silence.

'Shall us go back?' he asked.

'We'd be too late to help them. Tide's too low already. They must fend for themselves.'

'You always 'ave an answer off pat,' he grumbled. 'That be why you 'aven't never fired they pistols.'

'And I don't propose to now. I don't need a death on my conscience. This is business we're engaged in, not slaughter. Come now, take the oars for a bit and pull us back to Armouth.'

''Ee knowed summat, didn' 'ee, your Frederick,' said Jan as he took up the oars. 'Why didn' 'ee say so outright. Why didn' 'ee tell us not to go further.'

'Because he knew I wouldn't've listened. He knows his Grace Pensilva better than you do.'

Optimus smiled to himself. He had become so absorbed in the writing that Mrs. Lackland had entirely slipped from his consciousness. Grace Pensilva, however, was a person he could rely on. She was not playing cat and mouse with him like the Vicar's wife, she was playing cat and mouse with Jan King. Optimus could feel the stifling fog of jealousy that lay between Jan and Grace as their boat dropped back to Armouth with the tide.

As he stood there at his desk, chewing his pen, he tried to put himself into Jan's shoes. Did he trust her? Not completely. Though he wanted to, that was certain. No longer was it the memory of her reaction to Frank's death that made him uneasy. No, the real trouble was that there was a line, an invisible barrier between them, and it was all of her making. It was this barrier that made him fume at the easy intimacy that existed between her and Frederick Genteel. How long could he live with his idol and never touch her?

Grace was aware of this, she had to be, and indeed the situation was of her own making, but she remained true to herself, invariably so cool, so collected. She had known passion, long ago it seemed now, a passion others condemned as reprehensible, but that was over and she had become restrained, reasonable, calculatingly adventurous and successful, almost as if she had wanted to become a man in a man's world, the man her Frank would have been.

Optimus heard the clock strike. Ten o'clock: he still had time to follow them a little further. He sucked his nib and it clinked against the side of his glass inkwell before taking up its familiar scratching progress across the paper.

Across the road, a light still burned in Dr Cornish's window. The old man seemed scarcely to sleep at all now, but dozed and rambled on at the chimney corner. What was it he had said about not having much time when Optimus had first arrived at Branscombe? He was still alive, wasn't he? But his intellect! A pity he had not learned more from the Doctor while it was still possible. Now he was full of sententious nonsense:

'History explains nothing. At the best, it imposes a kind of order on brute fact and idle hearsay. It is no more than a fairy-tale. History makes us what we are, we listen to our own stories and try to live up to them –' and more of that ilk. So much for the cool, rational, scientific Doctor.

There was a faint jingle of harness and a slither of unshod hooves coming down the hill. Low voices cursing as they came closer. When they stopped in the lane, more whispered conversation. A rattle of gravel against the Doctor's bedroom window, then a short wait. The Doctor's young head, in a nightcap, stuck out of the window. What he saw in the starglow was the slack body slung across the donkey's back, with its hands and feet trailing. Behind the animal and the man who had thrown the gravel, a long line of squat figures and panniered donkeys straggled into the obscurity.

'A man've been 'it,' croaked the spokesman in a hoarse whisper.

'I can see that. Who is he?'

'Never mind that. 'Ee be 'urt bad, 'ee do need attention.'

'Bring him round to the back. I'll open up for you.' As the men carried their wounded comrade across the threshold the Doctor's candle revealed that blood was still dripping from his fingers.

'Bleeding like a stuck pig! Haven't any of you fellows ever heard of a tourniquet? Quick, lay him on the table. One of you draw water and set it on the trivet. Stir up the fire a bit.' Dr Cornish was in control now. The strangers stood around the walls or obeyed him dumbly as he made his preparations. As his mineral oil lamp flared up he saw them for what they were: Ashburton tinners, wild men in torn, earth-stained clothing. And the same spurt of flame revealed the face of the man on the table. Dr Cornish knew him: he was Jack Lugger the rabbit-trapper.

The man was far gone, a pistol ball in a ragged flesh wound and a cutlass slash across his forehead. His face was pale and his breathing shallow, becoming intermittent. He was practically a goner.

Soon the Doctor's forearms were red with blood as he cut away clothing and probed the wound. His patient was so far gone that he seemed to feel almost nothing. Only a feeble groan escaped him. 'He'll have to be left,' Dr Cornish said finally. 'He can't travel.' There was a long silence.

'You'll not 'and 'im over?' said the spokesman doubtfully. 'They'll transport 'im if they don't 'ang 'im.' He was a particularly villainous-looking fellow with a knife in his belt, but this was not what influenced the Doctor's decision. He shook his head.

'He'll be safe here so long as you chaps know how to keep your mouths shut.'

As they shuffled out and trotted off down the lane, he looked at the man on the table. With luck, he would live. As a doctor, Cornish knew he had fulfilled his oath and done his duty, but if the authorities got wind of this, it was going to be particularly bloody, worse than the stain upon his table.

Optimus awoke with his nose stuck into the paper alongside a huge blot where his falling head had overturned the inkwell. He was cold and his neck was stiff. His candle had burnt right down and was guttering.

The lane outside was deserted and silent. Through Dr Cornish's amber window he could make out a corner of the long table. What had Jack Lugger been saying as Optimus slipped across the desk and was jerked back into consciousness? He had to search a long time before it came back to him.

'That woman,' the sick man spat out in a gasping fashion. 'That woman were at the back o' this: that Grace Pensilva.' Surging up through his weakness were anger and spite. For the nonce, he was impotent. Optimus seemed to feel the same exhaustion.

Uncle Bill Terry was sitting splay-legged on his low stool in the cellar he used when making crab-pots. He was absorbed in his work and took some time to hear the noise of shrill

239

voices coming from the Plain. When it continued, he stood up slowly, careful to avoid striking his head on the low beams, and ambled down to observe proceedings. It was part of the advantage of plying an independent trade that he had no hard taskmaster to tell him when he might or might not set his labour down.

The hub of the small group of complaining women was Jan King; they were mobbing him like a crowd of rooks about a buzzard.

'Jack Lugger be at death's door!' Uncle Bill heard one of them say. 'And whose fault be it? Why, yourn and that cursed Grace Pensilva's.' On closer approach, Uncle Bill saw that the chief tormentor was Janet Coyte. It didn't surprise him that she was employing her sharp tongue, but he was astonished to hear about Jack Lugger.

'What be the trouble?' he asked, trying to be conciliatory.

'My Jack didn' come 'ome last night,' declared Mrs Coyte, 'that's what! 'Ee were off on that moonlightin' trade with Jan King 'ere and 'is fancy woman. The preventives 'ave shot un, but Jan and Grace did get clear away without a scratch. That be what I'd call a coincidence.'

"Ee bain't dead, be 'ee?' asked Uncle Bill solicitously.

'Near 'nuff,' continued Mrs Coyte angrily. 'Jack Lugger be my brother. I never 'eld with 'is carryin' on, but blood be thicker'n water. 'Ee wouldn't never 'ave gone back to it if 'tweren't for that Grace Pensilva. Jan King do follow that maid about like a sheep, 'ee do. There bain't a bit of a man in un.'

'No, I don't!' cried Jan King. 'I does what I likes and if that be smugglin', why, that be my business. And Jack Lugger didn' need askin' twice to take an 'and in it; 'ee bain't backward in comin' forward where money be concerned.'

"Ow was it you and Grace got clear away last night when Jack Lugger caught it?' demanded another woman.

'Us weren't in the same place, us was 'arf way down the river; us couldn't go back.'

'And no one never 'inted, no one ever suggested, no one tried to tip 'ee off that there were trouble brewin'?' the woman persisted. Jan King shook his head.

'Look 'ere, I never left Jack Lugger in the lurch, 'tiddn' my nature.' It was clear to Uncle Bill that Jan King was full of blind anger and was close to tears. He pushed into the circle and dragged the younger man out of it.

'Get on 'omealong!' he ordered the woman. 'I'll talk to un.'

''Aven't you made all the money you want to already?' he demanded once they were safely tucked away among his crab-pots.

'There bain't never enough,' said Jan.

'No, I suppose there bain't. But you was 'appy enough, I thought, when us was partners. Why couldn't us 'ave kept on with that? It were legal, nobody got shot doin' it.'

'She didn' want to. She 'ad this idea 'bout smugglin' and makin' money.'

'Well, she weren't no different from 'er brother before 'er. And what, may I ask, do you get out of it?'

'I gets me share.'

'That bain't what I mean and you knows it. The question be this: be Jan and Grace livin' together as man and wife?' Uncle Bill studied Jan's face thoughtfully. 'I guessed as much,' he added. 'Well, let me tell 'ee this: it did grieve me when you said us should no longer be partners, but it do grieve me even more to see 'ee now. That Pensilva maid don't bode no good for 'ee. Go 'ome and tell 'er so if you care to, I don't mind. But it must be make or break now, while there be still time.'

Uncle Bill watched Jan set off into the rain for Armouth and wondered how it would turn out. Would a worm turn? He could imagine all the fine angry phrases Jan was rehearsing in his head but, when he saw her, would they be like all the others, turned to dust in his mouth? What he did not imagine was that Jan would find his cottage deserted.

' "There was a time when meadow, field and stream –" ' Frederick Genteel began reciting, with his closed book clasped in his lap, one finger separating the pages.

' "Meadow, *grove* and stream," ' Grace corrected him. Genteel stole a peek at the printed page.

' "Meadow, grove and stream" – you *are* a pedant

Grace – "The earth and every common sight –" '

' "To me did seem," ' she continued.

' "Apparelled in celestial light," ' he smiled. ' "The glory and the freshness of a dream" – How wonderful Wordsworth is! How well he expresses himself in the language of common folk!'

'Common folk, what do you know of common folk, Frederick Genteel?'

'More than you think!' He straightened himself on the grassy bank where he sat facing her. They were concealed in a small natural arbour overlooking a corner of Leet Park and a stretch of the River Arun. Today, more than ever before, Grace's eyes had that bewitching sparkle that made him catch his breath and stumble over his quotations. He thought back to their first real encounter after the brushes he had had with her at the hunt and the harvest home. Shortly after he heard she had left Langstone Mill, he saw her rowing up the narrow River Arun among the flags and willows at the lower end of Leet Park. Turning away strangers was properly the game-keeper's work, but Genteel was almost certain of the intruder's identity when he strolled with deliberate non-chalance down to the water.

'I ought to be warning you not to come trespassing on my estate, Miss Pensilva,' he told her with a humorous glint in his eye. She lay on her oars and looked back at him solemnly.

'You'll do no such thing, Mr Genteel. This is tidal water I'm travelling on. The sea is everyone's highway; I'll ask leave of no one to use it.'

'Well, if I can't prevent you from crossing my park I must make the best of it. You won't give me a fee, I know that, but perhaps you'll accord me a favour. Will you stop and talk a little? I wanted to tell you how sorry I was that I offended you at the harvest home. It was not my intention. I was trying to be helpful. You're welcome here at Leet at any time, and not in any dubious capacity. Won't you step ashore a moment and take a walk? The trees are lovely at this time of year; I'd like to share them with you.'

Grace hesitated, but complied gracefully, and he felt a

242

peculiar yearning as her cool hand slipped into his when he helped her ashore. That had been months ago and was the first of many meetings. Frederick would linger by the riverside, now with his fishing rod, now with a book. From the first he sensed that there was another motive for her visits, she was not merely rowing for pleasure as she claimed, but spying out the land for another activity. He refrained from questioning her on this. There was a tacit compact between them: they could converse on a thousand and one topics, but Grace's personal affairs were not to be alluded to. Gradually they drifted into an easy intimacy, a marriage of true minds that he had never experienced with another woman. Their seemingly chance encounters and long bantering conversations on the fringes of Leet Park had come to mean more to him than he cared to admit to himself. Her faintly sad expression, her lovely face bewitched him. He sighed as he listened to her next assertion.

'Harberscombe folk don't say "grove".'

'I suppose not. But you do, and you're from Harberscombe. That's what so remarkable about you, Grace, you're so different. There's no one else round here with whom I can have a serious conversation.'

'There's your sister.'

'You don't know her, Grace. If you did, you wouldn't say that. Education doesn't imply sensibility. What about Charles Barker, you'll ask. Well, Charles is a nice old stick, one of the best, but a dull dog when it comes to poetry. No, I don't know how I'd stand it here without you to talk to. You're the one bright ray in a dull landscape.'

'Why did you come home if you find Leet so unappealing?'

'Not much choice. Their Lordships had no more use for me as a captain. Father had squandered so much money there was none for my allowance. I tried another job but didn't like it. So there was nothing for it but to come here and try to put the estate on its feet again. In a way, I like it really. There's something gratifying about seeing improvements made: new barns, strong gates, well-bred stock. It's heart-warming. Not like the blood and thunder I knew earlier. If I'd been hotter on

243

prize money than glory, I'd have been a rich man after all the fights I've been through, but I wasn't and it's no use mumbling sour grapes about it. If I hadn't come home I'd never have met Grace Pensilva.' He stopped speaking and his words hung in the air. He had never thought to be so explicit. She was looking at him with that cool stare of hers. It was not unfriendly. In fact he sometimes thought she returned his affection. Since he had known her, he had studied that face often until he knew it better than his own. Now, he looked away towards the river, unable to meet her eyes for fear of betraying untoward emotion.

'But you'd leave again if you had the means, wouldn't you?'

'If you must know, I've had a letter from my old friend Captain Fell, he's Governor of Malta. Fell says he can offer me something to keep body and soul together. He wants me to marry his daughter Felicity. It's tempting: the life, the sunshine, the wine, old friends – but I'll not take it. Not while I've you to talk to.' Grace's brow clouded briefly and she looked off into the distance.

'Don't turn down a good offer for my sake. I won't be here for ever.'

'What do you mean?'

'I'm taking your advice, giving up the trade, it's becoming too dangerous. Oh, I know you've been sheltering me, I realize you've been keeping the preventives off your estate, but you can't do that indefinitely. Now that they've seen one party and tasted blood, there will be no stopping them. So I'm turning it in; it was good while it lasted. Now I'll leave Harberscombe.'

'Where shall you go?'

'I don't know – somewhere.'

'And Jan King, is he to go with you? I have been meaning to ask, what is he to you exactly?'

'My partner.'

He leant across and took her hand, meeting her grey eyes solemnly.

'Dear Grace, if I were to ask you – if I were to suggest –'

She in turn reached across and put a finger to his lips.

244

'Hush!' she reproved him. 'You must not say it. I should be bad for you. You must not even think it. You are Captain the Honourable Frederick Genteel, son and heir to Lord May-berry. Take Captain Fell's offer if you cannot abide Leet House, and forget me.'

'That I shall never do. You ask too much, Grace Pensilva. But go away you cannot, Leet will be impossible without you. Can't you see? I want you to live here.'

'Cross your threshold as a servant I will not. The offer is unthinkable.'

'But, Grace –'

'I must leave now.' She rose abruptly. For an instant he thought he had seen confusion at the back of her eyes. Did she really know her true feelings for him? He followed her, moving stiffly for his leg still troubled him. In a moment she would have left the arbour and be lost to him, perhaps for ever. She turned. 'What was the last thing you did before you came here?' she asked unexpectedly.

'Nothing I want to talk about now. I'll tell you later.' He dropped his book, caught her by the elbows and held her fiercely.

'Promise me something,' he almost shouted, 'promise me you won't forget me.'

'I'll not forget you.' He pulled her closer and leaned down until their brows were touching.'

' "A slumber did my spirit seal",' he began.

' "I had no human fears",' she responded.

' " She seemed a thing that could not feel," ' he went on.

' "The touch of earthly years," ' she seemed to sigh.

' "No motion has she now, no force" '

' "She neither hears nor sees" '

' "Rolled round in earth's diurnal course," ' he intoned.

' "With rocks, and stones, and trees" ' she completed. They stood in silence a while.

'Oh, Grace!' he said hoarsely. 'Where shall I find you again?'

'I shall find *you* – when I want you,' she answered in a strangled voice. 'Have patience.'

He kissed her lips for the first time, perhaps the last also, and she was gone running, running down the parkland towards the Arun, too fast to follow.

Concealed in the garden hedge Optimus stood and watched the Vicarage. He felt ashamed of himself, yet unable to do otherwise since Diana Lackland had cast him off and Mrs Treebie had been forbidden to play the intermediary. The letter he had sent Mrs Lackland had been returned unopened.

The Vicarage, standing on a knoll at the boundary between Harberscombe and Bigmore parishes, was an ivy-clad, mock-baronial travesty of ancient Leet House, home of the Genteels. How curious, he ruminated, that he should have imagined Frederick Genteel to stand concealed in a hedge at the outset of his story and now himself to do likewise. Nature imitating art, an example of the obscure workings of divine providence.

Not far away, old Treebie was digging in the vegetable patch. Otherwise, there was no sign of life in the sunlit garden. Optimus was becoming impatient and debating within himself whether to try to attract his attention and obtain news of his tormentor, but he would have to shout so loudly that the whole household would hear him. The Bigmore church clock struck the hour and Optimus knew that he ought to be going home to prepare his lessons. He would count to a hundred and then, if he had had neither sight nor sound of her, he would leave.

Before he reached ten, Diana Lackland appeared round the end of the building. She looked radiant, in a bright gingham dress under a flowered parasol. The garden suddenly rang with her laughter. Her joy was salt in the wound which already pained him.

And she was not alone. Another, deeper, laugh pealed out beside her. As she threw back her head in wild merriment, the parasol which had shaded them both tipped up enough for Optimus to discern their faces. The man who had so amused her was that vile, pudgy-faced, sleek-headed wonder who had just arrived in Harberscombe, John Carfax, the curate, still full of himself after the tripos. How could Diana, any woman for that matter, find anything interesting in *him*? Optimus remembered his unctuous voice leading the congregation in their responses at the last choral evensong.

As the pair of them stopped midway along the walk, confronted each other and exchanged meaningful looks under the spinning parasol, Optimus found himself close to tears. He bit his knuckle, then turned and blundered off through the bushes. He no longer cared if they heard him. He was, if he could bring himself to admit it, like Jan, enamoured of a faithless woman.

''Ow do I know I can trust 'ee?'

Grace looked round swiftly at Jan's words. For a long time he had sat silent, morose, pretending to watch the fire while she busied herself with the evening meal. He had been brooding over something ever since their expedition two nights ago.

'What do you mean?' She turned away again and carried on cutting vegetables for the pot. There was a long silence, punctuated only by the small noise of her knife slicing into the flesh of the carrots.

'Stop that!' he said suddenly, loudly. 'Stop that I tell 'ee! Come over 'ere so us can talk proper.' There was exasperation in his voice, and an unwonted authority, born perhaps of despair. After a moment she obeyed, wiping her hands on her apron as she took the few steps across the small room. She halted at the opposite side of the hearth and faced him. This time his eyes did not slide away from hers. They stared her out and it was her turn to feel uncomfortable, wondering what he was thinking, how much he knew of her thoughts.

'Come on, you'll spoil our supper.' She was trying to keep the initiative, but he knew it.

'I don't care. Supper don't mean nothin' to me, not now. What I wants to know is this: where be I, Grace Pensilva?'

'Why, where you always were. No better.'

'I wants to know 'ow you do see me.'

She chanced a smile at him before replying.

'Like a brother.'

It was his turn to smile, laugh even, but bitterly.

'Your Frank! I did think you 'ad put un out of your 'ead, but I were wrong, weren't I? Oh, 'tis no use lookin' at me that way, as if I was mazed or somethin'. I know as 'ow you've kept 'is things, I've seen 'ee moonin' over 'em.'

When, she thought to herself. She had been careful, very careful, but Jan, for all his outward slowness, was sly. He must have spied on her.

'What if I have kept a thing or two as keepsakes. He *was* my brother.'

'If that were all, I wouldn't care. 'Twere *what* you kept: that be what I couldn' stomach.' He had been at her things. From the way that he spoke, that much was obvious. He must have found the letters. He had been reading them, her precious letters, the ones that Frank had sent her while he was away. What he had done was a sacrilege, an unpardonable intrusion into her private territory.

'If you respected me, you'd never think of prying. You're no better than a peeping Tom!' Even as she spoke, she was regretting it. She was coming over too strong, in danger of losing him.

'They books,' he exclaimed. 'I won't 'ave they things in my 'ouse!' The books, she had never looked on them as important, not to Jan that is. If it were only the books he was complaining of . . .

'What's wrong with them?'

'Foreign nonsense, wrong 'eaded revolutionary stuff. I've got rid of 'em.'

'Where are they?' She felt an unreasoning panic, a dull ache in the pit of her stomach. It was all very well for her to tell herself it was only a few old books.

'I've gived 'em away. Should've burned 'em. No need to keep askin' neither, I shan't tell 'ee who 'as 'em.' He stopped speaking and, for a while, sat gazing glumly into the fire. 'But 'tiddn' that, 'tiddn' that what be the trouble between us,' he burst out suddenly, rising from his seat and confronting her.

'Oh, Grace, Grace, give us your 'and and listen a minute.' He took her hand willy-nilly and crushed it in his own hard sailorman's palm. "Ow long 'ave 'ee lived 'ere, maid? 'Ow long? And I still can't get close to 'ee!' She tried to remain calm. His agitation was contagious.

'But our bargain, have you forgotten our bargain? When I came here, wasn't there a bargain?'

'Bargain! Bargain! God damn your bargain. A man be a man. I be flesh and blood, bain't I?' She felt his anger. It was like a blow to the face. He had no need to strike her, she felt it all the stronger.

'You must give me time, Jan, time to forget, time to get used to you.'

'Time! Time! 'Aven't you 'ad enough already? Want a whole life time do 'ee? No, no, no, and no. You can't 'ave it. Speak frank, tell me once and for ever, what do you feel for me?'

She paused before she spoke, trying to be honest as well as careful.

'You're a good man, Jan. You're honest, you're just, and you're a good seaman. I don't think there's a better. I know I can trust you.'

'Aye,' said Jan with even more bitterness, 'You can trust *me*. One law for Jan King and another for Grace Pensilva. Well, I won't have it. There will 'ave to be an end to it.' She had driven him too far. Without realizing it she had pushed him to the point where he would have no more to do with her.

'Is it because of Frederick Genteel?' she asked as gently as she could, propitiatingly. 'If it's that that's galling you, you've no cause to be jealous. There's nothing between us. I use him. He can have intelligence of the preventives.'

'You do use *me*, Grace Pensilva. Like you do use everyone when it do suit 'ee. And as for intelligence, if that be what you d'call it, what be the use of it if you don't take no 'eed of it?'

'It was too late then to change our plans. Jack Lugger and the tinners were waiting. They'd have been ambushed even if they carried nothing. As it was, they got off with only a scratch.'

'I bain't so sure they did.' In the firelight his face showed flushed and his eyes were burning, but she sensed that, having said his say, he might be vulnerable.

'So you want to split up, Jan King, dissolve our partnership. Well, I don't see why not. There's a good profit to share between us and I can be going. There's a whole world out there, beyond the Barrow, beyond Salcombe, beyond Plymouth. If you're not man enough to stay with me, I must go alone, but I'm going.' She had called his bluff. He was deflated, sure that she meant what she said.

'That bain't what I want, Grace, and you knows it.'

'We'll go on then, renew our bargain?'

'Not the way it was, no,' he shook his head slowly as he spoke, like an ox, she thought, obstinate. 'I 'as to 'ave hope.' Hope, that was easy enough to offer, a cheap commodity. Apparently impulsively, she took both his hands in hers and planted a kiss on his forehead.

'While there's life . . .' she murmured. 'No, that's not kind enough, is it? What I mean is, Jan, I'm getting to know you slowly. I'm coming to appreciate you, respect you. It takes time, Jan, oceans of it. I've come a long way, Jan. There was such a gulf between us.' Awkwardly, he put his arms round her and pressed her to him, seeking her lips for a kiss. When he found them, she responded slightly, but broke away before he had had all he wanted.

'If you want your supper, Jan King,' she chided playfully, 'you must let the cook perform her duties.' With a peck on the cheek, she was off across the room, leaving him wondering. He had touched her, he knew that. She had been frightened. And she had looked at him in a new way. Yes, there had been progress. He would give her a week or so, maybe a bit longer.

Perhaps she divined what he thought, for she called to him over her shoulder. Her voice was confident again and compelling. 'Just one more run,' she told him. 'It'll be a good one. We'll run rings around that Scully customer. You'll see. Your Grace knows how to do it. I have a plan. I'll tell you the details after supper. This time, I'll share the whole thing with you. And we'll make a mint of money, enough to retire on.'

'Retire! I can't see Grace Pensilva retirin', not ever.'

'Oh, but I *will*,' she assured him. 'All good things come to an end, Jan King, as you'll discover. For now, have patience if you want to know me better. Come on now, help me lift this pot to the trivet.'

They talked late into the night, until his head drooped forward and he slept. Grace was pleased with herself: he seemed to share her dream. If he were caught up in it, he would not distrust her.

She crept up the creaking stairs to her room and latched her door. Frank's chest lay across the window in the dim light that the night provided. She knelt beside it, feeling in the secret place where she had stowed Frank's letters. She heaved a sigh of relief as she felt the bundle. They were still safe. Then she heard Jan's footfalls in the stairwell. She closed the chest and stepped away from it, throwing herself fully clothed under the blankets.

When the door opened, she feigned sleep. She knew, without opening her eyes, that he was watching her. She prayed that he would not dare advance further, that he would go away and leave her.

'I know you bain't sleepin', Grace.' His voice was a sorrowful whisper. 'Undress yourself, you'll be more comfortable.'

She opened her eyelids the merest fraction. There he was, a formless shadow in the doorway. He must not have been dead to the world as she had thought when she left the kitchen. Perhaps he had been pretending, suspicious. She would have to be careful.

'I was tired,' she murmured, 'It's all this tension. Don't worry, Jan. Wait a little. Don't rush me. I'll come to you when I'm ready.'

3

Optimus banged his fist on his desk in frustration. Why couldn't his Grace Pensilva have been a sweet, gentle home-body, faithful and true, adoring and melting, devoted to her Jan King, instead of being a calculating, scheming, money-grabbing, ruthless smuggler? She had certainly been the lat-ter: her reputation was still strong in the neighbourhood. He had the certitiude that Grace, like Diana Lackland, had used men for her own purposes. To be reminded of Mrs Lackland was to feel a stab of pain, a burst of angry frustration He stumped downstairs and paced his kitchen like a caged beast. How could she be so callous, so flighty? Was she deliberately distressing him? He had to know. There and then, he decided he would go and see her. From what she had told him, she slept alone. He knew the window; it was only a matter of waiting for dark and scrambling up there. Yes, he thought, he would have it out with her; he couldn't take no for an answer. This curate fellow was but a blind, a man of straw set up to taunt him, he was persuaded of that. Once he and Diana were face to face, she would surrender to him. Already he could feel her warm softness in his arms.

Just as he was putting on his coat, Mrs Kemp came to the door. He was used to her comings and goings and imagined she was there to collect the supper dishes, though it was rather late for that. Before he could walk past her, she spoke.

'The Doctor would like to see you special.'

'Sorry,' he shouted close to her ear, 'must go out – urgent business. Tell him I'll call tomorrow '

''Ee be lookin' proper poorly.'

'Keep him warm, Mrs Kemp – give him a good grog with lime in it.'

'Won't you come over when you gets back? Doctor won't mind what hour you d'call. I'll leave the door unbolted.'

'I'll drop in to see him, if his light's still burning.'

'Thank 'ee, Maister, 'ee'll be glad to 'ear it.' Optimus hardly heard her final remark, he was so anxious to be off, trotting across the open country that lay between Branscombe and Bigmore Vicarage. As he approached, he ran faster; his heart pounded; his breath shuddered in his chest; but he was strangely at peace. No longer was he the timid, bookish schoolmaster: he was Leander swimming the Hellespont, Romeo approaching Juliet's balcony.

Reality was different. The romantic bulk of the Vicarage was etched against the starry sky as he approached it. He was perturbed to see that a light still burned in Mr Lackland's ground floor study. Another glimmered from Diana Lackland's first-floor bedroom. Optimus waited, hoping that Parson Lackland would retire to his own room at the back of the house. It was a chill night and Optimus shivered.

With the time that slipped away, his resolution wavered. He was loath to give up his determination to confront Mrs Lackland and declare his passion for her, but he was afraid of the consequences.

When he could bear the cold no longer, he stole forward until he could peer through the curtains into the study. Parson Lackland had his nose buried in books, preparing a sermon. How pathetic he looked with that long face of his, set in a perpetually disapproving expression under the wire spectacles. No wonder Diana found him lacking, his passions were all inverted into negations.

Optimus proceeded round the corner of the house, skirting the flower beds. When he came under Diana's window, he called to her in a whisper. She did not appear to hear him, so he picked up a handful of gravel from the path and tossed it at the window panes. The clatter they made was startling. Optimus was sure the whole house must hear it. He stepped back into some shrubbery.

There was a change in Diana's room. The candle flickered and shadows danced on the walls as it moved. Moments later, Diana's face appeared behind the casement, lit by the flames in the candlestick she held out before her. She was peering ineffectually into the dark. The low-placed source of light cast grotesque shadows across her features. She looked older, menacing. She raised the stay and pushed wide the casement.

'Who's there? Is that you, Mr Carfax?' Optimus heard her whisper. A pang caught at his heart. He bit his lip till the blood came.

'It's me,' Optimus called back, his voice tinged with bitterness.

'Me, who's me?'

'Optimus, Optimus Shute,' and he stepped out of the shrubbery.

'Hush, you young fool! Be off with you!'

'But there's something I must tell you.'

'I don't want to hear it.' Their raised voices were causing a commotion in the house. A light glimmered in another of the upstairs windows.

'What is it?' came Vicar Lackland's hollow voice from the study.

'I thought I heard an intruder,' Diana called over her shoulder, 'someone in the garden.' Then, dropping her voice again, she hissed, 'Go home with you, boy. If you stay a moment longer, I'll denounce you and your days as a school-master will be numbered.'

Optimus heard the french windows creaking open. Mr Lackland must be stepping out on to the lawn. There was nothing for it but to leave.

'You're a flirt, Diana, damn you, nothing but a flirt!' he shouted in final frustration as he blundered off across the flower beds, almost shattering the conservatory.

'Did you see him?' he heard Mr Lackland inquiring. 'I've heard him too. Must be a burglar.'

Optimus did not hear Diana's reply. He rushed away into the night. His boots were heavy with mud from the flower beds and his body was sticky with sweat. He felt unclean, ugly, besmirched. Now that Diana had clearly rejected him, he hated her. How could he ever have loved her?

The night breeze fanned his burning cheeks, but failed to cool them. He was too hot with the injustice of it all, too deep in youthful despair. He was so wrapped up in himself that he failed to note that the light in Dr Cornish's kitchen was out when he passed it. He did not give it a second thought, though it was often kept burning well into the small hours. He had forgotten the invitation Mrs Kemp had brought over. Optimus ran into the schoolhouse, threw himself fully clothed on to his bed, buried his face in the pillow, and wept.

The latch clicked upward abruptly. Dr Cornish looked up from his game of patience. He had been too absorbed to notice any arriving footfalls. There had been no knock however, he was sure of that. The faintest of groans from the next room reminded him of Jack Lugger. For days now he had been half expecting the preventives' arrival to arrest the wounded man. Was this them on the threshold? His hand reached towards his pistol in the drawer, but drew back. Resistance would be useless. He could not expect to hold at bay the combined forces of law and order.

As the door swung back, a single figure was revealed in the growing dusk. A woman, slightly built, her true proportions lost in an ample cloak, she hesitated momentarily as she became aware of his presence.

'Dr Cornish?' Already the voice had given him a clue to her identity.

'Don't just stand there, come in and shut the door. You're letting all the heat out.' The twilight filtering through the small windows and the fire's glow confirmed his suspicions. She stopped, facing him across the table. Her face, seemingly serene, fascinated him. Shadowed by the boat-cloak's hood and a wayward lock of hair, her eyes glistened. Only the way she held her hands betrayed her tension. He raised his eyebrows interrogatingly.

'I've come to see Jack Lugger,' she announced. 'I know he's here. Where is he?'

'You may want to see Jack Lugger, but I doubt if *he* wants to see you.'

'I'll be the judge of that. You're his physician; you're not God, are you?' Dr Cornish smiled a wry smile. This woman was so direct, so challenging, even if he had not seen her face, he might have guessed who she was.

'He's still a sick man, Miss Pensilva, a very sick man, he should not be troubled. Might I know your intention?'

'Oh, you needn't worry about that, my intentions are honourable, of course they are. We're in business together.' She smiled, a smile that was shy at first, but became radiant until it swept Dr Cornish's doubts away.

'Of course you are. You'll find him over there in my surgery. I'll open the door for you. But don't stay too long, he's still weak, can't take excitement. You'll bear that in mind, won't you?' She nodded as he escorted her down the length of the kitchen and ushered her into the surgery where he had installed Jack Lugger on a truckle bed. For the while he had been seeing his other patients in the kitchen.

As she closed the door behind her, Dr Cornish vacillated. Should he return to his seat at the table or should he follow his instinct and mount the steps that led to the chamber which gave on to the surgery where, ordinarily, he installed himself during consultations? Would the latter be ethical? Jack Lugger *was* his patient; Grace Pensilva wasn't. To eavesdrop on their conversation might be excused as protective of his patient's interests. In the end he was ruled by impulse. Three cautious strides and he was in his consulting chamber which was divided off from the surgery proper by a thin wainscoting partition. Providentially, the hatch was closed; he remained invisible and the sound of their voices came through to him clearly.

'What's the word, Jack? Are you mending?' she was asking quietly.

'Who be askin'?' The bed creaked as Lugger rolled over. 'Oh, 'tis you. I don't need your condolence. Leave me be, I be sleepin'.'

'How long before you'll be fit again, Jack? We need you.'

256

'Once be enough, more than enough. I 'aven't no wish to risk my skin too often, not with your schemes. If I 'adn' been caught up in the last one, I wouldn' be lyin' 'ere, sweatin'.' His voice was thin and hoarse, full of reproach and anger.

'There's always a risk, Jack I run the same risk as any of you, I share it.'

'You weren't there when I bought this one, Grace. No, you was far too clever. Far off you were and who could blame 'ee?'

'I know what you're getting at. It's a lie, and you know it! What you're saying is: you don't want to take your part in future runs nor share the profit.'

'I didn' say that.'

'But you meant it. Well, no hard feelings, Jack. Here, take this purse, you'll find what I owe you in it and a bit over to pay the Doctor and to make up for your trouble.' There was a short silence and Dr Cornish thought he heard the faintest of clinking as Jack Lugger took the purse.

'Money don't pay for a man's life,' he muttered.

'It doesn't, but you're still living, Jack, and don't forget it. I'm sorry you'll not be with us, not even in spirit, but it's your decision. Let me know if you change your mind about it.'

''Ow long do I 'ave to get well?'

'Can I tell you safely? Can I trust you, Jack Lugger?'

'Course you can, Grace. God's honour! Jack Lugger 'aven't never betrayed no one.' Another pause before she spoke.

'I suppose so, but there's always a first time. Never mind, here goes: Friday fortnight, same place, top of the tide.'

''Tis too soon, I shall never be better in time for it. As for the place, well, the preventives 'ave been there once and found us, they'll come back for certain.'

'Not so soon, they won't be expecting us, they'll think we'll try another landing.'

'Might be somethin' in that, I 'spose, but I wouldn' count on it.'

'Pity you don't agree, pity you won't be with us, there'll be good pickings. Think it over. I can't stay now, Jan will be worried about me. If you change your mind, you'll know where to find me.'

Dr Cornish sensed that the interview was coming to an end. If he remained where he was much longer and Grace emerged from the surgery, she would guess he had been listening. He stepped into the corridor, gliding on slippered feet to his place at the kitchen table where he busied himself with the lamp. It ought to be burning before she came out again. As he removed the chimney, trimmed the wick and approached with a taper from the fireplace, something bothered him. Why had she told Jack Lugger the time and place so easily? It wasn't like her, from what he'd heard. She left him little time to ponder, she was back in the kitchen before the lamp flame had steadied properly. If he hadn't spoken, he suspected she would have swept straight past him.

'Sit you down!' he insisted. 'Sit down and take a glass of brandy. Jack Lugger's tinner friends were not ungenerous. They've more spirit than money. You may enjoy a drop of your own produce.'

'No thanks, I rarely touch it.'

'Coals to Newcastle, eh? Well I can't blame you. A dish of tea then, you'll not deny me. It's a lonely life for a bachelor physician, nobody to talk to.' While he spoke, he was propelling her by the arm to a seat at the table. She resisted at first, but he had an impression that she was not unhappy to be given firm direction. 'What's your impression of Jack?' he asked as he filled the teapot.

'He'll live.'

'Indeed he will – outlive us all, I fancy, tough as old boots is Jack Lugger. And you, dear lady, how's the world treating you?'

'Well enough.'

'It would seem so. You have money, though you can't spend it; a devoted partner, Jan King's got a heart of gold, I hope you know that.'

'Look here, I don't care to be preached to.'

'No, I suppose not . . .' He busied himself with pushing back his papers and setting the table. 'I'm a physician, you know. I can't help seeing things in terms of sickness and health. Did you know you'd an illness?'

'An illness – I'm as fit as a fiddle.'

other questions about your boy Andrew's mother. Something's been intriguing me of late: why does he spend his Sundays at Leet House with Mistress Nancy?'

'You've been pumpin' the lad!' said Scully angrily.

'I didn't need to, Andrew just told me.'

'Well, what if 'ee do? There ain't nothin' wrong in 'is goin' to Leet and keep 'er company.'

'Presumably not, if you say so, but if it got about, if someone let the cat out of the bag, people might put two and two together. You know what sharp tongues they have in Harberscombe. There's more than one already that says you're not a proper person to have charge of the young man.' Optimus was watching Scully's face closely. For all his bold bluster, the miller's eyelid twitched when the boy's name was mentioned. He was convinced that Scully's feelings for the boy were pathologically possessive.

'You don't give an honest man much choice, Mr Shute. What you're a-sayin' do sound like blackmail.'

'Then you should be the first to recognize it. Well, what's your answer? Will you sing or no? It's all long gone and it can't hurt you.'

'Don't know about that, but I don't seem to 'ave no choice in the matter. What sort o' questions will you be askin'?'

'For a start, you can tell me how you came to be a tenant here at Langstone Mill.'

'Miss Nancy thought I couldn't be a worse farmer nor miller than that Coyte beggar what 'er brother turned off 'ere.'

'That's not what you said last time, you said it was Charles Barker that owed you a favour.'

''Tis all of a piece. Miss Nancy, as then was, did tell un to oblige me.'

'And why should Nancy Genteel owe you a favour?'

'I bringed 'er news of 'er brother.'

'Ah, what kind of news, I wonder? But before we come to that, there's another question. You didn't come straight here after Coyte, now did you? The place was run by a bailiff for a year or so. Where were you during that time? You'd left Salcombe, I've checked that.'

'Sailin',' said Scully, shifting his one eye uneasily.

'Sailing?'

'I 'ad command of a brig. The '*Ecate*.'

'The *Hecate*, privateer, if I'm not mistaken. And where did you sail her?'

'The Levant.'

'And to get there you passed by Malta. You were looking for someone, weren't you? Someone from this village, go on, admit it, saying so won't hurt you.' Scully nodded slowly.

'There were a price on 'er 'ead. You can't blame me.'

'No, I don't blame you. She wronged you didn't she?' Scully put up an involuntary hand to the place where his eye had been.

'More ways than one.'

'And did you come up with her?'

'I never did catch 'er. They called me Blood'ound Scully, on account I never gived up, but I never did catch 'er. I were close to 'er once, but she got clear away.'

'She got clear away, you'll swear it?'

'She must 'ave or she'd never 'ave come 'ome to 'Arberscombe. She did that, didn' she? D'you think I'd've left 'er go if I'd 'ad 'er? Not for love nor money. She 'n I 'ad too long a score to settle. I'd've 'ad 'er, too, if it 'and'n been for that damned interferin' Frederick. But she gived un no thanks for 'is 'elp, quite the contrary.'

'What do you know about that?'

'Only what were common knowledge: that they were seen together, and then they vanished. Grace turned up 'ere, Frederick weren't never discovered, though 'is wife did try all ways to seek un.'

'His wife?'

'Felicity, Felicity Fell were 'er maiden name. Ah, I can see there's some things you don't know already. Oh, I could tell you many a thing if I 'ad a mind to, but 'tis long since and me mind's gone sodden, never been the same since I 'ad this trouble.' Again he put his hand to his head.

Optimus fished in his pocket, found a guinea and held it up glinting. Scully's solitary eye never left it for an instant.

'Perhaps this'll help revive your memory, loosen your talk-strings. Telling the truth for once isn't so painful as you thought, is it? If I put this on the table, would it remind you about Salcombe for instance? There's something I've heard about a plan hatched between you and Mr Hawkins, a noose prepared for Grace Pensilva to put her neck in. If it comes back to you now, I'll not be ungenerous. How's that for a bargain?'

'I allus said you was a gennulman,' smirked Scully, 'there's allus an arrangement to be 'ad between gennulmen. Come into the parlour and I'll accommodate you.'

The Custom House in Plymouth was a four-square, no nonsense building with a granite façade and a severe Classical pediment enclosing the Royal Arms. The adjoining quays around the Barbican were thronged as usual with fishermen, fishwives, sailors, crimps, warehousemen, shipwrights, sea-captains, caulkers, topers, whores, rogues and scoundrels.

Mr Hawkins scarcely accorded them a passing glance as he stepped into the Custom House to be greeted by his chief clerk as usual.

'I'm a little late,' Hawkins remarked. He thought a punctual man could always afford to apologize for an occasional lapse and it helped inspire punctuality in others. 'Got caught up in some business in the Mayor's parlour. Anything worthy of my attention?'

'You've a person to see you, waiting in your office as you instructed.'

'Good, see we're not disturbed.' Mr Hawkins hurried up the stairs. He had been trying to get Captain Scully over from Salcombe for some time now. They needed to coordinate matters, have a conference, and he felt it was time he put Scully in his place and instilled some discipline in him. The Salcombe preventives were becoming a law unto themselves and a blind, flailing kind of justice at that. He had recommended discretion when calling because he didn't want every Tom, Dick and Harry along the coast to know that a determined operation was in the offing.

When he opened his office door, he found his visitor at the

window, looking down into the street from between the curtains, which were partly drawn. Clad in a poke-bonnet and a full skirt, the figure was unrecognizable.

'If you think that's funny, Mr Scully; if you think that's a suitable disguise, I can assure you I don't share your opinion,' he snorted.

His visitor whirled round in alarm and he saw in a trice that, whatever the disguise, and this person was keeping her face half covered, this *was* a woman. An involuntary action caused him to twitch the head of his cane, ready to unsheath his sword stick if needful. It was not unknown for women with a grievance, a husband or son transported to the colonies, or a lunatic, some deranged creature, to pull a weapon from under her clothes and assassinate even the mildest of men, and Mr Hawkins saw himself in that category.

'Beg pardon, your honour,' the woman began, fawning and showing him a thin smile, 'I'm come to see you on most particular business.'

'Well, for a start, who are you? I haven't time to beat about the bush.'

'I be from 'Arberscombe, your honour, a poor farmer's wife from 'Arberscombe. I've comed over because I've 'eard that – I've 'eard there be certain cases when –'

'Come on, woman, out with it!'

'I've 'eard that, if a person turns King's Evidence, or gives certain information, it might be taken into consideration when certain other matters were being decided.'

'What other matters?'

'Like whether prosecution would be brought against a certain party what's lyin' wounded not far from 'ere.' Mr Hawkins had a flash of illumination.

'Such as the man who's being treated by Dr Cornish? The old rogue says he's too sick to be moved, still less to stand trial, but we know he's got 'im in there in 'is surgery; he'll have to discharge him in time and my men are waiting to take him. He'll stand trial like any other felon. No jury would dare to acquit him.'

'But if you was to let un go free, when 'ee were mended

like, 'ee'd know when there were goin' to be a shipment and what would be more likely than that 'is sister'd know about it.'

'What if she did?'

'I be Jack Lugger's sister.'

'And you're offering to tip off the Revenue: you must have good reasons.'

'I've told you one already: to save me brother. T'other be personal.'

'You'll have to be more explicit if I'm to believe you.'

''Tis that woman; I can't abide 'er. She did try to seduce my boy Ronald, that and other things.'

'So you'll deliver up Grace Pensilva?'

'In return for a free pardon for Jack Lugger, your honour.'

'I'll think it over.'

'There bain't no time for that your honour. Comin' 'ere once to talk to 'ee were fool'ardly enough. Twice would be madness and they'd never trust me brother no more neither if I was seen 'ere. Now what be your answer?'

'A bargain, it's a bargain,' said Mr Hawkins, wondering whether she expected him to shake hands on it. 'But how shall I know the day and the time and the place of it?'

'I'll send you my young Ronald, 'ee be a bright lad, Miss Nancy 'ave just took un on at Leet to care for 'er 'orses, 'ee do ride to Plymouth often; no one'll mark un.'

Almost immediately she had left, Captain Scully burst into the room. He was mud-bespattered, stank of harness and horse sweat, and had brandy on his breath.

'I comed as quick as I could,' he said by way of apology before Hawkins could blame him for his lateness. 'They turnpikes be a disgrace.' Mr Hawkins put up a lace handkerchief to his nose and recoiled a little. Scully was not his choice of officer, but one took whom one could in the preventives.

'When we talk about putting down the brandy trade, Mr Scully, we don't infer that you should be putting it down your throat before nine in the morning. A man in authority has a duty to remain sober.'

'Sober as a judge, your honour!'

'Did you notice anyone on the stairs as you came in?' inquired Mr Hawkins casually.

'Nary a soul.'

'So much the better. Well, let's to business. Before many days are out there's to be a concerted operation against that Grace Pensilva and her gang. It won't be allowed to go off at half-cock like last time when you only winged one of them, and a cipher at that. This time we shall catch them red-handed, for I have certain knowledge –'

'Someone's peached on 'er. I knew they would, they allus does at last when they start to smell money!' interrupted Scully.

'I have certain knowledge,' Mr Hawkins reiterated coolly, 'that will enable us, provided there is no incompetence, no insubordination, no wiseacre among us, to concentrate our forces at the right moment and put an end to this insolent woman's activities.'

'I can't wait to get back to Salcombe to make things ready for 'er,' proclaimed Scully.

'Better stay here and sober up first,' grunted Hawkins. 'I've some plans drawn up that I'll go over with you when you're in a fit state to see them. In the meantime, take a walk on the Hoe, and stay out of taverns, d'you hear me?' Mr Hawkins had no illusions about Scully, the man was riff-raff, but a potter doesn't always choose his clay. It was up to the Receiver of Customs to frame his plans in such a way as to minimize the element of human error. He sat down at his desk and pulled his maps from the wide top drawer. That woman's activities were written all over them.

Grace Pensilva was not thinking of Mr Hawkins that day as she rode a small fish-cart down the steep hill into Salcombe. She had heard of His Majesty's Receiver of Customs, but she had never seen him; she recognized him as an adversary, but a distant one. The person who preoccupied her was Scully and she kept a wary eye out for him when she reached the centre of the town. She doubted if he would know her if he saw her, dressed as 'a youth as she was, but she was always prudent. She hitched her cart outside the Fortescue tavern and stepped inside with a crab in her hand.

'Where can I find Ben Barlow?' she inquired of the tapster.

'Can't be disturbed,' said the latter.

'Why not? It's urgent; I've come all the way from Harberscombe to see him.'

''Ee've urgent business to attend to – with a lady,' smirked the tapster.

'Never mind that. Go up and tell him I've brought him a present from Harberscombe.'

''Ee don't need no crabs; crabs be the last thing Ben Barlow'll be lookin' for at the moment!' The crowd of dedicated drinkers burst into a volley of laughter. Grace tried to keep a straight face.

'Shall I have to go up and fetch him myself?'

'Oh, no, that would never do.'

'Would this help to convince you?' The tapster saw the glint of a small gold coin.

'I'd say 'twould 'elp matters no end. Who shall I say's below to see un?'

'A friend, a friend from Harberscombe.'

When Ben Barlow appeared a few minutes later, the topers were astonished to see that the ill-humour vanished from his face the moment he saw his visitor. The two of them stepped into the snug and closed the door behind them.

'Well, if that don't beat all!' whistled the tapster. 'I didn' know Ben 'ad inclinations that way as well. Did you see 'ow that young lad did blush?'

'Talked funny too,' said a customer, 'sort o' lah de dah. There bain't many like that out to 'Arberscombe. Pity Cap'n Scully've ridden over to Plymouth today, 'ee'd've liked to make 'is acquaintance.' There was more laughter at that, but when Ben Barlow re-emerged and ushered his guest to the door, there was no more comment.

'Come on, you layabouts,' Ben said to them, 'give us an 'and to unload they crabs.' He turned to his visitor who was untying the pony, 'and come on over again as soon as you've a mind to.'

'I'll take you up on that, sooner than you think.'

'Mr Shute, you are a disgrace to your calling, a disgrace to your college. It is my duty to see that you are no longer entrusted with the education of Christian children.'

Before Optimus was properly aware of his arrival, the Vicar was already glowering down on his desk at the head of the classroom. Behind the intruder, a sea of startled faces looked up from their slates and primers. It had been quiet enough before, but now there was absolute silence. Mr Lackland's keen eye fell on the sheets of paper that Optimus was trying to cover with his hand. He tried to snatch them from him, but the schoolmaster resisted, won the battle and stuffed them into his jacket pocket.

'I know what you're up to,' snapped the Parson, 'you're frittering your time away on some deplorable nonsense while your pupils are left to their own devices. Mrs Lackland has told me about that too, she tells me *everything*. That's not why I'm here, however, there's a far more serious matter, something we can't discuss in front of the children. Come outside this minute. I insist. I'm going to have it out with you.' Optimus realized that there was nothing for it but to obey.

'Pray return to your work,' he instructed the class. 'Andrew,' young Scully looked up again. 'Take charge of the class while I'm away. Write names on the blackboard if there's misbehaviour.'

'Misbehaviour!' snorted Lackland as they left the room. 'You could teach them something about misbehaviour.' Optimus knew what to expect. Diana Lackland had denounced him to her husband who was about to dismiss him from his post as village schoolmaster. He expected a storm of reproach: it was not to be so. The moment the two men stepped into the road, Mrs Kemp descended upon them.

'I see'd your carriage, Vicar,' she shouted, buttonholing them. 'You'm come at the right time, just when you'm wanted. Dr Cornish do need 'ee now, if ever.'

'What the blazes do you mean, woman?' hissed Mr Lackland. 'You don't expect me to come gossiping with that old sinner, do you? Can't you see I'm busy?' Mrs Kemp looked blank. She was twisting her hands nervously in her apron. Optimus understood the problem.

'The Parson's busy,' he shouted.

'But 'ee be dead,' moaned Mrs Kemp, 'stone, rock 'ard dead, poor man. 'Ee do need a clergyman for 'is soul.'

'That old rogue? He never had one,' asserted Lackland firmly. 'And it's too late for repentance: he should have thought of that earlier. Call the carpenter to make him a coffin.' Optimus was white with shock and fury, he caught the Vicar by the shoulders and propelled him towards Dr Cornish's kitchen. He was oblivious to the consequences of his violence and, if he were to be dismissed anyway, what did it matter?

'Do your duty!' he told Mr Lackland who hovered on the kitchen threshold. Over the Vicar's shoulder, he could see the Doctor crumpled up in his fireside chair, almost as usual. Only a peculiar angle of the neck showed there was something amiss. 'But before you go in, tell me exactly what it is you reproach me with!' Optimus held the Parson by his lapels and watched his Adam's apple working convulsively.

'I've had a complaint,' he spluttered, 'a complaint from Mr Scully. You've been harassing him; he says it's blackmail.' Optimus almost laughed. It was so petty, so ludicrous. He pushed Mr Lackland into the kitchen and turned away. He strode blindly down the lane. Why hadn't he noticed that something was wrong at Dr Cornish's that night? Had the light been burning or not when he returned? He had been full of his own frustrated lust and damaged pride, his old friend had been forgotten. How long had the old man sat there dying, while the candle flame guttered to extinction, out of reach of his nerveless arm. There had been no one to share his last confidences with, the young fellow he had considered his friend and treated like a son had failed to come to him in the hour of his need. Deaf old Mrs Kemp lay drowned in her wordless dreams on her hard bed at the far side of the house.

Optimus thought he could see the Doctor's lips moving, but what was he saying?

Oh God! Hot tears flooded down his cheeks. He had not known how much he cared for the man. What was the link between them? Master and student. Dr Cornish had started him off on the school of life. God! Why hadn't he known earlier? Why hadn't he shown some gratitude? He was a self-centred, thankless young dog and he deserved a whipping. But a lifetime of self-reproach would not, could not, atone for his selfishness.

He turned back towards the school; life would not wait. Before his eyes as he walked, swimming through his tears, he saw the face of the woman that Dr Cornish had introduced him to. He was close to her now, tantalizingly close; why hadn't he told the Doctor? And over her shoulder, closed lips smiling enigmatically, was Frederick Genteel. Where was Jan King? Washed out in the blur that covered his reddened eyes. But he would find him. Back in the classroom, Optimus rapped on his desk with the pointer.

'Pack up your things and go home, all of you. Dr Cornish is dead. Go quietly, go respectfully. Don't let me hear a sound. Tell your parents to remember him.' He sat at his desk. So his time at Branscombe School was all but over; Mr Lackland could always find a pretext to discredit him with the Parish Council and the School Board. Well, they could take his job away, but they couldn't rob him of everything: they couldn't take Grace Pensilva.

He was glad that the Vicar did not return to the school after he left the Doctor's kitchen. Once he had clip-clopped away, Optimus unlocked the desk and took out the locket. It spun gently at the end of its thin golden chain. He had no need to open it. The interlaced calligraphy of the initials glinted almost imperceptibly. He remembered showing it to Dr Cornish and asking him to identify them.

God! Optimus crumpled the chain in his hands and buried his face in them. What a fool he had been! Dr Cornish had been his friend. And he had betrayed him.

*   *   *

The carpenter's hammer made Optimus put down his pen. Across the road lay another reality. If he hurried, he could see the old Doctor's face for the last time. He wanted to and yet he feared to. There was the fear of death, and the fear of unspoken reproach. Mrs Kemp must have washed her master's body and, with the carpenter's help, dressed him and laid him out. What had her relationship with Dr Cornish once been? Optimus had only known her old and deaf, wrinkled and ugly, but she had been young once. She had been in the Doctor's service this thirty years. Who could say how beautiful she might have been in the early days? And Mr Kemp, who was he? Where was he? Who had he been? Optimus did not think that these were questions which he would ever dare ask her.

Mrs Kemp was old enough to have known Grace Pensilva, yet he had never associated the two of them. The Doctor's servant seemed to come from another world, a world whose extreme limit was the weekly market, but which was normally as closely bounded as a convent and, like a self-humiliating nun, she scraped and slaved, she cooked and washed, till her hands were raw and her old eyes grew pale and dim. No, Mrs Kemp knew no one beyond her employer, and cared less. Though she crossed the road daily with food from the Doctor's table, Optimus realized he had never really noticed her, she was like the dried-out shell of a person, a person whose existence he had never suspected until it was too late.

Mrs Kemp was the only woman at the Doctor's funeral; Optimus and Charles Barker were the only other mourners; Vicar Lackland officiated and the carpenter led a party of four stolid, sluggish bearers. Optimus had the impression that Mrs Kemp deliberately ignored him afterwards, taking refuge in her deafness and scurrying off immediately the service was over. From her sidelong looks, he imagined that she harboured a deep well of resentment for his having failed to answer the Doctor's summons; he could not blame her. The Steward also departed quickly after exchanging a brief handshake. Optimus thought he looked suddenly older, but that was probably an illusion encouraged by his suit of rusty black.

He himself was ready to follow the other mourners when the Vicar tapped him on the arm and drew him aside from the carpenter and bearers who were filling in the grave quickly with their long-handled shovels.

'There is something – something I find difficult to say to you, Mr Shute, but I must say it – I have been wrestling with my conscience and I find – perhaps I have been too hasty, too quick to heed my wife's accusations – yes, yes, she is a romancer, she will invent anything to hurt people – me in particular, if I were to tell you the things she – But it isn't your cross, it's mine and I have to bear it. No, what I wanted to say is that, from all accounts, and a vicar gets to hear a great many, you're a good schoolmaster; the children like you; you're firm but fair; you have the gift for instilling the elements of literacy, numeracy; you do not neglect the moral virtues. I feel I must ask you, Mr Shute, to consider that my outburst in your classroom never happened. I'm asking you to stay, Mr Shute; the children need you and it will be extremely difficult to obtain a suitable replacement at this time of year if you –'

'If I decide I've had enough of Harberscombe and its narrow ways,' Optimus completed for him. He had been astonished by the Vicar's change of tack, the man was a weathercock, and half ready to accept the offer until the last few words sickened him. What did it matter that he had no other prospects, he was not a toy to be discarded and taken up at will by his employers. 'I won't be used, Mr Lackland. Your wife used me for her "good works" and you would like to use me for yours. I'm not available, Mr Lackland. You came and forced my freedom upon me: I intend to keep it.'

Optimus could not account for his anger. He did not care if the bearers heard him shout. Perhaps it was the manner in which Dr Cornish was being shovelled away expeditiously, in a remote, overgrown corner of the churchyard, that troubled him.

He turned his back on the Vicar and walked off among the ivy-clad graves. There was an iron wicket-gate or stile in the wall there which he had never noticed. Optimus let himself out and found that he was on a small patch of waste ground, rank with elder and bramble. What caught his eye was a railed-off rectangle, like a tomb, but inexplicably outside the consecrated ground. He pushed his way into the undergrowth, grasped the rusty fleur-de-lis heads on the railings and pulled himself up on to the granite plinth so that he could look down on the flat slate memorial. It was cracked and long tendrils of ivy were growing across it, obliterating some of the cursive lettering and making it difficult to decipher. When he began to grasp its meaning, he shook, as if with a fever; the coincidence was too great to be accepted lightly.

GRACE PENSILVA

said the first line, then there was a broad open space and in smaller letters that he had to guess at in several cases,

Not Wisely
But Too Well

Why had he never seen this monument? Why had Dr Cornish never mentioned it? Why had no one ever referred to such a tomb?

Optimus hurried away, half running, half walking, not caring where he went. Only later did he realize that he was passing through Okewell Court and that Armouth was not far ahead of him.

The beach was deserted, the cottage was more dilapidated than ever, the fishermen's huts were barred and bolted. Optimus halted where the tiny wavelets of the flood tide were lapping at the dried seaweed. The estuary was a pewter sheet, it called him and he could not answer.

Suddenly he took a decision: he ran back to the boathouse where old Uncle Bill habitually sat mending pots, pulled back the bolts and threw the doors wide open. Scrambling on to a pile of gear, he unslung one end of the gig from the rafters, then went round to disengage the other. He felt a slight sense of guilt, a fear of what Uncle Bill Terry would say when he found out, but he suppressed it.

273

The gig was astonishingly light, he might almost have carried it unaided, but it was long and unwieldly and he was obliged to drag it over the grass to the tide mark. The paddles lay ranged neatly inside it, hitched to the thwarts with a loop of twine. The twine was so old that it came apart in his hand when he knelt to untie them. When he shoved the boat into the water, tiny leaks, glistening like diamonds, spurted all along the clinker planking. He ran for a bailer. The hull was so dry it would leak like a basket during the first hour or so, while the wood took up.

Rowing the gig was like a dream; he made no attempt to guide it, but slid over the calm water haphazardly, leaving long curls of wake. He had a strange sense of perfection, of fulfilment. Worsted-grey water, dove-grey sky, slate-grey hills, he hung, he floated among them, and he knew something, he knew something he had suspected, but had been unable to confirm, he knew how it must have been.

The sea called him. Oblivious of the water lapping over his feet, he pulled southward, till the Barrow appeared, and the Bolt, and the Carracks. He felt no fear. He was alone and not alone. Grace Pensilva was there. Jan King was there. The pattern of spliced planks where he had mended the gig was there. So were the marks where she had gouged the gunwale.

It seemed as if their spirits were skimming around him like terns. They dipped and wove on unquiet wings. Optimus felt his eyes dampen with tears. The oar blades left the water with a sucking noise like the carpenter's shovel. The falling drops pattered from their extremities with a sound like crumbs of earth. But they spun and glistened on the sea's skin, perfect pearls in which was mirrored all God's grey creation. The thought had been; to achieve perfection it had taken on existence. All that remained, the Doctor reminded him, was to take it down. It was all there, noted in the water by the gig's scrawling keel.

4

Frederick Genteel lashed his horse with his whip and the animal, unused to such treatment from his indulgent master, sprang off down the ride. As soon as Frederick was out of sight of Leet House, he had dug in his spurs, cantering over the rolling parkland; now he was fairly galloping down the winding ride that followed the estuary's contours through the woods towards the sea.

It was several hours since Mr Hawkins had driven over unexpectedly in a closed carriage and announced that a body of preventives would be arriving at nightfall.

'You'll be as glad as I shall to see an end put to the illegal activities of these smugglers who are making free of your lands for their purposes,' he announced to Frederick as soon as they were cloistered in the saloon. 'I rely on you to see that no one leaves here this afternoon to give word of my presence. I've had to take a hand in this myself; that Scully isn't worth a brass farthing. If only his predecessor had continued at work, we'd never had had to put up with this new outbreak of lawlessness.' He looked straight at Frederick Genteel. 'You don't think he might be persuaded to collaborate? Even at this late hour, I'd drop Scully like a hot potato if I could replace him with a man of action, a man of honour.'

Frederick shook his head. 'A man might enjoy the action, particularly if he had been used to life on a ship of the line at sea, but he would seek in vain for honour.'

'I feared as much. However, I'm sure I can rely on the fullest assistance from Lord Mayberry's son.'

'Naturally. Now, as I'm sure you're fatigued from your

journey, I'll ask my sister Nancy to join us for tea in the drawing-room.'

'You're most kind. But I wish your assistance went further.'

'My dear Hawkins, the place is yours, you have your duty to do, but don't expect me to volunteer to turn out and shoot my own tenants in cold blood.'

Later, when Nancy had joined them in the drawing-room, she was full of enthusiasm for the coming action and scornful of Frederick.

'These are strange times when the Squire hasn't the stomach to go out and confront a woman. It shines no credit on the Genteel family name,' she complained when she heard that Frederick did not propose taking part in the expedition. 'You can take *me* with you, Mr Hawkins, I'm not afraid to hold a pistol.'

'If the trap springs as it should, Miss Nancy, I already have men aplenty. This kind of scrimmage is no place for a lady.'

'It's a place for Grace Pensilva, isn't it? She's the one you're hoping to catch, isn't she? Why shouldn't it be a place for me? Are you really sure she'll be there?'

'Perfectly sure; this time we've had certain information.'

'I must congratulate you, Mr Hawkins,' said Frederick Genteel, ''tis not every man's luck to meet a reliable informant. I did not think this Pensilva woman had many enemies; I thought she was rather admired in the locality.'

'One is enough,' said Hawkins drily.

'And one well-wisher to tip her off,' said Frederick. 'I've noted that that boy Ronald's been absent from his place at the stables. I'm going out to do my rounds and see there's no untoward activity. Do you attend to Mr Hawkins while I ride the bounds, Nancy, I'll not be long.'

'Have a care for my men,' said Hawkins, 'they'll be arriving soon and they're trigger-happy. An hour after dusk, they'll cover every lane in and out of Leet and Harberscombe. You won't be able to rely on your quality to protect you.'

Frederick Genteel bowed politely and left the room. He had made a show of patrolling the house and its dependencies before he saddled up and trotted out of sight among the parkland trees. Now, having circled back, he was hastening seawards.

His powerful chestnut hunter was thundering down the ride, but it was slower than his thoughts which were already far ahead, at Armouth, where he knew a certain person was oblivious to her danger. The ride was a roughly metalled road, cut through the woods by his father Lord Mayberry so that he could take his Arab race-horses down to the sands for exercise. Overgrown by the oaks on either side, it was like a tunnel enclosed by contorted grey ribs. They sped backwards in a blur as Frederick spurred on.

At a point where a brook had cut a gully in the hillside, the ride looped back inland in a series of tight turns. Frederick did not slacken his pace. The first bend was clear, but as he came out of the second he saw a fallen log partly blocking the roadway. His horse saw it too, shied and skidded on the carpet of wet leaves. Frederick gripped the animal's back with his knees and swayed dangerously. Had it not been for a projecting branch, he might have carried it off, but the knuckled limb struck him on the temple, partly stunning him. He wavered a moment in the saddle then slumped over the withers and slid to the ground. His horse whinnied in fear, curvetted and stamped, then trotted off a little way and halted. Frederick lay in the mud, trying to instruct his indifferent limbs to help him rise. It was like a nightmare; there was a person in danger, he was trying to warn them, but was being prevented.

If Grace Pensilva was aware of any danger, she was not showing it. She and Jan King were sitting in his small lugger waiting for the tide to reach them. In the still of the late afternoon, the overcast day was like an oil painting by one of the Dutch masters, all liquid flowing greys and blues, indeterminate misty patches, smears of cloud, and dun-coloured sands, in which the only object with a formal, clear-cut outline was their boat.

'This be the last, the very last time us'll get up to this damn fool caper,' Jan was insisting. 'You've promised, 'aven't you,

Grace?' There was still doubt in his voice, but also resentment.

'I've promised. This is the last time. I've told you a hundred times if I've told you once. Now cease your fretting.'

'Something's going to go wrong. In my bones I know it. The preventives've got wind of this. And I'm not sure of Jack Lugger, 'ee've been actin' peculiar.'

Grace smiled at him gently. She put a finger to his lips and shook her head reprovingly. 'You worry too much, Jan King. There's no need for it. Leave the worrying to Grace. Your Grace will handle it.'

'But what be it all for? Us don't need the money, us can't spend what us already 'ave without attractin' attention. What be the sense in puttin' our 'eads in a noose? *You* may be too 'ooked to let go, but why should *I* go on when I needn't?'

'For my sake, Jan King.'

'You never give me nothin'. All this time and us still be strangers to each other. When be it goin' to change?'

'Tomorrow.' Jan King laughed at that. His lips curled in disbelief. Then he became suddenly serious, his attention attracted by something behind her shoulder.

'What be that, Grace? There be someone comin'.' A horseman, not much more than a speck at first, was hastening towards them. As he crossed the shallow ponds in the sandflats, the spray flew up in a cloud around him. She raised her eyebrows quizzically a moment then stood up.

'Nothing important. It's only someone out exercising a horse. Come on Jan, take one of the sweeps and help me push off; the boat's lifting.' She seemed totally unperturbed, as though she were preparing to set off on a pleasure trip. There was no sign of anxiety as she braced her bare feet on the bottom boards and leaned on the oar until the drag of the sand broke and the lugger started moving. She did not bother to look over her shoulder, but Jan did and saw that the horseman was close upon them. Already fetlock-deep in the weedy water, he had slowed to a splashing canter.

'Friend o'yourn,' he said bitterly. 'Bain't you goin' to speak to un?' The rider had come up alongside the boat now and Grace turned to face him.

278

'Mr Hawkins is at the house,' said the rider breathlessly.
Jan had already seen he was Frederick Genteel. He hated the
direct, unpatronizing way the Squire addressed her. There
was a kind of complicity there that rankled. It rankled that
Grace was neither insolent nor deferential.

'What's that to me?' she asked, as though the Receiver of
Customs was a person of no consequence.

'He's filling the place with preventives. Stop a minute,
Grace, I must talk with you. This time you're in real danger,
terrible danger.'

'We have a tide to catch, Frederick. Jan and I are putting to
sea on our lawful occasions, what could Mr Hawkins have to
say against that?'

'Only that he and that Scully fellow will be waiting to catch
you red-handed when you step ashore.'

'Is that so? Well, give them my best regards and say I've
turned to fishing.'

'As far as they're concerned, I haven't seen you.' By now,
the water was right up under his horse's belly and he had
bent his knees to keep his boots out of the water. 'Turn back,
Grace!' he implored. 'Won't you listen to me?'

'What shall us do, Grace?' asked Jan uneasily.

'Do what you like,' she answered shortly, 'there's still time
to jump overboard and wade back. I'm not stopping you. If
you're man enough to come with me, you can hoist the sail
while I ship the rudder.'

Frederick Genteel had finally reined in and his horse stood
steaming while the lugger slid away from him with an almost
imperceptible wake in the water. He wished that he, not Jan
King, were sailing alongside Grace Pensilva, but he was
Frederick Genteel, heir to the Leet acres, and in the gilded
drawing-room his sister and his uninvited guest sat and
waited. Before he had ridden half across the sands and looked
back, the lugger had vanished, lost in the haze or some cleft
in the headland.

The ship loomed out of the half dark, slow-moving, creaking, enormous. The lugger was almost crushed beneath its

forefoot, but Jan King tugged at the oars and they slid along the planking to the chain-plates where a man in foreign clothes was looking down at them.

'Your navigation is almost too accurate, Monsieur Caradec,' said Grace in French. 'Do you think you can find the mouth to the Kingsbridge estuary just as easily? If you can, Jan here pretends to be able to pilot us up to Salcombe.'

'Keep it short,' grumbled Jan King. 'I can't abide to 'ear all that Froggy lingo. Just find out if 'ee've brought the stuff with 'im.'

'Can't you smell it?' said Grace. 'He says you're to jump aboard and pass him a painter so his men can stream the lugger astern.'

'Why didn't you tell me about this plan until the last minute?' Jan insisted once they were together on the quarter-deck. 'Didn't you trust me?'

'I didn't tell anyone, not even Caradec knew our destination until I told him just now.'

'Who gives a damn about Caradec, I be your partner, damn it, Grace, I've a right to be let into the secret.'

'The only real secret is the kind only one person knows: a secret shared is a secret sold.'

'If that be the way you feels, well, be damned to 'ee. Don't expect Jan King to pilot this hooker up river to Salcombe.'

'Why do you have to be so touchy, Jan?'

'Touchy? I'll tell 'ee why: because you've stayed so damned stand-offish, because you've done nothin' but lead me on, lead me on for your own purposes. You let me think that we'd come closer together, but it 'aven't 'appened; us be just as cool as when you comed to Armouth. I tell 'ee, 'tiddn' for the money, I'd never've done it for the money. 'Twas for you, Grace Pensilva, that I took up with this. I won't be used I tell 'ee! Tell the skipper I want to be put back in the lugger.'

'Hush, Jan, hush!' Grace caught him by the arm as she spoke and ran an arm around his shoulders.

'You won't get around me so easy,' he protested.

'Hush, Jan; it's going to be different.'

'How do you expect me to believe that? That be the same song you've been singin' all along.'

'I swear to you, Jan, 'tis all going to change henceforth,' she whispered soothingly. 'Now sit by me here on the rail and we'll watch out for the Little Mew Stone and the Gregory Rocks. We're in your hands, Jan, to pilot us in, no one else could do it, not in this mist. Sit down and I'll tell you how it's going to be once we've given over smuggling.'

Jan sat in the darkness, wondering at the strange sensation that went through his body when she held his hands. The ship was dark, the sea was one with the misty sky, the rocks, when they loomed to larboard, were darker still. The French captain brought them neatly to the estuary mouth and then called Jan over to the helm, speaking his usual broken English. For a while the wheel hung slack in his hands and then, suddenly, the current caught them like a blow and every nerve in Jan's body was engaged in a life and death struggle to save the ship, taking advantage of every flaw of wind and shift of stream, sensing out the unseen shore and straining his ears for the rush of the overfalls. The *Ar Mor* tacked and tacked again in the narrow stretch of water between Poundstone and Blackstone until Jan began to doubt his bearings and wonder if he could ever fetch Salcombe.

On the hill above the town, Captain Scully had already reviewed his troop of preventives and sent them trotting off to their appointed stations behind the hedges on the lanes that led out of Harberscombe. Haranguing them had given him a devil of a thirst. Consulting his watch, he decided he still had time to return to the Fortescue for a jar of ale before following them towards their night-long vigil.

In the stable-yard at Leet House, another preventive troop was forming up under Mr Hawkins' jaundiced eye, sidling around on their jaded nags.

'What they lack in smartness and *esprit de corps* I hope they make up for in numbers,' he muttered to Nancy Genteel. 'We'll have to move off in a moment, but I wonder what's happened to your brother, I'm worried about him, he's been gone far longer than he said.'

'You could save your concern for more serious matters,'

replied Nancy. 'If he's not here immediately, you can take me with you; I can handle a pistol.'

Just then there was a small commotion at the far side of the yard and a rider entered, forging his way through the preventives to the steps where Mr Hawkins and Nancy were standing. A groom held up a lantern and they recognized him; it was Frederick Genteel, his face muddied and bloody, his hat awry.

'I had a fall,' he explained curtly. 'It's nothing. By the way, Hawkins, I've thought things over, I'll ride out with you. As Squire, it's my duty.'

'What about me?' asked Nancy. 'I'm coming too, aren't I?'

'No, you shall stay at the house and prepare dressings; there may be wounded.'

As the Leet troop jingled quietly down to the bridge and the pool beyond it, Frederick reflected that the noose was closing around Grace Pensilva. Well, he had tried to dissuade her, but she hadn't listened. When Mr Hawkins had dismounted his men and stationed them in the wood, they stood together under a willow at the meadow's edge. A solitary light burned in Leet House; it shone from Nancy's chamber. It was chilly there, down by the water, and long wraith-like trails of mist were creeping across the parkland.

'You've forgotten your pistol,' whispered Hawkins.

'Have I? There's no lack of them round about.'

Mr Hawkins examined his face as carefully as the dim light allowed.

'You puzzle me, Genteel. Why've you come out here if you're not set on catching smugglers?'

'To see fair play,' murmured Frederick.

'Fair play!' spluttered Hawkins. 'Where does "fair play" come into it? They're criminals.'

'Hush,' said Frederick, 'they're also my people. Don't you think they're human?'

They stood silent after that, while the cattle padded about the park, thudding their hooves at the drinking trough, and the sea-trout splashed in the pool. It was a long wait and Mr Hawkins began increasingly to wonder. He wondered if the

282

troop he had sent up past Uglington to take the tinners on their way to their rendezvous with Jack Lugger at Leet had been successful. He had heard no shots; did that mean they had given in tamely? He wondered if Captain Scully had disposed his men in all the strategic points around Harber-scombe as planned. It was a comprehensive but simple scheme, a child could have done it. But Scully was certainly a soak and probably a scoundrel, not to mention a coward and the best-laid plans of mice and men . . . He wondered about Mrs Coyte and her son Ronald; they had seemed sincere enough in their dislike of Grace Pensilva, but it wouldn't be the first time that such smuggling families had hoodwinked the Revenue with false information. Well, if the Coytes *had* misled him, he congratulated himself that he still held a trump card. He would send their precious Jack Lugger up to Exeter Assizes for his part in the earlier affair. That would be worth at least transportation. Devon would lose an idle rogue and Van Diemen's Land would gain an unwilling settler. For the while, Lugger, at his own request, was lying, bound and gagged, in the midst of the wood.

Captain Scully was calling for one for the road, but he was in no hurry. Since he had entered the Fortescue's taproom he had discerned something odd, a strained atmosphere. Ben Barlow, the landlord, was putting on an air of forced joviality; beneath it there was worry. The old fox was up to something; he had probably decided to profit by the preventives' absence to pull off some trick or other. Scully began to wish he had kept back two or three of his men; whatever was in the wind, he didn't fancy facing it on his lonesome. He knew he had no friends in Salcombe; the usual crowd of drinkers on the settles around the chimney corner kept their faces turned studiously away from him and they were forever muttering and murmuring, with an occasional burst of laughter which he guessed was in his direction. Well, he would put paid to that; he strolled over to join them.

Shortly afterwards, the landlord went to the door in response to a gentle knocking. He opened it, stepped outside and, a moment later, returned, crossed the room and murmured to Scully deferentially. 'There be a person to see 'ee.'

'Tell 'im to come in,' said Scully briskly, not to be caught out that easily.

''Tis a lady, Cap'n, a proper lady, 'er don't look like the sort that comes to taverns. But she was most insistent.' Scully hesitated. He was curious to know the woman's identity.

'See who she is.'

Ben Barlow went outside again while Scully sipped at his mulled ale.

'She says you'll know 'er when you do see 'er,' Ben Barlow dropped his voice. 'She be a right 'andsome lady, she do belong to the quality, I reckon.'

Scully drained his mug. All the topers were watching him. If he failed to go to the door, he would be a laughing stock; after all, it was only a woman, he did not think the landlord was lying.

As he crossed to the door, he unobtrusively loosened the pistol in his sash. Scully knew how to be careful. When he threw back the door, he stepped to one side swiftly to spoil the aim of anyone who might have been waiting to draw a bead on him. He need not have bothered; the narrow street seemed empty except for his horse, tethered to a ring by the door.

'Captain Scully?' Only when he swung his head did he see her; she had been concealed in the dead area masked by his bad eye. The impression given by her soft voice was matched by the quality of her grey silken dress. Her face, framed by a poke-bonnet, was lost in shadow.

'Madam, at your service.'

'Close the door, if you please; I have some important intelligence for you, for your ears only.'

Scully studied her; she was unarmed and, as the landlord had said, uncommonly handsome. He pulled the door to with his foot.

'Well?'

'Come.' She beckoned him and set off down the lane. He followed unwillingly. At the crossroads, she turned. When he came up with her she whispered something, but he could not catch it. She beckoned him closer with her crooked little finger. He cocked his head to listen as she formed the words again. 'The woman you seek is here in Salcombe.' Scully started. He was not stupid, he could put two and two together. At one and the same time, he reached to pull off her bonnet and, with the other hand, began to free the pistol from his sash.

Before he could complete either movement, two strong arms came from behind his back and locked around him. Someone had been lurking in a doorway.

'Got un!' muttered a man's voice beside his ear. 'What shall us do ? Kill un?' What a fool! Scully spat in the gutter and squirmed in the stifling arms.

'What for? He's but a worm. We'll tie him. He shall enjoy a ringside seat. He was looking for smugglers wasn't he? He shall hear some working.' As she spoke, the woman stuffed her handkerchief in his mouth, choking and gagging him. Then she wrenched the pistol from his grasp and covered him while the man behind him tied his hands with a cord.

'Lie down!' she ordered. 'Tie his ankles to his wrists,' she told her companion. Scully still had not seen her face; it was too dark here, away from the lighted tavern. Now he cursed inwardly; the man was taking his sash and winding it round his head.

'Us can't afford to leave 'ee see too much, can us, me beauty,' muttered the man confidentially, 'but you shall 'ear the sound o' the casks rollin'; it do make sweet music.'

Scully understood, he understood how easily he had been duped, he even had a glimmering of understanding how not only Mr Hawkins also had been duped, but Mrs Coyte into the bargain. He hated this woman for her intelligence, he hated her more when he heard the casks bumping on to the quay, when he heard the clopping of hooves, the low voices of the drovers, when he smelt the unmistakable reek of brandy. He hated her because he was sure she had planned all this, down to the last detail, as though she had known he would stay behind to drink in the Fortescue, so that she could taunt him

285

with the sounds of his discomfiture. Meanwhile, Ben Barlow and his mates were sure to be still drinking quietly in the taproom. They would hear nothing, naturally. And they would be amazed to find him trussed like a fowl when they left for home.

The noise went on and on, this was no ordinary landing: the smugglers were unloading their ship right under the Custom House. Scully heard French voices; they had dared to bring the Frenchman right up the river, had they?

Scully writhed and pulled at his bonds. They were well tied with seamen's knots, he was getting nowhere. But he did achieve some success with his sash which was of smooth material. By rubbing his head against the wall he gradually slid it over the crown of his head until his one good eye could just see under it.

At the end of the street, he could see the Frenchman's bowsprit. Around it there were lanterns burning while the last of the casks were swung out of the hold with improvised cargo-booms. But that was not what caught his attention. What engaged his intense study was the face, the face of the bare-headed woman who stood on the prow and directed operations. He had only a minute or two to fix that face in his memory for the lights were doused and the last of the pack-animals, draped with casks in slings, trotted past him. She was the woman who had put his eye out. The ship was cast off and dropped back out of sight into the unlit vastness of the estuary.

Within minutes, as he had suspected they would, the landlord and his cronies were fussing over him. He shoved them aside and ran to his horse. He had two choices; he could ride after the moonlighters or he could try to cut off the ship. If he rode after the former, he would no doubt catch up with some of them, though their fellows would be scattered all over the country, but they would be small fry, determined to sell their lives and liberty dearly. If he rode out to cut off the ship he might reach the old battery, unmanned since Nelson's day, charge a rusty cannon and try a shot at the Frenchman. He decided on the latter course; there was but a small chance of

286

success, but he judged the odds were worth it. To get a shot, just one shot at point-blank range, with a possibility of destroying that woman, was all he asked for. He rode down the shore towards the battery like a wild thing, heedless of life and limb. With God's help, he would have her.

Mr Hawkins had given up hope of success; he had heard no word from his men who had gone after the tinners, and the time for high tide had come and gone, the water was gently receding. And then they heard it, both he and Frederick Genteel heard the sound at the same moment: there was no mistaking the rhythmic thudding that was coming from a boat being rowed up the river.

The preventives in the wood must have heard it too; there was a slight crackle of twigs and foliage as if a breeze had swept through the undergrowth. Mr Hawkins turned his head to the nearest sentinel. 'Alive! I want her alive!' he hissed. 'Pass the word down the line. I'll flay the man alive who fires without I give the order.'

They had not long to wait; the noise grew louder, a vague shape could be seen approaching along the Arun's meanders. It was lighter now; although there was no moon, the clouds were breaking and timid starshine was coming through. The two men under the drooping willow stood slightly hunched in their coats. Hawkins was holding a silver-chased pistol. Then, inexplicably, there was a spell of silence, as if the rower had taken fright at something. Hawkins allowed his pistol muzzle to droop; Frederick saw lines of frustration forming about his mouth.

The boat slid into the pool quite swiftly; one moment they were seeking it vainly through the willow fronds, and the next it was there, right in front of them, with the rower standing in the middle of it, guiding its course with the trailing blades.

Frederick coughed. Hawkins flashed him a glance of cold fury. So that was why he had come! The person in the boat looked round wildly and must have discerned some movement ashore, the glint of steel. In an instant the boat was empty, rocking wildly while its ertswhile occupant was scrambling ashore on the far bank.

'Stand!' bellowed Mr Hawkins, stepping away from the tree and levelling his pistol. At the same moment, the ring of preventives disclosed themselves. The fugitive floundered to a halt and stood dejected. 'Quick, bring lights!' Hawkins continued, leaping into the drifting boat with an agility unusual in a man of his age, and using it to ferry himself to the other side.

The fugitive clung to his knees in supplication and he found himself embarrassed by his pistol. One of his men came forward with a dark-lantern. When the shutter was pulled back, Hawkins saw that his captive was not a woman but a boy, and a boy he had seen all too recently.

'You, Ronald Coyte? What the devil are you doing here at this time of night?' Ronald Coyte was too terrified to answer coherently. He stammered and bit his lip; he was like a rabbit in front of a stoat. 'Speak out boy, or I'll kill you,' exclaimed Hawkins. 'Are you too in league with that damned woman?'

Ronald Coyte shook his head. Two of the preventives had pulled him off Hawkins' knees and were holding him upright. 'I comes 'ere often,' Ronald managed to say at last.

'At night?'

'She do call me over.'

'She?' Ronald Coyte's lips quivered; the name would not come out, but his eyes, cast in the direction of the single lighted window, high up on the wall of Leet House, told Hawkins everything.

Frederick Genteel laughed. He had waded the pool and was standing beside them. It was a bitter kind of laugh.

'Didn't you have the wit to know this wasn't the night to come courting?' he asked.

'She told me she'd 'orsewhip me if ever I failed 'er,' muttered Ronald.

'Bloody fool!' exclaimed Hawkins. 'But you're just one more of 'em. why do I have to be surrounded by goddamn, half-witted bloody fools?' He slipped his pistol in his pocket. 'I say, Genteel, you don't have any decent port or brandy up at the house, do you? I shall need some consolation. And you, I fancy, will be celebrating.'

'Celebrating?'

'Well, we haven't killed or caught anybody, have we? Wasn't that what you wanted?'

'Larboard a little,' said Jan King.

'*Bâbord, un peu*,' translated Grace for the benefit of the helmsman. She and Jan were sitting on the rail while Caradec ranged the quarter-deck and one of the crew steered the ship seawards with the current. They were all in a jovial mood; hadn't they just made fools of the Revenue? Salcombe town was slipping astern and the estuary mouth was opening up ahead. It was still dark, but getting lighter. The faintest of night breezes filled their sails and gave them bare steerage-way. The steersman's pipe glowed fitfully as he puffed on it.

'We did it!' exclaimed Grace impulsively.

'Aye, us did,' echoed Jan King. 'Know summat, Grace? You'm the greatest smuggler as ever was.' He put his arm round her shoulder and kissed her on the mouth. To his astonishment, she did not resist. The blood seethed in his head as he prolonged the moment. Then, afraid of being repulsed, he broke it off himself and sat back, holding her at arm's length.

The shot passed between their heads like the screech of violently tearing cloth. It shook the heads on their shoulders and left them dazed, almost unaware of the loud crack that followed it. Only Caradec had seen the flash, all the others had been facing away from it. He waited anxiously for a second detonation. They were sitting ducks, moving seaward with unbearable slowness. He glanced into the rigging to see if any of the stays or halyards had been sectioned. Only Jan King saw that the helmsman was slumped over his wheel. The ship was yawing slowly, spilling the wind from her sails; she was losing steerage-way and drifting towards the Blackstone Rocks. He sprang to his feet and threw the headless helmsman to one side, spun the wheel and stood there, poised like a cat on the balls of his feet, straining every sense to catch the mood of the ship and tease her back to life. Grace came and stood beside him, watching the muscles of his broad back flexing. Caradec stared at the shore, waiting, waiting for the fuse's glow, the red blossom from the next shot.

It never came. The seconds crept by, the ship hung, practically backwinded until Caradec pushed the boom over by main force and the mizzen filled with a quiet flap. Even then it was a long time before Jan felt some life come into the wheel.

All the earlier jubilation had evaporated. The sense of strain continued until the first Channel swells lifted the *Ar Mor*'s forefoot and the longshore breeze set them heeling. It continued while the crew came aft from the forecastle and busied themselves about their stricken comrade. It hung about them long after the corpse had been bundled in sailcloth with a shot at its feet and consigned to the deep when they were off the Bolt. It was with them still when the ship hove-to to allow Grace and Jan to embark in the lugger. Grace lingered a moment, talking quietly with the captain.

'What were you saying to Caradec just now?' he asked her when they had been cast off and were hoisting sail for the return to Armouth. 'Didn't you say "*demain*"? That means tomorrow, don't it?'

'I was wishing him a safe return. I said I hoped he'd be back in the Aber-Vrac'h tomorrow.'

'Good, I 'opes so too, and I 'opes us don't see un again in a twelvemonth, a lifetime for that matter. Us've done with this smugglin', 'aven't us, Grace. You swore it.'

'Yes, Jan, it's all over, all done as it was meant to be. From tomorrow, it will be all different.'

'Thank God for that, us 'aven't got nine lives to play with.'

For a while they sat silent, while the wavelets lapped past the clinker hull. They could see the high, brooding mass of the Devon coast, like a wall, culminating in the Dartmoor tors.

'Why aren't we sailing straight to Armouth?' asked Grace, with a trace of alarm in her voice. 'The wind's free, we can make it in one board without tacking.'

'Clever Grace, always one jump ahead, Grace bain't so

smart as Jan King this time.' She looked at him narrowly. What did he mean? What thoughts were seething about behind those steady eyes of his? She had seen that the course he was steering would carry them well to the east of the Barrow. It loomed increasingly high above their larboard bow.

'Clever Grace never thought about the money, did 'er? Us'd 'ave to be bloody fools to sail into Armouth Pool with all this money. Ten to one, the preventives'll be waitin' for us. They'll want nothin' better'n to take our money.'

'What shall we do then?'

'Sail to the Carrack Rocks and bury it. Then us'll catch a fish or two before us reaches Armouth. By that time, 'twill be mornin', 'Arberscombe folk'll be about and the preventives won't dare touch us without evidence.' He was right. She hadn't thought about that, the money had slipped from her consciousness, she had been one jump ahead, but had overlooked the obvious. This was a new Jan King: prudent, decisive. Until now, it had been all Grace; she had set the course and stemmed the tide, now she sat back in her place and let Jan do it.

'Another thing!' said the newly self-confident Jan King as they clambered back aboard the lugger after burying the money. 'I 'opes that Genteel feller won't be 'angin' about when us gets back to Armouth. I've took all I can stand, you must 'ave done with un.'

'I don't intend seeing him, not in your lifetime, not while we're together.'

They sailed quietly under the overhanging brow of the Barrow; Armouth was tucked away in the bay ahead of them.

'Glad to 'ear it. Bain't no use, maid, 'angin' about the gentry, their kind and ourn don't mix, not no more'n oil and water.'

'Frederick Genteel's not a bad man.'

'No, I never said that. Funny thing –' he paused and steered reflectively, 'there be summat 'bout Frederick I never told 'ee –' Again he sat silent.

'Well?'

'Frederick Genteel were there the day o' Frank's funeral. 'Ee were watchin'. I see'd un.'

'Why didn't you say so before?' her voice had a new sharpness.

'Wouldn've changed nothin', would it? Wouldn've changed 'ow you felt about un. 'Twaddn' fair to tell 'ee, neither, not while I thought you cared for un.' Now it was her turn to sit silent. She kept her peace till they crossed the bar and brought up in the estuary.

'You're a good man, Jan, better than I thought. Dr Cornish is right. I don't deserve you.' She had always known it was going to be hard, but this was harder, much harder. Only a word and her resolve was shaken.

5

'Wake up! Wake up, sleepy-head!' She took him by the shoulder and shook him. He rolled on to his back, pulling the sheet across his naked chest with an instinctive arm while his eyes flew open an instant, then closed again.

'Leave a man be, can't 'ee?' he grumbled, but without rancour. 'I needs me sleep, I bain't no machine, to run without rest.'

''Tis such a wonderful day, Jan King. The sun is out, 'tis hot, and the river is shining. 'Tis a day to go swimming, 'tis a day for a holiday. You can't waste it sleeping.' Jan King opened one eye. His hand flew out and he caught her wrist, dragging her towards the bed. She resisted, but only mildly, sitting on its edge propped on her arms above him.

'I knows 'ow us can waste un,' he declared knowingly. 'Give us a kiss, Grace, like the one last night.' With his arms about her neck, he tried to pull her down to him. She allowed him to bring her close, but twisted away when his stubbly cheek grazed hers.

'You're like a hedgehog, Jan, too prickly for pleasure. Let me go, I'll fetch some hot water and see you shaved first.' He released her reluctantly and she went downstairs to blow up the fire under the kettle. The door stood open and a bird sang in the hedge opposite.

'Little bit of bread and no cheese,' sang the bird in the hedge, cocking its head on one side to observe her. Grace felt a sudden pang. Her mother had taught her that. It was strange how a place caught hold of you. This valley, with its steep lane and small, high-banked fields, rising towards invisible

Okewell Court, was part of her now. So were those puffy clouds hovering over Harberscombe. She had always said to herself that it would be a blessed release, that the dust of that place would never darken her feet again and no regrets, and yet.

And yet she put her hand to her mouth and bit her knuckle. And tears were close to her eyes. She fought them down, squinting into the brightness where the black boathouses glistened in the late morning sun. Not a soul was about; it was Sunday and the fishermen were at church, praying for safe returns and silver harvests. How credulous they were. The sea made men superstitious.

The gig sat on the close-cropped grass where she had visited it half an hour before, stowing a bag in the stern locker and a basket of provisions in the bow. Jan had repaired it well and painted it blue and white. She had glanced up through her hair at his window as she closed the stern locker. He had not seen her; drowned in sleep, she would have to revive him.

Harberscombe bells rang out. How fast the time was flying! She snatched the singing kettle from the fire and climbed the stairs. She hoped she had managed to compose her face, but she need not have worried, Jan was too impatient to study her. He was lurking behind the door and embraced her as soon as she stepped into his room.

'Careful, you're like to scald yourself in a painful place!' she teased him. 'Come on, fetch me your razor and mug, be quick, I haven't all day. We're going on a picnic; it'll be your wedding breakfast, Jan King.'

'And they be weddin' bells, bain't they?' asked Jan eagerly. 'You've made me wait powerful long, Grace Pensilva. It 'ave been 'ard, so much I've wanted you.' She smiled over her shoulder while she drew the razor across the strop. Seeing her dexterity with it, he wondered where she had learnt the skill. With Frank? His eyes clouded.

But Grace was full of infectious excitement and he soon forgot to be sulky. The sun was indeed shining and he had never known her so playful. She set the broken scrap of looking-glass in a corner of the window frame, then lathered his face for him. She handed him his razor and stood behind him with her arms round his waist while he raised his elbows for the first tentative stroke. He could feel her breasts against his shoulder-blades; there was only her thin cotton dress between them. Her chin was on his shoulder so that she too could see into the mirror.

'I always wondered what 'twas like,' she confided as the razor blade rasped against the first stretch of stubble.

'Wondered what what was like?'

'To be a man – have all those whiskers – to shave.' She giggled, upsetting him.

'Hey, don't jog my arm like that; you'll make me cut myself.'

'Let me do it for you.' He paused in mid gesture, undecided. ''Tis terrible sharp.'

'Go on, let me try; I won't hurt you.' While she spoke, he felt her cool hands dragging across the tight flesh on his belly. He sighed and failed to resist when her fingers slid up his arm and took the razor from him. She pressed tight against him, breasts to his back, belly to his buttocks; it was a sensation that made him feel faint.

The razor's long blade dragged slowly across his cheek and he felt the stubble resists, then capitulate like massed soldiery mown down by musketry. It was so quiet that they could both hear the scrape of the razor's edge. She was staring into the glass intently and guiding the blade with increasing confidence. Was this how she had done it for . . .?

She felt him relax, his apprehension waning. 'What does it feel like?' she whispered.

'I can't tell 'ee. 'Tis like –' he sought the words, ''tis like bein' a lord, a prince. 'Tis like 'avin' an 'andmaiden, a slave, a . . .'

'A whore?'

'Don't say that!' He was angry with her; his body stiffened.

'Careful, I'll cut you.'

'Then don't say that no more. I won't 'ear you say it.' She stopped shaving him and her hand holding the razor was poised an inch from his face.

'What's wrong, Jan?' Her voice was soft, coaxing.

'I won't 'ave no one say that, not about the woman who – who's goin' to be . . .'

'Going to be what, Jan?'

'Goin' to be my – wife.' Merely to utter the word was a struggle for him.

'Then I won't.'

'Nevermore?'

'Nevermore.'

The hand holding the razor slowly approached again and the cool metal skimmed the skin under his chin. Once more he relaxed, surrendering himself to the unwonted, dangerous pleasure, confiding himself to another being, exposing himself at his most vulnerable to a hand directed by another consciousness, in which it pleased him to confide implicit trust.

Only when he sensed the slightest of hesitations, with the blade lingering under his Adam's apple, did he rouse himself from the delicious lethargy into which he had subsided. Something made him look into the mirror, a desire to see his beloved's features. What he saw unnerved him. Her face was lined with unusual concentration, but more than that, the eyes were set on a reflection he could not see but which seemed to be within his flesh beneath the razor's edge, and their expression held nothing of loving. She seemed more like a sleepwalker or a person in a trance than her normal self. Careful to avoid shocking her out of her spell, he raised his own hand gently and took the razor from her.

'I must have been dreaming.' She rubbed her eyes and he believed her. They brightened again with kindness. She had told him it would take her a long time to forget.

'I'll finish meself,' he told her. 'Do you go down and find some breakfast; I be 'ungry as an 'unter.'

When she had gone downstairs, he finished shaving himself with minute care. What had made him apprehensive? She had not even nicked him. He heard the familiar clicking of pans in the kitchen as he rinsed his face in cold water from the ewer and ran his fingers through his hair. Not such a bad lookin' chap after all, he told himself silently as he fluffed out his side whiskers; his hair was naturally curly, he rarely combed it. What girl could resist him? With his shirt in his hand he ran barefoot down the stairs. She was standing by the table, putting a few final items into a basket. Her look was level, friendly; he had been wrong to distrust her, but when was she going to surrender to him?

"Ow about that kiss now?' he demanded, advancing swiftly and catching her by the shoulders. 'I could eat 'ee.' She held him at arm's length, laughing, then darted forward, planting a kiss on each cheek.

'That's enough for now,' she told him, with her palms against his chest, 'two for the price of one. That's good measure. Now, pick up the basket, I'll carry the cider.'

'What about me breakfast?'

'Didn't I tell you? We're going to have a picnic.'

'A picnic?' said Jan dubiously.

'We're going to take the gig, row round to the Carrack Rocks, have a feast and count the money. How's that for a jaunt?'

'I dunno, I'd rather stay 'ome.'

'Get on with you, Jan King, don't be a dog in the manger. Come on, put that shirt on, the sun is burning. And smile a little, you can't refuse me that, not on my wedding. Take your time, Jan, we'll drink the cider and we'll go swimming.' He pondered a moment, she could see him relenting; he would be remembering the time he had come upon her in the cave; that had been near the Carracks. He slipped on his shirt and picked up the basket. 'How handsome you look, a proper gentleman,' she told him as they left the cottage.

'Gennulman? I don't want to be no gennulman,' he scowled. 'If you wants gennulmen, you must go after that Frederick o' yourn.'

'Oh no!' she laughed. 'Come on, hurry, the tide's falling.'

Frederick Genteel came down the last few stairs painfully. He held on to the newel post at the bottom of the Elizabethan staircase at Leet before crossing the hallway to the saloon. His ribs were exquisite agony; he must have bruised them worse than he thought when he took that tumble. However, the pain had provided a good excuse for staying in bed until Mr Hawkins had taken his own rest, left the house and was in the stable-yard harnessing up for departure.

Each step he took brought him a suffocating twinge that stopped him in his tracks. The journey from stairs to doorway was a long calvary, but he looked forward to subsiding on to the sofa for a spell of rest. After that, he would see. To be held up like this by a bit of physical discomfort was something he could not easily admit, still less consider calling for the doctor. To give in would be damnable weakness. All the same, the sofa looked as attractive as a tropical island after a long year's difficult navigation.

But the saloon was not empty; his sister was there already, standing in one of the tall windows and holding the frock-coat he had thrown down on a chair that night when he returned with Mr Hawkins. Nancy Genteel had a knowing smile on her face and she did not snap at him as usual. These were not good portents.

'I shall be getting that thoroughbred, shan't I?' she announced sweetly. 'You can't refuse me that now, can you? Nor all the cambric handkerchiefs in creation.'

'Oh, can't I?' Speech itself was painful. Frederick hoped he wasn't about to be drawn into yet another quarrel. He stood swaying beside the sofa.

'There will be changes at Leet, big changes.' There was an acid certitude in her voice that Frederick did not like.

'What makes you think that?'

Nancy did not reply directly. Instead, she held out the coat, displayed over her forearm and gripped by the collar like some poor miscreant evil-doer caught in the act.

'Our Mr Hawkins wasn't very observant, was he?'

'What d'you mean?' Already, he was beginning to suspect what she had discovered.

'You fell in the woods, didn't you? At least, that's what you told us. So you did: this coat's plastered with mud – but that's not all, there's something else isn't there? – Sand – sand all up the back – a layer of sand and then another layer of mud

– now what does that tell us? No need to pain yourself answering – Frederick Genteel did more than ride the bounds of Leet Park yesterday, he rode beyond it, he rode across the beach, didn't he?' Nancy Genteel was all too aware of her advantage; she was pressing it mercilessly. Frederick subsided on to the sofa, he felt faint, as though the world were slipping away from him.

'And what would Frederick Genteel be doing, riding helter-skelter across the sands, if he weren't trying to find someone, if he weren't trying to warn them? Or was it only a coincidence that he rode that way the very day Mr Hawkins arrived with the preventives?' Nancy threw the coat back on the chair and approached him, leaning over him sarcastically. 'Poor Frederick, is it terribly painful? What's it like to have a broken heart, Frederick? To be turned down for an illiterate fisherman, or should I say smuggler? She didn't listen to you, did she? Well, whether she did or not is immaterial, what matters is that you, Squire Genteel, rode out to warn her. That coat over there provides the evidence. Do you deny it?'

Frederick sat silent.

'No, I thought not. At least you're honest, painfully honest. Well, now that I have the evidence, I intend to exploit it.' She took her riding crop and bent it between her slim fingers until it was arched so tight it seemed it had to break. 'You have bent me like that, brother Frederick, bent me often enough, to your man's will. Now, it is you who will bend, you who will cut your clothes to suit your cloth. It is you who will leave Leet. It is you who will marry for money.'

'And if I refuse?'

'I have the evidence. The crime: hampering the King's justice.'

Frederick looked over his shoulder into the stable-yard. Mr Hawkins was already seated in his carriage, ready to drive away. He had not been observant enough to see the sand on his coat. What was to prevent Frederick from washing it? Where would the evidence be then?

There was a grinding of wheels in the courtyard. Nancy's face showed that the same thought must have occured to her.

But she had only to run to the window and shout; Hawkins would return immediately. Frederick caught her by the wrist.

'You expect me to go quietly and leave you to lord it over here with your Ronald, your precious Ronald? Well, you shan't have that satisfaction. Hawkins shall never see that coat.' To his astonishment, she did not struggle, attempt to pull free. She did not shout either.

'What do you take me for? A green slip of a girl? A looby? And what makes *my* Ronald any less honourable than *your* Grace Pensilva? I knew you despised me, but I didn't think you purblind enough to consider me stupid. What d'you think's been afoot while Frederick Genteel's been reclining in his chamber?' She paused, and Frederick released her wrist. The coach had left the courtyard and was out of sight down the drive. She massaged the bruised skin delicately. With a thin-lipped smile she continued.

'Why, chatting with Mr Hawkins, talking things over. We came to several interesting conclusions. First of all, unless you wish it, there shall be no scandal. Nothing shall be said in public. In private, I shall be magnanimous and keep it from Father. It will be up to you to write to him and explain that you have decided to return to your travels. And, as you are of a generous, almost equally magnanimous turn of mind, you will tell him that you are making over your interest in the estate to your sister and that your decision is final. Mr Hawkins agrees that that is the elegant thing to do; there is no advantage in soiling the public's view of the nobility with some unpleasant case at the assizes, and I must say that it would be of no advantage to me to have my brother shackled at Rougemont Castle and branded a felon; that does not help in polite society. You have three days in which to make the necessary provisions and take passage out of the country.'

'Is that all?'

'Mr Hawkins told me something else about you, something I had half expected, about you and Salcombe, about you and Grace Pensilva's brother . . .' Nancy was smiling her thin-lipped smile as she spoke. She waited a moment before continuing. 'You'll have told her yourself, of course. It's always best to have that sort of thing out in the open. And she's forgiven you too, hasn't she? Just as she's forgiven Jan King and charmed him to love her! How wonderful! How convenient! I shan't need to let her know, or rather, when I *do* send word to her, it will be no more than a reminder.'

If Frederick had not been paralysed by his bruised ribs, he might have sprung forward and throttled her. He knew he was defeated, not by his sister's cunning, but by his own imprudence.

'You win,' he muttered. 'I'll go. The estate will be yours to run, and much joy may you have of it.'

'Take your coat,' said Nancy, tossing it onto the chair beside him. 'Mr Hawkins has already examined it. Furthermore, I have shown it to Charles Barker, without saying why, of course. Now he's seen it, he's too clever a lawyer to commit perjury on your behalf. Ronald Coyte took care of your horse. He remembers its coat was sandy. So it's all cut and dried . . . When all's said and done, it pains me, Frederick, to see a well-meaning moral man like you suffer as you must at this moment. I'll call Dr Cornish to examine you. He's said to be good with smugglers.'

When she had left the room, Frederick Genteel took stock of his predicament. He must leave. He had no choice in the matter. At least he had Captain Fell's offer of employment to fall back on. What rankled most was that Nancy was sure to betray his secret to Grace Pensilva. If only he had told her himself! He had been afraid to break the spell that bound them together. Perhaps she suspected already, she did not seem to. Now, sooner or later, she would be told that he had been the instrumental cause of the death of her brother. His impulse was to ride over and tell her directly, before Nancy's malicious message could reach her, but he knew that his cracked ribs made that impossible. All he could do was to send her a message.

The schoolroom was tidy; Optimus had just gone round a final time, stacking the primers neatly in the windows, straightening desks. Although they were empty, the desks

301

still contained his schoolchildren. That was Alice Terry's place, she was the one with the halo of golden hair and the pert nose and the mischievous eyes. Uncle Bill Terry, who was uncle to all the Terrys and a great many besides, must be her great-uncle. Here, where the floorboard was already worn away by scuffing boots, Bob Kingdom sat. He was an absent-minded boy, but that wouldn't matter; his father was a farmer with a hundred acres and more. Bob could afford to go wool-gathering a little and lose his cows in the corn; his maternal grandfather had been a man called Wroth, Eric Wroth. He too had a touch of capriciousness; what's bred in the bone will come out in the beef. And the Scully child, Optimus had found it difficult to like young Andrew: sly, quick to throw suspicion on others, grasping; like father like son. But it was uncharitable to visit the sins of the fathers on their progeniture, however unpromising. Optimus wiped a slate, it was Albert Triggs' and Triggs was a big, slow-moving, sensible boy who was probably the teacher's pet. Triggs was endowed with a peculiar intuitive intelligence and grasp of logic. And yet there was a flaw, a quirk that went beyond mere imagination, like the phrases and scrawled drawings which Optimus had just effaced, that made him doubt his reason. Had Ivor married? Who would have wanted him? It had been Optimus' intention to consult the parish register, but that project, like others, would have to be abandoned now. There were no Pensilvas, no Kings, and for that he was grateful; he did not like to imagine the same drama being played out by another generation.

'I hear you're leaving, Mr Shute, there will be a great void in Branscombe.' Optimus looked up in astonishment; he was not expecting anyone and the Steward had crept up on him.

'Decidedly, there are few secrets in this community,' he replied drily. 'I'm sure it will survive the departure of a common or garden schoolmaster. There may be a few more Methodists and a few less Church of England scholars, but that's hardly a cataclysm.'

'You undervalue yourself. You'll be missed, Mr Shute.'

'I hope you haven't come over to dissuade me. I'm not to be shaken.'

Charles Barker shook his head.

302

'No, I'm here as executor to settle up some matters concerning poor Dr Cornish. It's in connection with that that I've come over to see you. Would you mind stepping across the road a moment?'

'I doubt if Mrs Kemp would welcome –'

'What's Mrs Kemp to do with it?' interrupted Barker. It was the lawyer speaking. 'I'm calling you over, I'm the executor. It's only a formality, but better seen to in the house than elsewhere or by correspondence.'

It was just as Optimus had expected. Mrs Kemp sat and scowled in a corner, pointedly refusing to join the two of them at the long table. Optimus sat down on one of the long benches and could not help remembering the evenings he had spent here, when the air was full of tobacco smoke and the whiff of brandy. A lump formed in his throat, he felt curiously sick. There was a smell of dead ashes in the room now; in the past it had always smelt of burning; the hearth had always had a warm heart to it. He shifted uneasily, gripped by an involuntary urge to run outdoors, but Charles Barker was keeping a firm eye on him. The lawyer sat down in the old man's chair at the head of the table, shuffling some papers. Optimus was reminded of his first encounter with Dr Cornish, there had been a heap of papers in exactly the same place. The scene was strikingly similar, yet fundamentally different: one of the characters was missing. Falstaff had been replaced by Shylock; no, that wasn't fair, Charles Barker was a dry stick of a man with gold pince-nez that made him look like an insect, but there was no vice in him.

'Ready?' asked Barker, adjusting his glasses and, not wanting a response, plunging into the reading of a curiously folded piece of paper.

'I, Edward Anthony Wyatt Cornish, being of sound mind do by this my last will and testament dispose of my worldly goods as follows . . .'

So that was it; Charles Barker had required his presence to witness the reading of the Doctor's will. Optimus subsided into a kind of brown study while the lawyer detailed a long series of bequests to people whose names sometimes suggested that they were cousins, a sum for the Royal College of Physicians, a donation to University College in London, Optimus lost track. And then, just as his imagination was finally taking over, he heard something that shocked him into careful attention.

'. . . and all the remainder of my possessions, whether in coins, lands, hereditaments, investments in Government Stock and venture companies, I will and bequest to Optimus Shute, Schoolmaster, of this parish, to have, hold and dispose of as he wishes, with this one stipulation, that he do allow Mrs Kemp the free use of this house during her lifetime and that he maintains her in the style to which she is accustomed – Witnessed by Charles Barker, Lawyer, of Leet, and William Terry, Fisherman, of Harberscombe.'

A deep silence settled on the shadowy kitchen. Without turning his head, Optimus was sure he knew Mrs Kemp's expression. She would be spitting, metaphorically at least, into the dust. With what an ironic twist the scheming, manipulative old Doctor was tying Optimus and Mrs Kemp's destinies together from his station beyond the grave. Well, at least, after all the various bequests, the residue could not amount to much. He stood up and approached Mrs Kemp who had sat through the reading immobile and apparently uncomprehending.

'Nothing has changed,' he shouted at her. 'I want you to know that nothing has changed, you are to live as ever.'

'I know, I know,' she muttered and dropped her eyes into her lap. 'Go as you please, young master.' What did she know, wondered Optimus? There was much that was puzzling in all this, but he could not afford to be drawn into it. Making a sign to the lawyer to follow him, he walked out and, once they were in the cobbled yard, he tackled him.

'Well, it was nice of Dr Cornish to remember me, though I never did anything to deserve his generosity. But at least it won't add up to much. I shouldn't like to think I was depriving Mrs Kemp of the reward for her years of devotion.'

'That's where you are mistaken,' said Charles Barker, folding his pince-nez and slipping them into his waistcoat pocket.

'You will find, I assure you, that you are provided with what is known, I think, as "an elegant sufficiency". Dr Cornish did not earn much from his practice, but he was of a family with some standing and came into property. As you know, he was not an extravagant man. You need never want, unless you yourself turn spendthrift.'

'But Mrs Kemp –'

'I am sure the Doctor considered the matter and came to the conclusion that you would manage matters to the best of your ability to ensure that she would never want.'

'But she detests me, she must; I let him down, I betrayed him. At the last moment, I failed him.'

'Who knows what another person really thinks, least of all a deaf old woman who speaks in riddles – Now, if you'll excuse me, I must tidy those papers. Probate may take up to six months, but there should be no undue complications. In the meantime, you will be able to draw money for your expenses from Dr Cornish's bank; I shall send them instructions. Five hundred pounds ought to see you through that period, shouldn't it? What are your intentions?' Optimus reflected a moment. Then, impulsively, he punched the fist of one hand into the palm of another.

'I shall go to Malta,' he said. 'Yes, I shall go to Malta.'

Back in the schoolhouse, he continued his packing with renewed vigour. Grace Pensilva and Frederick Genteel were beckoning to him. The old Doctor must have anticipated this; he was a man who enjoyed playing God. It was he who had brought Grace to Optimus' notice; he was close to her now, closer than ever before, but still he could not grasp her, she fled before him.

She eluded him, something in her nature eluded him each time he attempted to fix her on the written page as Dr Cornish seemed to have wished, but at least he now had the means to pursue her.

They were skimming along, close under the Barrow among the crab-line buoys and their retinue of fleeters, bobbing idly in the slack tide. Jan rowed on the gig's bow thwart, Grace took a pair of oars amidships. Her strong young back rocked rhythmically as she pushed the looms away from her, dipped the blades and swung back into a long smooth pull. It excited him, making him occasionally miss his stroke. She laughed at him over her shoulder, but did not slacken her effort. In places, where submerged rocks approached the surface, long oarweed fronds like brown hands clutched at their paddles. On their larboard beam the steep shillet slopes that formed the cliffs beyond the Barrow glistened like sheets of milky glass in the blinding light. Jagged rocks, in fantastic shapes, jutted out of the sea, leaning over deep channels where lurked lobster and conger. Inquisitive cormorants poked their snaky necks out of the water as the gig swept by, then sounded, giving a brief glimpse of their arching bodies. Further off, others perched on rocky summits, their tattered wings outspread to dry in the sun.

The Carrack Rocks appeared ahead: low islands that were entirely washed over in winter gales, but in summer were topped by a mantle of turf and sea-pinks. In the lee of these islands was a narrow channel, a natural harbour where in fine weather a boat might lie, secured to ringbolts that for some purpose had been driven into the rock. On the seaward side, invisible from the land, was a tiny beach of floury white sand. Seals sometimes sunned themselves there, but today Grace found it empty when she topped the rise with her picnic basket. She gave the cider flagons to Jan so he could set them in a rock pool to cool and set the food in the shade.

Now they were alone in the kind of place in which Jan's imagination had so often pictured them. Strolling a few steps away from her, he began to toss pebbles into the sea. What should he say? How should he begin?

Presently, oppressed by the silence, he turned round to see what Grace was doing. To his astonishment, she was completely naked, placing the last of her folded garments on a rock. Conscious of his stare, she met his eyes calmly and beat them down.

'You're coming in, aren't you? It's such marvellously clear water. I couldn't wait, it's too perfect.'

He watched her take the few strides down the sand to the water and sink into it gradually. As she lifted and swam, he saw her body's whiteness tinged with green, flecked and distorted by the surrounding fluid as she progressed over the sandy sea-bed towards the rocky depths, blue shadows and purple patches of sea-anemones.

Moments later, as he followed her down the slope, he felt the sharp coldness of the water. It was ocean here, unwarmed by the estuary sands. The coldness rose from his ankles to his knees, his thighs and the tumescent staff of his sex. It numbed him, conflicting with the warmth of his desire, and yet the water's caress led him into a new realm of sensual enjoyment; he slithered and plunged after the woman of his dreams. As he approached her, his world narrowed down to a small orb of blueness whose summit was a dome of heat-hazed sky and whose base was a bowl of aquamarine shot with cold sapphire and rich purple.

She dived and he followed, lured downwards by the pale flash of her limbs and her hair's weed-like tendrils. They tumbled and twisted like otters at play, passing close, but not quite touching, spraying chaplets of bubbles wavering upwards to linger under the sea's fishy skin. Strange lances of light struck down at them from the place where the invisible sun hung in a different space.

They rose, gasping for air, and swam together till their noses touched. Her eyes probed into his with a new gravity; her lips blew him a bubbled kiss. Then she laughed, as a mermaid might have laughed and slanted away down into cool isolation. They played until a lethargy seized them and they swam gently to the ramp of wheaten sand. They hauled themselves out on to its warm, hillocked surface.

He touched her then. Her own hand swung over, imprisoning his. His desire mounted, mingled with anger. Why, for each small advance she permitted, did there have to be a new barrier, a fresh prohibition?

'Grace,' his voice was hoarse and strangely strangled. 'Grace, I can't wait no longer.'

'You want me?'

'I needs 'ee.'

'And you're prepared to pay?' Her question astonished him, it stirred his anger. He sat up, leaning over her and glowering.

"Aven't I paid enough already? Damn you, woman, when will you be satisfied?' This was a new Jan King, fierce and strong, crushing her in his arms, straddling her. She tussled with him, but he was powerful, overwhelming. His lips were hot upon her neck, her cheeks, her mouth. Unexpectedly, she found herself responding to him. Her nipples hardened, her body arched against his. Still she tried to resist.

'If you don't stop that, I'll beat the hell out of you,' he whispered, and she knew he meant it. Her eyes closed; she was lost in red darkness. Grace Pensilva was gripped by fear, not fear of Jan's brutality, but fear of enjoying it, fear of succumbing to his domination. A tidal wave of pent-up emotion carried her further than she had ever thought possible. She was being unfaithful and she was enjoying it. Her body was betraying her.

The shadow of a rock crept across the heat-soaked cove, laying its chill across their interlaced bodies. Jan sat up and looked around him. A whitish smudge on the horizon, just where the sun struck it, caught his attention. He rubbed his eyes; the sail pattern looked just like the Frenchman, but it couldn't be. Caradec must have sailed her half-way to Brittany by now. It was only a fleeting impression; the ship, if it was one, vanished into the haze almost immediately.

'God, but I'm hungry,' he declared. 'See to the food, Grace, while I fetch the cider.'

They dined on a check cloth spread on the sand between them. Grace carved the meat and bread with a sharp knife, feeding him small morsels. They drank cider from the bottle and amber drops dribbled down her chin on to her breast. Jan leaned over and lapped it up. No longer was he self-conscious; he was all animal.

'You made me forget the money,' she laughed at him. 'Wait here a moment while I go and fetch it.' But when she climbed on to the grassy knoll behind the cove she failed to find it, though she searched in one rabbit hole after another. After trying five holes in succession, her face registered astonishment and dismay.

'It's not here,' she wailed. 'Someone has taken it!' She searched a further hole and then another. It had to be here; she had watched Jan conceal it. When she looked up, he was standing nearby, smiling at her. 'There's nothing to grin at,' she told him. 'It isn't funny. We risked our lives for that money and now it's gone. It's not there!'

'Money isn't everything,' remarked Jan smugly.

'Don't just stand there looking ridiculous with no clothes on. Do something. Help me look for it. Can't you see we've lost our earnings? Who can have seen us hide them?' Jan King did not reply. He did not hurry either, but picked his way over the sharp, cutting rocks until he had passed her. Then he sat down on the rim of turf, facing away from her, lifting one foot so he could massage it. After a minute, he set it down and bent over the other.

''Tis terrible 'ard on the feet; I can't go no further.'

'Doesn't it matter to you?' she shouted at him as she climbed on to the grass and ran across to him. She grasped him by the shoulders and shook him violently. But he was already shaking with suppressed laughter. She shook him more fiercely still; he only laughed the louder. She bit his shoulder.

Then she stopped. What stopped her was the sight of something gold glinting in the grass: a coin, spilled from the buckskin bag in his lap.

'Why didn't you tell me you'd found it?'

'Didn' 'ave time to.'

'You were just being cruel, teasing me.'

'Never 'ad much of a bump for direction, did 'ee?' asked Jan, but not maliciously. ''Ow d'you think you'd've fared without Jan King to 'elp 'ee?'

'I'd've kept looking,' said Grace, but she knew she would not have found it. 'You're a clever boy, Jan King; now let's see if you're clever enough to count it.'

''Tis a terrible lot,' said Jan a little later when the coins were

set out between them on the cloth and they had broached the
second flagon of cider. 'Whatever shall us do with it? Us'll
never spend that pile in 'Arberscombe.' Grace lay back on the
sand with her eyes closed and her hands behind her head.

'Don't worry, I have a plan for it.'

'I knowed you would,' chuckled Jan. 'Grace Pensilva 'as a
plan for everythin'.' He felt wonderfully close to her now that
her ambition to be rich was realized. She had managed her
life so as to bring about that result; he was sure that her future
enterprise would come to an equally successful conclusion.
How wonderful she was! And she was his! He took the flagon,
poured a trickle of cider on to her belly and fell upon her.

'Jan, Jan, the money, the money! It's all in the sand; you'll
lose it.'

'You'm all the wealth I wants,' said Jan. 'Us'll drink to the
day I discovered it.' She caught his mood. They drank cider
till drowsiness conquered them and they slumped down on
the cloth among the guineas and sovereigns. The gold of her
skin was a living gold, darker than the gold of their treasure.
He took up handfuls of coins and showered them upon her.
Then he lay back and kissed her puffed and contented face.

The blazing sun swung westwards. The sea-breeze sprang
up and put a sparkle on the sea. Flights of cormorants, long
necks outstretched and wingtips kissing the wavelets, beat
their way home to roost on the Carracks. Shadows formed
and lengthened in the coves along the coast. Faint bells for
evensong rang out from Harberscombe. Grace and Jan shivered and groped for their clothes.

They found the gig with bottom-board awash. It hung in
the cleft as though suspended in space. As they climbed
aboard, Jan King put his hand to the stern hatch, preparing to
take out the bailer.

'This boat allus did leak like a basket,' he grumbled. Grace
pushed past him.

'Let me do that,' she told him. 'You load the gear and ship
the paddles. Careful with that bag, we'll hide it ashore later.'

'Time us was gettin' 'omealong,' said Jan and remembered
the time he had been here with Uncle Bill Terry. Uncle Bill

was a wise old bird, but he had been wrong about Grace Pensilva, she had come to love him.

'There's just one favour before that,' she told him.

'A favour?'

'You won't deny me a favour now, will you?'

'S'pose not.'

'I want you to show me the place.'

'What place?'

'The place where it happened, where Frank . . .'

'You won't see nothin', there bain't nothin' out there, nothin', it be a place like any other.' He sounded angry.

'Never mind that, I need to go there, set my mind at rest, lay a ghost.'

''Tis a long pull.'

'I know, but we must do it.'

They set out over the flat, misty, evening sea. High on the Barrow, a solitary man rose from the place where he had sat all afternoon by the cliff and took a last look at the coast and sea. Mackerel shoals were surfacing in the evening light and seething like boiling patches in the bay. Above them, isolated, predatory gannets hung, swung and plummeted, crookwinged till they vanished in a spurt of foam, then emerged and flapped lazily away as they swallowed their prey. Ships, white-sailed, were stealing by hull-down between Eddystone and Bolt. Close in, a narrow rowing boat suddenly emerged from its hiding place between the Carracks and began to crawl away seaward. There were two rowers in it and the watcher knew who they must be.

As they rowed southward, Grace Pensilva saw a small movement on the skyline, above the Barrow, as though someone were quitting a look-out. But she was not sure; it had been only an impression; perhaps the fox setting out for Harberscombe. Soon, she forgot it, her attention fully absorbed in watching for the marks, waiting for the end of the Rame to appear beyond the nearer headland. Eventually it appeared and began to poke out, dark blue, almost black under the sunset sky over Cornwall. That was the first rise; they would have to pull onwards till the second rise came clear, and on again until they opened up the third, highest rise.

While they rowed Grace kept staring at the killack which lay at her feet. The killack was a large kidney-shaped stone with a line hitched on, used as a crude anchor for the gig. Seeing it started a dream in which the line became twisted round a man's bare foot. She imagined herself flinging the killack over the gunwale and the line rushing after it, burning into the gunwale until it yanked him overboard and there was silence. What would Jan do if he knew what she was thinking? Was it possible for him to sit so near and yet have no inkling? She had an almost irrepressible urge to swivel round and search his face. Was it full of reproach, condemnation? Instead, she concentrated on the mechanics of rowing, leaning to the oars, feathering them with a backward flick of the wrist, pushing the blades skittering over the water towards the bow, dipping them and pulling again, and again and again, until all conscious thought had ebbed away.

Jan King rocked in unison with her arching back. What a woman, he thought. How shall I ever understand her? Whenever he had the impression that he was taming her, she did something that puzzled and confused him. But he would humour her. He could have taken her anywhere, she would have known no different, but it pleased him to find, as near as possible, the very spot. If, as she claimed, she hoped to exorcise a spirit, he would help her do it.

'This be the place,' he announced after a final survey of the fading coastline. Grace backed water and the gig stopped suddenly.

'How do you know?' she asked him.

'Third rise of the Rame and Malborough church half-way from Bolt Tail to the Crickstone.' Grace scanned the shore for the marks he mentioned. The dusk was coming on so fast that, to her untrained eye, they were invisible. The gig might be anywhere. Jan King could tell her anything, it would make no difference.

'It's too dark. How can you be sure?'

'I just knows. Sure as I sits 'ere, this be the place. But I told you 'twouldn' look no different.'

312

'How did you find it that night? Ivor said it was pitch black, much darker.'

'I just knowed. Us comed the usual way. And I were right, weren't I? The buoys were there, the kegs were there . . . Better if we 'adn' never found 'em. Better if I'd've lost my way entirely.'

If Grace had expected to feel some special mood hovering over the place like an unquiet spirit, she was disappointed. She lay on her oars and studied her surroundings. In the sunset lull, there was nothing but calm water, with just a swirl here and there that might have marked the presence of a deep-water reef. Outside the inner circle of her perceptions, a thin mist was rising, veiling what well-defined features remained in the landscape. Her feeling was one of anticlimax, of doubt. If she had expected her brother to come to her as an apparition, imploring her aid with twisting hands, she was mistaken. And though she had imagined Jan King floundering in a sudden descent to oblivion after the killack, he was still in the boat behind her, still kind, still helpful, still seated firmly in the thwart, waiting patiently for her decision to set off homeward. For the first time, she was full of indecision.

If Jan had not spoken at that moment, or if he had said something different, she might have accepted; she might have conceded defeat and called it forgiveness, but, trying to express good advice that was also meant for consolation, he murmured, 'Well, Grace, now you can begin to forget un.'

She stiffened. Forget Frank? Never. On the instant, Frank's face, pale, troubled, accusing, took shape in her mind's eye, as though she saw him staring unwaveringly through water.

'Just one thing before we row home; your pipe.'

'My pipe?'

'It's true what Ivor Triggs told me, isn't it? You lit your pipe. Just before the preventives arrived, you lit your pipe.'

'I've cursed meself for that, don't think I 'aven't. If they 'adn' seen that, they'd never've found us, 'twas black as the inside of a sack.'

'Why didn't you stay and fight?'

'There weren't no way; the gig was sunk.'

'Ivor Triggs stayed.'

'Ivor couldn' do no other; Ivor can't swim.'

'Frank was your friend, you should have stayed with him.' Jan King was fully awake now, the weight of the implied accusation had beaten all the drowsy expectancy out of him. Instead, he was swamped by a vision of the fatal event. He remembered his long shallow dive away from the capsizing gig, his arms threshing as soon as he broke surface. He remembered pausing for breath. He remembered wondering why Frank wasn't there beside him. Ivor had vanished too; there was no hope for Ivor, he must have foundered right away. He remembered hearing splashing and shouting, Frank's voice calling to the cutter's captain for help, for pity. 'Pity,' he had cried, 'pity!' and then there had been the crunch of the cutlass severing flesh, bone and sinew across the gunwale. It made him sick even now, to think of it.

'Forgive me, Grace,' he asked, with a break in his voice.

'Forgive you?'

'I lived, I swimmed away. I should 'ave stayed and died with un.' There was pain in his voice, pain in the lines on his face, pain in the hangdog way he sprawled behind her. She reached out and clasped his hand. For a long time, he sobbed uncontrollably with slow tears coursing down his cheeks.

'There, there, isn't it better when the truth's been spoken? And you gave him away, didn't you?'

'I s'pose I must've done, though I never meant to. But you'll forgive me, won't you Grace?'

'I've tried to,' she replied in a tired voice. Then with more decision, 'It will do no good to stay here. Let's change places before we go home, I'm tired of rowing stroke.'

'All right, Grace,' he sounded dubious, 'but take care when you stands up, this gig be terribly cranky.' He was right; once they were both on their feet, it rocked dangerously, but they were both used to life in small boats and moved in unison to sidestep the centre thwart simultaneously.

'Jan.' She halted him when he was almost past her.

'Yes.'

'You may kiss me.'

314

Wondering at this new alteration in her behaviour, he hesitated. The frail gig moved gently under their feet, but Grace stood motionless, lips parted, inviting. It was just like her to catch him off balance. If she was asking for a kiss, that was a good sign, a kiss meant reconciliation. For Jan it meant reassurance, a new solid foundation to their relationship. Standing there in the gig, responding to the unstable inconstant sea, he knew himself to be poised on a precipice, ready to fall into a dizzy chasm of love. His only grip on reality was the touch of his hands on hers and his tongue in her mouth.

He was falling, tumbling, gyrating. He did not care. His blood hissed in his ears and his closed eyes were full of coloured lights.

The next moment, the coldness struck him; the wetness closed over him, he was gasping for air. He was in the water. Somehow he had tumbled over and gone right under. With a powerful swimmer's reaction, he jack-knifed and drove swiftly upwards, fighting the drag of his clothing. When his head broke surface, the gig was still close to him, rocking wildly. Grace was still in it; she was in the act of sitting down and grasping a set of paddles.

'I'm all right,' he called to her and saw her glance at him briefly. Her face was an expressionless blur. One of the other pairs of oars was in the water, alongside the boat, but she was making no attempt to retrieve it. Jan King was a bare six feet away; a couple of strokes would bring him to it. As he struck out he saw, to his amazement, that she was rowing away from him. Even then, it took a while for the full realization to dawn on him: she had pushed him in and now was abandoning him.

'Grace!' he called to her. 'Grace, don't do that. Wait for me.' It seemed as if she slowed a little, but even without being rowed, the light gig slipped through the water incredibly quickly. And Jan was being held back by his sodden clothes.

She had tricked him, he saw that now. It was a bad joke. There had been method in her madness. She had always intended to abandon him out here in the place where her brother had drowned. It was no use appealing to her.

All was not lost. He was a strong swimmer and had reached the shore from here on a previous occasion. He had been lucky then. He might be lucky now. He paused to get his bearings. The stars were out and the Plough showed him the way north, toward the land.

'Jan, Jan, where are you?' She was calling to him. It was already so dark that she could scarcely see him.

'Poor boy, did he fall into the water then?' Her voice was soft, cajoling. 'Where are you? I was only teasing.'

'Enough of that foolin',' he shouted. 'A joke's a joke. This is past that. Let me aboard again.'

'Wait a minute, keep talking so I can find you.'

'Stay where you are, I'll soon swim over.' Before he reached the gig, he saw that Grace was standing in the stern. She was holding out an oar to him. When he was within reach, he made a grab for it. Instead of letting him take it, she lunged forward unexpectedly, jabbing him in the face with it. The blade's copper tip dug into his flesh, breaking his nose and half blinding him. He could taste the salt blood in his mouth in the moment before she lunged again and he ducked under. The woman was mad! She was trying to kill him! It wasn't enough for her to abandon him, she must have reached the conclusion that he was capable of swimming ashore again.

He swam a few strokes underwater to get clear, but had to come up for air. She was just out of reach, still jabbing at him.

'You're crazy, woman' he spat at her, 'you're bloody crazy!'

There was no sign that she had heard him. The oar blade continued to slice the water just in front of his face. Suddenly, he hated her.

Driven by a wild unreasoning anger, he swam under water again until he reached the gig's small transom. She was still plunging the oar down at him in repeated stabs, bruising his back with it.

Jan King kicked downwards and flung himself up so that he could grab the top of the transom. As he came clear, she struck him again, a blow that glanced off his temple, opening a cut, and dug into his shoulder. The pain was exquisite, but he hung on, trying to drag his heavy body into the boat, but his clothes were weighing him down. He could no longer see properly. Dizziness was engulfing him and he felt his strength ebbing away. Dimly, he saw Grace step back as though to leave him room to fall forward into the boat.

Then she hit him. She struck him three times, brutally, deliberately. The first blow was like a battering ram to his throat. It choked him. The second bludgeoned his head as he slumped into the water. Even then, he did not give in, but did what he ought to have done in the first place: he pulled down on the gunwale on one side with all his might. If he could capsize the boat and get her in the water they would be on equal terms. He would catch her and kill her. The third blow was a frantic raking swing which she took when she realized what was happening. It fell on his hands and destroyed his fingers. He felt himself slipping away.

It was the first time she had used violence. Though she had carried pistols, she had never fired them; never raised her voice even. But within her was a woman whose existence he had never suspected, whose ferocity was a revelation to him. Numbed by stabbing pains, he slipped under water and paddled away from her as best he could. The gig was out of reach and he was safe from her blind vengeance, at least for the moment. But he would never catch it; he knew that now.

Jan moved his limbs feebly, trying to tread water. He was done for: that much was certain. In the state in which she had left him he would never swim anywhere. His lungs were already burning with the water he had swallowed. He had to struggle to avoid drifting away into unconsciousness, but he forced himself to speak.

'You'll be sorry, Grace; you'll pay for this and you'll be sorry – but why, woman, why –?'

She was still erect in the gig, leaning on the oar and crooning her answer.

'Betrayed, he was, betrayed to the Revenue, on a night that was as black as a sack and only one man knew how to get there; that man's name was Jan King; Jan King betrayed my brother.'

317

'No!' he whispered, choking as he swallowed more water. 'No! No I never!'

She made no response to that, but sat down to the oars and maintained herself a boat's length away, waiting to see if he would recover. She sat there until night closed in on them completely and the small hump of his head faded and vanished. She sat there until the stars brightened and their wavering light revealed her alone on an empty sea.

Only then did she set herself to row; the dull thud of her oars was lost in the vastness around her. She rowed south.

When she was gone, the mist closed in and there was nothing, nothing but silence and smooth water. Nothing but bitter memory remained.

Part Three

Revenge is a kind of wild justice, which the more man's nature runs to, the more ought law to weed it out.

Of Revenge, Francis Bacon, 1561–1626

1

'Land ho!'

The look-out's cry summoned Optimus back from the dreamy state in which he had been lying on his bunk during the final hours of the packet-ship's voyage from Falmouth. Increasingly, as he approached his destination, he had found himself mulling over the few scraps of information in his possession, wondering whether they could still lead him to Grace Pensilva. He had read the letters that Charles Barker had passed on to him, read them over and over, seeking a pattern. What emerged was that there were two sets of them; one series sent by Frederick Genteel to his friend Barker, telling him of the events that marked his arrival and stay on the island; the other, more fragmentary, undated in many cases, were from Grace to Frederick and had, according to the Steward, been sent home in an envelope addressed to him with the other personal effects that were returned after his disappearance. In the letters Frederick wrote to Charles Barker, Grace Pensilva had never been mentioned. On the other hand, Grace's letters, some unmistakably sent before she herself reached Malta, showed that a correspondence existed between them. What Optimus did not know was whether their meeting in Valletta was the result of a pre-arranged plan, or had evolved out of circumstances once contact had been re-established. Apart from the letters, there was the slender clue contained in the locket: the name of the artist might lead him somewhere if he could discover him.

'Land ho!'

The repeated cry tumbled Optimus out of his bunk and

sent him groping up the companionway. If land were in sight, it must be Malta and he couldn't wait to get a first look at it. The place names in the letters were ringing in his head: Valletta, Senglea, Vittoriosa, Mdina, Attard, Rabat. He had tried to imagine them, but had nothing much to go by in their brittle, dried-out pages. Only a feeling of heat, of stifled emotion came through to him unmistakably.

The deck, when he emerged, was almost deserted. Only a few ghostly figures were scattered about under the limp, barely-drawing sails. A clinging mist hemmed in the packet on all sides and a feeble sun was trying to burn through it, but could do no more than produce a faint glow to the eastward. Of the land the look-out had signalled, there was no trace. He turned inquiringly to the skipper who, swaddled in a pilot-coat with its collar turned up to protect his neck from the heavy drops of condensation that fell from the sails and rigging, was planted like a statue beside the helmsman.

'Where is it? I can see nothing.' By way of an answer, the skipper pointed high in the air on the port beam. Following his finger, Optimus saw a clear-cut skyline with a few rectangular buildings etched on it. The ship was close in, very close, and the mist must be masking the tall cliffs that lay right alongside her.

'Gozo,' said the skipper. 'Malta's little sister. That's the southwestern shore you're looking at; we're off course a little. No wonder with the calms we've just had. It would try the patience of a saint to keep track of our tacking. Now we'll have to beat up to Valletta through the Comino Channel. When the wind comes, that is. For the moment, we're drifting.'

During the Biscay crossing the packet had faced hard weather and she had met unseasonable storms in the Mediterranean, but they had hurried the ship onward until she rounded Cape Bon two days earlier. Optimus had seen little of his fellow passengers. For the most part they had kept to their cabins and only a hardy few had graced the saloon tables at mealtimes. Somewhat to his own surprise, Optimus had found he had a taste for heavy weather and had spent long hours on deck, jammed in the lower rigging, watching the ship's plunging course across the combers. It was this that had brought about a kind of complicity between him and Captain Angove, a bluff old sea-dog who drove his ship relentlessly. If he was off course now, it wasn't by much, Optimus recognised.

As the sun struggled upward and cleared the opaque horizon, it burned off the mist and bathed the steep cliffs in a blood-red glow. A chill breeze blew down off the heights and urged the ship onwards. Before long, Optimus observed a deep horseshoe bay with a precipitous rock almost closing off the seaward side of it. He shivered.

'Fungus Rock,' said the skipper who had ranged alongside him. 'There's a story attached to that place. It seems the Knights of St John, the order that used to rule Malta, knew of a plant that grew on that islet. Every year they'd come and gather it. They said it was a specific against all wounds.'

'Even a broken heart?'

'A broken heart?' chuckled the skipper. 'Not yours, I trust? You're far too young to be afflicted with that malady.'

'I wasn't thinking of myself,' said Optimus with a wry smile. A few weeks ago, he *had* imagined himself heartbroken, but every mile he put between himself and Mrs Lackland diminished his grief.

'First time here, isn't it? What are you, Navy?'

'Just a traveller. What sort of a place *is* Malta?'

'You'll soon tire of it: no one to talk to outside the Service families and a few expatriates. The Maltese are Papists to a man, clannish; they speak a strange lingo, more like Arabic than any Christian language. The place is barren. Look at it, not a tree in sight, and dry, dry as an Irishman's gullet for most of the year, and hot, hot as Nebuchadnezzar's furnace. in midsummer.'

'If you go on like that, you'll make me wish I hadn't come here.'

'Oh, there must be compensations. That, for example.' The skipper jerked his head towards the two women who had already been standing in the waist of the ship when Optimus came on deck. Until now, he had scarcely spared them a glance. During the passage out from England they had kept to their cabin almost continuously and from the rarity of the meals he had seen carried there by the steward, he assumed that they had been prey to persistent seasickness.

Today, in the growing light, he saw that they were both pretty; the younger who might be a maid or companion was pert and lively, but the elder, her mistress, was frankly beautiful. She was tall for a woman, with well-shaped arms with which she leant on the bulwarks. Her cloak was flung back from her shoulders so that she could bask in the warming sunshine and it revealed a breast that heaved with emotion as she gazed at the moving coastline and talked animatedly with her companion. She was like a butterfly that had lain dormant throughout the long voyage but was now spreading its wings in delight at the summer heat and brightness.

'Fair-weather creatures,' said Optimus dismissively.

'None the worse for that,' said the skipper. 'If I didn't have a wife and family in Falmouth, I'd be tempted to linger here for either one of 'em.'

In the hours that followed, while the packet threaded her way up the Comino Channel between Gozo and Malta and then coasted down towards Valletta, Optimus found himself spying on the two women, particularly the elder, wondering who she was, why she was coming to Malta. With sidelong glances he compared her precise oval features with the image he retained of the Grace Pensilva enclosed in the locket. This girl, for she was little more than that, had a rounded, Mediterranean cast to her features, a peach-like bloom to her, a slight olive tint to her skin that seemed slightly at variance with her prepossessing figure. One thing seemed certain from the way she talked: she was a woman of spirit.

Grace Pensilva too. It was Grace Pensilva's spirit that drew him on to this place and now, with the island's low northern shore unfolding before him, Optimus became wrapped in conjecture about how she had arrived here, in what frame of mind, with what fixity of purpose. One thing was certain: Malta was utterly unlike her native Harberscombe, not only by reason of its flat-roofed villages patronized by high-domed churches, not only for its arid tawniness, but the essence of the difference he perceived was something else. The explanation did not come to him that first day; when it came it was a revelation. It lay in the quality of the light.

That light now shone on the harbour the packet was approaching. Nothing had prepared Optimus for this vision. Whole hillsides had been sculpted into redoubt and curtain wall, cavalier and ravelin, great glowering slopes impregnable from seaward. Within them, regular house-terraces of honey-coloured stone rose towards the summit. As the packet wove round the first walled headland and entered the haven, other massively fortified tongues of land on the far shore were disclosed to him.

'Isn't it splendid!' Optimus remarked brightly to the young woman whom he had approached imperceptibly during his examination. 'How happy you must be to arrive here.'

'What makes you think that?' she answered sharply. 'I can think of more cheerful occasions. For all your staring, you're not very observant.' Optimus felt his cheeks go hot as he moved away, a deep blush must be mantling them. Why hadn't he noticed that the young woman was dressed entirely in black? What he had taken for fashion had another significance, a fresh conviction that was to be borne out shortly.

After ghosting past a line of moored frigates in the windless mid-harbour, the packet let go her anchor close under the main gateway to Valletta town. Even before the cable had begun to rattle out of her hawse-pipe, a bevy of small, elegant, gondola-like craft with high stem and stern posts came swarming towards the ship from all parts of the harbour. Meanwhile, the packet's passengers had been snatching up their luggage and were lining the rail, itching to get ashore.

'No one's to disembark till we get pratique!' bawled the skipper. 'Keep those damned *dghajsas* away, Mr Snell,' he instructed the boatswain, pronouncing the word 'dicer' like the old Malta hand he was, 'use the boathooks if needful'. He turned to Optimus and showed him the launch approaching from the classical building that he took to be the Custom

House. 'Scared stiff of plague here,' grunted Captain Angove. 'If we don't wait for the doctor to give us a clean bill of health, we'll be cooling our heels in Lazaretto Creek for a month or so. You've got plenty of time to collect your luggage if you've a mind to. Anyone expecting you? – No? – Well, I can give you the name of a cheap lodging-house if you need it. Don't bother to join the rush for a *dghajsa*, I'll book one for you.'

Optimus was in a subdued frame of mind as he packed his valise with the bits and pieces that were strewn about his cabin. Only now did he realize the daunting nature of the task he had set himself. The secret of Grace Pensilva's life on Malta was walled up in a citadel and he was far from sure he held the key.

Leaving his cabin, he bumped into the lady's maid, laden down with two heavy valises. Gallantly he took one from her and followed her on deck with it.

'What's your mistress's name?' he murmured.

'I'm not sure as I should tell you.'

'Go on, there's no harm in it.'

'Maria, Maria Kirkbride.'

With all the boldness he could muster, Optimus approached the lady in question and laid the bag at her feet.

'Excuse me, Miss Kirkbride, I did not mean to annoy you just now, I was merely – '

'Making polite conversation,' she completed. 'Well, if you're determined not to annoy me, you'll leave me in peace now also. Unless, and it's most unlikely, you have something worthwhile to say to me.'

'Only that you're a very beautiful lady,' Optimus heard himself blurt out. He could hardly believe he had said it. 'And you have my condolences, I was insensitive not to have noticed.' She made no reply. Her face seemed frozen and now, instead of seeing him, she was looking beyond him towards a jolly-boat in which a slight figure, likewise all in black, was regarding her. The moment the boat touched the packet's side he sprang aboard and ran to clasp her. He was an old man, Optimus noticed, but sprightly. Sensing that his own presence was an embarrassment, Optimus retreated a little.

'My poor dear,' he heard the old fellow murmuring, 'so good

326

of you to come all this way, but really you shouldn't have done it. No use wasting your life on an old fogey like me. I know what death is, a close companion. Loss is loss, and one must bear it.' Though he spoke perfect English, Optimus noted a peculiar accent.

'It will be easier for the two of us,' whispered Miss Kirkbride. 'I miss her too, more than you know. She was like a mother, my real mother, when I think of it.' Optimus schooled himself to listen no further. It was unseemly to intrude on private grief. He returned to the captain.

'You'll be needing that plant from Fungus Rock for your heartache, if you persist with that one,' grinned Angove. 'I wish you a jolly stay here, and incidentally, if you ever should have a notion to take up seafarin' I'll give you a berth on this hooker.' Optimus could see the skipper was half serious. It cheered him.

'You never know, I just might take you up on that,' he answered. 'You've been in this trade a long while by the look of you. Don't you ever tire of it?'

'A man don't tire o' the sea, never. I've been sailin' now, man and boy, for thirty years. Started in the Delaluna Line as a nipper and left as soon as I could buy me own vessel. Here I am today, still as moonstruck about it as ever. The sea's a hard mistress, but a man can't leave 'er.'

'Tell me something else,' said Optimus, 'you must know people here if you've come so often. Does the name Scicluna mean anything to you?' Before answering, the skipper placed a hand on his shoulder and pushed him a little aside so that he could see beyond him.

'Scicluna? There's more than one o' that name on Malta. But there was one who answered to that name aboard here two minutes ago. He's gone now, but you saw 'im. He was the old chap who came to meet that young lady you fancied. How's that for a coincidence?' Optimus in his turn looked over his shoulder. The jolly boat was already receding, with the old man and the two young women in the sternsheets.

'R. Scicluna, that's the one I'm looking for, some kind of artist.'

'Well it's not 'im, that's for certain. That's Count Pietro

Scicluna, the shipowner as was – the Delaluna Line. We don't talk much, not since I left 'is Line. He wanted me to stay and help 'im – ancient history now, all of that – Well, if you'll excuse me, I've work to do. Your *dghajsa*'s waitin'.'

'You said you'd tell me the name of a lodging-house.'

'Oh aye, but I don't know if it'd be up to your standards, it's very plain and ordinary. What *is* your line of business exactly?'

'I'm a schoolmaster.'

'Don't dress like one. That coat's too fine a fabric. Never mind, if you don't like the place, it's your funeral. Try Battery House, on St Ursula Street. I'll tell the boatman to take you there.'

All the way across the harbour, Optimus kept watching the jolly-boat, far ahead of him. He saw its passengers disembark and disappear into a chaise which set off into the city. Something was puzzling him: he was sure he had come across the name Delaluna somewhere, possibly in the letters. As soon as he reached the lodging-house, he would get them out of his valise and go through them.

Battery House turned out to be better than he had expected from the captain's description. The room its proprietor ushered him into was high-ceilinged and comparatively cool, with whitewashed walls, a white counterpane on a black iron bedstead, and a tiny balcony enclosed in minute lattice-work that allowed him to look into the street without himself being observed.

The life in the steep streets had astounded him; nothing in English life had prepared him for the bustle, the strident milkman crying, '*Halib! Halib!*' and milking his goat into a mug on the pavement; he had no proper defence against the urchins who had insisted on carrying his bag and then demanded money; the old women who sat on chairs in the street clicking their lace-bobbins in gnarled fingers and scrutinizing him with bold stares had been oddly unnerving, making him feel foreign, a stranger. It was a relief to be alone in the quiet room, rinse his face and hands at the wash-stand, and survey the world from his window. Before the afternoon

328

heat descended, he would go to the Governor's Palace and find the archivist. There must be some record of Frederick Genteel to provide a foundation that he could build on.

Already Optimus was trying to fit Grace Pensilva into these unfamiliar surroundings. In his mind's eye, he saw her climbing the steep streets. The clothes she was wearing were of a style and quality far above what she had worn in Harberscombe. With her velvet and taffeta, she was unmistakably a lady, and her eyes were smiling and self-assured. But who was that other woman who strolled beside her, sharing her laughter and banter?

The stranger was smaller, light and quick, with flaxen ringlets that cascaded in artificial confusion about her shoulders. Her face was winsome, though her nose was a trifle prominent and gave her a bird-like appearance. As she passed, she put her hand on Grace's bare forearm and whispered to her confidingly.

Then he remembered who she was, who she must be: Felicity Fell. Her name was frequently mentioned in the letters from Frederick to Charles Barker, but it was a curious quirk of his imagination to place her alongside Grace Pensilva in such easy familiarity.

Grace was still on Optimus' mind half an hour later when he entered the Governor's Palace. The archivist, a Mr Osborne, was a gangling fellow, spare and dry as a stick-insect, with a face of wrinkled parchment.

'Yes, I did receive your letter,' he murmured in almost ecclesiastical tones when Optimus had introduced himself. 'However, I've little enough to tell you, and before I do, I'll need to know your interest.'

'I'm something of an amateur historian, doing research on the Genteels and other Devon families.'

'Historian, eh?' The archivist warmed to him suddenly. 'Did you know that this place we're standing in was once the Grand Master's Palace? It had style in those days: the Knights of St John came from the noblest families in Europe. Now we hear nothing but moaning about money and bickering about

329

the constitution from the Maltese aristocracy who're two a penny. But I digress. Where was I – Oh yes – Genteel – well, here are some facts for you.' He handed over a paper with a few lines in his own copperplate handwriting. 'You'll see that he wasn't here long really, but there are certain documents like his appointment as victualling clerk, a very profitable post if a man wasn't above taking a few back-handers, his marriage certificate – '

'He married, then?' Optimus was shocked.

'I traced it through the pro-cathedral, and here are the inquest proceedings after he vanished.'

'What was the verdict?'

'Missing, presumed drowned, if I recall correctly. You can see for yourself later. I'll dig out the documents for you if you need them.'

'And Grace Pensilva?'

The archivist pulled a long face and tapped his finger on the table.

'You've given me a deal of work for nothing there, Mr Shute, a wild goose chase, absolutely. If you'd had to pay for my time . . . You're lucky I'm a government servant. What makes you think this Pensilva person was ever present in Valletta?'

'Some of her letters – hearsay.'

'Who was she, if that's not an indiscreet question?'

'A friend of Genteel's, from Devon.'

'A *friend* eh?' Osborne's thin lips twisted into a smile. 'Well, if she were that sort of friend, it isn't surprising that she's not in the archives.'

'Felicity Fell? Mrs Genteel?'

'Ah, Felicity, she had the undoubted merit of being legitimate didn't she? There's quite a bit about Felicity, mostly court proceedings, tradesmen who had the bad taste and presumption to dun her for money. I know we pride ourselves on the fairness of British courts, but it takes optimism or gall, or both, to sue the Governor's daughter. She left a trail of unhappy Maltese haberdashers, tailors, wine merchants and what not when she finally went home with her father. Looking

330

at the evidence, it's hard not to be condemnatory, but perhaps she was compensating for her loss. The child didn't survive long either; went down with Malta fever, less than a year old, a daughter. You know that?' Optimus shook his head.

'You've taken a deal of trouble on my behalf, far beyond the call of duty. How can I hope to reward you? Can I invite you to dinner?'

'It would be inappropriate. Thanks anyway. For the present this office must close, it's past twelve o'clock.'

'Just one last question: do you know of a shipping firm called Delaluna?'

'Delaluna – Delaluna.' The archivist bit his lower lip as he pondered. 'It rings a bell, but I can't place it. It seems to me that I've seen it somewhere, over in Conspicua or Vittoriosa perhaps.'

'Can you tell me how to get there? I think I'll go straight over.'

'You'll need to take a *dghajsa*, it's on the far side of the harbour, but you'll be wasting your time, haven't you heard of siestas? You're not looking for a passage home already, are you?'

'No, not yet, but I've been warned I won't like it here.'

'Who said that? No, don't bother to tell me, they all say that. But to an historian, ah – a genuine historian as I imagine you to be, Mr Shute, this place is full of interest, these stones could tell you stories . . .'

When Optimus stepped out of the vaulted cool of the palace into the street the canicular heat hit him like a blow. The unrelieved sunlit stones forced his eyelids into quivering slits. The air was hard to swallow. Though he had planned to disregard the archivist's advice and proceed immediately to Conspicua, he changed his mind and made for the shelter of his lodging-house. Within a few yards his wet shirt clung to his armpits and shoulders. The street was already deserted.

Perhaps it was the intensity of the light, perhaps it was the attention he was concentrating on finding the right side street, perhaps it was the peculiar white clothing: whatever it was exactly, he cannoned into a kind of apparition. Taking a step back, he saw a strange, almost deliberately horrific figure. The person he had encountered might have been either male or female, though the hands suggested it was a man. Apart from the gloved hands, not a single portion of its body was visible. From shoulders to the tips of its shoes, it was draped in a flowing white cassock. Above this was an ample hood which extended like a chasuble over chest and back. This too was white, as were the gloves and a flat-crowned wideawake hat. Apart from the tips of its shoes the only sombre items were the rosary knotted into the girdle round its waist, and a kind of funnelled box decorated with a religious medal; these items and the dark holes behind which, presumably, lurked the eyes. If it was a phantom, it was a very substantial one, for it had stopped him in his tracks, but it was none the less unnerving.

Croaking a few words in an unknown language, the figure shook the box at him. It jingled. Was he being asked for money? Thankful to get off so lightly, Optimus dug in his pocket for a small silver coin and thrust it into the funnel. The figure raised its free hand in a gesture that might have been a blessing and stepped aside. Optimus huried onward. He was not content until he was in his room with the door fast shut behind him. Even then he was still shaking with agitation. He lay down on the bed and compelled himself to re-read some of the letters. With his fresh information, they should hold a new meaning. Five minutes later he was asleep with the letters scattered around him. He had not realized the depth of his exhaustion. He slept fitfully, taking refuge in dreams from a bizarre reality.

Frederick Genteel took the last of the Barracca Steps at a run and burst on to the wharf where Captain William Fell, Governor of Malta, was already waiting. Rotund, self-important, it was not *his* way to come running, even when greeting his only daughter.

'Why come flyin' down at the last minute?' he growled in the bearish manner he affected. 'Don't you ever stop dreamin'?'

'There's more paperwork to the job you've given me than I expected. I've got a backlog already. Isn't that them arriving?'

Putting his hand across his eyes to shield them from the glare, Captain Fell followed his pointing finger. A barge had just left the side of a newly arrived frigate and was crawling towards them.

'I imagine so.'

'I think I can see her already, in the pale blue dress, isn't that her?'

'You've better eyes than I have, young feller, if you can see a figurehead at that distance. Look here, Frederick, you don't have to play up to me. I know you're marrying my daughter out of a false sense of duty. You don't need to, you know that. But I could go blue in the face telling you. You're a stubborn pup, d'you know that?'

'I have a great regard for your daughter. I think she's a fine person.'

'Humph – How long is it since you saw her?'

'Five years.'

'And how old was she then?'

'Thirteen.'

'Well, at least you're not marrying her for money. God knows, her father has little enough of it.'

As the barge neared the wharf it became apparent that there were three women grouped about the midshipman at the tiller.

'That'll be Aunt Harriet sitting beside her, but who's the other person?' asked Genteel.

'Some friend or other – picked her up in Palermo. You know what women are, always wild about their latest acquaintance.'

The two men stepped forward to the edge of the wharf and Frederick extended an arm to help the ladies ashore. He peered intently at the young woman who sat facing him. The one beside her *was* Aunt Harriet, her foster mother ever since Fell's wife had died in childbirth. She was easy to recognize with that bulldog face of hers. Still, her bark was worse than her bite; she was a mild soul really. The third woman had kept her back to him and the light cloak she wore told him nothing of her identity.

'You don't know me, do you?' piped the girl with a wide smile and an arch look. 'I knew you wouldn't remember. I'm Felicity, the girl you're going to marry.'

'You've changed so,' he muttered lamely, '– for the better.'

'Oh, wasn't I nice enough for you last time? she rallied him. Genteel's face stiffened, he wasn't good at banter. But she was pretty, oh ever so pretty, and the fault was not that she was too lively, but that he was too stuffy. His voice was gruff when he spoke to her.

'Take my hand, your father's waiting.' She sprang ashore lightly, barely touching his hand as she did so. He was astonished how that touch affected him.

'Papa, Papa,' she was crying behind his shoulder, clinging to her father in an unseemly display of affection. He could see the sailors grinning behind their hands already. 'How serendipitous to see you! – Oh, damn!' she broke off with a stamp of her foot. 'I've left my blue gloves on board. They're the only ones I have to go with this dress. You'll have to send the boat back to fetch them, I feel *naked* without them.'

'Felicity! You know you can't ask your father to do that!' Genteel found himself expostulating.

'Of course he can! Don't they call him King Billy here? Fetching my gloves won't strain the royal prerogative. You *will* send it, won't you, Popsie?' Genteel winced. She's twisting him round her little finger, he thought wryly.

'Anything you wish, dear,' grunted Fell and, for an instant, Genteel seemed to see his wife, not his daughter, standing beside him.

'But I'm forgetting someone terribly important!' cried Felicity, turning towards the boat where the others stood waiting. 'I want you to meet my new friend, Miss Delabole. We've had such splendid times together at Palermo. Don't look at her like that Frederick, she's not a ghost. You're going to love her. Take her hand, she won't hurt you. She's sworn to me she's not a man-hunter; she's come to Malta to make her fortune.' Mechanically, Genteel extended his arm and confronted the grey eyes under the boat-cloak's hood.

'Charmed,' he muttered, trying to contain the wild feelings

that the face he now saw re-awakened.

'What about *me*? What about your poor Aunt Harriet?' wailed Felicity's aunt. 'Why don't *I* get helped ashore? I'm too old, I suppose. Where's your consideration?'

'What the devil are you doing here like this, Grace?' whispered Genteel urgently. 'Didn't I tell you not to? We must talk somewhere – soon.'

'A cat may look at a king,' said Miss Delabole, gathering her skirts as she dropped her hand from the crook of his arm. 'I'm come to see King Billy.' She beamed at Captain Fell. 'I've heard so much about you.'

'Didn't I hear you call her "Grace"?' asked Felicity a few moments later.

'Did I?' said Frederick, with a show of absent-mindedness. 'I didn't give her Christian name when I introduced her.'

'Your father must have told me.'

'Then why did you look at her like that?'

'She reminded me of someone – but it was a mistake, she wasn't the same person. I don't much like the look of her.'

'Come on!' Captain Fell was calling. 'You'll have all the time in the world for tête-à-têtes later. For the time being, duty calls. I've got to govern Malta. Stir yourselves, the coach is waiting.'

'Grace Delabole is my best, my dearest friend, I love her terribly,' Felicity was murmuring to Frederick, 'and you must love her too. Today, however, I must have you all to myself. I want to feast my eyes on my future husband. Tomorrow morning, while I'm with the sempstress, you shall make your peace with Grace and show her round my father's palace.'

'Come on, you two lovebirds!' Captain Fell shouted. 'We will leave without you.' He offered his arm to Grace Delabole, helping her into the carriage. 'I've told Frederick that my daughter will ruin him with her frivolity and extravagances, but he won't believe me,' he told her. 'Marryin' her for the wrong reasons, he is: out of gratitude to me for givin' 'im an appointment, and because he was struck with 'er years ago when he was my first lieutenant – but you'll know that part already, Felicity will have told you how they met at Naples.

She wrote and told me you'd become inseparable. I'm not sorry, you seem a quiet, sensible sort of gel who knows how to hold her tongue. What did you say you name was?'

'Delabole, Grace Delabole.' Fell wrinkled his brow.

'Delabole – seems to me I knew someone of that family once, a maiden lady, lived near Frederick's place in Devon, you're not related . . .?'

'I'm from the Cornish branch of the family.'

'Humph, thought they were extinct year ago. You'll have to tell me about them – at dinner tomorrow. And incidentally, you know they call me King Billy, well, consider that more a command than an invitation. I know I shall like you, young lady. The sooner we get acquainted the better.' He turned away from her as Felicity and Frederick followed them into the carriage. 'You've made a wise choice in your friend for once,' he told her daughter, 'this Grace knows how to keep her peace, a rare gift in a woman.'

'Pay no attention to him, Grace,' said Aunt Harriet with a wave of her fan. 'He revels in his bearishness. Look out of the window, isn't Valletta charming?'

The coach lumbered upward.

2

'You won't find no one in there mate.'

The voice came from across the street where an aproned man stood in an alehouse doorway with a straw broom in his hand. Optimus had just tried a door adjacent to the nameplate he had been deciphering. The brass was worn from years of polishing, but there was no mistaking its inscription:

DELALUNA & CO. SHIPPERS

The first time he walked down the street, he failed to notice it. The *dghajsa* owner who had rowed him across had pretended to know of the firm when Optimus questioned him on it and had directed him to this street in Conspicua, but the dull brass plate had escaped his attention. He had wandered on, finding himself in Vittoriosa before turning back in frustration. It had been a surprise to find the door locked against him, he was practically certain it had been ajar on the occasion when he first passed it and, though he couldn't swear to it, he thought he had seen someone step out and walk off in the opposite direction at the very moment it came in sight again after his peregrinations.

'Will they come back later?' he asked swiftly.

'No use your waitin', no one ain't never there nowadays. Mebbe I can 'elp 'ee. What was you lookin' for zackly? Are you a merchant?'

'In a small way.' Optimus was surprised at the ease with which the small falsehood passed his lips, but in the world of equivocations he felt he had entered since he set off after Grace Pensilva, it hardly mattered and a new identity might make his inquiries seem more natural. He realized that the

337

sober clothes he wore were of the right quality and cut to aid the deception. Adopting a casual air, he strolled across the street and lowered himself into one of the chairs set out on the pavement.

'Would you be wantin' a drink or somethin'?'

'That would be the general idea.'

'You see, 'tisn't the time of day I usually – and 'tis all topsy-turvy and dirty – 'tisn't shipshape –'

'Never mind that, I shan't be incommoded. Fetch me something cool, if you have it. What can you offer?'

'There's ale – that's local, and I've a good beer shipped out from Faversham.'

'That will do nicely.' While the landlord was away in the back of his shop, Optimus studied the house opposite. By now he was certain that there *had* been someone in the downstairs room when he went by earlier. The curtains had been open. Now they were tightly drawn. A spider was busy reconstructing his web in one corner.

'Here y'are,' the landlord announced, breaking in on his thoughts, 'you'll like that, I'll warrant. Now, tell me 'ow can I be of assistance. I knows plenty of shippers.'

'Well, Mr –'

'Bentley, your 'onner.'

'Well, Mr Bentley, this Delaluna firm has taken my fancy, must be the name or something. You see, it's not just a firm to ship goods I'm after. I'm thinking in terms of an investment. I'd make it worth your while if you'd put me in touch with Mr Delaluna.'

'Mr Delaluna!' The landlord laughed and slapped his thigh. 'Ain't never been no Delaluna in this business.'

'Mr. Bentley,' Optimus pretended to be angry, 'I'll thank you not to make merry at my expense. If the owner's not an Italian with lunar connections, who *is* he?' Landlord Bentley wiped his hands nervously on his apron.

'I'm not sure as I ought to say. 'Ee's retired like.'

'Go on, I shan't eat you. Do I look like a scoundrel?'

'You d'seem like a gennulman to me, but these days a man can't be too careful –' Optimus waited; the silence lengthened. '– Name o' Scicluna.' Optimus sipped his beer slowly.

'But that's not Delaluna. You're a mite too clever for me, Mr Bentley. You'll have to give me the reason.'

'Why, 'tis simple when you knows, sir. 'Tis two names put together.'

'Well, if Scicluna's the second name, what's the first one?'

'Don't make much difference, 'tis long gone now, sir.'

'Never knew a man beat about the bush so. Out with it!' The landlord's apron was in a tight knot. He was much older than he had at first appeared. His speech and his tattooed forearms suggested that he had been a sailor, like many others who kept taverns around the harbour. Optimus had never seen such a collection. This Bentley fellow was evidently reluctant to talk, whatever the reason. Was Optimus pushing him too far? He decided to change the subject. He already had a shrewd suspicion what the name would be! Delabole. There was no point in estranging this man, he might be useful in the long run.

'D'you know Captain Angove?' he continued. 'He's a friend of mine – told me I ought to come and find Delaluna. He sailed with the Line, didn't he? I suppose you know that?'

'Aye, long since, 'ee did. A good man, Angove. Pity 'ee left. The Count, Count Scicluna, were terrible put out when Skipper Angove weighed 'is hook and set sail on 'is own account.'

'That's it, that's it exactly, that's what made me think Count Scicluna might like a new partner.'

'Oh, 'ee might've done. Not now, 'ee's past tryin' that kind o' venture. 'Ee ain't been to that office in a twelvemonth.'

'You know him then? What sort of a chap is he?'

'No one to touch 'im. Afore I'ad this place, I did crew for 'im. Boatswain I was. Them was good days. There's many a tale I could tell 'ee.'

'And so you shall. I'll come back, if I may. I like the brew you sell here. Now, where shall I find the Count? I have a proposition to put to him; he can take it or leave it.'

'I don't rightly know now. 'Ee's'ad to sell 'is old 'ouse in Notabile.' Optimus was sure the man was hedging, but there was no point in making an issue of the matter. Malta was a small island, finding Count Scicluna should present little difficulty.

'Oo shall I say called, if I 'appens to run into 'im?'

'Cornish, my name is Cornish, but he won't know me.' Optimus had hestitated momentarily to use this supplementary deception, yet it came as easily as the first one. Was it his assumed personality, the unease it generated, that made him feel as the day progressed that he might be followed?

'Floggin' a dead 'orse you'll be, tryin' to do business with Count Scicluna, but I s'pose you won't learn till you've tried it. I think perhaps I've let on too much, but I'll tell 'ee straight, though I may be proved wrong, you do seem a decent young feller.' Optimus felt an urge to take the landlord by the hand and shake it, he sensed such warmth in the old sailor, but he held himself back, that might be unseemly and appear out of character.

'I'm flattered by your trust. I'll try hard to live up to it. Now I must be off, I've an appointment across the harbour.' This was only half true. Optimus had made no definite arrangements to see Mr Osborne so soon, but that was now his intention. One of the things he was eager to question him on was yesterday's strange encounter.

'There's a down to earth explanation to everything,' the archivist expounded later, with a monitory flick of his folded glasses, 'and it's all too easy for the young and inexperienced to read something irrational and superstitious into an everyday occurrence.'

'It didn't seem everyday to me,' protested Optimus. 'I was petrified.'

'Well, here in Valletta we all know the Brotherhood of the Rosary when we see one of them. They make a collection: alms to pay for Masses to save the soul of some poor felon condemned to execution.'

'It's still spooky to me.'

'Familiarity breeds contempt,' said Osborne sententiously, as though he had invented the expression. 'Likewise, yesterday's mystery has a simple explanation. I could find no refer-

340

ence to Grace Pensilva. Now you tell me she had another name, thus was another person, and here,' so saying he placed one hand on a pile of papers, 'is proof positive of her existence. While you've been waiting, I've found out a great deal about her: when she arrived, the house she purchased, her business relations with Count Scicluna.' A faint smile flickered across Optimus' face at the thought of paper proving a person's existence.

'What're you grinning at, young man? Have I said something amusing? *I* wasn't aware of it.'

'Of course not. My mind was wandering. I say, would you mind if I took those papers home with me? If I could read them quietly –'

'It's not strictly legal –'

'I promise I won't run off with them. There isn't far to run to either, is there?'

'Well, if you sign for them . . . Did you find Delaluna?'

Optimus nodded.

'Gone out of business though.'

'Oh, has it? I saw in these papers that one of the original partners was Count Scicluna. Poor fellow, he's frittered away his fortune in lawsuits. No one ever wins against the government. Now that I come to think of it, I might be making a grave mistake in letting this,' and here he tapped his glasses on the pile of documents, 'out of my possesion. The whole Scicluna affair is probably still *sub judice*. If you, or any one else for that matter, were to air it publicly, it might be a great embarrassment to the government.'

'It might also serve the cause of justice.'

'Justice! What has justice to do with the matter? Old Scicluna had a bone to pick with Captain Fell over some payment he thought he was due. If he'd had the sense to sue discreetly, ask the Governor to make an *ex gratia* payment, as a favour, you understand, he might have got it. But no, Count Scicluna had some idea of honour at stake, wronged honour, and took Fell to court. He's still waiting for his money. Between ourselves, these Maltese nobles are a jumped-up bunch, not your true aristocracy. Papal creations for the most

341

part, so I can't see what they're so finicky about. Haven't we let them hang on to their titles? Aren't they elected to the Council? They can't overrule the Governor, of course, but they get all the honour a man could wish for. I'd settle for half their ceremony and a quarter of their money, even old Scicluna's, though he pleads poverty.'

'How about lending me those papers all the same? I've no axe to grind on Scicluna's behalf; I haven't even met him. The only interest he holds for me is marginal, in so far as he may know something about Frederick and Grace. Come now, we're both English, we're both gentlemen, don't you think you can trust me?'

'They'll be back in my hands tomorrow noon at the latest?'

'Here's my hand on it.'

'I don't need that. You're a historian, a scholar, or say you are, my best guarantee is your detachment. Now run along with you – and keep clear of those Rosarians,' he called after Optimus, 'they may not get your soul, but they'll hit your wallet.'

As he entered his lodgings, Mrs Mifsud the proprietress accosted him from the foot of the stairwell.

'Was someone 'ere lookin' for you, Mr Shute,' she shouted in an unmusical voice. He pondered.

'What sort of a person?'

'A lady – I think.'

'What d'you mean, you think? Don't you know a lady when you see one?' Optimus was annoyed at having his private business broadcast about the house like this.

'She come in a carriage; her coachman ask for you; I not see her directly.'

'If she calls again, come up and tell me. Otherwise I'm not to be disturbed. If she calls when I'm out, take her name, find out where she comes from.'

This was a new distraction. Optimus couldn't help wondering who the woman was and what she could want with him. But he had the papers Osborne had lent him, nothing must keep him from studying them. He cleared the ewer and basin from the wash-stand and laid them out across it. Within seconds he had forgotten all about his unknown visitor. Grace Pensilva was here in these dog-eared pages, beckoning him. He seemed to see that peculiar smile of hers; the moist lips barely parted, the faintly ironic curl to their corners, the sparkle in her eyes whose look, so direct and challenging, was for him alone.

Oblivious of the heat, he was still reading when dusk descended.

Frederick Genteel was going through the motions of showing the Grand Master's Palace to Grace Pensilva. In the quietness of the empty rooms he turned to her with his questions.

'What happened to Jan King?' he demanded.

'We went our separate ways. I took ship to France on the *Ar Mor*, with Caradec. England held nothing for me. Much of the rest you know; you've had my letters.'

'That's not what they say in Harberscombe; they tell another tale; they're not forgiving.'

'All the more reason to be glad to be away from them. Out here, life is so different. You told me it would be, remember?'

'I remember. But why have you followed me here now, when I am engaged to be married? If you had come earlier – Now, I distrust you. Do you know what I suspect? I think your association with Felicity is deliberate. I don't know why you've accomplished it, but you have. Providence could not have thought of it.'

'You credit me with too much guile,' said Grace. 'I just happened to stop in Palermo. I have been studying the advantages of various ports for the business I intend to embark on. English society in Palermo is a small world. Can you wonder we were thrown together? Furthermore, she knew you, an added attraction.'

'Even if I could accept that, there's the new name. How do you explain it?'

'Perhaps you would tell me, Frederick Genteel, how a girl called Grace Pensilva, without connections, could make her way here in this society?'

'I should have helped you,' Genteel blurted out. 'If

only – why did you not join me immediately, why did you delay until –'

'I told you, I have my pride. You knew the conditions.'

'And I should have met them. Dear Grace – I have made a terrible mistake. I know it. But it is not too late. I can see Captain Fell and talk to him. He told me himself I was making a mistake in asking the hand of his –'

'Hush!' she whispered, putting a finger on his lips. 'Hush Frederick! I should not be good for you, not proper. Felicity is such a pretty girl, so full of life, and she thinks she loves you.'

'*Thinks* she loves me! That's it exactly. Whereas you, Grace, whereas I . . . You know I'd do anything for you.'

'There is *one* thing, only one favour I shall ever ask of you.'

'Name it.'

'That you will never, while I live in Malta, mention the name of Grace Pensilva. She has never existed. Swear to me you do not know her.'

'I swear it.'

She took his hand. For a brief moment, he felt the old uncomplicated joy he had known with her in Leet Park return, electric, suffocating.

'Come,' she was saying as she led him towards the next room, 'you still have much to show me.' He tried to hold her back.

'Grace, Grace, you're not going to leave me.' She stopped and looked him straight in the eye with that unwavering grey stare of hers.

'Frederick, while you live, I shall be with you always. Now we must hurry, Felicity is waiting, she will be worried about you.'

'Damn Felicity!'

'Felicity is best for you. I want you to have Felicity. In the end, you will see how right I have been.' Reluctantly, he followed her.

The room which they entered was a long gallery, lined on the one side with suits of armour and on the other a succession of tall windows. At the far end, two men were involved in animated discussion and, seeing them, Genteel's first reaction was to withdraw as quickly as possible, but a shout from one of them forestalled him.

'Frederick! Thank God you're here. You must deliver me from this leech, this jackanapes.' Genteel had recognized his employer, Captain Fell, the Governor. The other man, about Fell's own age, slim, olive-skinned, was dressed in an Italian fashion affected, as was the language, by the Maltese nobles. Genteel knew him too: he was Count Pietro Scicluna. By the same token, he knew what they must be discussing. That had been his reason for trying to withdraw before Fell noticed them. Count Scicluna held his ground, unabashed by the Governor.

'Mr Genteel,' he appealed, standing straight at his full height; he was not a tall man, but he appeared larger, 'I call you to witness. You, more than anyone, must be aware of the justice of my cause. You know that in the war with the French, I dispensed my fortune, furnished ships and men to fetch viands from Sicily. Victory has left me ruined. I have bills of hand signed by various British officers, but no one will honour them. When we Maltese put our hearts and souls into the fight to get rid of the French tyrant, we supposed we were fighting for freedom, for justice. And what do we find now . . .? Another tyranny. Mr Genteel, I insist, say it is true. You have seen the recognizances.'

'Tell 'im he's wrong, Genteel, don't stand there cogitatin',' urged Captain Fell.

'I'm sorry, I can't,' said Genteel quietly. 'I've seen his bills on the government and they're all in order.'

'I thought I'd get proper support from one of my staff, let alone an old friend as you are,' said Fell bitterly. 'These recognizances are two a penny, every Maltese seems to have sacks of them. They were incurred in Captain Ball's time, long before Great Britain undertook this island's protection. If I honour yours, the floodgates will be open, I shall have to pay all of them; the government will be bankrupt.'

'But, Captain Fell,' broke in Grace, 'surely you're confusing two different governments. These bills are on the British Government, not Malta's. The British treasury isn't so poor

345

that it will be emptied by a few pounds paid back in Malta.'

'You're a bold hussy,' said Fell, somewhat taken aback by her intervention, 'for all your misplaced perspicacity, this is men's work and I'll trouble you not to dabble your pretty little fingers in it . . . As for you, Count Scicluna, I'll have you know there isn't a penny here to pay you, or in London either. It would be more than my job is worth even to suggest it. You have your remedy, you mentioned freedom, well, you're free to press your claims through the courts, and much joy may you have of them. Now you may leave us, this audience is at an end.'

When the Count had left, Fell adopted a quieter tone. 'Really, Frederick,' he chided, 'you must learn a thing or two about diplomacy. It's not done to break ranks in the face of the enemy. And as for you, young lady, I resent your interference, but I like your spunk. I could wish to have more men of your spirit about me . . . I tell you, Frederick, if you weren't marrying Felicity, you could do worse than marry this gadfly creature.'

Optimus heard wheels turning in the street. For a while it had been quite silent and the approaching sound drew him from his writing. He peered through the latticework balcony. A closed black chaise was grinding up the slope towards Battery House, passing through the blinding shafts of early morning sunlight from the cross-streets as it approached them. Its paintwork had lost its sheen and was browning in leprous patches, there was an old coachman lolling behind the dashboard, encouraging the bony horses with idle flicks of his whip. When the vehicle juddered to a halt beneath his window, Optimus saw a mark on the nearside door that might once have been a blazon. There was a kind of inevitability about its stopping here, just as it had been inevitable that he should have looked up from his writing and turned to the window.

The coachman climbed down stiffly and came to the door where he knocked briefly. The echoes had long died away in the hallway when Mrs Mifsud came to open it. There ensued a brief conversation that Optimus could not understand. The horses pawed the ground and chomped at their bits, slavering. Otherwise there was silence. The coachman returned to his perch.

Someone was scratching at the door. When he pulled it back, Mrs Mifsud, still in a nightgown, confronted him.

'A person call for you.'

'The same?'

'I do not know.'

Pausing only to slip on his shoes, Optimus followed her. He was dressed already, having slept only a few short hours until the dawn awoke him. The burnt-down candle he had used still sat in a pool of grease on the table.

The coachman did not speak, but motioned with his folded whip towards the chaise's doorway. Inside, all was dim. At first, he could perceive nobody, but laid his hand on the top of the door, leaning forward. A small gloved hand released the latch and beckoned. Like a somnambulist, Optimus complied. Immediately, the chaise jerked forward, depositing him on one of the benches.

Optimus endeavoured to regain his composure. As his eyes accustomed themselves to the gloom, he observed the tattered grey headlining, the sagging unholstery, but what concentrated his attention was the person opposite.

She, for it was a woman, sat bolt upright in the middle of her seat, with her gloved hands clasped in her lap before her. Everything she wore was black; so complete was her costume that, from sharp-toed black shoes to heavily veiled hat, the only scrap of colour, the only sign of animation came from her mouth and chin.

For a while, although the lips twitched slightly, she did not speak. Then, as the chaise rumbled through the city gate, she addressed him.

'Your purpose, Mr Shute, what is your purpose?'

'My purpose?' As he countered her question with his own, Optimus was trying to place that voice. Her reply gave him the answer.

'Ever since you arrived, you have been ferreting about,

pursuing Count Scicluna. You have been at his offices; pretending to be a man of affairs, don't bother to deny it.'

'I did call there, Miss Kirkbride.'

'But you are no merchant. A real merchant, a real financier would never disclose his business to a tavern-keeper – and your name is not Cornish, perhaps it is not Shute either –'

'It *is* Shute,' Optimus insisted, 'and, for all your accusations, my intentions are honourable.' The woman laughed, it was a sharp, bitter laugh. 'My intentions *are* honourable, the real reason I've come here is to –'

'Is to cheat my grandfather,' she completed for him. Optimus clenched his fists until the knuckles showed white. This woman was totally unfair, unreasonable.

'The real reason I'm here,' he enunciated slowly, almost vindictively, 'is to find Grace.'

A long silence descended upon the carriage. Apart from the clopping of the horses' hooves and the creak of harness, there was a tense quietness in which he could hear his companion's panting respiration. She too was agitated now, stiff with anger.

'Don't expect me to believe that. What can that woman possibly be to you. No, she's just a pretext, a lever, a way of getting at my grandfather. I distrusted you from the moment I saw you on shipboard. Why did you travel on that ship with me?'

'It was a coincidence.'

'Coincidence – coincidence, there is no such thing as coincidence. You planned it. It could never have been coincidence.' There was, Optimus reflected, something in her accusation. *He* had not planned it, of course, but was there such a thing as coincidence, or was it only part of the working out of some strange providence, the same providence that had sustained Grace Pensilva and provided her with the means to exact her vengence.

'Where are you taking me, Miss Kirkbride?'

'My grandfather has asked me to fetch you.' She paused, rubbing her interlocked fingers together in her lap. 'He has asked me to fetch you to him. He wants to know the nature of your proposition, the proposition *we* both know is but your deception. Count Scicluna is an honourable man, Mr Shute, and trusting. It has been his downfall. He wants to give you the benefit of the doubt, but I want you to know that *I* distrust you. If you are come to compass his ruin, I shall protect him.'

The sheer far-fetched injustice of her observations staggered him. Nothing had been further from his thoughts than a plot to defraud Scicluna, it was preposterous. He blustered.

'I assure you, the only reason why I followed up the Delaluna connection and stumbled on your grandfather was his past association with Grace Pensilva – Grace Delabole, as she was known here.'

'I don't believe you. Grace Delabole is long gone; there can be no possible profit in searching for vestiges of her. No, as far as I am concerned, there is no possible point in pursuing the matter further. But my grandfather wishes to meet you; I must respect his wishes . . . If you possess a scrap of the good intentions you say you have, you'll not claim his attention more than strictly necessary.'

Optimus gave up the attempt to communicate with her. Far ahead of him, on a small eminence, stood a walled city with domes and pinnacles. Nearer at hand, small stone-walled fields lay parched already to either side of the dusty highway. Here and there were small houses, farms probably, flat-roofed, with an outside staircase to the upper floor. It was something of a surprise when the coachman pulled up at one of them.

3

'If you want to understand what happened between Grace and Frederick, the answer lies in Argostoli.'

Count Scicluna was explaining to Optimus in that quaint academic English of his, with the peculiar accent. The old man had met him at the door, sent Maria off to the kitchen in search of a bottle, and ushered him down a dim corridor to a large, almost equally dim room, lit by two half-round windows set high in the wall. It was cool like a cave, an impression heightened by the ponderous stone beams that roofed it, and furnished simply with a large polished-wood table and high-backed chairs around it. Between the two men as they sat was a decanter flanked by two glasses.

'Where's Argostoli?'

'In Cephalonia. The Seven Islands as it was then, Greece as it is now. More marsala?'

Optimus nodded, remembering how Maria had brought it half an hour ago and thumped it angrily upon the table. 'You mustn't mind Maria,' the Count had murmured when she was gone, 'she's been terribly hurt by the loss of her grandmother. So was I, of course,' he had stopped and sat gazing into his wineglass whose foot he held pressed to the table top with the fingertips of both hands, 'she was a good woman, more of a mother to Maria than anything else. Her real mother, who married Major Ian Kirkbride of the garrison here, found she hadn't much time for child-rearing when they were posted to London. It was all balls, and picnics, and parties. We did not hear from her much. Just recently, since her mother's death, she's taken to writing. Poor girl, she must be lonely. Anyway,

350

I'm digressing, am I not? To get back to Maria, she's appointed herself my guardian in my old age and she's trying to protect me. God knows, that's an ungrateful task she's set herself, fighting imaginary foes. All my life I have been my own worst enemy. When I started, I lived in a fine house in Notabile; you saw the town on the way here; and look at me, reduced to a farmhouse. But I'm happy here, now that she's come, contented.' He had sighed and poured their first glass of marsala. 'Now tell me again about this Grace Pensilva who is, you say, the same person as our Miss Delabole. I'll help you if I can. She was an extraordinary person. We loved her.'

Optimus had sketched Grace's early life for his host, but had deliberately omitted to mention Jan King and what he assumed had happened to him. For one thing, he did not want to prejudice his informant; for another, he wanted to concentrate on Grace's relations with Frederick. But first he asked about the genesis of Delaluna and Company.

'She came to see me the day after I first met her,' Scicluna recollected with a slight puckering of the brows as though re-living a scene long past. 'She came to my office on the wharf, and she apologized, she apologized for the boorishness, the unfairness of her compatriots. Then she came to the point: she questioned me about my business. I had to tell her it was in a poor way, for I only had one ship left, a schooner, and had not the money to fit her out and man her. She asked where there were cargoes, what trade would bring most profit. I said currants from Argostoli. Grace pondered. Then she said she knew someone who might be an investor, take shares in the vessel, but who, by reason of his position, could not be seen to take part in business ventures. I thought she meant Mr Genteel, but I refrained from asking. Next day she came with the money: gold pieces in a canvas belt, and more in a buckskin bag. That's how we started.'

'And Frederick Genteel didn't have anything to do with it at that stage?'

'No, he was too busy getting married to Felicity Fell. She ran him a merry dance. A young girl can do that to a man, you know, sometimes against his better judgement. No, it wasn't

351

till the *Marathon*'s fourth or fifth voyage, that was what we called our ship, the *Marathon*, that Genteel became involved in it. By then Frederick was hard up, very hard up, she'd spent all her dowry and what little he had saved besides on her extravagances. He needed money. Grace offered him a secret share in the venture if he'd captain the ship to Argostoli. Angove, her usual skipper, had just left the firm without notice, without so much as a by your leave, and no one of the right stamp was available. Frederick and Grace weren't on good terms then. I sensed it, you understand. He took the job because he had to. She could afford to pay him generously. We weren't just shipping currants back to England. On the outward journeys there were other goods. There was a war on in Greece and there were cargoes that, if handled discreetly, were worth a fortune to the shipper. I had next to nothing to do with that part of the business, Grace handled it, as she handled Genteel's hiring. She was in control up to then. I just watched he work and marvelled. I wondered why she bothered to share the business with me; she could have done without me. I thought she had induced him to come along to protect his investment. I didn't understand anything. That voyage opened my eyes to something I hadn't suspected. As I said, if you want to understand what happened between Grace and Frederick, the answer lies in the Argostoli episode.'

When he had topped up Optimus' glass with marsala, he filled his own, swirled it round and sniffed it. 'Yes, until the Argostoli episode, Grace had always sipped at the wine of life, the wine of pain, the wine of happiness, but never drunk. I think it drove her mad, the realization, and the folly of it.'

'What was it? What did she realize?' Optimus was on the edge of his chair, excited.

'It was more of a revelation. Perhaps it was something that had not properly existed before. Living that voyage together made it happen. Bentley can tell you more about that voyage, he was on it. So was I, but I'm tired now. You'll come back. You'll come often. Just name the day and I'll send the chaise to fetch you.' He rose with a slow courtesy, taking Optimus by the sleeve in a delicate, bird-like grip as they approached the door.

'Did I tell you Grace lived in this house until she bought her own in Floriana? Well she did. She and my daughter Rita, Maria's mother, were thick as thieves. Rita worshipped her, she was so free, so modern, so independent. Ah –' he sighed a long sigh, 'Maria is so like her, she is so like both of them, she frightens me a little.' He smiled a thin smile, and Optimus felt a gust of sadness, like a hot, tear-inducing breeze, blow over them. The old man caught himself, straightened and ushered Optimus into the hallway. Maria appeared in a moment.

'Allow me to show Mr Shute to the carriage, Grandfather,' she asked winningly, as if all her fears were forgotten. 'It's too hot for you to go out at present.'

'You see what it's like to be an old man, to be molly-coddled,' laughed Scicluna. 'By the way, had you noticed this painting?' He pointed to a small oil in a gilt frame. 'It is my wife. Rita painted it. She was very artistic.'

Optimus realized that he had completely forgotten to ask about the miniature and its painter. Now here was the answer to his question coming to him unbidden. One more of the pieces in his puzzle had fallen into place. The face had something of Maria but fuller, more kindly.

As he went to step up into the chaise, Maria detained him. Her face was unveiled now and he was struck by her beauty. He was unprepared for what she had to say to him.

'Don't imagine that, because my grandfather has taken to you, I have, Mr Shute. *I* still distrust you. Whatever your motive may be, I shall find it out and I shall baulk you. If I were you, I'd drop this business at once, leave Malta and never come back here. You English are determined to ruin my grandfather, but you shan't, do you hear, you shan't. I think I know where you're leading with your tales of Grace Pensilva, but your pound of flesh will cost you dear. Now, be off with you.'

She was so vehement that Optimus really felt himself guilty of some crime he could not even imagine. Her wild face haunted him as the coachman set the chaise in motion. Suddenly, on impulse, Optimus stuck his head out of the window and shouted back at her. She was at the door, but turned to listen.

'I *am* going,' he cried excitedly. 'I'm going to Argostoli. Will that satisfy you?'

Without a change in the lines of her face that he could discern, she entered the house and shut the door behind her.

'I've made too many concessions already,' complained Frederick, keeping his voice as calm as he could. He sat perched uncomfortably on the edge of a gilded chair in Felicity's bedroom while she absent-mindedly brushed her hair. 'I've agreed to a marriage in the cathedral to satisfy your Romish tastes; I've agreed to your priest's demands that the children be brought up in that superstitious faith; now you're insisting on having Grace Delabole as your bridesmaid –'

'Why not? I haven't objected to your having that gruff Major Kirkbride as best man, have I?'

'That's different: Kirkbride's an old friend. Grace is practically a stranger, we know nothing about her.'

'But she's my best friend, my only friend. I thought you liked her too and I can't think what you have against her.' Felicity had stopped brushing her hair and held the brush limply across her lap, staring blankly into the swing-mirror on the table in the window embrasure. All around her, the bedroom was in its usual state of feminine confusion. Hats, silk stockings, dresses, petticoats, lay scattered where she had discarded them, drooping over the furniture, expiring on the floor. She herself wore a loose white gown in the classic manner, just sufficiently diaphanous to show the outlines of her anatomy. 'You know something about her, don't you, and you won't tell me. Is she one of your old flames or something?' Their eyes met in the mirror as she put the final challenging question.

'Most certainly not!' Frederick lied with all the conviction he could muster. If he was honest with himself, he had to recognize that Felicity had put her finger on the very reason why he did not want Grace to participate in the ceremony. Was it feminine intuition that led Felicity to this conclusion? Or had Grace said something to make her suspicious? He thought not. Grace seemed to be clinging too fiercely to her new identity to want to jeopardize it by admitting to such a compromising acquaintanceship.

'What *is* it then?'

'It's just that – it's just that you don't know who she is, do you? How did you come to bump into her at Palermo?' Frederick was persuaded that their meeting had not been an accident; he must have alluded to Felicity in one of the replies he sent to Grace's notes in the time she spent wandering before reaching Malta. If she had arrived earlier . . . but there was no use in such speculation. Grace herself wanted him to have Felicity. 'What did she give as her reason for being there?' he concluded, thinking how bewildered Felicity looked, with her hair in disorder and her hands to her temples.

'Oh my head! My poor head! Oh, how you do confuse me,' she wailed, swaying on her chair as though she would swoon. 'Stop pestering me! Grace Delabole is the one friend I have here and I don't *care* who she is or where she comes from. She's a lady: that's evident from the moment you meet her. I wish I could say you were as much of a gentleman.'

'I'm only trying to protect you against any possible exploitation.'

'*Grace* isn't marrying me for my dowry.'

'That's unfair. That's not why I'm doing it.'

'Well, why are you? You don't talk as if you loved me, you just keep telling me I can't do this or the other. I don't need that. You're not my father.' Frederick felt momentarily uncomfortable. He *was* much older, but he was a young man for all that.

'I'm marrying you because I've always wanted to; I'm marrying you because I've promised your father I'd look after you. Money doesn't come into it.'

'And money doesn't come into *my* friendship with Grace. You can set your mind at rest; she has never discussed such matters. And Papa has quizzed her, he told me. She's rich in her own right and has good connections; she's from an old Cornish family. She's just a modern woman, like Hester Stanhope. I'd be like her myself if I had the money and half her courage. But I shan't, shall I? I'm going to marry you, and I'd be perfectly content about it if you weren't such a dog in a manger. Why can't you just agree to her being my bridesmaid and not make a mountain out of a molehill?' Felicity had turned to face him and was looking at him in wide-eyed sad-mouthed supplication. 'She'll be back here shortly, and I want to tell her it's agreed to.'

'Where is she?'

'She's off in the country, seeing some Maltese person called Scicluna.'

'She's making a mistake,' said Genteel, 'she can't afford to go hob-nobbing with the Maltese. She won't be accepted in good society if she persists in it.' Frederick felt aggrieved. It was one thing to stick up for Count Scicluna in his quarrel with the Governor; it was quite another to cultivate the Maltese and make friends with them. There was something else that rankled; why was Grace rejecting him, pushing him into Felicity's arms when he could so easily have turned to her? He knew he would have fallen for her, if only she . . . And he had been practically certain the feeling was mutual. Why else had she kept corresponding with him? At first he had felt awkward with her: he had feared her, but that was all past and now he resented her seeming indifference. She was a mass of contradictions: one moment she was fascinating him with her bold seriousness; the next she was enraging him at the way she had curled herself round Felicity so tight that he met her at every turning. He wished he could understand her, but all he could do was make the best he could of it.

'Shall I have her?' Felicity persisted.

'I don't know.'

'Oh, you are such a solemn, serious fellow, Freddie! Can't you ever forget about politics and talk to a girl about important matters like bonnets and blouses? Tell me,' and she stood up to take something from the bed, 'how do you think this lavender sash will go with my wedding gown?' Pulling the sash tight around her, above her waist and close under her pert young breasts, she flounced towards him, swaying her hips with deliberate voluptuousness. 'This shall be my wedding gown and Grace shall be my bridesmaid,' she half-whispered.

'You won't get round me that way. It isn't that easy.' His own voice sounded rough and strained. She was using her body to manipulate him. He resented it, but knew he could not resist her. He already sensed that a man might even enjoy being thus exploited.

'Oh, but I shall, dear Freddie, and you shall have your reward.'

'My reward?'

'You shall have a kiss on account!'

'A kiss is not enough.' Against the light, he saw her body's outline, close, available. Her musky perfume intoxicated him. It would be so easy to capitulate. That was what Grace wanted, wasn't it? He found himself breathing deeply. 'I want you. I want you now,' he murmured. He rose to his feet and threw his arms around her.

'Nay, Frederick, you must learn to wait – it is only for a few days now. Tell me you agree, tell me Grace shall be my bridesmaid.'

'You use me!' he almost shouted. 'How can I marry a woman who does nothing but bargain over everything?' Felicity's shoulders drooped. She tried to turn away. She was weeping. He took a handkerchief from his sleeve and dabbed at her eyes with it contritely.

'I'm sorry. You shall have Grace. I've been unreasonable.'

'You'll make your peace with her?' she asked hopefully. 'For my sake – if you love me a little.'

'I'll try.' Genteel sensed he was making a mistake, but that it was inevitable.

'Then you shall have your kiss, Freddie. Just one for now, but in earnest of more hereafter.'

She melted in his arms. She was skittish, coquettish, and he suspected that she enjoyed tormenting him. But her body stirred him more than he had thought possible. He kissed the nape of her neck. He sought her lips. When he found them, they were more responsive than he had ever known them. Encouraged, he crushed her breasts against his chest, feeling her nipples through his shirt. A warm tide of desire was drowning him.

'Do you want me?' he murmured, brushing her ear with his lips.

Through half-closed lids, he saw the divan behind her and imagined himself already thrusting her down upon it. When she failed to reply, he kissed her again, more urgently. With eyes shut, he saw himself kissing her before the priest in the cathedral. A woman was watching them: her face showed neither grief nor joy, yet her eyes were burning. The face was Grace Pensilva's. Her hot stare was driving him on, launching him deliberately into the commitment that neither of them really desired.

'I must have you,' he gasped involuntarily.

'No, no, Frederick, not now. Grace will be back directly.' He bit his lip until the blood came. Was this what Grace wanted? Fiercely, he flung her away and left the room. He would not be denied much longer.

There had been no ship that week to take Optimus to Argostoli. To go there had been a sudden impulse provoked by Maria Kirkbride but, once his resolve was made, he had felt thwarted. The enforced days he spent in Valletta were like a prison sentence, an illusion heightened by the walls around him. He had endeavoured to put his time to good use, talking to Osborne, searching for the house where Grace had lived in Floriana and the one nearby where Frederick and Felicity had set up their married home. There was nothing conclusive to prove it, but Optimus had the impression that their union was something that Grace might not have instigated but, when she discovered its impending occurrence, she manipulated events to ensure its successful conclusion. By the time she embarked on the Argostoli voyage with him, a routine had been established, a *modus vivendi* in which Grace played the role of Felicity's confidante.

The accounts and writs for non-payment of debts provided by Osborne were ample evidence of Felicity's extravagance. It was clear that her dowry, which was not substantial, was soon frittered away in clothes and furnishings, not to mention her Maltese servants.

Now that this background was available, several of Grace's undated notes to Frederick acquired a context and Optimus understood the way in which an intermittent, clandestine relationship had persisted between them. That it survived at all was probably her achievement for, in the early months, Genteel appeared to have been completely in thrall to his Felicity. Even when her fecklessnes had pushed him close to ruin, he had remained loyal, grateful for the joys she had given him. If he fell in with Grace's plans at all it was not from any romantic motive on his part; he had dismissed that possibility from his mind; but one of absolute necessity.

After the drama of Malta, Greece at first was a disappointment. Argostoli, on the eastern arm of a vast roadstead from which the land rose gently, was not much larger than a village. There were a few buildings in the Classical manner, built while Cephalonia was under the protection of the British Crown. One of these was the hospital, part of the legacy of Colonel Charles Napier, the enlightened Governor of Cephalonia. As he expected, Optimus drew a blank here. There was no one who remembered the arrival of a particular wounded officer all those years ago. And yet, from what the tavern keeper Bentley had told him, Frederick had been brought here, and here he had lain until Grace had taken him off to a house in the town to tend him herself.

The grandeur of Argostoli, Optimus discovered that evening when he grew tired and slumped on a chair at a taverna overlooking the port, was in the mountains. Away to the east, unsuspected in the daytime haze, the sleeping giants slowly revealed themselves in the light of the setting sun. They were like huge beasts, heads lolling forward over their paws. Their faint reflections lay scribbled on the shifting waters of the bay. Sipping his coffee, Optimus was strangely move. The barefoot fishermen loading their gear into their boats; the bemused shepherds, dazzled by the brightness of the city they were visiting for the day; the kilted klephts, looking more like the brigands they were than the freedom fighters they had briefly been against the Turks; all were the same walkers-on, or nearly, as Grace must have known during the troubled days she spent here. The evening air seemed to have become transformed into a soft, jelly-like substance, and Optimus imagined he knew how Ulysses, whose Ithaca lay just beyong those mountains to the east, had felt in Lotus Land. His quest seemed to have fizzled out in a dead end. There was nothing for it but to retrace his steps.

The fact that a man in European dress was threading his way through the thin crowd towards him did not, at first, register with him. Only when he realized that the newcomer was regarding him with a fixed stare as he came closer and closer did Optimus pay him more than casual attention. The man wore a close-fitting, high-buttoned serge jacket with worsted trousers of a lighter grey. His craggy face was topped by a tumultuous sea of grey locks that contrasted strangely with the primness of the rest of his appearance. His humorous mouth spread in an elastic smile as he settled himself on a nearby chair, tugging at his trouser knees as he did so. Under bushy brows, a pair of deep-set black eyes twinkled.

'You are welcome to Argostolion, Mr Shute. Do you lack anything? Are you lodged comfortably?'

'Well enough, I did not expect luxury,' replied Optimus warily. He had thought himself unknown in Cephalonia, yet here was a perfect stranger who knew his name and was pretending to be solicitous about his welfare. 'I didn't think I had had the honour –'

'Spiro Marcopoulos, at your service. I am official *transitaire* at the port here. But you wonder, I see you wonder, how I come to disturb you – I hear you inquire about a certain person.' Part of the explanation seemed obvious, this fellow had heard of his inquiries at the hospital. It would have been easy for him to obtain Optimus' name from the arriving ships' manifests if he was really the shipping agent he claimed to be.

'I *am* making a few inquiries.'

'What is your interest? No doubt you are a relative and have inherited a share in the Delaluna business. Perhaps I can help you to –'

'Before I accept such aid, I think I should know *your* interest.'

Before replying, Marcopoulos called to the taverna proprietor in Greek and a jug of wine appeared on the table.

'If we were to drink to the health of Count Scicluna, that would content you?' It was Optimus' turn to smile. Evidently Scicluna still had a long arm in this part of the world.

'To Count Scicluna,' he echoed, sipping the amber wine.

'In fact,' Marcopoulos assured him, 'it is I who am in your debt. Without your coming I should have had no news of my old friend on Malta. How is he? His letter says nothing of himself, it is typical.'

'He is in mourning, his wife . . .'

Marcopoulos crossed himself in the Orthodox manner. 'God rest her soul. A good woman. He is alone then?'

'No, his granddaughter Maria is with him.'

'I knew her well, a gentle creature.'

Optimus could not repress a smile; gentleness must lie in the eye of the beholder. He decided not to pursue the matter. During their conversation, he had been absorbed in conjecture over Marcopoulos' age. Despite his sprightliness, the nest of wrinkles that cupped his eyes suggested that he was as old as Scicluna or older.

'Did you know Frederick Genteel?'

The Greek shook his head slowly. '*Ochi*,' he replied, 'no, I had not that honour, though I once saw him. He was not in a state of talk poor fellow. But Grace Delabole, that is a different story; we were in trade together.'

'What kind of trade? Was it legal?'

Marcopoulos sat back and laughed.

'What a question! Well, perhaps at the time it wasn't absolutely – but it was for a good cause. I see you know more than I thought.' A cloud seemed to spread over his features and he stared off across the roadstead. In the sunset it was as if some half-demented follower of Salvator Rosa had dragged his oily

361

brush across the landscape in stripes of vermilion, cadmium, burnt sienna and umber over the lustrous water. 'Those were good days,' Marcopoulos continued. 'We all thought ourselves immortal, that is the way with the young. And Grace, Grace had a touch of genius. Whatever she touched, it prospered. Until the voyage with Frederick ... When she reached here, she had changed; when she left, she was a different woman.'

'How?' Optimus was interested now.

'She had been so sure of herself, but with Genteel here, she was like a ship without a rudder. Count Scicluna thought it had something to do with that scoundrel Captain Scully's arrival in the roadstead, but I know better. I had been watching her while she nursed Frederick; I saw her change.'

'What did she feel for him?' Optimus was surprised at his own directness. 'Did she love him?'

'*She* didn't think so,' Marcopoulos became absorbed in the landscape again. 'What is this woman to you? Why have you come so far to ask questions about her?'

It was Optimus' turn to lose himself in the sunset. 'I didn't mean to – I stumbled on her story – or rather, it was thrust upon me. My Grace Pensilva, your Grace Delabole, was someone who wormed her way into your heart by being herself, distant, different, almost unapproachable. I think now that, had I known her personally, had I been mixed up in her life, I should have feared her – at least I ought to have. But that doesn't lessen the attraction. For me, she's just as real as you are.' Marcopoulos reached across the table and covered Optimus' hand with his own.

'I believe you. It is reason enough. All passion, all desire is unreason. I knew her. I knew her face. I knew how she acted. Grace was a person who did all, apparently, according to reason, and then ... You know, of course, that this is the country that invented tragedy? And you know what it is that makes misfortune into something more than a passing sadness, the work of blind chance, an accident ...? Partly, it *is* fate: perhaps some small detail that was overlooked in the beginning. Partly, it is in a commitment, a passion, a great love. Partly and above all, it lies in the wilful destruction of such a love for some supposedly noble purpose.' He stopped speaking and gave a nervous laugh. 'But I am boring you with my pedantic nonsense . . . Have you noticed?' He pointed out into the bay where it seemed that hundreds of tiny lights were twinkling. 'Do you have that in your country, the *lamparos*? The fishermen light a fire in a brazier and hang it out over the water. The fish swim to it. They cannot resist the lure. They are caught. They die. So it goes . . . If I had known that that was the last time I should see Grace – but how should I have known what was in store for her? I should have known: it was the first time that I saw her troubled. Grace Delabole was a real person.'

'Surely you remember more of what exactly happened here?'

'It is late for me, I grow tired. Tomorrow morning I will take you somewhere – it is not much, but it may help you see things, and I will show you the *katavrothes*, they are a phenomenon and a mystery, unique to Argostolion. You must not feel you came here for nothing.'

Optimus found it hard to sleep that night. It was not the heat, though his room was stuffy. It was not the noise of the klephts singing and quarrelling in the tavernas. He was consumed with impatience to know what Marcopoulos would show him, and above all, he was desperate to know more of what had happened between Grace and Frederick. He already knew that on the way here their ship had been involved in some kind of battle and that Genteel had arrived wounded. Both Count Scicluna and Bentley had told him about that. The events were clear enough. The intriguing part was how they had affected Grace Pensilva. When at last he slept, he was haunted by that face, its lines grown haggard, its grey eyes troubled.

Grace was riding along a track on the steep flank of a mountain. Her horse was lathered with spume and sweat, for she had ridden him hard on the way here. When she left Argostoli, it had been barely dawn. She had galloped across

363

the causeway as if into a battle, her hair flying, the cool morning air reddening her face. To her left, the landlocked harbour lay wrapped in ghostly mist through which the topmasts and yards of the *Marathon* and other ships poked out like fire-burned trees on some strange battleground. Only when the rolling foothills gave way to the mountainside did she slow her headlong course, allowing her mount to pick his way along the cornice between cliff and mist-shrouded sea. Far below, on some unseen beach, the waves sighed in the shingle.

She had left Argostoli, she had left Frederick there because she could bear it no longer. At first, when there was but the wound to contend with, she had been full of confidence and hope, but now, now that he was wasting away with every hour, she could not bear it. That was what had made her knock at the taverna door at first light, demanding a horse and saddle. She had paid little heed to where she was riding.

At first, the pounding rush of her flight relieved her of some tension. To be doing something, to be doing anything, was a catharsis. She had struggled for so many days and nights she had lost count of them. Now, with the horse gingerly picking its way along the narrow track, she had leisure to think. For herself she felt no fear, though one misplaced hoof might send her tumbling hundreds of feet down the precipitous slope. Her fear was for him. Every step she moved away increased her disquiet. She seemed to see his dry, feverish lips move. He was whispering something.

She came to a place where three ways met. The horse stopped of its own accord, waiting to know her decision. One of the ways before her trended down. There was a smiling village among vineyards at the end of it. She imagined herself riding there with Frederick, in another time, when he was happy and strong, strong as the Venetian fortress which topped the peninsula beyond the houses. The other road was a hard road, struggling up between the rocks to a pass in the mountains. It was cold up there and lonely. Was that her way? She feared so.

Before she could jab her horse into motion along it, she

heard a whirring overhead. Looking up, she saw the reason. A black bird was soaring above her. As she watched, it spiralled down, until it seemed enormous. When it was within feet of her head, it jerked itself to the opposite direction, swinging behind her, so her eyes could not follow it. When it reappeared, it was even closer. She had a blurred vision of gaping beak, tattered pennons, and grasping talons. In frantic fear she struck out at it. The bird merely avoided her. She heard it croak and smelt the rank smell of it.

It was her eyes she feared for; they were so vulnerable. There was nowhere she could go for shelter, nothing but low heath all round her. And the bird was there, soaring and swooping. It passed so close to her she felt its dusty wing-tips brush her face. Her hands felt her horse tremble, it would shy at any moment.

She wrapped her arms about her head and screamed. She screamed again, and her scream was met by a mocking echo from the cliffs above her. She screamed again, but the scream was choked in her throat.

Silence.

When she dared drop her arms once more the bird had vanished. Her eyes sought it in all directions. Her breath came in short gasps and her heart was thudding.

Was that it, high up, so high that it was a mere speck, right in the hazy sun?

Now that it had left her, she was disorientated. She no longer dared to travel onward. That was not all. In the abrupt quietness, with the insects scraping among the stones, she had leisure to think of another significance. What if the bird had been a warning? She shrugged it off; she could not afford to allow her life to be ruled by the irrational. And yet, was it possible that this had been a bird of ill omen? Did its blackness mean something she was not ready to admit? Was she ready to accept the loss? Did she accept that loss it would be? If he were to slip away, would it not be the better way, saving her from the execution of her purpose? Was she sure that she still had strength to accomplish it? She had been waiting, waiting for the time, the right time to come and reveal itself to her. She had waited to see him woven into a cocoon of felicity. She had schemed to trap him in a net of dependence on her financially. In all these things, time and the fates had aided her. It had been all too easy, but now, on this bald hillside, there came to her a terrible realization: she did not want him to die. Not now. Not ever. Perhaps, at this very moment, he was lying dead without her.

She screamed again, but silently, a scream in the head. With savage hand, she wrenched the horse's head to turn him homeward. Reckless of life she rode like one possessed.

The woman ushered the two of them into the chamber. They had just spent several minutes in the adjoining room which doubled as kitchen and parlour, though there was not a single comfortable chair in it. The only concession to luxury was a piece of lace spread across the table. Marcopoulos had talked to her animatedly in Greek and Optimus had wondered how, such a small matter could provoke such noise and gesticulation. The woman had appeared hard, with hatchet-face to match her manners. Now, as the door closed behind them, he breathed a sigh of relief.

The chamber they had entered was relatively spacious, with a high ceiling, walls washed with a pale blue distemper, and a single window, set high up in one wall. The light that came through it flickered constantly and Optimus saw that the reason was that a fig tree reached right across it and its leaves were shaking in the sea breeze.

Spiro Marcopoulos had brought him to this house without much explanation, threading his way through the lanes behind the seafront. It was as if he assumed that Optimus would know their destination.

'This is where he lay,' he announced quietly, with a wave of his arm towards the corner where an iron bedstead extended under a cross and a silver-framed, blackened icon. 'Of course, it is not the furniture. But the room is the same.'

'You saw him here?'

'Once. She would not let others enter. It was early one morning. Unaccountably, she had left him. He was there, in the corner. For a week, he had remained unconscious. I see him now, in my mind's eye.'

It was at this precise moment that Optimus finally understood what he had earlier suspected about the quality of the light. There was a terrible clarity about this Mediterranean light. It was all or nothing. Optimus did not have to try to imagine Grace listening to Frederick's shallow, slightly erratic breathing. She saw him as he was; poor clay, but more than that, a spirit. Did she remember what Dr Cornish had told her about the soul, her soul? She had no need of a mirror to see her own face and know that whether or not she had forgiven him, it made no difference. She was bound to him, bound with a bond that was both more or less than marriage. Whatever she did, this revelation, borne in on her by a flawless light, would remain with her. Optimus saw her put her knuckle to her teeth. She was both made and broken.

'You did not hear what I said,' Marcopoulos was reproaching him.

'I'm sorry, I must have been dreaming.'

'I was telling you about the arrival of the *Hecate*. Two weeks after I saw Frederick here, a brig sailed into the roadstead: HMS *Hecate*. Naturally, I was one of the first to know of it, I used to do the victualling. I went out in a bum-boat and met her captain, a man called Scully. I remember him well, he had one eye and was fresh from England, via Malta. He gave me a letter for Frederick Genteel. I remember he said he knew him and I thought it peculiar. He did not seem the type with whom Genteel would be familiar. Well, I mentioned it to Count Scicluna when I gave him the letter to deliver to Grace to pass on to Frederick, and he didn't seem affected by it, but when I told Ben Barlow, he was beside himself.'

'Ben Barlow?'

'Haven't you met him? He worked for Delaluna. He lives in Malta.' Optimus schooled himself to keep a straight face. Another piece had fallen into place.

'I may have met him, but the name is unfamiliar.'

'Perhaps he goes under another one now. Well, Barlow went running to tell Grace about it. Within twelve hours, she was gone from here for ever. They all were gone, though the *Marathon* wasn't really ready for sea. The crew were still repairing her.' He paused. 'Have you seen all you wanted to here? There wasn't much: I warned you.' Optimus nodded and began to leave the room. Marcopoulos detained him.

'Oh yes, there was this. I almost forgot to give it to you. I found it on the table after they left. I meant to send it on, but by the time I could, I heard about what happened and it was useless to do so, so I kept it.' Optimus took the letter. Its seal was dusty and had been broken long since. The hand-writing was unfamiliar to him, rounded and degenerating into a scrawl at the end of sentences. He had no need to read the signature to know who had been the sender. As he scanned its contents, he was filled with impatience at her selfishness and insensitivity.

'May I keep this? I should like to study it again quietly.'

'I have no need of it now. When I first found it, there were small stains visible, tears I thought. They are faded now. Even I cannot see them. Come, I must show you the *katavrothes*. You will see, out in the sunshine you will feel better. There is still a sadness in this room. I feel it.'

As they passed through the outer room, Optimus tried to place a small coin on the table. The woman was on him at once, almost shouting as she shook him by the arm and thrust the money back at him. Decidedly, he would never understand these people.

'Why have you brought me here? There is nothing to see,' said Optimus in disappointment. 'I have seen mills before aplenty. What difference is there between this one and all the others? There is just a house and a wheel turning.'

'The difference is in the water. In the *katavrothes* it flows from the sea downwards. In all other mills, it flows down to the sea. Grace and Frederick walked here one morning. He was still weak and leant on her shoulder. I saw them, they went slowly, slowly. From the way she held her head I knew the sadness. There was a brig in the bay, at anchor, but she did not know then that it was Scully. I remember I thought as they paused beside here, that Grace is like the *katavrothes* water, she flows downwards, downwards and deep. Did you know that this water flows under the island and comes up in a grotto near Sami? So it goes with our lives, Mr Shute, a story dies and then, long after, like your coming here, it is alive again ... Well, I have told you all I could, you must be satisfied, though it was but little.'

'Just one more thing,' Optimus said, anxious to clarify a point that had been nagging him, 'you had a letter about me, from Malta, from Count Scicluna, was that where you got the idea that I must be related to Grace and a claimant to a share in the Delaluna partnership?'

'Not at all, it was a simple deduction. Not many men would make the voyage you have without hope of gain, merely to seek the truth about a woman.'

'But that woman is Grace Pensilva.'

'And I believe you. I hope you find her.'

'I shall. I shall follow her back to Malta.'

The clatter of hooves as she rode up brought Count Scicluna to the doorway. She scrutinized his face for a sign. There was none. In her mind, she had pictured the sickroom. All the way back while she rode helter-skelter, her heart had been tight with a premonition about Frederick. Now, as she dismounted, she felt sick, sick with fear, she had to compel herself to ask the question.

'How is he? I saw an omen. I came back immediately.'

'He has been restless.'

He was not dead then. She took a quick breath and brushed past Scicluna, half running across the outer room until she was in the chamber. She leaned against the doorframe, panting. Watching Frederick, she saw that the bedclothes were tumbled as if he had ridden out a nightmare. His face was twitching slightly and it seemed as if his eyelids were trying to open. His shallow breathing was the only sound in the room and, to her fearful imagination, it looked as if a dark hand was clutching at his throat. As she watched, it fluttered slightly, resting on his windpipe where it emerged from the crumpled sheet. With another gasp, she crossed the chamber

369

and knelt beside him, reaching out to brush away the clutching hand.

It was insubstantial, her own fingers passed through it and came to rest on Frederick's throat. His flesh felt cool, cooler than she remembered it. Now the shadow lay across her own hand also. She looked across the room and upward to the window and laughed. Outside, in the bright sunlight, a fig leaf trembled.

When she looked back his eyes were open. For the first time in weeks they were studying her lucidly. She felt another pinch of fear; was this a last surge of consciousness? She had heard that this might happen. He was whispering to her. His voice was so thin that she had to put her ear to his lips to hear it. Even then, she could not believe it. One tear, then a second, ran down her cheek and splashed upon his pillow.

'I'm hungry,' he repeated. How long since he had eaten? She had watched him wasting away each day while the bowl of gruel on the table remained uneaten. It was there now, cold from the day before, indigestible. She must make more. If he was hungry, if he could eat, then he would live. She felt like singing. Placing a finger on his lips to make him silent, she kissed his brow and left him.

He is alive, she sang to herself in her head as she lit the charcoal and fanned it into flame. He's alive, she sang as she stirred the pot. He will live, she prayed as she warmed it up. The smell of burnt charcoal caught in her nose, a reminder of another occasion, not long since, when for the first time she had seen the real Frederick, not the awkward, reluctant official, bending to Fell's will, but a man of action, cool, decisive, brave to the point of folly. She had not suspected Frederick of harbouring this character when she embarked with him. Her eyes clouded as she stirred automatically, reliving those hours together on the ship.

The sail had been there on the horizon behind them since morning. It was a russet triangular scrap that dipped and swung. The ship which carried it was hull-down and invisible. Grace kept catching Count Scicluna throwing a glance at it whenever he thought she was not observing him.

At midnight they had left Valletta, hauling the *Marathon* out of the port with sweeps. When the wind came, just before dawn, she had breathed a sigh of relief. It might have been awkward to be discovered under the guns of Fort St Elmo with Genteel aboard as captain and without proper papers for the cargo. She had stood quietly to one side while Genteel gave instructions to Ben Barlow for the running of the ship. It was as if he had known her all his life, and she sensed that he was sailing her like a yacht, adjusting the sheets till the sails pulled sweetly. Grace caught Barlow nodding to himself in approval in the half-dark.

'This *Marathon* of yours is a fine hull,' Frederick confided in her at dawn, when they were romping along on a loppy sea, with Malta melting astern of them, 'she's a flyer.'

Grace too was proud of the *Marathon*, as was Count Scicluna who had bought her as a prize laid up in Marsa Creek. In her first youth, she had been an American ship, built on the Ipswich River for the Mediterranean trade, but had made only one voyage. Becalmed off the North African coast, she was taken by pirates and her crew sold into slavery in Algiers. Turned round again with a corsair crew, she herself became a pirate until, bottled up at anchor under Cape Farina, a British squadron took her. When Scicluna bought her she had been a sorry sight, her paint blistered, her seams gaping in the dry heat, but now with new gear and her black upperworks shining, she was a real thoroughbred. Slim, low-waisted, fore and aft rigged with a huge spread of canvas, there wasn't a vessel that could catch her when beating to windward.

If they had been beating now, the lateen that was dogging them would have been left standing, but they were running free and the breeze was dying.

'I don't like the look of things,' Frederick murmured as if he read her thoughts. 'That ship is tracking us and I think she's gaining. If she is, that can mean only one thing: she's a galley. If she is, we'll be needing something stronger than those popguns.' He gave a dismissive wave at the four brass cannon that were secured, two to a side, like toys in the waist behind the bulwarks.

371

For a long while no one spoke. The sea smoothed, and the sails hung slack and the triangular sail crept closer. For all her speed, the *Marathon* was impotent in these conditions. Manning the sweeps might defer the encounter a while, but could not prevent it.

They smelt the galley almost as soon as they saw the banked oars and could identify it with certainty. There was a foul, pestilential reek that drifted down from it on the slack breeze, an odour of abused humanity. There was no doubt now about their adversary. Only a few galleys were left and these had but one purpose: piracy.

Genteel's long features seemed longer than usual. His nose was pinched, otherwise there was no visible change in his demeanour.

'Have you visited Tunis or Algiers?' he asked Scicluna drily. 'We're likely to try the accommodation there before long, I fancy.'

'Is there nothing we can do?' asked the latter.

'Whistle for a wind, a big one. That would serve us nicely.'

During the next quarter of an hour, Genteel stood apart, grasping the jerking rigging while the *Marathon* wallowed. But for the preventers on her booms, they would have swung across incessantly. Her sails were almost empty. Her crew of four men had come out of the forecastle and had joined Barlow under the mainmast, looking anxious. The galley was so close they could see a white moustache under her forefoot. Her oars beat rhythmically.

'Are you game to try something?' Frederick was asking her. Grace turned around.

'What is it?'

'Will you play the decoy? Johnny Turk has a weakness for ladies. If you stay on deck here, well in view, it might distract him and stop him raking the ship with his bow-chasers.'

'I hadn't intended hiding below.'

'Well, slip down now and put on your smartest dress and a hat to match it. Meanwhile we'll see if we can't prepare a frolic that'll astonish that fellow.'

While she was below, she heard Genteel giving orders in a

low voice, and Barlow answering him. Then there was a rumble as something was dragged across the deck.

When she emerged on deck, she saw the reason: the starboard side cannon had been dragged to larboard and secured there between the existing pieces.

'Double shot 'em,' Genteel was ordering. 'We shall fire through our own bulwarks, a man to each gun, to fire in succession when I give the order.' He turned to Grace. 'You see what I'm planning: if we can induce the galley to range alongside our larbord quarter, we can give him something to remember us by, before he hits us. With the sails boomed out to starboard and no sign of resistance, it ought to work nicely. It's the part after that I'm not so keen on. We haven't the firepower to keep him from boarding. If only we had a bigger crew and plenty of muskets –'

'We *have*,' Grace blurted out, 'we've whole boxes of them!'

'Muskets?' His puzzled frown was matched by a tone of anger.

'Those crates of Birmingham goods,' she explained, 'they're for the Greek soldiers.'

'No wonder you wanted me to captain this vessel,' Frederick exclaimed bitterly, 'it was a nice way to avoid suspicion. You know as well as I do that you're not supposed to take the Greeks munitions under the British flag. Of course you knew it. And you tricked me. I was a fool to trust you . . .' Still, we must make the best of a bad job. Are they serviceable, is there powder and ball?' She nodded. Genteel turned to Scicluna. 'I'll ask you to do down in the hold with Barlow and take care of the loading. If you can hand the muskets up fast enough, we'll have a chance to beat 'em. It'll be a small chance, but a chance nevertheless, and better than a life in prison.'

Genteel's hostility was heavy in the air while the final preparations were made and the galley bore down on them. He sent Barlow to fetch his pistols and cutlass. When he returned, there were just the three of them visible on deck: Genteel himself at the wheel, Grace close behind him, and Barlow beside the open main-hatch, ready to leap below and help Scicluna at the start of the action. The seamen were all lying concealed in the scuppers, match in hand and muskets beside them.

The galley's stench swept across the *Marathon* like a fetid wave. Grace could see the gun crews on either side of its two bow-chasers. Behind them stood a slim, blue-coated officer in a fez. She stared at him. That was what Frederick would want her to do. If she willed him to hold his fire, the *Marathon* might not be disabled. She tried to appear unperturbed, as if the *Marathon*'s small crew were unwary. The officer's face was set in a thin smile.

'What's happening?' asked Genteel quietly, without turning round. 'Are they coming alongside us?'

'I think so.' It did look as though the galley's bow was veering away and its guns were no longer pointing at them.

'Aftermost gun fires first,' Genteel was reminding Barlow. 'Fire when I stamp my foot. Don't open the gun ports.'

The long metal-shod beak that stuck out from the galley's forefoot showed clearly through the water. The two vessels were overlapping more and more, with just enough space between them for the galley's oars to operate. Genteel waited. He turned his head enough to take in the situation and to avoid looking too wooden. It seemed to Grace that his eyes were dancing. He's enjoying this, she thought to herself. What sort of a mind does a man have to revel in danger?

'Number four,' she heard Frederick say, in the same tone as at a whist party. Then he stamped his foot.

The shot tore out through the *Marathon*'s bulwarks projecting a shower of splinters that sent the galley's gun crew reeling. The officer, however, was miraculously intact. Of the shot there was no immediate trace. Then, from inside the nearby hull, there came an agonizing yell, a hopeless cry that Grace was sure she would remember to her dying day.

'Poor devils,' said Frederick. 'We've hit 'em between wind and water . . . Number three,' and he stamped his foot.

Unable to halt her progress, the galley was reaching further along the *Marathon*'s side. Her own bow-chasers could not be brought to bear. She carried no side armament. However, the blue-coated officer was signalling to her helmsman, under an awning in her stern, to put her to starboard, and he was shouting, evidently calling for reinforcements. A squad of shouting corsairs came rushing forward along a catwalk.

Marathon's second shot made a new hole a little further aft than the first one. Once again the screaming was frightful. Fellow Christians were dying in there. The galley, deprived of its starboard oars, was slewing towards them.

'Take my pistols,' said Frederick. 'I suppose you can fire them.'

In quick succession, the *Marathon*'s remaining guns spoke and were echoed by screaming. Their adversary was down by the bow, taking water, but not fast enough to incapacitate her. Her ram grated harmlessly against *Marathon*'s side, but the gap was now so small that the corsairs could jump across it.

'Fire muskets!' cried Frederick above the yelling and detonations.

As the first muskets poked over the gunwale, the leading corsairs came leaping across. Three reached *Marathon*'s deck behind the kneeling gunners. Barlow accounted for one of them with a stab from the hold. Another had time to disable one of *Marathon*'s gunners before Scicluna shot him. But Scicluna himself was in danger. The third man was taking aim at him with a pistol.

The following moments were confused in Grace's mind. She remembered aiming one of her pistols, she remembered firing it, but she did not see the result. A long-robed corsair had sprung into the rigging and dropped down on her. With her arms pinned to her sides and winded by her fall to the deck, she was unable to bring her pistol to bear on him. She bit his neck, tasting the hot blood and smelling his sweat, but she guessed that his free hand was reaching back so that he could stab her. She dropped one pistol and then the other, writhing until her hands were free and she could grope for the man's dagger whose pommel was stuck in her midriff.

'Grace!'

Genteel's shout stung her to fresh effort, she twisted to one side and the corsair's sword dug into the deck beside her. The next instant, she was fighting with a dead weight. When she pushed it aside, she saw that Genteel had left the wheel and cut her assailant down.

But he himself was in danger. The blue-coated officer was on the gunwale, levelling a pistol. He fired and Genteel spun across the deck with a hand to his shoulder. His right arm was useless. The officer was pursuing him with a scimitar. Genteel snatched up his cutlass and swung it awkwardly in his left hand. It was evident he was no match for the officer. Grace looked round. Down in the waist of the ship, the crew had their own preoccupations. She remembered the unused pistol and searched for it. When she found it, Genteel and the Turk were grappling so close that she did not dare use it. She approached warily, hearing their panting while their feet skidded on the bloody deck. The officer was manoeuvring to keep Genteel's body between them. The muscles in Genteel's good arm were knotted with effort.

Suddenly, he butted the Turk in the face and flung himself sideways. The Turk was left standing in front of Grace, half-blinded, but drawing back his scimitar to strike Frederick.

'Fire, goddamit, don't just stand there!'

Obediently, she pulled the trigger. The Turk's face was flattened by a look of amazement as the shot caught him in the chest and drove him staggering back to the rail. He fell over, but was still strong enough to grab at the rigging and hang in the space between the two vessels. The smoke from Grace's pistol was wafted away. She saw Genteel looking at it. Then he looked up at the sail.

'The preventer, Barlow, cut the preventer!' A fresh wave of attackers was massing on the galley. The *Marathon*'s crew were hopelessly outnumbered. In time they must be overwhelmed; the odds were against them.

Barlow must have heard Genteel; he was hacking at the preventer with his cutlass. It parted and the mainsail, which had been backwinded by the breeze that had sprung up from a new quarter, swung across with a loud swoosh. Genteel ran to the wheel and watched the boom sweep by, first skimming his own head and Grace's, then scything over the front of the galley, taking all with it. Only one corsair escaped by leaping up and clinging to the leech.

The *Marathon* was edging ahead. If she could be turned away, she could escape the bow-chasers which were already depressed now the galley was down by the head.

'Quick, Grace, haul the mainsheet!' Frederick shouted. For the first time, she detected excitement in his voice. She hauled on the rope as if her life depended on it.

It did. The *Marathon* gathered way and her stern swung across, pinning the Turkish officer between the two vessels. Grace heard his ribs crack and he dropped away. Someone, Barlow she thought, took a pot shot at the Turk silhouetted against the mainsail. He too fell away. The firing slackened.

Behind them, the galley was sinking. The chorus of screams went on unabated, diminishing only as the distance increased between the two vessels.

Grace looked at Frederick. He appeared to be smiling, though it might have been a rictus of pain from his wound.

'Are you all right?' she asked him.

'As well as might be expected. I suppose, finally, I ought to forgive you for smuggling the muskets – I thought you'd turned to legal commerce. So much for my illusions.'

'Was *I* all right?' she asked him.

'You were amazing, Grace, amazing.'

Grace remembered him saying that now as she carried in the gruel. She remembered how Barlow had carried him like a child into the cabin, and how Count Scicluna had fussed over him, and how she herself had nursed him while the *Marathon* butted into a moonlit sea towards Argostoli. His half-humorous eyes were watching her from the pillow. She smiled back at him. He was lost and was found, was dead and was alive again.

4

Four days after Frederick regained consciousness he awoke in the early morning. A gecko was sunning itself on the wall beside him, its flanks expanding and contracting regularly as it breathed. Across the room, her head drooping, Grace sat uncomfortably on a chair, asleep. Her hair was unkempt, her clothes were wrinkled, her cheeks were puffy and her eyes were lined with fatigue. He knew the reason, she had been caring for him. Intuitively, he realized, he owed his life to her. She had given so much of herself that now she was drained, exhausted.

There was a small commotion in the outer room and the gecko scuttled away into a crevice beside the window. The door opened and Count Scicluna's head appeared. When he saw that Frederick was awake, he came in quietly, trying not to disturb Grace.

'A letter for you,' he whispered, placing the sealed paper beside Frederick's hand on the bed. 'There's a ship from Malta, her captain brought it.'

Without moving, Frederick could see and recognize the handwriting. He was impatient to open it and know its contents, but wished to read it in private.

'Thank you. I'll look at it later,' he murmured.

'Anything else you want?' Frederick shook his head, letting his eyelids droop and feigning sleepiness until Scicluna left.

As soon as he was alone, Frederick tore the letter open. He was astonished at the effort it cost him; until then he had underestimated his weakness. He read the letter once, then he read it again. An indulgent smile creased his features.

When he looked up, he discovered that Grace was watching him. Perhaps she had been observing him all the time; he had paid no attention to her.

'What is it?' she inquired, straightening herself on her chair and brushing a wisp of hair from her forehead.

'A letter – from Felicity. It's about the ball. Her father's giving a ball for Captain Pelham who's visiting. She's worried I won't be back in time for it. She says she misses me. She's ordered a new dress for the occasion, it'll be a tragedy if I'm not there and she can't wear it. She says a married woman can hardly go to a ball without her husband.'

'*I* should.'

'Yes, but you're Grace Pensilva, you're not Felicity. How stands the wind for Malta?'

'But you're not strong enough to travel.'

'I'm getting up.'

She crossed the room quickly, trying to restrain him, but already his feet were on the floor and he was leaning against the wall while he pushed himself upward. She could see he was dizzy, swaying alarmingly. She put an arm round his shoulder.

'What day is it?'

'Tuesday.'

'I mean what date? How long have I been lying here?'

'Two weeks.'

'Two weeks! I must leave immediately.'

'The sirocco is blowing, it will be dead against us. The *Marathon* isn't seaworthy, the repairs aren't completed.'

'Don't try to hold me back. Felicity mustn't be disappointed. If I'm not back for the ball she'll be heartbroken.'

'Oh yes, the ball,' said Grace flatly, 'she mustn't be allowed to miss that.'

'Don't be such a dog in the manger, Grace. It isn't like you.' Then, noticing her silence. 'Have I said something to hurt you?' Grace shook her head. 'I'm feeling better now, thanks to you. It's only natural I should want to get moving.'

'I'll cook you an egg. You ought to stay resting, but get dressed if you must, in the meantime.'

'Women!' she heard him mutter as she went to the kitchen.

For all his reviving independence, he was grateful for her shoulder to lean on as he took his first walk outdoors later that morning. With his good arm across her neck they strolled slowly along the Argostoli waterfront. It had turned into a dazzlingly bright day. The sirocco was over. The *Marathon* sat calmly on her own reflection. From her decks came the sound of shipwrights hammering. Further off, a newcomer, a brig, swarmed with men putting a harbour stow on her sails and rigging. Closer at hand, the streets were full of life: tall swaggering Suliot klephts; swarthy blue-jackets in straw hats, squinting at Grace from taverna doorways; milkmaids, their donkeys laden with yaourti, cheese and milkchurns; pastry-cooks setting out their sticky wares.

Grace was fearful that Frederick would exhaust himself, but his strength seemed to return miraculously with each step he took, each breath he breathed. His illness had wasted him terribly: his cheeks were hollow and wan; his sinewy torso was become so bony and thin that his clothes floated on him.

'Stop looking at me like that,' he complained, 'I'm not Dresden china!'

'You're not Tom Cribb either,' she countered, squeezing his biceps between finger and thumb.

'No, I wouldn't make much of a pugilist, would I?' he grinned, and they both laughed gaily. This was the Grace he liked, the provocative one he was at home with.

'Come on,' he challenged her, 'race you to that house over there!' and set off at an awkward loping run with his wounded arm hanging useless beside him. Why am I so fearful of his falling, thought Grace as she followed him, but he crossed the rocky ground safely and leant against the end wall of the building, awaiting her. She knew this place, she had walked here once or twice while Count Scicluna had been watching over him. She came up to him slowly; she did not feel like running.

'Can you hear it?' she asked him. He listened. From around the corner came the sound of gentle splashing and a steady rumble of machinery. 'Doesn't it remind you of something?'

380

He took the few steps needful to see round the corner.

'It's a mill,' he announced, furrowing his brow in thought. 'Ah, I see what you mean: Langstone. That was where you lived when I met you. It seems so far away now, doesn't it? You were unhappy there, Langstone Mill was full of sadness.'

'This mill is different,' she told him, 'it's special. Taste the water.' She regretted it, seeing the difficulty he would have to scramble down to the channel. He slipped and she caught his arm.

'Leave me alone, woman, I can manage.' The brusqueness of his tone shocked her. He was like an ungrateful boy. That was all he was really, a boy dressed up as an officer. He knelt and tasted the water.

'It's bitter.'

'Salt. It's ironic really. You find me at one mill and I find you at another.'

'You find me?'

'I'm just beginning to see you properly.'

'I can't present a pretty picture,' he remarked, rubbing his cheek, 'but soon you'll be relieved of my dull-wittedness.'

'You don't have to say that,' she replied thickly, and he saw that her eyes were moist and her lip quivered.

'You've been good to me, Grace,' he added quickly. 'You're the sort of woman who needs a good man to care for. I hope you find one soon. There are plenty of good fellows on Malta, Kirkbride for instance.'

Her face remained clouded. 'Tell me, Frederick, why did you marry Felicity?'

'You told me to – not only that, there were the other reasons: I like her, she's terribly pretty, she dotes on me. And I had promised her father. I had given my word as a gentleman.'

'Damn being a gentleman. Tell me something else: how exactly did Nancy cheat you out of your inheritance? You tell me nothing unless I push you?'

'Blackmail. She saw the sand on my coat the day I rode to warn you about the preventives.'

'So it's *my* fault .   . Oh, Frederick, I'm sorry, so sorry.'

'It wasn't the end of the world. Aren't we both here, alive in Argostoli?'

'Do you know who you look like with that arm of yours?' He raised his eyebrows quizzically. 'Your hero: Nelson,' she completed. 'You're like him in another way too, if only you knew it.'

'I hope not,' he laughed in embarrassment, 'the arm's enough. I'll keep my two eyes, thank you.'

'I didn't mean that, I meant your Emma.'

'My Emma? I could not wish any woman into the part of Emma. Don't you know how she was treated? It's not worth the risk, Grace.'

'Men take their risks in battle; women take theirs in love. Didn't you know that?'

Before he could answer, they both saw Ben Barlow running towards them. When he was within earshot he stopped and pointed.

'That brig over there, the 'Ecate, d'you know who 'er skipper is? – 'Tis Scully!'

'My God!' muttered Genteel. 'Is he after you?'

'I don't know,' said Grace. 'It's possible.'

'We must sail immediately, before he comes ashore and finds you.'

Grace nodded dumbly. Whatever she had dreamed or hoped since she came to Argostoli was blighted. There was no way to go but onward.

The battered chaise pulled up outside Valletta Cathedral and a familiar figure descended. Before she had vanished into the building, Optimus was running towards her, but by the time he himself stepped inside, she had vanished. The broad nave was almost empty, only a robed priest, preceded by a verger in knee-breeches, disturbed its vastness. On both sides, the nave was flanked with ornate, gilded chapels and it was easy to deduce that the person he followed had slipped into one of them.

At the fourth attempt, he found her. She was kneeling at a candle-bedecked shrine with her face turned away from him, but he knew from the fall of her shoulders under the veil she wore that he was not mistaken. Placing a coin in a box on the wall, he took a candle from a nearby sheaf, lit it from one that was burning and spiked it in a vacant place on the rack along the altar.

If she noticed him, she gave no immediate sign, her lips moved constantly in silent prayer, but when he knelt beside her he could feel the hostility.

'Go away,' she hissed. 'Can't you leave me in peace to pray for my grandmother?'

'Not before you tell me something,' Optimus insisted. 'Tell me why you wrote to Spiro Marcopoulos!' He could hear the anger in his voice and it pleased him to see the start it gave her to hear his implied accusation.

'He told you, did he? I thought he could be trusted.'

'He told me nothing of the sort. I thought it was your grandfather who had written, I thought it was your grandfather who had the delusion I was trying to defraud him by getting the details of Grace Pensilva's share in his business so I could pass as an inheritor and claim it. Of course, I should have remembered it was *you* who affected to distrust me. It was only when he told me he had not written to Marcopoulos that the truth dawned on me. Well, I've had enough of it! I won't stand your meddling in my business. If you'd had your way, Marcopoulos would have distrusted me completely and I'd have learned nothing!'

'Hush! Don't you know you're in a holy place? Have you no respect for people's feelings?'

'What about *my* feelings? How do you think it feels to have to put up with false accusations?'

'Keep your voice down. I'll call the verger.'

'Call whoever you like. I shan't stop till I've had this out with you.'

'Have you no respect for the dead?'

'I never knew her, but I much regret your grandmother's passing. That candle was sincerely meant, believe me. But if you want to avoid a scene in here, you'll agree to meet me outside and talk in a few minutes.'

Optimus knew his cheeks were hot. His anger had been overpowering. Now, seeing the slight twitching of her lips and the almost tearful brightness of her eyes behind the veil, he felt himself weakening. He fought it.

'In five minutes, at the main door. Don't try to sneak off, I'll be watching you. If you do, I'll be forced to tell your grandfather you've been playing tricks on me. He's a good man, an honest man, *he* won't disbelieve me, and he won't like to hear the truth about his favourite granddaughter. Well, will you agree to have this out with me?' He confronted her, one hand on her shoulder to twist her round to face his glare. Her eyes met his and, for a moment, he thought they would blaze up and she would refuse, but they dropped suddenly.

'I'll come.'

'Promise!'

'Will you swear to God that you mean no evil to my grandfather?'

'I swear it.'

'Then you have my promise.'

As he made for the door, across the marble-encrusted armorial tombs of the long-dead knights, he knew he had no need to look back, no need to doubt if she would follow. He would question her and she would tell him about her mother, Rita Scicluna, the girl who had painted the miniatures, the girl who had married Ian Kirkbride, who himself had been best man at Genteel's wedding in this very place. Without looking, Optimus could see the four of them standing before the priest at the high altar: Kirkbride, Genteel, Felicity and Grace, with Captain Fell a step or two behind them. The words were in Latin, but he knew their purport. Rings were exchanged, the bride and bridegroom kissed, but it was not *their* faces that engrossed him, his attention was all on Grace Pensilva as she too observed the act. He watched her eyes, he scanned her lips, seeking the sign he expected, the token of her inner strife. Her face was a mask. It had been so then, but today he was getting behind it, Frederick and Grace were sailing back from Argostoli; soon they would be at the ball. Both knew that time was short, the horizon was closing in on them. Maria Kirkbride's mother had attended that ball, per-haps her daughter knew the secret of what had passed there. Optimus hoped so. If she did, he now believed she would tell it to him.

'How do I look?' Felicity was asking.

'Splendid – absolutely,' said Frederick, tugging at the wings of his waistcoat that no longer fitted him.

'You're a beast! I know you don't mean it. You haven't even glanced at it – or me either for that matter. Oh, I know you're tired of me already, I know you've tried to forget me. And now you're trying to make up for it with insincerity. I'm losing my looks, I must be.'

'My dear Felicity, I never was more honest. You have never looked lovelier. I care for you so that I have brought you a little present. I thought you deserved it for waiting so patiently.'

'A present? Let me see it, I'm so excited.' He fumbled in his pocket with his left hand, eventually extricating a flat leather case of the kind used by jewellers. She almost snatched it and opened it eagerly.

'Well? Do you like it?'

'It's lovely, absolutely lovely; I've never seen anything lovelier. Put it on for me.' Genteel lifted the thin gold chain from the box and undid the catch. As he bent to fasten it round Felicity's neck, he smelt the intoxicating musk in her perfume and her bronzed ringlets brushed his cheek. She watched him in the glass while he adjusted the locket on her breast, her eyes steady as a cat's.

'It suits you ever so well. Grace said it would.'

'Grace! Grace! Can't you ever stop talking about her? Ever since you've come back it's been Grace this and Grace that. I'm fed up, fed up to the back teeth with it.'

'You're being unfair, Felicity. Grace saved my life – for you too, if you could only see it.'

'She had the easy part of it. *She* didn't have to wait here all alone with no news, just waiting, waiting. I've done nothing but sit here and worry. I've worried myself sick about you.

You've changed, you know; you're no longer the same person you were when you left here. We were so *happy* before you left on that silly journey. Why wouldn't you tell me the reason for it? *She* was at the back of it, wasn't she? That was the real reason. Captaining the ship was only a pretext.' Felicity dragged at the locket's chain, trying to find the catch so she could undo it. 'Where did you get the money for this?' she demanded accusingly. 'It must have been expensive. You're always saying you have no money. I suppose *she* paid for it. Well, I don't want it.'

Tears began to well from her wide, tragic eyes. She made no attempt to staunch them. Her arms hung limp at her sides like a rag doll's. Was she shamming? The pathos in her voice was still troubling but, instead of evoking love, it stirred him to anger.

'I thought you loved me,' she wailed. 'I was so *proud* to be Mrs Frederick Genteel. Now I know they must all be laughing at me. Why did you have to spoil it for me? I had a secret to tell you. Now I can't. I don't want to.'

Genteel's face hardened in its turn. He took the locket back from her and stuffed it into its case.

'We went to all the trouble in the world to get that locket for you. We scoured the goldsmiths' quarter for the finest workmen. Grace's friend Rita painted day and night to complete the pictures: one of me, your husband; the other of her, your best friend, or so you called her.'

'She *was*, until you did this to me.'

'I can't help it if you don't know who your real friends are.'

'That woman, I thought she was my friend, but she's a viper. You were a fool to trust her. She enticed you away, but you can't see it. You're the only one who can't see it.'

Genteel turned away from her and made for the stairs. 'Come on, madam, cease that weeping, straighten your face and get a move on. The carriage is waiting. You know your father, he'll be in a foul mood if we're late again.'

The ball was being held in the Auberge d'Aragon, a hall in which one of the various *langues* that comprised the Order of St John of Jerusalem had once resided. Tonight it was full of the froth of British society and when Frederick finally escorted Felicity into the ballroom, the dancing was in full swing. There were smells of spilt liquor, powder and perspiration. The shimmering chandeliers and candelabra shone on a lively throng engaged in a cotillion. At the far end of the room the band was scraping away merrily on a platform. Nearby, Captain William Fell presided bibulously, slumped in a golden throne. Around him, a group of hopelessly unattached young officers stood drinking and gossiping. At this early stage of the evening, all the eligible females, hopelessly few in number, had been snapped up already, their cards marked for all the dances by enterprising, rakish fellows who were preening themselves on the dance floor. The bystanders were reduced to an occasional wink at another man's partner.

'You can leave me at Aunt Harriet's table,' said Felicity coldly. 'Go and pay your respects to Papa. I can't face it: I know what he's thinking. Tell him I find it too hot, and so it is. I know I shall swoon directly.'

Genteel handed her over to her aunt with relief and joined the Governor's party. Captain Fell saw him coming and rose unsteadily.

'Give Mr Genteel a glass, Kirkbride,' he instructed his aide-de-camp. 'Here's to a very gallant officer who's just given Johnny Turk a bloody nose. Your hand Frederick. Let me congratulate you.' Only when he saw the anguish on Genteel's face did he cease pumping the hand he had just seized.

'What, that arm still not better? Forgive me.' He turned to Kirkbride. 'That's right – a bumper. Now bring our wounded hero a chair. He shall sit beside me. You'll be pleased to hear the squadron's being augmented; Captain Pelham in *Parthian* and a new fellow called Scully or something commanding *Hecate*. Did you meet him in Argostoli? – No? Well, no matter. What I'm coming to is that I'm going to ask you a favour. I'll be going away – taking command of the squadron, and I've a host of things to attend to. Now tomorrow there's some kind of frolic on Gozo, one of their blessed saint's days or something and, in a weak moment, I said I'd go over and grace it with my gubernatorial presence. Well, you know how I *hate* ceremonies, so damned gentlemanly. I want you to say you'll stand in for me. It won't be that much of a sacrifice really; you're in no fit state to go off fighting when the fleet assembles tomorrow; Pelham's frigate's already here and I've recalled *Hecate* from Argostoli. What d'you say, Freddie, will you do it for me?'

Genteel hated to be called Freddie and he detested being cornered like this by a man who, instead of using his authority, preferred to create the fiction that his servant was volunteering. Still, the Gozo assignment would keep him away from Felicity. He had suddenly begun to find her impossible.

'What's kept you so long?' she hissed as he subsided into a chair beside her. 'I've been watching you. You've been boozing and talking on and on, about women no doubt.'

'Your father was asking me to stand in for him at the Festa on Gozo tomorrow.'

'And you accepted?'

'I had to, Captain Fell doesn't take no for an answer, but you'll enjoy it.'

'You mean you expect me to accompany you?'

'You'll like the excitement.'

'But you *know* how I detest sea voyages.'

'It's only a mile or so across the water.'

'That's more than enough. I shall be sick as a dog and you'll glory in it.'

'Don't talk like that, Felicity. I won't have it. I have my duty to do and yours, as my wife, is to share it. And now, if you don't mind, you'll join me in the next dance. I'm sure you've been burning to show off your petticoats.'

'I don't think I'll dance this evening.'

Genteel looked at her blankly. 'What do you mean? You implored me to come back here for this ball. I did so against my better judgement, before I was really fit to travel. Now you tell me you won't dance. Explain yourself!'

'Hush!' whispered Felicity in a contrite tone. 'Everyone's looking.' She bit her lower lip, then dropped her voice until it was a whisper so faint that, even bending towards her, he could barely hear it above the music. 'I believe I'm in what they call an interesting condition.

Genteel stared at her. So that was it : she was pregnant, or thought she was. That would help to explain her recent unreasonableness; explain it, but not excuse it. How different her face looked in this light to the visage he had found so attractive when he greeted her on the wharfside. He ought to be feeling pleased, he ought to be whispering that he loved her. Instead, he felt trapped. How long had he married this creature for? A lifetime?

'In that case you'd better stay at home tomorrow. I'll excuse you.'

After that, they sat for a while unspeaking. There was a lull in the music, with dancers drifting back to their seats. Then a peculiar, awkward silence fell upon the room. Two women had just entered. Everyone turned to look at them. It was not merely that they were beautiful, though Frederick had never seen Grace dressed so splendidly. Indeed, he had never imagined her in any kind of finery. The ivory watered-silk of the gown, trimmed with a grey like that of her eyes, shimmered as she paused momentarily, scanning the ballroom. However, it was her companion who was the cause of the embarrassment. Beside her, almost equally stunning, was another dazzling creature: smaller, more buxom, darker. Arm in arm, the two of them made their way across the empty floor to the place where Captain Fell was sitting.

'I've brought a friend with me,' said Grace quite loudly enough for all to hear. 'Rita Scicluna has no official invitation, but I knew *you* would love to see her.' The silence lay even heavier upon the room until Felicity's aunt broke it with a horrified stage-whisper.

'Scicluna! Why that's a Maltese name, ain't it?'

Grace affected to ignore this comment. She and Captain Fell were exchanging glances. He liked her, she knew that, and she was capitalizing on it.

'Well?' she challenged him.

'A filly like that don't need an invitation,' he grunted, struggling to his feet in an access of gallantry. 'With advantages like that, she's welcome anywhere. I'd take 'er out to dance meself if I weren't so plagued with gout, so I would, damn me ... I say, Kirkbride, give these ladies a drink, won't you. When that's done you can partner Miss Scicluna in a waltz. That's if she'll have you.' Fell slumped into his chair and then looked up roguishly. 'Don't I know your father, Miss Scicluna? I fancy I may have crossed swords with him.'

Rita Scicluna nodded.

'Well, tell 'im I much prefer to see 'is daughter. Has that Kirkbride feller filled your glasses for you? Here's a toast: to the two loveliest young ladies in Valletta! Who'll join me in it?'

The air around them was suddenly full of waving glasses as the young officers echoed his proposal. When they had drunk, Grace raised her own glass in return.

'To frolic!' she proposed unexpectedly. 'To frolic and gaiety!'

'Are those damned musicians dead or something?' demanded Captain Fell, catching her mood. 'A waltz! A waltz! Play up you idle rogues or I'll keel-haul you!'

As the music struck up and Major Kirkbride offered his arm to Rita Scicluna, Grace slipped away to Felicity's table. With her black satin bag swinging from her hand and her foot tapping, she addressed her.

'I'm sorry I'm late. I had to fetch young Rita. Isn't she a peach? These Maltese girls have so much charm they make us feel envious, don't they, Aunt Harriet?' and she shot a meaning look at that lady, who blushed furiously. Then, noticing the glum looks that reigned around the table, she added, 'What the matter? Cheer up, Felicity! Frederick's home again. Why aren't you dancing?'

'*I've* nothing to dance about,' huffed Felicity.

'Well, I have, and in that case you won't mind if I borrow your husband. Frederick, will you dance with me?'

'Would you take a refusal?' His wry smile set her laughing as he rose to his feet. No one could ignore the hostility emanating from the two women he was leaving, but he was unrepentant.

Starting to waltz was difficult. His arm was still stiff and painful, but Grace held him and the excitement of the dance soon made him forget about it. Initially, as they spun, he saw fragments of the frieze that ran round the walls above them, but it soon blurred and he was conscious only of his partner. Instead of the throb in his arm, it was his heart-beat that troubled him. He realized that he must have been smiling.

'You look pleased to be back,' Grace was saying, half teasing.

'I'm pleased to be here at this ball, but not for the reason you're thinking.' They danced on and Grace abandoned herself to the pleasure of being turned, turned, turned, in the torrential rush of the waltz. It was a fleeting joy that might have lasted for ever.

'Are you happy?' she murmured.

'Happy? What has happiness got to do with it?' Then, abruptly, a cloud crossed his features, the ease and confidence went out of his step and he piloted her to the adjacent doorway. Outside, in the dim corridor, he stopped and leant his forehead against the wall. A kind of groan escaped him.

'What is it? Are you unwell? Is it your arm or something?'

'I had forgotten. There is bad news to tell you!'

'Then tell me, I can take it.'

'Captain Fell has ordered *Hecate* back to Malta. It will be two days at most before she arrives here. You must take precautions, hide. Scully will come ashore. He must not see you. I myself cannot stay to protect you. The Governor has ordered me to represent him at the Gozo Festa.'

'That's why Felicity's sulking, is it? She hates water worse than a cat.'

'Felicity isn't coming, but that's not the reason.'

'What is it then?'

'I don't want her with me.'

It was Grace's turn to pause in disbelief. 'Can *I* come with you?'

Genteel's mind raced at the preposterousness of it. What was it they said about its being as well to be hung for a sheep as a lamb? And it was even possible that the inward-looking

391

British community would never learn of it. Gozo was like another continent, peopled by strange natives and seldom if ever visited.

'I can't stop you.'

'But do you want me?'

'You'll need to be at the Marsa ferry by eight. I shan't wait for you.'

'I don't intend to sleep,' she answered, 'I intend to dance and dance. You must partner me often.'

'Wait!' He was fishing in his pocket for something. When he found it, he put it in her hands and clasped them both about it.'

'But it's not mine,' she whispered. 'It's Felicity's.'

'That was a mistake,' he told her almost roughly. 'I want you to wear it. Here, let me help you fasten it. I did not really understand what we were doing when we chose it. We are both in that locket, aren't we? Keep it and we shall be together always.'

They did not kiss, but their eyes met. In a few moments, they were back in the ballroom.

5

'Are you embarrassed?' Grace asked discreetly. Her question was drowned in the grinding of the wheels and the shouts from the population who lined the road into Rabat, the principal town on Gozo. 'About me, I mean.'

'Not particularly,' replied Frederick, nodding and waving in restrained greeting to the Gozitans.

'You aren't looking very cheerful. I thought it was because they'd taken me for Mrs Genteel.'

'I hadn't the heart to disabuse them.'

'Or me either.'

'It's just for a day.'

'Yes, just for a day.' She smiled to herself, smiled to the people who were pressing ever closer to the landau which had been waiting for Genteel at the Mgarr landing. The horses' plumed heads nodded as they laboured up the final slope into the town. It was the usual collection of three-storeyed town houses built of honey-warm stone. Brooding over Rabat, when seen from a distance, was a ponderous fortress. Beside it rose the twin towers of a cathedral, dazzling white in the morning sun. She felt as if she and Frederick were royalty. The whole situation was both real and unreal. Yet there could be no possible doubt about that flawless blue sky. She stole another sidelong glance at Frederick. He was sitting ramrod straight, with both white-gloved hands clasped on the pommel of his old sword that stood sheathed and clamped between his knees. What perturbed her was his face: its lines were drawn and haggard. She felt her heart go out to him. She checked herself. What of her resolution? If she were so careful of him, where did that leave her vow of vengeance? Looking at that sad face, she feared that the will to harm him had left her. When he winced involuntarily, it felt as if a knife in her bowels was being twisted. She took a deep breath.

'What's the matter?'

'My arm, it's paining me.'

'Poor Frederick.' She laid a hand on his knee as she spoke, but withdrew it when she realized he found it unseemly. 'Did you know there was a herb that grows here in Gozo that the Knights used to cure such troubles with? We'll try and find some for you.'

'Humph!' It was clear that Frederick had little faith in such nostrums.

By this time their landau was passing under the first arcade of decorations. The narrow street was spanned by a succession of elaborate arches that formed a moss-like calligraphy over the brushed and whitewashed pavements. It was like riding into a magic cave.

'I'm not going to enjoy this,' Genteel told her pointedly, 'nor you either. Nothing but bells, chanting, incense, bands, feasting and fireworks. Nothing but Maltese being jabbered away all day around you. Nothing but standing around for hours on end, pretending to be interested. Nothing but sweat and indigestion. You'll wish you'd never had the silly idea you'd like to accompany me.'

'It wasn't a silly idea. We're going to enjoy it. Unless, of course, Frederick Genteel is determined to be a wet blanket.' She thought she provoked a ghost of a smile with this.

They emerged into a sunlit square at the end of the tunnel and, as they did so, there was a volley of church bells and a fresh outburst of cheering. A covey of ecclesiastics and civil dignitaries stood waiting for them and their spokesman launched straight into a flowery speech.

'What're you grinning at?' demanded Genteel through his clenched teeth. 'I wish I understood the lingo.'

'They're still assuming I'm Mrs Genteel,' smiled Grace. 'Shall I undeceive them?'

'Hardly the moment,' Genteel sniffed, 'and they'd hardly

believe you. This is farce, a crazy bloody farce, but we needs must play it out. Take my arm and we'll proceed to the next scene of it.'

It turned out to be exactly as he had predicted; an interminable round of formal greetings, handshakes, bows and curtsys. Grace found herself protecting him as best she might and wondering at the determination that kept him going.

He had been right about the indigestion too; the food in the Bondi Palace where they took luncheon was heavy and cold, swamped in viscous olive oil. The heat was overpowering, despite the open windows through which came chanting and incense from the square outside where the images of saints looked down from high wooden plinths disposed to either side of the cathedral steps. Grace knew she could bear the heat, but would it be too much for Genteel in his enfeebled state? She leant across and had a whispered conversation with the master of ceremonies. The latter's face darkened with shame, the proceedings were abridged and, within five minutes, they were out in the street again.

'What did you say to that chap in there?' grunted Genteel. 'It isn't your place to interfere with their ceremonies.'

'I told him you were expecting a baby,' Grace giggled. 'Naturally, he thought that *I* was. It's half true anyway.' Genteel looked sour. He regretted he had told her about Felicity.

'What's next on the agenda?'

'The racing.'

'Racing? In this place? In the street?'

'Yes, horse racing, and that fellow is waiting to lead us to it.' She pointed to a stocky fellow in a sailor's jersey under a wide straw hat that practically concealed his face from them where they were standing.

'Well, there's nothing for it, I suppose, but to go through with it. Your Maltese is good, Grace, tell him we're ready, and find out how far it is.'

'If it pleases your honour, the paddock is distant about three cables,' said the man directly.

'I know that voice,' exclaimed Genteel, suddenly more cheerful, 'Barlow, isn't it? What the devil brings you to Gozo?'

'Courting a local filly, your honour. They know me as Bentley hereabouts, sir, I'll thank you to forget Barlow.' He added in a whisper. 'I can't risk remaining the same person now that Scully's so close upon us.'

Genteel smiled inwardly at the irony that made the Fortescue's erstwhile landlord adopt a disguise while he, the masked revenue captain, now showed his true face to the light of day.

'Lead on then, but first give me your hand. I swear I did not know you.'

'This way, sir,' Barlow announced once Genteel had freed his hand. Frederick had, Grace noticed, ignored the pain the greeting occasioned him. Once they were on their way, Barlow took her discreetly aside and murmured to her.

''Ave you 'eard about Scully? 'Ee's back in Valletta. One o' me mates 'as seen the '*Ecate*. Take care, Grace, that man won't never forgive and forget, I know 'ee's after you.'

'I can look after myself. This is no time to discuss it, but thanks for telling me.'

Before they could say more, there was a commotion in the balconies on either side of them. All heads were turned to look downhill. Conversation dropped to a low buzz and, moments later, they heard a clatter of hooves. Excited shouts, like a breaking wave, rolled along with them.

'Here they come!' cried Grace. As the horses breasted the rise, she could see their riders whipping them unmercifully. Hooves, arms and whips were flying in all directions. Luckily, by this stage in the race, the contestants were sufficiently strung out to engage in the human funnel that led to the finish near where she stood. A chestnut suddenly shot forward and began to overhaul the leader. The crowd flinched back, terrified of its pounding shoes. Its rider was standing in the stirrups, shouting and lashing it on. The whole street rocked with a wild yell of mingled excitement and apprehension.

'Which one was it, sir?' asked Barlow. 'I'm too short to see over the people.'

'The chestnut, by a whisker, at least, I think so. This is a damned dangerous sport, if you ask me – cruel, into the bargain.'

'Don't change your mind, whatever you do,' whispered Barlow, 'they know you're impartial.' Then, raising his voice to a shout he cried, 'Huzza for Windfall! Three cheers for Windfall!' Finally, in a murmur to Grace, he explained. 'Thank God for that outsider, 'ee's saved me a fortune. I makes the book, see, and a win by the favourite spells ruin.'

'You're more of a rogue than I took you for,' she grinned.

'So're you,' said he with a wink and a toss of the head towards Frederick.

At the bottom of the hill they came to a kind of ring in which a band of dejected donkeys was being saddled up. Barlow poked at them knowledgeably and peeled back their lips to examine their teeth. 'This one'd do fine for you, sir,' he told Genteel solemnly. 'Last time the Governor was 'ere 'ee distinguished 'isself as a rider.'

'I'd rather not. That animal doesn't look as if it would carry me.'

' 'Tis expected, sir, I can't say nothin' further.'

'Oh, go on, Frederick,' said Grace impulsively. 'Don't be a spoil-sport. They'll love you for it. And I will if you will. Here, give that silly sword to Ben Barlow.'

Genteel didn't like to be dragooned into anything, but the Gozitans were all round him, smiling, friendly. 'All right, then.'

Instantly, Grace regretted having talked him into it. The stiffness in his arm as he handed his sword to Barlow, the fatigue in his features, told her it was a mistake.

'Stop, Frederick, I was wrong. You really don't have to.'

Genteel ignored her. 'What's the name of this specimen?' he was asking Barlow.

'Cannonball, your honour. 'Ee's got a lovely temper. You won't 'ardly need to flog 'im.'

From the moment he cocked his leg over Cannonball's back, Genteel knew him for a mean and roguish animal. The donkey ignored his tugging at the reins and sidled round to face in the opposite direction. The crowd were laughing.

Grace had succeeded in making a laughing stock of him. Out of the corner of his eye he saw that she had already tucked up her skirt and jumped astride one of the other animals.

With what seemed like a huge explosion, the starting cannon went off. All the other donkeys shambled off uphill to the delighted shrieks and hoots of the spectators. Cannonball pawed the ground, but refused to move. Genteel dug in his heels. Cannonball lowered his head and glowered. Genteel felt light-headed and angry.

'Pull 'im by the ear!' Barlow was shouting. Genteel did as he was told and the donkey responded grudgingly. ' 'Old on tight, sir!' cried Barlow and jabbed the animal in the rear with Genteel's scabbard.

The result was instantaneous. The reason for Cannonball's name became apparent: he *was* a flyer. Genteel found himself tearing up the slope between two blurs of faces. So fast was Cannonball moving that the bunch that had set off earlier seemed to be drifting back towards him. He saw Grace among the leaders, her hair and shawl streaming. The hill steepened and Cannonball began overhauling the stragglers. As they dropped behind, Genteel found himself riding along a wave of applause. He began to feel better. He wouldn't admit that he was enjoying it, but he had had worse moments. His hat was jogging loose and he let go of the reins with his left hand to ram it down again.

Less than a furlong ahead, the close-packed spectators showed where the finish must lie. Cannonball had caught up with the bunch. Grace was several lengths ahead of them, but her donkey was flagging. Cannonball began pulling up on it. Behind him, Genteel heard the thunder of hooves. The walls were closing in on him. The shouts rose to a crescendo. Grace looked back and saw him coming. She belaboured her mount, but he was no match for Cannonball. Only lack of space could baulk him now and he was determinedly boring into the narrow gap where the crowd shrank back before him.

Genteel saw the child step out and he was horrorstruck. A tiny infant, not more than three years old, had just emerged between the spectators' legs as they shrank back. The child just stood there, undecided whether to run. If Cannonball didn't stop, he would kill it.

Genteel hauled back on the reins with all his might. Cannonball did not respond; he was running out of control. Only a few yards separated him from the child. None of the people beside it seemed to have noticed anything amiss. No one would snatch it back. What a fool, what a fool, Genteel thought, what a fool he had been to have allowed himself to be dragged into this stupid race. The child's eyes looked straight at him, mutely appealing.

He flung himself forward across the donkey's neck, sliding to one side so that he unbalanced it. He hit the paving stones with a dull thud. A stabbing pain went through his shoulder. Cannonball was half on top of him. He was sliding along in a cloud of dust. The shouting had stopped utterly. Only a single piercing scream told him that someone had recognized the child's plight.

Genteel clambered to his feet unsteadily. His hat had gone. His uniform was thick with dust. One epaulette lay damaged at his feet. Everything was ruined.

Unexpectedly, a woman with a child in her arms rushed up and kissed him. At first he did not make the connection.

The crowd was all over him, cheering, clapping, patting his shoulders, brushing his coat, handing him his epaulette, bringing him his hat. He could not understand what they were saying, but it did not matter. It did not matter that he had been ridiculous. It did not matter that his clothes were in disorder. All around him was a sea of tearful and smiling faces. Pushing between them was another with a concerned and contrite expression: Grace.

'You were wonderful,' she told him fervently and kissed him. There, in full view of everyone, she kissed him on the mouth.

The next moment, Genteel found himself rising inexplicably. Swaying awkwardly, using his good arm to hold on for dear life, he found himself being chaired up the street. Beneath him wavered a dense carpet of upturned faces. Arms were reaching out to touch him in the way the Maltese touched the images of their saints as they passed in procession. His own right arm, the wounded one, hung limp at his side. Immediately he became aware of it, the pain returned, shooting, burning, searing, overwhelming.

'Can't you see he's hurt?' he heard Grace's voice crying. 'Be careful!' He twisted round in an attempt to see her. Before he could find her, he fainted.

'This is the place, Mr Shute.'

'Looks unoccupied to me, Ben,' said Optimus after considering the tall, rather austere house with its windows shuttered.

'This is where 'ee told me to bring you,' said Barlow, 'and now, if you'll excuse me, I 'ave work to do 'elpin' the artificers.'

Before Optimus could detain him, he was off down the quiet street and into the busy square which was dominated by the blue and white robed image of the Virgin on a three-storeyed pedestal surrounded by minor statuary. Optimus struck the panelled door with the knocker. It was in the form of a hand holding an iron ball and its banging seemed to echo into emptiness. He listened for footsteps. Instead, a voice called to him from an upper window.

'Come up, the door will open.' Optimus lifted the latch and pushed it back, letting himself into a high-ceilinged hallway with an iron-framed lantern hanging in the centre. To the rear, a winding marble stair led upward. It was cool in the house, but also slightly musty, as though his first impression of abandon had been the right one.

'Shute, my dear fellow, how wonderful to see you! Come on in and share a glass with me,' insisted Count Scicluna the moment his feet touched the *piano nobile*. 'You must not mind the dust. Maria is ashamed of it, but what can you expect. This house lies empty for most of the year, but I can't bring myself to sell it, it holds too many memories. Did you have a good journey? Did Ben look after you properly?'

He ushered Optimus into a spacious saloon furnished with

400

Italianate chairs and an inlaid marble table. What caught his attention was a cluster of framed miniatures around the fireplace.

'Do I know the artist?'

'I expect you can guess. That one is my dear wife's portrait; how young she looks there! And that is Rita herself. I remember her sitting by the mirror as she did it. She loved it here. We came for all the holidays. I miss her you know. Since she accompanied her husband to England, I've never seen her, though she writes occasionally. Families drift apart, don't they? That's why I find Maria's generosity and devotion in coming out here to look after me all the more remarkable. I'm trying to talk her out of it. A young woman ought not to throw away her life like that. But she won't listen. Women can be as pig-headed as men when they choose, can't they? For a long time she insisted she detested you. I suppose you know that.'

'She distrusts me. Nothing I can say or do will change that.'

'Oh, Mr Shute – Optimus, I can call you that, can't I? It's no earthly use judging a woman by appearances. When you're as old as I am, you'll know that you can't take her statements at face value. She doesn't even know herself what she thinks, she can be the victim of her own duplicity. But hush, here she come. She's been out shopping.'

Maria entered the room, bearing a basket of pastries. After an initial semblance of surprise, she took Optimus' proferred hand briefly and he returned her cool clasp gently.

'You're becoming a Maltese institution, Mr Shute. One finds you all over the landscape. Are you determined to stay here?'

'Not at all, I shall be leaving shortly. My ticket is bought and I am passing the time as agreeably as I can until my departure. Your grandfather was kind enough to invite me here for the celebrations. You'll soon be rid of me.' While he spoke, Optimus was watching Maria's face for a sign of her reaction. The lips remained bland and smiling, but was there the slightest alteration in the eyes?

'I see you have been looking at my mother's miniatures,' she remarked, and he suspected her of deliberately changing the subject. 'There is one in particular that ought to be of interest to you. Have you noticed it?'

Optimus scanned the collection again. There *was* one portrait that stood out from among the rest, one that showed no family resemblance, no Maltese cast to the features. He knew where he had seen its fellow, it was in his possession. He pointed. 'This one.'

Maria unhooked the tiny frame and held it up to the light. 'You think you know her?'

'Sometimes I think I do.'

She turned the frame over so that the reverse side became visible. There, scrawled across the backing paper, in the now familiar handwriting was the name:

Grace Delabole

'This is no time to be fussing over old relics,' interrupted Count Scicluna, presenting them both with glasses. 'When you've drunk this, I have a plan for you. There is a two hour wait until the main procession. You shall take our chaise, Maria – I've arranged to have it made ready – and show our friend the ruins at Ggantija. Now where are those pastries I sent you for?'

'To you, Count Scicluna,' said Optimus raising his glass, 'with all my thanks for all your kindness. I find it hard to think that I have known you for so short a time. It seems as if we had been friends for ever.'

'And so we shall be,' replied Scicluna, clinking glasses. 'And so I suppose we were beforehand, since Grace brought us together.'

'Then I'll drink to Delaluna too,' exclaimed Optimus. 'There's something I've been wanting to discuss with you ever since I returned from Argostoli. When I was talking to Spiro Marcopoulos I learned there were fresh commercial possibilities if you were ready to take an interest in them. Delaluna could be revived, put on a new footing –'

'I'm far too old,' laughed Scicluna, 'and you know I haven't the money.'

'I was coming to that,' insisted Optimus. 'I think I could

make an investment. If I could rely on your experience and contacts . . .'

'It is nice to dream,' said Scicluna wistfully. 'If I were young again . . . If the truth were told, I was never the mainspring of Delaluna, Grace was that. It was never the same without her. I kept it going, of course, just ticking gently but, from the day she left us, the heart wasn't in it. It was here in Gozo that the last scenes happened, you know that already. Well, Maria's been asking some questions round about and she has plenty to tell you, if she decides to. She's a wilful girl, but I love her. A bit like her mother. Perhaps I love her for it . . . Off with you now, leave me in peace, I have my memories.'

Maria herself drove to Ggantija. Alone with her in the chaise, Optimus found contact less easy. She drove confidently, her small gloved hands holding the reins with practised ease, but she said little. Was she at odds with him again? He supposed so.

It seemed even more tense when they left the horses tethered and entered the ruins together. Maria became withdrawn. In the mourning she still wore, she seemed almost tragic in these surroundings. The huge monoliths of which the ruins had been constructed were jumbled together as if by an earthquake, but it was still possible to make out the shape of the structure. What had it been? Palace? Granary? Temple? Perhaps all of these. Its builders were long dead and all that seemed sure was that they had tried to build for eternity. Their building lay heavy upon the land, and its great stones lay with equal weight upon the spirit.

Optimus drifted away from Maria and found himself in an inner chamber whose floor was made of bare, musty earth and whose roof was built of tightly spaced stone transoms. A solitary beam of light entered it from the far end, through a hole in an upright. He knelt beside it and looked out into a kind of courtyard. Maria was standing there, withdrawn and pensive. She had not seen him. A sudden whim seized Optimus. He cupped his hands about his mouth and whispered towards her.

'Who are you?' She looked round in a kind of panic, vainly seeking the speaker. It was as if the voice enveloped her. 'Why do you live for the dead?' he continued. She had lost all composure. Her hands went up to her cheeks. Her fear was so evident that Optimus almost relented, but he put one more question.

'Are you Grace Pensilva?' He did not know why he asked this question, it came to him and he pronounced it mindlessly. The effect on Maria was devastating; she ran from the courtyard with a stifled scream, blocking her ears with her hands. Optimus was full of remorse. He rushed to comfort her. When he emerged from the ruins, she ran to him and clung fiercely.

'What's the matter?' he heard himself ask, instead of confessing as he had intended.

'Oh, Optimus!' she gasped. 'Didn't you hear? You must have. It was so loud. Quick, take me away from here. This is a bad place. Can't you feel it?'

With his arm still round her, he led her to the chaise where the horses were still grazing peacefully. 'There, there,' he murmured quietly, patting her shoulder.

'Is it wrong to mourn?' she asked tearfully. 'Tell me it isn't.'

'It's very human,' said Optimus.

'I think, wherever she is, Grace – Grace Delabole – Grace Pensilva – is still mourning. I think she must have known this place. There is something so austere about it. Even in sunlight it feels inhuman, as though terrible sacrifices took place here. There is a hardness, like the hardness Grace showed to Frederick. I didn't tell you, did I, that my mother met Grace just afterwards. I should have, but I kept it from you.'

Optimus settled her in the chaise. She was still shaking. This time he took the reins. When they had put sufficient distance between them and the ruins, he tried a question. 'What did your mother say about Grace? Did she love Frederick?'

'Of course she did, but she was hard. My mother says I'm like her. She says she thinks her spirit entered my body. Perhaps it did. I don't know . . .'

'You're different,' said Optimus, putting a reassuring hand over hers. 'You don't know how different.'

He let the horses amble on. There was no hurry. Far ahead,

over the town, a white puff stained the sky and they heard an explosion. 'That'll be Ben setting off the fireworks. He told me about it.' They rode on in silence while the maroons exploded in volleys.

'Is it true you're leaving?' she asked woodenly.

'I'm sailing back with Captain Angove the day after tomorrow.'

'We shall miss you – I shall miss you.'

'I have to go. I still haven't found Grace Pensilva. She went on from here and I must find her.'

'I think you're in love with her. You must be.' For the first time there was a ghost of a smile on her lips.

'Someone else told me that once. It's not true, not exactly, but she's like a familiar spirit, I have to exorcise her. What did your mother say about that time she saw her?'

'She said that she called at her house at dead of night. My mother still hadn't heard about Frederick. Grace must have been afraid to go to her own house. She took some money and clothes for a journey. My mother thought they were running off together. Grace let her believe it – she was in disguise.'

'What was she wearing?'

'She was disguised in the robes of the Brotherhood of the Rosary.' Optimus gasped. How much of life was fate, how much was coincidence? So much of what he had learned of Grace Pensilva seemed curiously bound up with events in his own life.

'Did anyone else see her? Did your grandfather?'

'No, but my father did. As he left the house, where he had been courting my mother, Major Kirkbride passed her. He mentioned it next morning, but he didn't recognize her. Where did she go? You know that, don't you? How did she end?'

Optimus had a sudden vision of the weed-covered tomb outside Harberscombe churchyard. 'She went home. But there are still questions without answers.'

The chaise was rattling into the outskirts of the town which was full of excitement and tumult. Optimus turned and looked at Maria's face. It was softer and more lovely than he had thought. When she became aware of his stare, her eyes dropped to her lap.

'And you,' he continued, 'when will you come back to England?'

'I don't know. Perhaps never. I've vowed to look after my grandfather. A promise is a promise. Would you have me break it?' Optimus shook his head slowly and soon they were swallowed up in the merrymaking. Moments later they passed under the windows of the Bondi Palace and Optimus looked at its windows, half expecting to see Grace Pensilva.

Frederick Genteel lay on the bed in a shallow sleep. When he was brought up into this room the doctor who came had administered laudanum. All that the patient needed, he insisted, was rest. Grace leaned over him and brushed a strand of hair from his face. He was balding already. It might be something to do with wearing that hat of his. The hat, coat and gloves had been carried off for cleaning. His epaulette was being sewn on. He lay there in his breeches and shirt, looking weak and vulnerable.

She heard hesitant footfalls on the stair. They stopped outside the door. She waited. Then, barefoot, she ran across the tiled floor and opened it. There, with Genteel's sword in his hand and an undecided expression on his face, stood Ben Barlow.

' 'Ow is 'ee?'

'He's resting?'

'I brought this over.'

'You can give it to me.'

'Before that, there's something I need to say to you, private.' With sudden resolution he pushed past her and pulled the door shut, leaving them isolated on the landing.

'What is it?'

'Frederick Genteel is a good man. I want to know your intentions towards 'im. I were the one what told you 'ee was the captain of the revenue cutter, weren't I. I told you when I comed out from England. Well, I've been thinkin' about it: the reason you wanted to find out, that was so you could take your revenge. You didn't know Frederick Genteel then, did you? Now you do. Both of us know 'ee's not capable of a deed that'd bring 'im dishonour –'

'Come to the point, Ben, what're you getting at?'

'I shouldn't like for Mr Genteel to come to no 'arm – can you look me in the eye and swear 'ee's in no danger?'

'If he's in danger, it's from trying to do too much before he's properly recovered. Don't you know how I've nursed him?'

'I know that,' he responded grudgingly, 'but can I trust you?'

'Of course you can.' She looked him full in the face and her eyes looked tearful. 'Do you think I don't love him?' As she spoke, she took the sword with one hand and patted his shoulder with the other. 'You want to protect him too, don't you? We all do.'

Barlow was more than half convinced. Either she was a far better actress than he imagined possible, or she was sincere and Genteel was in the safest hands he could have wished for. 'Can I see 'im?'

'The doctor says he must have quiet. Come back tomorrow morning.'

When Barlow had gone, Grace let herself into the room and paused. Genteel was still sleeping. She walked to the window, drew the sword-blade, and slid it through the bars of the evening light that came through the shutters, examining it. It was just another nondescript sword: a cutlass with a wired hilt and silver pommel. The guard was slightly rusty, but the blade was oiled and clean. She studied it, seeking a stain, but found none. One man at least had died by that sword, but there was no trace of it.

'Grace!' came the thinnest of dry whispers.

She turned round guiltily, fearful that he had read her thoughts. He had shifted on the bed. His lips were moving. 'Where are you?' he called weakly.

'I'm here.' She laid the sword on a corner table and knelt beside him. Her concern was so great it almost suffocated her. His eyes were shut; he had not fully awakened. He was trying

407

to say something else: what was it? At last she heard.

'Don't leave me.'

'I shan't leave you, Frederick. Not if you don't want me to. Not now. Not ever.'

She lay down beside him with his good hand clasped between hers. The light from the shutters crept round slowly, crossing the floor and staining the wall until it illuminated the sword on the table. Genteel was sleeping quietly now. The light faded. She also slept.

In her sleep, a voice was calling her, choked and hopeless in a drowning hiss. A face appeared to her through swirling currents. Whose was it, Frank's? Or Frederick's? The eyes were gone. A little crab peered out of one of the sockets. She shuddered.

Genteel felt the shuddering. The revenue cutter was riding over the gig. There was a crack of splitting timber. He strove to keep his balance, his sword arm lifted. A sharp pain in his calf, a voice calling:'Good Christ! Have pity!' He knew it. His sword swung down like an automaton's. Then he himself was falling, falling into a welter of hooves pounding, pounding.

He woke. The room he lay in was lit by flashes of real explosions. By their fitful light he saw the sleeping form beside him, a dear face he knew, asleep and fearful. Where were they? He swung his legs to the ground. The old wound in his calf was hurting. Haltingly, he went to the window and threw back the shutters. The night sky was so bright he could not believe it: gold flashes, ruby, sapphire, bright vermilion, stars bursting, lazy rockets sizzling over.

'Quick, Grace, come and look! It's wonderful. You'll never see anything like it.' She came to him and he put his good arm round her. In the light of the fireworks he saw that her face was still troubled. 'What is it?'

'A bad dream – a nightmare.'

'Don't worry, I'm here. I'll look after you.'

He kissed her. He kissed her brow, her eyelids, her cheeks, her neck, her lips. He felt the warmth and life she had lost come back to her. They kissed and clung together as though they were drowning. There, with the sounds of mock-battle behind them and the smell of acrid gunpowder in their nostrils, they kissed again. The quest was over.

'Look,' said Grace after a while, 'the doors, they're opening.' At the head of the steps across the square, the church doors were swinging back. Jolting unsteadily, the holy image on its palanquin was emerging. 'How lovely!' she exclaimed as the blue-robed figure swayed in the light of a hundred torches.

Frederick Genteel stood behind her. With his wounded arm, he circled her waist, with the other he fondled her breasts. A tension gripped her. All around them huge maroons went hissing into the air and blossomed into detonating fire-balls. The fireballs expanded into golden sheaves of streamers. A whiff of incense rose from the street and enveloped them. The image, hands uplifted in greeting to God, lurched towards them.

As it approached the window, he drew Grace back into the shadow, nuzzling her neck. She twisted towards him, cradling his face in her hands.

'It's all for us, all this,' he whispered. They kissed again deeply. The noise and light of the procession receded. After a while, she felt him fumbling at her dress fastenings. His bad arm was hampering him.

'Do you want me?' she whispered.

'Don't ask stupid questions.'

'But your arm, I can tell it's hurting.'

'Damn my arm. Why don't you help me?'

'Tomorrow morning we'll go to Fungus Rock. I'll climb up and fetch the specific to cure you.'

'I can't wait for tomorrow. I want you now. Can't you understand, Grace? I need you. I've always needed you. I didn't know till now.'

A kind of smile wreathed her lips, there was irony in it. 'But Felicity.'

'Damn Felicity.'

'She'll never forgive you.'

'I don't care. What's the matter, don't *you* want *me*?'

'Why do you think I followed you here?' She slipped away

from him. Now that the torches had gone, he could barely see her in the twilight. When he reached her, she was naked. He tried to embrace her.

'Wait,' she commanded, with a hand against his chest. 'Your arm, your poor arm, you must not hurt it.'

He felt her cool hands working at the buttons on his shirt. He felt his belt-buckle loosen. He felt her palms sliding his breeches down over his hips. He felt her lips on his chest. He felt her fingers exploring his sex. He gasped as the foreskin slid back. He felt enormous.

With a gasp he propelled her back to the bed and fell upon her, kissing her breasts, nipping them with his teeth until she cried out.

He entered her. Her mouth kissed him. Her tongue pushed past his teeth. Her nether lips enfolded him. Her heels dug in his back. He spoke to her in sounds not words, sounds like mumbled prayers, sounds like an agony.

His sword in her scabbard, darting, darting, killing her, killing her.

Fighting for life, wrestling together on the edge of dying, dragging each other under, locked in one flesh, one fate, ears singing, heads throbbing, hearts pounding and being pounded in waves of ecstasy.

'Oh!' A single desperate syllable, lost in the darkness.

When he returned to himself, a full moon was shining through their chamber window. She was nestled against him and blew a kiss across his chest as she saw his eyelids stirring.

'Have I slept?'

'Like a child,' she told him, 'the sleep of the just.'

'I'm not, I'm not just. I'm not perfect.'

'You are a man of honour.' He sighed, then stiffened slightly.

'There's something you should know, if you don't already.'

'I don't want to hear it.'

'You must. If you love me, Grace, if you love me enough, you will listen. I cannot keep it from you.'

'I love you, but you need not tell me.'

'It burns me. I need your forgiveness.'

'Forgiveness?'

410

'I was the man in the mask, the captain of the cutter, I was the one who –'

'Killed my brother,' she finished for him. 'I knew already.'

'But you never spoke.'

'Do you think I haven't forgiven you long ago? Jan King told me he saw you at the funeral. It wasn't hard to put two and two together.'

'You didn't forgive Jan King.'

'Jan King was different. He betrayed him.'

'You've got it all wrong, Grace, your brother deserved it –' he began, but suddenly she was sitting up, hard and catatonic.

'I won't hear you say that!'

'Hush! Stop it!' He too sat up and put his arm around her.

'I'm sorry,' she murmured much later.

'What shall we do?'

'You must go back to Felicity and I must be leaving.'

'That's impossible. We must stay together.'

'Have you forgotten Scully? I must leave Malta before he finds me.'

'I'll come with you.'

'No, you will stay, Frederick. You must. Sleep now. There will be much to do tomorrow. We must rise early if you want to come with me to seek the Knights' remedy.'

'Sleep? Sleep? When I've all that wasted loving to make up for?'

'You must eat something,' she told him severely. 'They have brought you wine and food for supper.'

'You are my supper,' he informed her, stopping her mouth with a kiss.

'There's something here that I'd like you to look after,' said Optimus, smiling to Maria in the candlelight. They were sitting together in the peaceful saloon, alone now that Count Scicluna had retired to rest and left them. It seemed a friendlier place than when he had first seen it that morning. The mahogany table glistened and its surface was littered with decanters and wine glasses. He fumbled in his pocket, feeling

411

a little awkward, self-conscious. When he found what he sought, he stood up and went round the table to where Maria was sitting on the sofa. He opened his hand and showed it to her.

'I can't take it. It's too precious.'

'I'm not giving it to you, not now, but you ought to have it. There's something of your mother's in there. Let me show you.' Delicately, he manoeuvred the catch and first one and then the other miniature was displayed to her.

'So that is what Frederick Genteel was like,' she said quietly, 'he was so handsome. I think I'd have loved him myself, if I'd have known him.'

'I didn't think you were free with your love.'

'Only with exceptional persons.' She was smiling at him. It was a smile like Grace Pensilva's in the miniature. He snapped it shut and passed the chain around Maria's neck, fastening it.

'There, it suits you – do you know you're lovely?' She put a finger across his lips. He saw her breast was heaving.

'Not as lovely as Grace. You still have to find her.'

'Different,' he told her, taking her hand, 'different, not less lovely. I mean that. You'll keep the locket for me until I return to claim it. No one else can wear it better.'

'Were you serious just now when you talked about going into business with my grandfather? He half believed you. He doesn't deserve disappointments.'

'When I have found Grace Pensilva, I shall return to Malta. I have some unfinished business to transact . . . You didn't trust me at first, did you? And now . . .?'

'I think you're a fine person.'

'You'll write to me.'

'I'll write to you.'

Outside the window, maroons still thumped and splashed the night with flame. Then, in a magical display that brought Maria and Optimus across the room to watch, the brooding citadel was outlined in red fire. He took her hand; her cheeks were flushed; was she blushing? He hoped so.

*   *   *

They rose in the cold blue light of dawn, before the town was stirring. They walked hand in hand down the dusty road between stone-walled fields, chill and dry in the last of the night breeze. The blanched moon still hung low in the western sky, so huge they felt they could reach out and touch it.

'I fear I shall not be able to climb the rock with you, my arm has stiffened terribly,' he told her.

'Never mind, I'll soon make it better. Come on now, keep moving, it's only a little further.'

Just as the sun cleared the horizon, they came to the lip of a deep declivity. At the bottom, like a lake, was a patch of water on which a few boats were resting. She hurried down the path ahead of him.

'Do you think it's all right?' he asked as Grace unmoored one of the little vessels. 'I mean, there's no one here to ask permission.'

'We're only borrowing. How fastidious you are. We'll bring it home, won't we? Jump in. If we're quick, we'll be back before they miss us.'

The water was perfectly clear. Frederick watched small fish dart away as she dipped the paddles. It was sea water, the weed and the sea-urchins told him that, but where was the open water? There seemed to be nothing but rock all round them. He sat facing Grace, on the after thwart, with his hand trailing the water. It brought back memories of a day with his father. When he looked at Grace, his heart seemed to expand in his chest, as though it was bursting. His love for her was more like pain, yet he could not forgo it.

And Grace, pulling at the oars, studied that long sad face, so lined and careworn. How strained he looked, how wan. If her life were linked to one man, it must be him, her Frederick.

He was looking past her, at the wall of rock that seemed to have no opening. When he spoke, he was like a man in a dream, recounting an illusion.

'I had a strange meeting yesterday,' he told her. 'It was after the ball. I was walking home alone, to Floriana. A figure accosted me, one of those fearful Brothers of the Rosary. He barred my path. I took a coin from my purse and offered it, thinking I could buy safe-passage. He dashed it down. He refused it. He whispered something: "You cannot buy back your own soul," he told me. Then he waved me on. It affected me. It ought not to, it is all superstition, but since that time, I have been crushed with melancholy.'

Grace seemed hardly to hear him. She too seemed to be acting in a dream, rowing instinctively towards the cleft in the rocks that was opening out before them. In her reverie her eyes strayed to the bait-knife that was stuck in the thwart beside her.

'Grace!'

She looked up quickly, almost guiltily. 'What is it?' she asked, returning from a vast distance. He sighed.

'So little time.'

Their boat was gliding through a cavern, a tunnel from the inland sea towards the open water. It was like a journey from one life to another. Beyond the far entrance, tiny waves were sparkling in the sunlight. They themselves were gliding through velvety darkness.

'I love you.'

She hardly knew that she had spoken.

'I know, Grace. I know.'

She heard him answer. They came into the light again and she saw that the gunwale was gouged with cuts where the bait-knife had scored it. The wood was steeped in blood, blood of a thousand sacrificed creatures. She thought of another gunwale, another creature's blood. She had a sudden urge to snatch up the knife and plunge it into her own heart.

'Look, there it is!'

His voice startled her and she dropped an oar which fell clattering into the boat. Had he read her thought? But he was looking beyond her, out to sea where tall precipitous Fungus Rock shot up out of the water. His face was lit by the light of a young day, suddenly cleansed and hopeful. In that sharp, early morning light, she saw him for what he was, a good man and, for all his hesitations, a strong one. She loved him. She knew that now with all the clarity the Mediterranean sunlight had to offer. And yet this was the man who had wronged her, wronged her Frank, who was doomed by her vow of vengeance. Did she still have the courage? Was she capable of the sacrifice its execution demanded?

'Are you happy?' she asked him, rowing seaward.

'You *know* that's a question without an answer,' he told her in a choked voice. 'It's killing me, Grace, killing me.'

6

When the carrier set Optimus down by the gatehouse at Leet, there was a tall gangling man exercising a horse in the park, taking the animal round in tight circles and making it lift its hooves in an elaborate trotting action. Optimus had decided to leave the cart here for two reasons: first, he wanted to speak to Charles Barker about his Maltese experience and second, he had formed the design of walking back to Branscombe via Harberscombe village. It was the longer way, but he had a special reason for taking it. His bags would be dropped off at the house by the carrier. It was a fine morning and the walk over the hills would be pleasant.

The lodge by the gate looked more forlorn than ever, but he was unprepared to find the windows boarded up and a padlock on the door. From the pile of leaves on the sill and the torn spiders' webs in the corners, the door had not moved in a long time. What had happened to Barker? It was easy to imagine: the Steward had only remained on sufferance. Shaking his head sadly, he set off towards Harberscombe.

Half-way across Slaughter Bridge, Optimus paused and looked across at the mansion. The autumn gales had already stripped most of the trees and the house was revealed more clearly than he had ever seen it. Was there a figure standing at one of the turret windows? It was too far off to be sure. He had to admit to himself that he had never plucked up the courage to visit Nancy Genteel. It was not out of deference, or fear exactly, but a strong sense of revulsion had kept him from knocking on her door.

Well, whatever was uncertain in Grace Pensilva's story,

Leet House was inescapable. It sat four-square on the land and glared arrogantly at the hills around it. But, oddly enough, it was not the house itself that Optimus was aware of. He envisioned a tall, pensive figure, with a book in his hands behind his back, strolling along the river. Frederick Genteel was seeking someone, someone who would be rowing up on the tide from Armouth. It was, of course, an illusion. Frederick had never returned from Malta. There had been theories about his fate. Some said that he had run off with Grace Pensilva, but this did not square up with her own subsequent appearance alone in Harberscombe. The general opinion was that he had met his end off Gozo, though the exact manner, for want of a body, was never established.

With an indefinable sadness, Optimus turned away and began the long walk to Harberscombe. This was a hilly road: three times it dipped and three times it rose, steep as the roof of a house, a road to daunt the stoutest pilgrim. It was the way the Harberscombe folk had once been obliged to bear their dead to Uglington and return to mourn them. It was a similar errand that had brought Grace Pensilva along this road on her last journey.

Optimus stepped out boldly. Walking refreshed him after a night spent cooped up in the mail coach from Falmouth. Although he had lived but a short time in this neighbourhood, there was a peculiar poignant joy in rediscovering it. To see the familiar clumps of trees, to see the red earth, already furrowed by the autumn ploughing, to see the red cattle browsing in the water-meadows, to see the distant, cloud-capped moors, brought a pain to his heart and a tightness to his throat. He was so immersed in this communion with nature that he did not hear the approaching horseman until he was right upon him. Optimus sprang to the side of the narrow lane to allow the rider to pass, but the latter reined in to a walk beside him.

'You're the one who was so curious about Grace Pensilva, aren't you? I recognized you when you stopped on the bridge. You're wasting your time lookin' for Charles Barker, we've done away with 'im. None too soon neither – don't know

417

why she kept the old fool on so long anyway. What did you want with 'im?'

There was something aggressive in the man's tone that Optimus disliked instinctively. His accent was odd, half broad Devon, the rest clipped county. He walked on in silence.

'Out with it!' the rider insisted.

'That's my business,' said Optimus curtly. 'You're Ronald Coyte, aren't you?' he added. 'You've done very nicely for yourself, very nicely. Has she married you, I wonder?'

'Mind your tongue.' Optimus could see him fingering his whip. The fellow was quite capable of lashing out if sufficiently provoked and, on this wild road, there would be no witnesses.

'I meant no harm. You didn't choose your life, none of us do. Tell me, why did you bother to ride after me? It wasn't to tell me about Charles Barker.'

'If you'd been more civil, I'd a mind to tell you something. Now I'm not sure I'll bother . . .' For what seemed an age, Ronald Coyte rode in silence.

'About Grace Pensilva?' Optimus prompted him.

'You'd like to 'ear 'ow she came to do away with herself, wouldn't you?'

They had come to a fork in the road at the top of the hill. After hearing Coyte out, whichever road he took, Optimus would take another. He could not say exactly why he disliked this man, it was visceral.

'Did away with herself?' Suicide, why hadn't he thought of it? That would explain the isolated tomb outside the graveyard. That would explain part of the villagers' silence.

'She told me, Mistress Nancy told me, that if ever I did see Grace again, to come to Leet House and tell 'er. She had somethin', somethin' o' Frederick's to give 'er – Well, Grace *did* come, just like you did just now. I went for the packet and rode after 'er. I met Uncle Bill on the way and he told me where I should find 'er. When I comed up with 'er, I gived 'er the packet – wouldn't take it at first till I told 'er it was Frederick's. Even then, she didn't open it directly. When she thought I'd gone, she carried it into the church and sat down

418

in a pew to unwrap it. I watched through a window.' Optimus could see the scene all too clearly: Ronald spying through the leaded panes, Grace intent on removing the wrappings.

'What was in the packet?'

'Interested now, aren't we?'

'You said you wanted to tell me. What's the use of breaking off in the middle of your story? What was it?'

'A book.'

'What kind of a book?'

'A kind of bound notebook.'

'What did she do?'

'She looked inside, she looked at the writing. Then she set to readin'. Didn't take more than five minutes altogether. Then she shut it. I never did see a woman so changed. One minute she was straight and proud like always, the next she was bent and broken.'

'What happened to the book? Did she keep it?'

' 'Ow should I know? Once I see'd what it did to 'er, I went on me way rejoicin'. I mean that, I'll not conceal it: I was 'appy to see 'er broken, broken like she broke poor Jan King, slighted like she did slight Ronald Coyte, injured like she did injure Frederick Genteel.'

'You say Uncle Bill saw her, who else saw her in Harberscombe?'

'Don't rightly know. I've 'eard tell she did call at Emma Troup's 'ouse.'

'And that's all?'

'What more do you want?'

'What was in that notebook, didn't Mistress Nancy ever tell you?'

Ronald Coyte shook his head. 'She just said it would open 'er eyes a little.'

'Do you think I could come and talk to Lady Nancy about it?'

Ronald touched a finger to his brow signigfcantly. 'You won't learn nothin'. And she won't see no one.' Optimus felt an unexpected twinge of sympathy for this isolated man. He had not really done as nicely for himself as he had imagined.

419

'Young Scully comes to see her.' Once again, it looked as though Coyte might strike him, but he held himself in.

'You know more than enough, Mr Shute, more than is good for you. Who Miss Nancy do see is 'er own business. She ain't never goin' to ask permission o' no horse-trainer.' Once again, Optimus was struck by the hopelessness behind the arrogance.

'What did *you* make of Grace Pensilva?'

'She put 'er mark on a man. I think I was proper mazed about 'er when I was younger.' He laughed in embarrassment. 'But that was long ago, 'tis ancient history.' He kicked his heels into his horse's belly. 'Good day to you, School-master.'

How strange, thought Optimus as Ronald Coyte rode back the way he had come, I used to despise this man and now, after five minutes' conversation, I see him as a victim. Once a servant, always a servant.

Optimus walked on, down one hill and up another, then down again, anxious to come to Harberscombe, pulling himself up the last long slope before the village. To one side lay Langstone Mill alone in its valley. A thread of smoke rose from its chimney. The turning wheel was groaning faintly. Pulling himself together, Optimus continued up the hill, through the outlying farms until the church appeared through the elms and he reached the graveyard. There, in the autumn sunshine, the dried grasses whispered peacefully. Dr Cornish's headstone still looked as new as the day it arrived there, but that too would pass. On Grace's tomb, the ivy had made fresh inroads. One particular tenacious shoot had lifted the slab slightly. Optimus knelt to look under it. He could see nothing but darkness, smell nothing but dust. Did Grace Pensilva really lie here? And if she did, could he bear to see her face?

'Stay away from 'Arberscombe, Grace, you bain't wanted.'

Grace looked up. She knew the voice: Uncle Bill Terry's. He was perched high on a great rock that overlooked the lane just above Langstone. She had been standing in a gateway

420

pondering, remembering the night when she went to the harvest home and stopped in this very same spot. Nothing seemed to have changed: the woods still drooped down to the mudbanks that shone like molten metal, the cattle still grazed peacefully in the meadow beside the dam where Farmer Coyte used to shoot mullet. The mill-wheel still groaned and turned.

And yet, everything was subtly different. She herself had changed. She had kept her vow, but was another person. Only the stones, she thought, do not change. She had made herself into a stone, she had hardened her heart but, as she soon was to learn, even stones break.

'Good day to you, Uncle Bill,' she answered, as bold as she could.

'What do 'ee want with us 'ere? Bain't one life enough for 'ee?' His voice challenged her from the rock that barred the road with its heavy shadow.

'I have come to pray for the dead.'

'You've not come to pray for Jan King, I warrant. Poor Jan 'aven't got no grave ashore to pray by.'

'Why should I pray for Jan King?'

'Pray for yourself would be better. I see'd 'ee, I see'd 'ee row off from the Carrack Rocks that evenin'. I were up on the Barrow. And I knows 'twas only you went off with the Frenchman. Caradec told me. There were but you in the gig when 'ee found un. So, if you was thinkin' to stay 'ere in 'Arberscombe, you've another think comin'. Us don't want your kind 'ere.'

'I shall go when I will.'

'If you'm still 'ere tomorrow, I shall tell the magistrates. I shall do my duty.'

'As I shall do mine. You'll not stop me with threats, but comfort yourself, there's no fear of my staying. What do I care for this place? I was never accepted.'

Grace crossed the shadow and walked into Harberscombe. She neither looked to left nor right. Who saw her she cared not, but the roads were deserted.

As she approached the churchyard, her heart quickened.

421

Frank, Frank, her mind repeated, they never accepted you either, they never trusted you. They cared not a whit when your life was taken. But you were a better man than any of them and I have avenged you. I have avenged you upon your betrayer; I have revenged you upon your murderer.

She searched for the grave. Where was it? The weeds had covered it over. There was no headstone. She came to a halt among the thistles.

'Frank, Frank,' she whispered, 'I have kept true to you. It has cost me dear, but I have avenged you. The men who wronged you are no more. Now you can rest. Rest, rest, sweet Frank, and I shall rest also. I have paid the price, but you have had justice.'

She stayed a little among the rustling thistles. Why don't I feel anything, she asked herself, why this emptiness?

'Grace! Grace!' a voice was calling her. She saw it was Ronald Coyte coming towards her. He was holding out a packet.

'What's that?'

'It's from Nancy.'

'Then I don't want it.'

'She said 'twas somethin' left behind by Frederick.' Grace was sure there could be no goodwill behind this present, but she could not refuse it.

As soon as she was rid of Ronald, she slipped into the church and untied the packet. Within, she found a notebook. It was in Frederick's handwriting.

Not for more than half its pages did she do more than grasp the general drift, understanding where and when Frederick had written it. Then, suddenly, she clutched it to her heart. She read the line again. There could be no mistake about the name and description. Frederick's writing was firm and clear.

She made herself read on and, as she read, the horror augmented. Now she knew why Nancy Genteel had sent the book to her. It was a poison, a poison she could not resist, a poison she must drink. She read on and her spine weakened until she leaned on the pew in front for support. It must be a forgery, an elaborate plot imagined by Nancy to destroy her.

She was capable of it. No, in her heart of hearts, she knew this could not be. There was no need of a plot when the truth itself was devastating. This was Frederick speaking to himself, she recognized the tone. Not only that, everything fitted in. There was a logic that was inescapable.

No! No! No! Her mind still refused to accept it. When she turned the last written page, she dropped the book and beat her fists against her head. No! No! It could not be true. And yet it must be. Poor Jan, her inner voice cried, and Frederick! Frederick!

She could not stay still. Blindly she took her bag and ran to Emma Troup's cottage. The door was on the latch; she pushed it open. The hearth was cold. She sat at the table and waited. She bit her thumb. She wanted to tell Emma all, pour her heart out, ask her if she might hope for forgiveness.

She almost cried to God, but she could not do so. What should she pray for? For help? For absolution? Then, in her next thought, she cursed Him. Without His aid, her vengeance would never have been compassed.

Frederick, Frederick, would he ever forgive her? Wherever he was, would he understand and pardon? The tears ran down her face, they stained the papers she had scattered about the table. Oh Emma, Emma, she implored, come home soon or I shall lose my reason.

'Are you much the wiser for your journey?' Mrs Troup asked Optimus when she saw him. She was at her knitting and showed no surprise at his arrival, only nodding to a fireside chair by way of invitation.

'A little.'

'I knowed you wouldn't find all the answers in Malta.'

'She came back here. She came back to this house. You saw her, didn't you?' Emma Troup shook her head sadly.

'No, I never see'd 'er. I were off to Salcombe – didn't come back afore next mornin'. Grace 'ad gone then – left 'er things upon the table. You've 'ad most of 'em.'

'What about the notebook, Genteel's notebook, have you still got it?'

423

'No, I never 'ad un.' Mrs Troup's reply was firm, he didn't think she was bluffing.

'But there *was* one. She read it, she learned something. It made her desperate.'

'Aye, she were desperate, all right, I could see that the moment I stepped in 'ere, but Grace were gone, I didn't know where to find 'er.'

'But she was found later, wasn't she?'

'Much later – they found a body, it might 'ave been Grace's, but you know what they'm like after an age in water. Anyway, Dr Cornish, 'ee paid for the gravestone and they buried 'er, outside the wall – Vicar wouldn't 'ave no suicides on church property.'

'I hope she's at rest.' For a long while, the only sound was the clicking of Emma Troup's needles.

'In life, she didn't know 'ow to. In death, I fear 'twon't be no different ... Did you 'ear there's a new schoolmaster at Branscombe? Not much of a scholar, not like you, Mr Shute, but us don't need that in such places. You was too bright for Branscombe. What will you be doin'? Do you plan to stay 'ere?'

'For a while, I expect. I still have unfinished business. I shall see you again before leaving. Now I must get home before nightfall.'

As he approached Branscombe, Optimus was still wondering about Grace Pensilva. Even now, with the evidence he had heard, it was hard to imagine her dead. She had been so alive that she must live on somewhere.

When he arrived at Dr Cornish's house, his house, he was astonished to find it locked against him. He had written ahead to warn Mrs Kemp of his arrival. He hammered on it with his fist, but was doubtful if she would hear him, even if she were in there. Something told him the place was deserted. He circled round to the other door, peering through the windows. Both fires were out, not a trace of smoke rose from the chimneys. He stood and listened. All that he heard was the monotonous muttering from across the road where the children were still at their lessons.

He returned to the back door. His two bags lay under the porch where the carrier had left them. This was a ridiculous situation. He beat on the door again and shouted. Silence.

'Mrs Kemp! Mrs Kemp!' Silence. He knocked hard again and put his ear to the door, trying to hear the slightest sound from inside the house.

'Mr Shute?' Optimus turned round, slightly embarrassed to be found in this posture. Facing him was a young man in a black jacket and stiff white collar. In his hand was an envelope.

'The same.'

'I was expecting you. My name is Clifford. I'm the new master. Mrs Kemp asked me to give you this.' The envelope was heavy; it contained the huge old key to the kitchen door. There was also a piece of paper.

'Dear Mr Shute,' he read, 'please do not blame me for leaving your house unattended. I trust you will find all in order. Mr Clifford will help with provisions. Forgive me, I cannot stay longer. This house is too empty.' It was signed F. Kemp. Optimus thanked Mr Clifford who returned to his teaching.

The key turned stiffly in the lock and the door swung back on the cold kitchen. Optimus felt its emptiness, the void that had once been Dr Cornish, his domineering personality. There was his fireside chair, untenanted. Optimus remembered the first time he had entered this room and stood, hesitant as now, upon the threshold. There, along the far wall, with its flanking benches, was the long table at which he had sat facing the Doctor with the heap of documents between them. In his head he still heard the roofers hammering as they finished the new schoolhouse.

The table was not empty now. It was just as Dr Cornish had left it. There was a clay pipe, a glass and an unfinished game of patience. He could understand why it had been so unbearable that Mrs Kemp had left it. Idly, he turned the last card over. It was the king of hearts. He completed the patience.

Then he saw the book. Its cover was so dark that it had escaped his notice. He picked it up, holding it up to the light from the small window, examining it. It was a ruled notebook with marbled endpapers. Was it? Could it be?

Before he had read a page or two, he was convinced he held it. It was three-quarters full of neat, closely-spaced writing; long paragraphs interspersed with dates; there was no doubt it was the journal and, from the handwriting which he knew well: Frederick's journal.

Sitting in Dr Cornish's place on the bench, with the light at his back, he read avidly. Though the name of the town was not mentioned, several details told Optimus that it was Salcombe. The writer was giving a personal, day to day account of his life as captain of the preventives. It started when he arrived from London and put it about discreetly that he was empowered to pay substantial rewards for information. Thenceforth, for a while, the journal was a fairly dull record of crew training and it was clear that he had a low opinion of his subordinates, particularly the cutter's mate, a man called Scully. There were details of the occasional, fruitless patrol. Then it happened.

'At last we are getting somewhere,' Optimus read. 'Nine of the evening. I am dozing by my fire. The landlord has just taken out the remains of my supper. There is a scratching at the window. I take my pistol and open it. The man outside is even more frightened than I am, worried about being discovered talking to me. I let him in through the window. He is well-spoken, not the sort I expected to be mixed up in smuggling, and he is ready to sell his information, betray his comrades, for remarkably little, far less that I was expecting to be asked for. He says he will give the bearings of the exact spot where the kegs will be moored, pending collection. In return, he will receive a hundred guineas, a free pardon for his involvement, and a passage to America. Naturally, I suspect him of double-dealing, but he is earnest and I must take him seriously. He says his name is –' Here the page had been scratched violently until the paper was almost worn through. The name had been obliterated. Who could have done this? Grace? Some other interested party? Optimus read on.

426

Two pages later, he found an answer. 'The agent I employed to check on my informant tells me that he is a person of known Jacobin opinions who lives in Harberscombe with his sister. He is fairly recently returned from France, and has lived several years in America. What can be his motive in this matter beyond pure greed? Is he punishing his fellows for their lack of revolutionary fervour? Whatever his reasons, his treachery will lead us to the smugglers and enable us to set an example. This man has made a deep impression on me. I should know him in a thousand, but I do not think that he would know me. There is no reason why he should. I have taken the added precaution of changing my voice in these circumstances.'

Despite the missing name, the informer's identity was obvious. It was Frank Pensilva. It was his treachery that had given away the gig.

Optimus pressed on, skimming through routine observations and the preparations for the expedition, reading Genteel's frequent soul-searchings about the honourability of the proceedings. It was evident that he had been driven to take up this uncongenial employment by only one thing: lack of money. His service appointment had come to an end and his spendthrift father was denying him a proper allowance. There was some question of his managing the Leet estate, but it had not been agreed on. Hawkins had talked him into this job, telling him only a man of honour could resist the temptation to come to terms with the smugglers. All his predecessors had succumbed to it.

Ten days later, the pace of the action quickened. The informer returned with a paper which had the bearing written on it. He pushed it through the window.

'Tomorrow night,' he whispered, and ran off quickly.

Optimus read on eagerly. There was the account of the revenue cutter's approach along a compass bearing, using dead reckoning. He caught the excitement of low voices as the cutter surged forward under muffled oars. He seemed to be inside Frederick Genteel's skin, perched in the bow, dark-lantern in hand when the cutter slammed into the gig. He too felt Jan King's knife-blade enter his leg. He too staggered, almost overboard.

But it was the next page that gripped him. The cutter had rammed the gig twice and it had gone under. One of the three men who had been flung out of it was trying to climb over the preventive boat's gunwale.

' "Don't you know me?" he shouted. I knew that voice. He had no need to add "I'm-from Harberscombe." ' Once more the name was scratched out. 'What were the thoughts that raced through my mind in that brief moment as I groped for my cutlass? Of course I knew him: he was the traitor who had betrayed his comrades. "Good Christ! Have pity!" the scoundrel implored me. My sword arm came down and put an end to his whimperings. Thus, with a kind of rough justice, did I send him to his Maker. If there is pardon for his deed, he will find it in Heaven. As for my own, I will take my chance at that same tribunal.'

Optimus passed his hand across his eyes. No, there could be no possible doubt. There was none, even with the name missing, and equally Grace, when she read this, would have had no need of more definite identification. Optimus felt slightly sick. He needed air. If it affected him thus, how must Grace have felt? *She* who was haunted by two sorrowful, accusing faces, those of Jan King and Frederick Genteel. He turned the last few pages.

'A dirty business,' he read near the end, 'and I shall be well out of it, though I fear it has marked me for ever. This day I saw the dead man's sister at the graveside. Her face still haunts me. Though I thought that the deed I did was just, nothing I can ever do can take it back, nothing can expunge that sorrow. Her eyes looked through me. Yes, a dirty business. I have asked Mr Hawkins to come over from Plymouth to see me and I have written my letter of resignation. Whether my father approves it or not, I am determined to return to Leet and take up farming. Time will tell if I can beat my sword into a ploughshare.'

Optimus sat with his chin in his hands and stared across the table into the shadows. Who had brought Genteel's notebook here? Would he ever know? Did it matter? Had Mrs Kemp held it all the time? Poor Frederick, upright, honour-able, self-questioning Frederick: he had been the man Grace had pursued for cold-blooded murder, convinced her Frank was faultless.

Under the last sentence in Frederick Genteel's writing was a short inscription in a different hand, sprawling nervously across the page. Optimus knew it from the Malta letters.

Not wisely but too well

He sighed and pushed the book away. A little later, he stood up slowly. There was a fire to light, food to prepare. He was light-headed with hunger. As soon as he had eaten, he would find candle, pen and paper and write to Maria Kirk-bride. He had so much to tell her. Already, from the moment he set foot on Angove's packet for the return to England, he had begun to miss her. Maria was so different, so straight-forward, so impulsive, so beautiful. He knew he could entrust his soul to her. She was kind and soft, so unlike Grace Pensilva.

Optimus knew he would not remain long at Branscombe. Before he left, he would find Mrs Kemp and see that she was amply provided for. Perhaps she would tell him how the book came to be lying on the table. Perhaps not. It did not matter. Where Grace Pensilva was concerned, one question's answer still led to another. Never mind, whatever the details might be, he was convinced he knew the essential answer. Few women, he thought, were like Grace Pensilva. It was her nature, more than anything else, that had led her to her tragic destiny. Any man might be lured to her, like moth to candle. He himself had felt the attraction. And, however harrowing his quest, he was grateful to Dr Cornish for having set him off upon it. Without that spur, he would still be, like Clifford, an ignorant schoolmaster, and he would not have met Maria.

As he knelt and blew the tinder into the first small flame and the twigs crackled, he felt the old Doctor's presence close behind him: rough, overbearing, friendly, reassuring. He did not need to turn to see him.

Outdoors, in the dark, he saw a woman standing, with the night wind in her cloak, and her wild hair flying. From just ahead of her, at the Barrow's foot, came the stern sea's grumble. One more step and she would be over. He shuddered. His arm went out to her.

Now, at long last, he knew the sadness that was Grace Pensilva.

Grace Pensilva was walking swiftly through the night. She was empty handed. All her possessions were lying where she had left them on Emma Troup's table. She no longer had any thought of telling her all, making a confession, seeking compassion, obtaining forgiveness. There could be none. She had weighed herself in the balance of life and had been found wanting. Even were Emma Troup to say she forgave her, there was one judge who would never forgive her: herself.

As she left Harberscombe, she had looked stonily at the gentle woods that hid Langstone Mill and through which towered Leet showed briefly. Both pain and joy were mingled there; she turned away from them.

In the swiftly closing dusk, Jan King's house stood gaunt and lifeless. No light burned in his window. He was gone, gone down the tide's secret way, where she had sent him. She saw the crab come out of his eye. Was she quite demented?

Set faced, she crossed the cliffside fields that climbed towards the Barrow. Harberscombe was behind her. So was Malta. All that had turned to horror. Ahead lay the cleansing sea: the sea that held Jan, the sea that held her Frederick, the sea that would hold Grace Pensilva.

THE END

DIANE PEARSON
THE SUMMER OF THE BARSHINSKEYS

'Although the story of the Barshinskeys, which became our story too, stretched over many summers and winters, that golden time of 1902 was when our strange involved relationship began, when our youthful longing for the exotic took a solid and restless hold upon us . . .'

It is at this enchanted moment that *The Summer of the Barshinskeys* begins. A beautifully told, compelling story that moves from a small Kentish village to London, and from war-torn St Petersburg to a Quaker relief unit in the Volga provinces. It is the unforgettable story of two families, one English, the other Russian, who form a lifetime pattern of friendship, passion, hatred, and love.

'An engrossing saga . . . she evokes rural England at the turn of the century with her sure and skilful touch'
Barbara Taylor Bradford

'The Russian section is reminiscent of Pasternak's *Doctor Zhivago*, horrifying yet hauntingly beautiful'
New York Tribune

0 552 12641 1   £2.95

CORGI BOOKS

A SELECTED LIST OF TITLES
AVAILABLE FROM CORGI BOOKS

WHILE EVERY EFFORT IS MADE TO KEEP PRICES LOW, IT IS SOMETIMES NECESSARY TO INCREASE PRICES AT SHORT NOTICE. CORGI BOOKS RESERVE THE RIGHT TO SHOW NEW RETAIL PRICES ON COVERS WHICH MAY DIFFER FROM THOSE PREVIOUSLY ADVERTISED IN THE TEXT OR ELSEWHERE.

THE PRICES SHOWN BELOW WERE CORRECT AT THE TIME OF GOING TO PRESS (FEBRUARY '86).

☐	12281 5	**JADE**	*Pat Barr*	£2.95
☐	12142 8	**A WOMAN OF TWO CONTINENTS**	*Pixie Burger*	£2.50
☐	08615 0	**THE BIG WIND**	*Beatrice Coogan*	£2.50
☐	99019 1	**ZEMINDAR**	*Valerie Fitzgerald*	£2.50
☐	12387 0	**COPPER KINGDOM**	*Iris Gower*	£1.95
☐	12637 3	**PROUD MARY**	*Iris Gower*	£2.50
☐	11944 X	**THE WAYWARD WINDS**	*Evelyn Kahn*	£2.95
☐	12182 7	**THE WILDERLING**	*Claire Lorrimer*	£2.95
☐	11959 8	**THE CHATELAINE**	*Claire Lorrimer*	£2.95
☐	12641 1	**THE SUMMER OF THE BARSHINSKEYS**	*Diane Pearson*	£2.95
☐	10375 6	**CSARDAS**	*Diane Pearson*	£2.95
☐	10271 7	**THE MARIGOLD FIELD**	*Diane Pearson*	£2.50
☐	09140 5	**SARAH WHITMAN**	*Diane Pearson*	£2.50
☐	10249 0	**BRIDE OF TANCRED**	*Diane Pearson*	£1.75
☐	12607 1	**DOCTOR ROSE**	*Elvi Rhodes*	£1.95
☐	12367 6	**OPAL**	*Elvi Rhodes*	£1.75
☐	12375 7	**A SCATTERING OF DAISIES**	*Susan Sallis*	£1.95
☐	12579 2	**THE DAFFODILS OF NEWENT**	*Susan Sallis*	£1.75

All these books are available at your book shop or newsagent, or can be ordered direct from the publisher. Just tick the titles you want and fill in the form below.

CORGI BOOKS, Cash Sales Department, P.O. Box 11, Falmouth, Cornwall.

Please send cheque or postal order, no currency.

Please allow cost of book(s) plus the following for postage and packing:

U.K. Customers—Allow 55p for the first book, 22p for the second book and 14p for each additional book ordered, to a maximum charge of £1.75.

B.F.P.O. and Eire—Allow 55p for the first book, 22p for the second book plus 14p per copy for the next seven books, thereafter 8p per book.

Overseas Customers—Allow £1.00 for the first book and 25p per copy for each additional book.

NAME (Block Letters) ....

ADDRESS ....

....